The
WITCHES
of KARRES

BAEN BOOKS by JAMES H. SCHMITZ

The WITCHES
of KARRES

James H. Schmitz

The Witches of Karres

Copyright © 1966 by James H. Schmitz

A Baen Book

Baen Publishing Enterprises
P.O. Box 1403
Riverdale, NY 10471
www.baen.com

ISBN: 0-7434-8837-7

Cover art by Kurt Miller

First Baen printing, July 2004

Library of Congress Cataloging-in-Publication Data

Schmitz, James H., 1911-
  Witches of Karres / by James Schmitz; edited by Eric Flint.
    p. cm.
  ISBN 0-7434-8837-7
  1. Space ships--Fiction. 2. Women slaves--Fiction. 3. Witches--Fiction.
  I. Flint, Eric. II. Title.

PS3569.C5175W58 2004
813'.54--dc22

2004009762

Distributed by Simon & Schuster
1230 Avenue of the Americas
New York, NY 10020

Production by Windhaven Press, Auburn, NH
Printed in the United States of America

10 9 8 7 6 5 4 3 2 1

This book is dedicated to
a very good little witch named
SYLVIA ANN THOMAS

Chapter ONE

IT WAS AROUND the hub of the evening on the planet of Porlumma when Captain Pausert, commercial traveler from the Republic of Nikkeldepain, met the first of the witches of Karres.

It was just plain fate, so far as he could see.

He was feeling pretty good as he left a high-priced bar on a cobbled street near the spaceport, with the intention of returning straight to his ship. There hadn't been an argument, exactly. But someone had grinned broadly, as usual, when the captain pronounced the name of his native system; and the captain had pointed out then, with considerable wit, how much more ridiculous it was to call a planet Porlumma, for instance, than to call it Nikkeldepain.

He then proceeded to collect an increasing number of pained stares as he continued with a detailed comparison of the varied, interesting, and occasionally brilliant role Nikkeldepain had played in history with Porlumma's obviously dull and dumpy status as a sixth-rate Empire outpost.

In conclusion, he admitted frankly that he wouldn't care to be found dead on Porlumma.

1

Somebody muttered loudly in Imperial Universum that in that case it might be better if he didn't hang around Porlumma too long. But the captain only smiled politely, paid for his two drinks, and left.

There was no point in getting into a rhubarb on one of these border planets. Their citizens still had an innocent notion that they ought to act like frontiersmen—but then the Law always showed up at once.

Yes, he felt pretty good. Up to the last four months of his young life, he had never looked on himself as being particularly patriotic. But compared to most of the Empire's worlds, Nikkeldepain was downright attractive in its stuffy way. Besides, he was returning there solvent—would they ever be surprised!

And awaiting him, fondly and eagerly, was Illyla, the Miss Onswud, fair daughter of the mighty Councilor Onswud, and the captain's secretly betrothed for almost a year. She alone had believed in him . . . .

The captain smiled and checked at a dark cross-street to get his bearings on the spaceport beacon. Less than half a mile away. . . . He set off again. In about six hours he'd be beyond the Empire's space borders and headed straight for Illyla.

Yes, she alone had believed! After the prompt collapse of the captain's first commercial venture—a miffel-fur farm, largely on capital borrowed from Councilor Onswud—the future had looked very black. It had even included a probable ten-year stretch of penal servitude for "willful and negligent abuse of entrusted monies." The laws of Nikkeldepain were rough on debtors.

"But you've always been looking for someone to take out the old *Venture* and get her back into trade!" Illyla reminded her father tearfully.

"Umm, yes! But it's in the blood, my dear! His great-uncle Threbus went the same way! It would be far better to let the law take its course," said Councilor Onswud, glaring at Pausert who remained sulkily silent. He had *tried* to explain that the mysterious epidemic which suddenly wiped out most of the stock of miffels wasn't his fault. In fact, he more than suspected the tricky hand of young Councilor Rapport who had been wagging futilely around Illyla for the last couple of years....

"The *Venture*, now...!" Councilor Onswud mused, stroking his long, craggy chin. "Pausert can handle a ship, at least," he admitted.

That was how it happened. Were they ever going to be surprised! For even the captain realized that Councilor Onswud was unloading all the dead fish that had gathered the dust of his warehouses for the past fifty years on him and the *Venture*, in a last, faint hope of getting some return on those half-forgotten investments. A value of eighty-two thousand maels was placed on the cargo; but if he'd brought even three-quarters of it back in cash, all would have been well.

Instead—well, it started with that lucky bet on a legal point with an Imperial official at the Imperial capital itself. Then came a six-hour race fairly won against a small, fast private yacht—the old *Venture 7333* had been a pirate-chaser in the last century and still could produce twice the speed her looks suggested. From then on the captain was socially accepted as a sporting man and was in on a long string of jovial parties and meets.

Jovial and profitable—the wealthier Imperials just couldn't resist a gamble, and the penalty the captain always insisted on was that they had to buy.

He got rid of the stuff right and left. Inside of twelve weeks, nothing remained of the original cargo except two score bundles of expensively-built but useless tinklewood fishing rods, one dozen gross bales of useful but unattractive allweather cloaks, and a case of sophisticated educational toys which showed a disconcerting tendency to explode when jarred or dropped. Even on a bet, nobody would take those three items.

But the captain had a strong hunch they had been hopefully added to the cargo from his own stocks by Councilor Rapport; so his failure to sell them didn't break his heart.

He was a neat twenty percent net ahead, at that point—

And finally came this last-minute rush delivery of medical supplies to Porlumma on the return route. That haul alone would repay the miffel farm losses three times over!

The captain grinned broadly into the darkness. Yes, they'd be surprised . . . but just where was he now?

He checked again in the narrow street, searching for the port beacon in the sky. There it was—off to his left and a little behind him. He'd gotten turned around somehow.

He set off carefully down an excessively dark little alley. It was one of those towns where everybody locked their front doors at night and retired to lit-up enclosed courtyards at the backs of the houses. There were voices and the rattling of dishes nearby and occasional whoops of laughter and singing all around him; but it was all beyond high walls which let little or no light into the alley.

It ended abruptly in a cross-alley and another wall. After a moment's debate the captain turned to the left again. Light spilled out on his new route a hundred yards ahead where a courtyard was opened on the alley. From it, as he approached, came the sound of doors being violently slammed and then a sudden loud mingling of voices.

"Yeee-eep!" shrilled a high, childish voice. It could have been mortal agony, terror, or even hysterical laughter. The captain broke into an apprehensive trot.

"Yes, I see you up there!" a man shouted excitedly in Universum. "I caught you now—you get down from those boxes! I'll skin you alive! Fifty-two customers sick of the stomach-ache—YOW!"

The last exclamation was accompanied by a sound as of a small, loosely built wooden house collapsing, and was followed by a succession of squeals and an angry bellowing, in which the only distinguishable words were: "threw the boxes on me!" Then more sounds of splintering wood.

"Hey!" yelled the captain indignantly from the corner of the alley.

All action ceased. The narrow courtyard, brightly illuminated by a single overhead light, was half covered with a tumbled litter of empty wooden boxes. Standing with his foot temporarily caught in one of them was a very large fat man dressed all in white and waving a stick. Momentarily cornered between the wall and two of the boxes, over one of which she was trying to climb, was a smallish, fair-haired girl dressed in a smock of some kind which was also white. She might be about fourteen, the captain thought—a helpless kid, anyway.

"What *you* want?" grunted the fat man, pointing the stick with some dignity at the captain.

"Lay off the kid!" rumbled the captain, edging into the courtyard.

"Mind your own business!" shouted the fat man, waving his stick like a club. "I'll take care of her! She—"

"I never did!" squealed the girl. She burst into tears.

"Try it, Fat and Ugly!" the captain warned. "I'll ram the stick down your throat!"

He was very close now. With a sound of grunting exasperation the fat man pulled his foot free of the box, wheeled suddenly and brought the end of the stick down on top of the captain's cap. The captain hit him furiously in the middle of the stomach.

There was a short flurry of activity, somewhat hampered by shattering boxes everywhere. Then the captain stood up, scowling and breathing hard. The fat man remained sitting on the ground, gasping about "—the law!"

Somewhat to his surprise, the captain discovered the girl standing just behind him. She caught his eye and smiled.

"My name's Maleen," she offered. She pointed at the fat man. "Is he hurt bad?"

"Huh-no!" panted the captain. "But maybe we'd better—"

It was too late! A loud, self-assured voice became audible now at the opening to the alley:

"Here, here, here, here, here!" it said in the reproachful, situation-under-control tone that always seemed the same to the captain, on whatever world and in whichever language he heard it.

"What's all this about?" it inquired rhetorically.

"You'll all have to come along!" it replied.

Police court on Porlumma appeared to be a business conducted on a very efficient, around-the-clock basis. They were the next case up.

Nikkeldepain was an odd name, wasn't it, the judge smiled. He then listened attentively to the various charges, counter-charges, and denials.

Bruth the Baker was charged with having struck a citizen of a foreign government on the head with a potentially lethal instrument—produced in evidence. Said citizen admittedly had attempted to interfere as Bruth was attempting to punish his slave Maleen—also produced in evidence—whom he suspected of having added something to a batch of cakes she was working on that afternoon, resulting in illness and complaints from fifty-two of Bruth's customers.

Said foreign citizen also had used insulting language—the captain admitted under pressure to "Fat and Ugly."

Some provocation could be conceded for the action taken by Bruth, but not enough. Bruth paled.

Captain Pausert, of the Republic of Nikkeldepain—everybody but the prisoners smiled this time—was charged (a) with said attempted interference, (b) with said insult, (c) with having frequently and severely struck Bruth the Baker in the course of the subsequent dispute.

The blow on the head was conceded to have provided a provocation for charge (c)—but not enough.

Nobody seemed to be charging the slave Maleen with any-thing. The judge only looked at her curiously, and shook his head.

"As the Court considers this regrettable incident," he remarked, "it looks like two years for you, Bruth; and about three for you, Captain. Too bad!"

The captain had an awful sinking feeling. From what he knew about Imperial court methods in the fringe systems, he probably could get out of this three-year rap. But it would be expensive.

He realized that the judge was studying him reflectively.

"The Court wishes to acknowledge," the judge continued, "that the captain's chargeable actions were due largely to a natural feeling of human sympathy for the predicament of the slave Maleen. The Court, therefore, would suggest a settlement as follows—subsequent to which all charges could be dropped:

"That Bruth the Baker resell Maleen of Karres—with whose services he appears to be dissatisfied—for a reasonable sum to Captain Pausert of the Republic of Nikkeldepain."

Bruth the Baker heaved a gusty sigh of relief. But the captain hesitated. The buying of human slaves by private citizens was a very serious offense on Nikkeldepain. Still, he didn't have to make a record of it. If they weren't going to soak him too much—

At just the right moment Maleen of Karres introduced a barely audible, forlorn, sniffling sound.

"How much are you asking for the kid?" the captain inquired, looking without friendliness at his recent antagonist. A day was coming when he would think less severely of Bruth; but it hadn't come yet.

Bruth scowled back but replied with a certain eagerness, "A hundred and fifty m—" A policeman standing behind him poked him sharply in the side. Bruth shut up.

"Seven hundred maels," the judge said smoothly. "There'll be Court charges, and a fee for recording the transaction—"

He appeared to make a swift calculation. "Fifteen hundred and forty-two maels." He turned to a clerk. "You've looked him up?"

The clerk nodded. "He's right!"

"And we'll take your check," the judge concluded. He gave the captain a friendly smile. "Next case."

The captain felt a little bewildered.

There was something peculiar about this! He was getting out of it much too cheaply. Since the Empire had quit its wars of expansion, young slaves in good health were a high-priced article. Furthermore, he was practically positive that Bruth the Baker had been willing to sell for a tenth of what he actually had to pay!

Well, he wouldn't complain. Rapidly, he signed, sealed, and thumbprinted various papers shoved at him by a helpful clerk; and made out a check.

"I guess," he told Maleen of Karres, "we'd better get along to the ship."

And now what was he going to do with the kid, he pondered, as he padded along the unlighted streets with his slave trotting quietly behind him. If he showed up with a pretty girl-slave on Nikkeldepain, even a small one, various good friends there would toss him into ten years or so of penal servitude—immediately after Illyla had personally collected his scalp. They were a moral lot.

Karres—?

"How far off is Karres, Maleen?" he asked into the dark.

"It takes about two weeks," Maleen said tearfully.

Two weeks! The captain's heart sank again.

"What are you blubbering about?" he inquired uncomfortably.

Maleen choked, sniffed, and began sobbing openly.

"I have two little sisters!" she cried.

"Well, well," the captain said encouragingly. "That's nice—

you'll be seeing them again soon. I'm taking you home, you know."

Great Patham—now he'd said it! But after all—

However, this piece of good news seemed to have the wrong effect on his slave. Her sobbing grew much more violent.

"No, I won't," she wailed. "They're here!"

"Huh?" said the captain. He stopped short. "Where?"

"And the people they're with are mean to them, too!" wept Maleen.

The captain's heart dropped clean through his boots. Standing there in the dark, he helplessly watched it coming:

"You could buy them awfully cheap!" she said.

In times of stress the young life of Karres appeared to take to the heights. It might be a mountainous place.

The Leewit sat on the top shelf on the back wall of the crockery and antiques store, strategically flanked by two expensive-looking vases. She was a doll-sized edition of Maleen; but her eyes were cold and gray instead of blue and tearful. About five or six, the captain vaguely estimated. He wasn't very good at estimating them around that age.

"Good evening," he said as he came in through the door. The Crockery and Antiques Shop had been easy to find. Like Bruth the Baker's, it was the one spot in the neighborhood that was all lit up.

"Good evening, sir!" said what was presumably the store owner, without looking around. He sat with his back to the door, in a chair approximately at the center of the store and facing the Leewit at a distance of about twenty feet.

" . . . and there you can stay without food or drink till the Holy Man comes in the morning!" he continued immediately, in the taut voice of a man who has gone through hysteria and is sane again. The captain realized he was addressing the Leewit.

"Your other Holy Man didn't stay very long!" the diminutive

creature piped, also ignoring the captain. Apparently she had not yet discovered Maleen behind him.

"This is a stronger denomination—much stronger!" the store owner replied, in a shaking voice but with a sort of relish. "*He'll* exorcise you, all right, little demon—you'll whistle no buttons off him! Your time is up! Go on and whistle all you want! Bust every vase in the place—"

The Leewit blinked her gray eyes thoughtfully at him.

"Might!" she said.

"But if you try to climb down from there," the store owner went on, on a rising note, "I'll chop you into bits—into little, little bits!"

He raised his arm as he spoke and weakly brandished what the captain recognized with a start of horror as a highly ornamented but probably still useful antique battleax.

"Ha!" said the Leewit.

"Beg your pardon, sir!" the captain said, clearing his throat.

"Good evening, sir!" the store owner repeated, without looking around. "What can I do for you?"

"I came to inquire," the captain said hesitantly, "about that child."

The store owner shifted about in his chair and squinted at the captain with red-rimmed eyes.

"You're not a Holy Man!" he said.

"Hello, Maleen!" the Leewit said suddenly. "That him?"

"We've come to buy you," Maleen said. "Shut up!"

"Good!" said the Leewit.

"Buy it? Are you mocking me, sir?" the store owner inquired.

"Shut up, Moonell!" A thin, dark, determined-looking woman had appeared in the doorway which led through the back wall of the store. She moved out a step under the shelves; and the Leewit leaned down from the top shelf and hissed. The woman moved hurriedly back into the doorway.

"Maybe he means it," she said in a more subdued voice.

"I can't sell to a citizen of the Empire," the store owner said defeatedly.

"I'm not a citizen," the captain said shortly. This time he wasn't going to name it.

"No, he's from Nikkel—" Maleen began.

"Shut up, Maleen!" the captain said helplessly in turn.

"I never heard of Nikkel," the store owner muttered doubtfully.

"Maleen!" the woman called shrilly. "That's the name of one of the others—Bruth the Baker got her. He means it, all right! He's buying them!"

"A hundred and fifty maels!" the captain said craftily, remembering Bruth the Baker. "In cash."

The store owner looked dazed.

"Not enough, Moonell!" the woman called. "Look at all it's broken! Five hundred maels!"

There was a sound then, so thin the captain could hardly hear it. It pierced at his eardrums like two jabs of a delicate needle. To right and left of him, two highly glazed little jugs went *clink-clink!*, showed a sudden veining of cracks, and collapsed.

A brief silence settled on the store. And now that he looked around more closely, the captain could spot here and there other little piles of shattered crockery—and places where similar ruins apparently had been swept up, leaving only traces of colored dust.

The store owner laid the ax carefully down beside his chair, stood up, swaying a little, and came towards the captain.

"You offered me a hundred and fifty maels!" he said rapidly as he approached. "I accept it here, now, see—before witnesses!" He grabbed the captain's right hand in both of his and pumped it up and down vigorously. "Sold!" he yelled.

Then he wheeled around in a leap and pointed a shaking hand at the Leewit.

"And NOW," he howled, "break something! Break anything!

You're his! I'll sue him for every mael he ever made and ever will!"

"Oh, do come help me down, Maleen!" the Leewit pleaded prettily.

For a change the store of Wansing the jeweler was dimly lit and very quiet. It was a sleek, fashionable place in a fashionable shopping block near the spaceport. The front door was unlocked and Wansing was in.

The three of them entered quietly, and the door sighed quietly shut behind them. Beyond a great crystal display counter Wansing was moving about among a number of opened shelves, talking softly to himself. Under the crystal of the counter and in close-packed rows on the satin-covered shelves reposed a many-colored gleaming and glittering and shining. Wansing was no piker.

"Good evening, sir!" the captain said across the counter.

"It's morning!" the Leewit remarked from the other side of Maleen.

"Maleen!" said the captain.

"We're keeping out of this!" Maleen said to the Leewit.

"All right," said the Leewit.

Wansing had come around jerkily at the captain's greeting but had made no other move. Like all the slave owners the captain had met on Porlumma so far, Wansing seemed unhappy. Otherwise he was a large, dark, sleek man with jewels in his ears and a smell of expensive oils and perfumes about him.

"This place is under constant visual guard, of course," he told the captain gently. "Nothing could possibly happen to me here. Why am I so frightened?"

"Not of me, I'm sure!" the captain said with an uncomfortable attempt at geniality. "I'm glad your store's still open," he went on briskly. "I'm here on business."

"Oh, yes, it's still open, of course," Wansing said. He gave the captain a slow smile and turned back to his shelves. "I'm taking inventory, that's why. I've been taking inventory since early yesterday morning. I've counted them all seven times."

"You're very thorough," the captain said.

"Very, very thorough!" Wansing nodded to the shelves. "The last time I found I had made a million maels. But twice before that I had lost approximately the same amount. I shall have to count them again, I suppose." He closed a drawer softly. "I'm sure I counted those before. But they move about constantly. Constantly! It's horrible."

"You have a slave here called Goth," the captain said, driving to the point.

"Yes, I do," Wansing said, nodding. "And I'm sure she understands by now I meant no harm. I do, at any rate. It was perhaps a little—but I'm sure she understands now, or will soon."

"Where is she?" the captain inquired, a trifle uneasily.

"In her room perhaps," Wansing suggested. "It's not so bad when she's there in her room with the door closed. But often she sits in the dark and looks at you as you go past . . . ." He opened another drawer, peered into it, closed it quietly again. "Yes, they do move!" he whispered, as if confirming an earlier suspicion. "Constantly . . . ."

"Look, Wansing," the captain said in a loud, firm voice. "I'm not a citizen of the Empire. I want to buy this Goth. I'll pay you a hundred and fifty maels, cash."

Wansing turned around completely again and looked at the captain. "Oh, you do?" he said. "You're not a citizen?" He walked a few steps to the side of the counter, sat down at a small desk and turned a light on over it. Then he put his face in his hands for a moment.

"I'm a wealthy man," he muttered. "An influential man! The name of Wansing counts for a great deal on Porlumma. When the Empire suggests you buy, you buy, of course—but it need not have been I who bought her! I thought she would be useful in the business—and then even I could not sell her again within the Empire. She has been here a *week!*"

He looked up at the captain and smiled. "One hundred and fifty maels," he said. "Sold! There are records to be made out . . . ." He reached into a drawer and took out some printed forms. He began to write rapidly. The captain produced identifications.

Maleen said suddenly, "Goth?"

"Right here," a voice murmured. Wansing's hand made a convulsive jerk, but he did not look up. He kept on writing.

Something small and lean and bonelessly supple, dressed in a dark jacket and leggings, came across the thick carpets of Wansing's store and stood behind the captain. This one might be about nine or ten.

"I'll take your check, captain," Wansing said politely. "You must be an honest man. Besides, I want to frame it . . . ."

"And now," the captain heard himself say in the remote voice of one who moves through a strange dream, "I suppose we could go to the ship."

The sky was gray and cloudy, and the streets were lightening. Goth, he noticed, didn't resemble her sisters. She had brown hair cut short a few inches below her ears, and brown eyes with long, black lashes. Her nose was short and her chin was pointed. She made him think of some thin, carnivorous creature, like a weasel.

She looked up at him briefly, grinned and said, "Thanks!"

"What was wrong with *him?*" chirped the Leewit, walking backwards for a last view of Wansing's store.

"Tough crook," muttered Goth. The Leewit giggled.

"You premoted this just dandy, Maleen!" she stated next.

"Shut up," said Maleen.

"All right," said the Leewit. She glanced up at the captain's face. "You been fighting!" she said virtuously. "Did you win?"

"Of course the captain won!" said Maleen.

"Good for you!" said the Leewit.

"What about the take-off?" Goth asked the captain. She seemed a little worried.

"Nothing to it!" the captain said stoutly, hardly bothering to wonder how she'd guessed the take-off was the one maneuver on which he and the old *Venture* consistently failed to cooperate.

"No," said Goth. "I meant, when?"

"Right now," said the captain. "They've already cleared us. We'll get the sign any second."

"Good," said Goth. She walked off slowly down the passage towards the central section of the ship.

The take-off was pretty bad, but the *Venture* made it again. Half an hour later, with Porlumma dwindling safely behind them, the captain switched to automatic and climbed out of his chair. After considerable experimentation he got the electric butler adjusted to four breakfasts, hot, with coffee. It was accomplished with a great deal of advice and attempted assistance from the Leewit, rather less from Maleen, and no comment from Goth.

"Everything will be coming along in a few minutes now!" he announced. Afterwards it struck him there had been a quality of grisly prophecy about the statement.

"If you'd listen to me," said the Leewit, "we'd have been done eating a quarter of an hour ago!" She was perspiring but triumphant—she had been right all along.

"Say, Maleen," she said suddenly, "you premoting again?"

Premoting? The captain looked at Maleen. She seemed pale and troubled.

"Spacesick?" he suggested. "I've got some pills."

"No, she's premoting," the Leewit said, scowling. "What's up, Maleen?"

"Shut up," said Goth.

"All right," said the Leewit. She was silent a moment and then began to wriggle. "Maybe we'd better—"

"Shut up," said Maleen.

"It's all ready," said Goth.

"What's all ready?" asked the captain.

"All right," said the Leewit. She looked at the captain. "Nothing!" she said.

He looked at them then, and they looked at him—one set each of gray eyes, and brown, and blue. They were all sitting around the control room floor in a circle, the fifth side of which was occupied by the electric butler.

What peculiar little waifs, the captain thought. He hadn't perhaps really realized until now just how *very* peculiar. They were still staring at him.

"Well, well!" he said heartily. "So Maleen 'premotes' and gives people stomach-aches."

Maleen smiled dimly and smoothed back her yellow hair.

"They just thought they were getting them," she murmured.

"Mass history," explained the Leewit, offhandedly.

"Hysteria," said Goth. "The Imperials get their hair up about us every so often."

"I noticed that," the captain nodded. "And little Leewit here—she whistles and busts things."

"It's *the* Leewit," the Leewit said, frowning.

"Oh, I see," said the captain. "Like *the* captain, eh?"

"That's right," said the Leewit. She smiled.

"And what does little Goth do?" the captain addressed the third witch.

Little Goth appeared pained. Maleen answered for her.

"Goth teleports mostly," she said.

"Oh, she does?" said the captain. "I've heard about that trick, too," he added lamely.

"Just small stuff really!" Goth said abruptly. She reached into the top of her jacket and pulled out a cloth-wrapped bundle the size of the captain's two fists. The four ends of the cloth were knotted together. Goth undid the knot. "Like this," she said and poured out the contents on the rug between them. There was a sound like a big bagful of marbles being spilled.

"Great Patham!" the captain swore, staring down at what was a cool quarter-million in jewel stones, or he was still a miffel-farmer.

"Good gosh," said the Leewit, bouncing to her feet. "Maleen, we better get at it right away!"

The two blondes darted from the room. The captain hardly noticed their going. He was staring at Goth.

"Child," he said, "don't you realize they hang you without a trial on places like Porlumma if you're caught with stolen goods?"

"We're not on Porlumma," said Goth. She looked slightly annoyed. "They're for you. You spent money on us, didn't you?"

"Not that kind of money," said the captain. "If Wansing noticed . . . they're Wansing's, I suppose?"

"Sure," said Goth. "Pulled them in just before take-off."

"If he reported, there'll be police ships on our tail any—"

"Goth!" Maleen shrilled.

Goth's head came around and she rolled up on her feet in one motion. "Coming," she shouted. "Excuse me," she murmured to the captain. Then she, too, was out of the room.

Again the captain scarcely noticed her departure. He had rushed to the control desk with a sudden awful certainty and switched on all screens.

There they were! Two needle-nosed dark ships coming up fast from behind, and already almost in gun range! They weren't regular police boats, the captain realized, but auxiliary craft of the Empire's frontier fleets. He rammed the *Venture's* drives full on. Immediately, red-and-black fire blossoms began to sprout in space behind him—then a finger of flame stabbed briefly past, not a hundred yards to the right of the ship.

But the communicator stayed dead. Evidently, Porlumma

preferred risking the sacrifice of Wansing's jewels to giving him and his misguided charges a chance to surrender . . . .

He was putting the *Venture* through a wildly erratic and, he hoped, aim-destroying series of sideways hops and forward lunges with one hand, and trying to unlimber the turrets of the nova guns with the other, when suddenly—

No, he decided at once, there was no use trying to understand it. There were just no more Empire ships around. The screens all blurred and darkened simultaneously; and, for a short while, a darkness went flowing and coiling lazily past the *Venture*. Light jumped out of it at him once in a cold, ugly glare, and receded again in a twisting, unnatural fashion. The *Venture's* drives seemed dead.

Then, just as suddenly, the old ship jerked, shivered, roared aggrievedly, and was hurling herself along on her own power again.

But Porlumma's sun was no longer in evidence. Stars gleamed in the remoteness of space all about. Some of the patterns seemed familiar, but he wasn't a good enough general navigator to be sure.

The captain stood up stiffly, feeling heavy and cold. And at that moment, with a wild, hilarious clacking like a metallic hen, the electric butler delivered four breakfasts, hot, right on the center of the control room floor.

The first voice said distinctly, "Shall we just leave it on?"

A second voice, considerably more muffled, replied, "Yes, let's! You never know when you need it—"

The third voice, tucked somewhere in between them, said simply, "*Whew!*"

Peering about in bewilderment, the captain realized suddenly that the voices had come from the speaker of the ship's intercom connecting the control room with what had once been the *Venture's* captain's cabin.

He listened; but only a dim murmuring was audible now,

and then nothing at all. He started towards the passage, returned and softly switched off the intercom. He went quietly down the passage until he came to the captain's cabin. Its door was closed.

He listened a moment, and opened it suddenly.

There was a trio of squeals:

"Oh, don't! You spoiled it!"

The captain stood motionless. Just one glimpse had been given him of what seemed to be a bundle of twisted black wires arranged loosely like the frame of a truncated cone on—or was it just above?—a table in the center of the cabin. Above the wires, where the tip of the cone should have been, burned a round, swirling orange fire. About it, their faces reflecting its glow, stood the three witches.

Then the fire vanished; the wires collapsed. There was only ordinary light in the room. They were looking up at him variously—Maleen with smiling regret, the Leewit in frank annoyance, Goth with no expression at all.

"What out of Great Patham's Seventh Hell was that?" inquired the captain, his hair bristling slowly.

The Leewit looked at Goth; Goth looked at Maleen. Maleen said doubtfully, "We can just tell you its name . . . ."

"That was the Sheewash Drive," said Goth.

"The what drive?" asked the captain.

"Sheewash," repeated Maleen.

"The one you have to do it with yourself," the Leewit added helpfully.

"Shut up," said Maleen.

There was a long pause. The captain looked down at the handful of thin, black, twelve-inch wires scattered about the table top. He touched one of them. It was dead cold.

"I see," he said. "I guess we're all going to have a long talk." Another pause. "Where are we now?"

"About two light-weeks down the way you were going," said Goth. "We only worked it thirty seconds."

"Twenty-eight," corrected Maleen, with the authority of her years. "The Leewit was getting tired."

"I see," said Captain Pausert carefully. "Well, let's go have some breakfast."

They ate with a silent voraciousness, dainty Maleen, the exquisite Leewit, supple Goth, all alike. The captain, long finished, watched them with amazement and—now at last—with something like awe.

"It's the Sheewash Drive," explained Maleen finally, catching his expression.

"Takes it out of you!" said Goth.

The Leewit grunted affirmatively and stuffed on.

"Can't do too much of it," said Maleen. "Or too often. It kills you sure!"

"What," said the captain, "*is* the Sheewash Drive?"

They became reticent. Karres people did it, said Maleen, when they had to go somewhere fast. Everybody knew how there. "But of course," she added, "we're pretty young to do it right."

"We did it pretty clumping *good!*" the Leewit contradicted positively. She seemed to be finished at last.

"But how?" said the captain.

Reticence thickened almost visibly. If you couldn't do it, said Maleen, you couldn't understand it either.

He gave it up, for the time being.

"We'll have to figure out how to take you home next," he said; and they agreed.

Karres, it developed, was in the Iverdahl System. He couldn't find any planet of that designation listed in his maps of the area, but that meant nothing. The maps weren't always accurate, and local names changed a lot.

Barring the use of weird and deadly miracle-drives, that detour was going to cost him almost a month in time—and a good chunk of his profits in power used up. The jewels Goth had illegally teleported must, of course, be returned to their owner, he explained. He'd intended to look severely at the culprit at that point; but she'd meant well, after all. They were extremely unusual children, but still children—they couldn't really understand.

He would stop off en route to Karres at an Empire planet with interstellar banking facilities to take care of that matter, the captain added. A planet far enough off so the police wouldn't be likely to take any particular interest in the *Venture*.

A dead silence greeted this schedule. He gathered that the representatives of Karres did not think much of his logic.

"Well," Maleen sighed at last, "we'll see you get your money back some other way then!"

The junior witches nodded coldly.

"How did you three happen to get into this fix?" the captain inquired, with the intention of changing the subject.

They'd left Karres together on a jaunt of their own, they explained. No, they hadn't run away—he got the impression that such trips were standard procedure for juveniles in that place. They were on another world, a civilized one but beyond the borders and law of Empire, when the town they were in was raided by a small fleet of slavers. They were taken along with most of the local youngsters.

"It's a wonder," the captain said reflectively, "you didn't take over the ship."

"Oh, brother!" exclaimed the Leewit.

"Not that ship!" said Goth.

"That was an Imperial Slaver!" Maleen informed him. "You behave yourself every second on those crates."

Just the same, the captain thought, as he settled himself to rest on a couch he had set up in the control room, it was no longer surprising that the Empire wanted no young slaves from Karres to be transported to the interior! Oddest sort of children. . . . But he ought to be able to get his expenses paid by their relatives. Something very profitable might even be made of this deal . . . .

Have to watch the record entries though! Nikkeldepain's laws were explicit about the penalties invoked by anything resembling the purchase and sale of slaves.

He'd thoughtfully left the intercom adjusted so he could listen in on their conversation in the captain's cabin. However, there had been nothing for some time beyond frequent bursts of childish giggling. Then came a succession of piercing shrieks from the Leewit. It appeared she was being forcibly washed behind the ears by Maleen and obliged to brush her teeth, in preparation for bedtime.

It had been agreed that he was not to enter the cabin, because—for reasons not given—they couldn't keep the Sheewash Drive on in his presence; and they wanted to have it ready, in case of an emergency. Piracy was rife beyond the Imperial borders, and the *Venture* would keep beyond the border for most of the trip, to avoid the more pressing danger of police pursuit instigated by Porlumma. The captain had explained the potentialities of the nova guns the *Venture* boasted, or tried to. Possibly they hadn't understood. At any rate, they seemed unimpressed.

The Sheewash Drive! Boy, he thought in sudden excitement, if he could just get the principles of that. Maybe he would!

He raised his head suddenly. The Leewit's voice had lifted clearly over the communicator.

" . . . not such a bad old dope!" the childish treble remarked. The captain blinked indignantly.

"He's not so old," Maleen's soft voice returned. "And he's certainly no dope!"

He smiled. Good kid, Maleen.

"Yeah, yeah!" squeaked the Leewit offensively. "Maleen's sweet onthu—ulp!"

A vague commotion continued for a while, indicating, he

hoped, that someone he could mention was being smothered under a pillow.

He drifted off to sleep before it was settled.

If you didn't happen to be thinking of what they'd done, they seemed more or less like normal children. Right from the start they displayed a flattering interest in the captain and his background; and he told them all about everything and everybody in Nikkeldepain. Finally he even showed them his treasured pocket-sized picture of Illyla—the one with which he'd held many cozy conversations during the earlier part of his trip.

Almost at once, though, he realized that was a mistake. They studied it intently in silence, their heads crowded close together.

"Oh, brother!" the Leewit whispered then, with entirely the wrong kind of inflection.

"Just what did you mean by that?" the captain inquired coldly.

"Sweet!" murmured Goth. But it was the way she closed her eyes briefly, as though gripped by a light spasm of nausea.

"Shut up, Goth!" Maleen said sharply. "I think she's very swee . . . I mean, she looks very nice!" she told the captain.

The captain was disgruntled. Silently, he retrieved the maligned Illyla and returned her to his breast pocket. Silently, he went off and left them standing there.

But afterwards, in private, he took it out again and studied it worriedly.

His Illyla! He shifted the picture back and forth under the light. It wasn't really a very good picture of her, he decided. It had been bungled. From certain angles, one might even say that Illyla did look the least bit insipid.

What was he thinking, he thought, shocked.

He unlimbered the nova gun turrets next and got in a little firing practice. They had been sealed when he took over the *Venture* and weren't supposed to be used, except in absolute emergencies. They were somewhat uncertain weapons, though very effective, and Nikkeldepain had turned to safer forms of armament many decades ago. But on the third day out from Nikkeldepain, the captain made a brief notation in his log:

"Attacked by two pirate craft. Unsealed nova guns. Destroyed one attacker; survivor fled . . . ."

He was rather pleased by that crisp, hard-bitten description of desperate space adventure, and enjoyed rereading it occasionally. It wasn't true, though. He had put in an interesting four hours at the time pursuing and annihilating large, craggy chunks of an asteroid swarm he found the *Venture* plowing through. Those nova guns were fascinating stuff! You'd sight the turrets on something; and so long as it didn't move after that, it was all right. If it did move, it got it—unless you relented and deflected the turrets first. They were just the thing for arresting a pirate in mid-space.

The *Venture* dipped back into the Empire's borders four days later and headed for the capital of the local province. Police ships challenged them twice on the way in; and the captain found considerable comfort in the awareness that his passengers forgathered silently in their cabin on these occasions. They didn't tell him they were set to use the Sheewash Drive— somehow it had never been mentioned since that first day— but he knew the queer orange fire was circling over its skimpy framework of twisted wires there and ready to act.

However, the space police waved him on, satisfied with routine identification. Apparently the *Venture* had not become generally known as a criminal ship, to date.

Maleen accompanied him to the banking institution which was to return Wansing's property to Porlumma. Her sisters, at the captain's definite request, remained on the ship.

The transaction itself went off without a visible hitch. The jewels would reach their destination in Porlumma within a month. But he had to take out a staggering sum in insurance. "Piracy, thieves!" smiled the clerk. "Even summary capital punishment won't keep the rats down!" And, of course, he had to register name, ship, home planet, and so on. But since they already had all that information on Porlumma, he gave it without hesitation.

On the way back to the spaceport, he sent off a sealed message by subradio to the bereaved jeweler, informing him of the action taken and regretting the misunderstanding.

He felt a little better after that, though the insurance payment had been a severe blow. If he didn't manage to work out a decent profit on Karres somehow, the losses on the miffel farm would hardly be covered now . . . .

Then he noticed Maleen was getting uneasy.

"We'd better hurry!" was all she would say, however. Her face turned pale.

The captain understood. She was having another premonition! The hitch to this premoting business was apparently that when something was brewing you were informed of the bare fact but had to guess at most of the details. They grabbed an aircab and raced back to the spaceport.

They had just been cleared there when he spotted a group of uniformed men coming along the dock on the double. They stopped short and scattered as the *Venture* lurched drunkenly sideways into the air. Everyone else in sight was scattering, too.

That was a very bad take-off—one of the captain's worst. Once afloat, however, he ran the ship promptly into the nightside of the planet and turned her nose towards the border. The old pirate-chaser had plenty of speed when you gave her the reins; and throughout the entire next sleep period he let her use it all.

The Sheewash Drive was not required that time.

Next day he had a lengthy private talk with Goth on the Golden Rule and the Law, with particular reference to individual property rights. If Councilor Onswud had been monitoring the sentiments expressed by the captain, he could not have failed to rumble surprised approval. The delinquent herself listened impassively, but the captain fancied she showed distinct signs of being impressed by his earnestness.

It was two days after that—well beyond the borders again—when they were obliged to make an unscheduled stop at a mining moon. For the captain discovered he had badly miscalculated the extent to which the prolonged run on overdrive after leaving the capital was going to deplete the *Venture's* reserves. They would have to juice up . . . .

A large, extremely handsome Sirian freighter lay beside them at the moon station. It was half a battlecraft really, since it dealt regularly beyond the borders. They had to wait while it was being serviced; and it took a long time. The Sirians turned out to be as unpleasant as their ship was good-looking—a snooty, conceited, hairy lot who talked only their own dialect and pretended to be unfamiliar with Imperial Universum.

The captain found himself getting irked by their bad manners—particularly when he discovered they were laughing over his argument with the service superintendent about the cost of repowering the *Venture*.

"You're out in deep space, Captain," said the superintendent. "And you haven't juice enough left even to travel back to the border. You can't expect Imperial prices here!"

"It's not what you charged *them!*" The captain angrily jerked his thumb at the Sirian.

The superintendent shrugged. "Regular customers! You start coming by here every three months like they do, and we can make an arrangement with you, too."

It was outrageous—it actually put the *Venture* back in the red. But there was no help for it.

Nor did it improve the captain's temper when he muffed the take-off once more—and then had to watch the Sirian floating into space, as sedately as a swan, a little behind him.

Chapter TWO

AN HOUR LATER, as he sat glumly at the controls, debating
the chances of recouping his losses before returning to Nikkeldepain, Maleen and the Leewit hurriedly entered the room.
They did something to a port screen.

"They sure are!" the Leewit exclaimed. She seemed child-
ishly pleased.

"Are what?" the captain inquired absently.

"Following us," said Maleen. She did not sound pleased. "It's
that Sirian ship, Captain Pausert!"

The captain stared bewilderedly at the screen. There was a
ship in focus there. It was quite obviously the Sirian and, just
as obviously, it was following them.

"What do they want?" he wondered. "They're stinkers but
they're not pirates. Even if they were, they wouldn't spend an
hour running after a crate like the *Venture*."

Maleen said nothing. The Leewit observed, "Got their bow
turrets out now! Better get those nova guns ready!"

"But it's all nonsense!" the captain said, flushing angrily. He
turned towards the communicators. "What's that Empire general beam length?"

".00r44," said Maleen.

A roaring, abusive voice flooded the control room immediately. The one word understandable to the captain was "*Venture*." It was repeated frequently.

"Sirian," said the captain. "Can you understand them?" he asked Maleen.

She shook her head. "The Leewit can."

The Leewit nodded, gray eyes glistening.

"What are they saying?"

"They says you're for stopping," the Leewit translated rapidly, apparently retaining some of the original sentence structure. "They says you're for skinning alive . . . ha! They says you're for stopping right now and for only hanging. They says—"

Maleen scuttled from the control room. The Leewit banged the communicator with one small fist.

"Beak-Wock!" she shrilled. It sounded that way, anyway. The loud voice paused a moment.

"BEAK-Wock?" it returned in an aggrieved, startled tone.

"Beak-Wock!" the Leewit affirmed with apparent delight. She rattled off a string of similar-sounding syllables.

A howl of inarticulate wrath responded.

The captain, in a whirl of outraged emotions, was yelling at the Leewit to shut up, at the Sirian to go to Great Patham's Second Hell—the worst—and wrestling with the nova gun adjustors at the same time. He'd had about enough! He'd—

SSS-*whoosh!*

It was the Sheewash Drive.

"And where are we now?" the captain inquired, in a voice of unnatural calm.

"Same place, just about," the Leewit told him. "Ship's still on the screen. Way back though—take them an hour again to catch up." She seemed disappointed; then brightened. "You got lots of time to get the guns ready . . ."

The captain didn't answer. He was marching down the

passage towards the rear of the *Venture*. He passed the captain's cabin and noted the door was shut. He went on without pausing. He was mad clean through—he knew what had happened!

After all he'd told her, Goth had teleported again.

It was all there, in the storage. Items of up to a pound in weight seemed as much as she could handle. But amazing quantities of stuff had met that one requirement—bottles filled with what might be perfume or liquor or dope, expensive-looking garments and cloths in a shining variety of colors, small boxes, odds, ends, and, of course, jewelry . . . .

He spent half an hour getting it loaded into a steel space crate. He wheeled the crate into the big storage lock, sealed the inside lock door and pulled the switch that activated the automatic launching device.

The outer lock door slammed shut. He stalked back to the control room. The Leewit was still in charge, fiddling with the communicators.

"I could try a whistle over them," she suggested, glancing up. She added, "But they'd bust somewheres, sure."

"*Get them on again!*" the captain said.

"Yes, sir," said the Leewit, surprised.

The roaring voice came back faintly.

"SHUT UP!" the captain shouted in Imperial Universum. The voice shut up.

"Tell them they can pick up their stuff—it's been dumped out in a crate," the captain instructed the Leewit. "Tell them I'm proceeding on my course. Tell them if they follow me one light-minute beyond that crate, I'll come back for them, shoot their front end off, shoot their rear end off, and ram 'em in the middle."

"Yes, SIR!" the Leewit sparkled. They proceeded on their course.

Nobody followed.

"Now I want to speak to Goth," the captain announced. He

was still at a high boil. "Privately," he added. "Back in the storage—"

Goth followed him expressionlessly into the storage. He closed the door to the passage. He'd broken off a two-foot length from the tip of one of Councilor Rapport's overpriced tinklewood fishing poles. It made a fair switch.

But Goth looked terribly small just now! He cleared his throat. He wished for a moment he were back on Nikkeldepain.

"I warned you," he said.

Goth didn't move. Between one second and the next, however, she seemed to grow remarkably. Her brown eyes focused on the captain's Adam's apple; her lip lifted at one side. A slightly hungry look came into her face.

"Wouldn't try that!" she murmured.

Mad again, the captain reached out quickly and got a handful of leathery cloth. There was a blur of motion, and what felt like a small explosion against his left kneecap. He grunted with anguished surprise and fell back on a bale of Councilor Rapport's allweather cloaks. But he had retained his grip—Goth fell half on top of him, and that was still a favorable position. Then her head snaked around, her neck seemed to extend itself, and her teeth snapped his wrist.

Weasels don't let go—

"Didn't think he'd have the nerve!" Goth's voice came over the intercom. There was a note of grudging admiration in it. It seemed she was inspecting her bruises.

All tangled up in the job of bandaging his freely bleeding wrist, the captain hoped she'd find a good plenty to count. His knee felt the size of a sofa pillow and throbbed like a piston engine.

"The captain is a brave man," Maleen was saying reproachfully. "You should have known better."

"He's not very *smart*, though!" the Leewit remarked suggestively.

There was a short silence.

"Is he? Goth? Eh?" the Leewit urged.

"Perhaps not very," said Goth.

"You two lay off him!" Maleen ordered. "Unless," she added meaningly, "you want to *swim* back to Karres—on the Egger Route!"

"Not me," the Leewit said briefly.

"You could do it, I guess," said Goth. She seemed to be reflecting. "All right—we'll lay off him. It was a fair fight, anyway."

They raised Karres the sixteenth day after leaving Porlumma. There had been no more incidents; but then, neither had there been any more stops or other contacts with the defenseless Empire. Maleen had cooked up a poultice which did wonders for his knee. With the end of the trip in sight, all tensions relaxed; and Maleen, at least, seemed to grow hourly more regretful at the prospect of parting.

After a brief study Karres could be distinguished easily enough by the fact that it moved counterclockwise to all the other planets of the Iverdahl System.

Well, it would, the captain thought.

They came soaring into its atmosphere on the dayside without arousing any detectable interest. No communicator signals reached them, and no other ships showed up to look them over. Karres, in fact, had the appearance of a completely uninhabited world. There were a large number of seas, too big to be called lakes and too small to be oceans, scattered over its surface. There was one enormously towering ridge of mountains which ran from pole to pole, and any number of lesser chains. There were two good-sized ice caps; and the southern section of the planet was speckled with intermittent stretches of snow. Almost all of it seemed to be dense forest.

It was a handsome place, in a wild, somber way.

They went gliding over it, from noon through morning and

into the dawn fringe—the captain at the controls, Goth and the Leewit flanking him at the screens, and Maleen behind him to do the directing. After a few initial squeals the Leewit became oddly silent. Suddenly the captain realized she was blubbering.

Somehow it startled him to discover that her homecoming had affected the Leewit to that extent. He felt Goth reach out behind him and put her hand on the Leewit's shoulder. The smallest witch sniffled happily.

"'S beautiful!" she growled.

He felt a resurge of the wondering, protective friendliness they had aroused in him at first. They must have been having a rough time of it, at that. He sighed; it seemed a pity they hadn't gotten along a little better.

"Where's everyone hiding?" he inquired, to break up the mood. So far there hadn't been a sign of human habitation.

"There aren't many people on Karres," Maleen said from behind him. "But we're going to the town—you'll meet about half of them there."

"What's that place down there?" the captain asked with sudden interest. Something like an enormous lime-white bowl seemed to have been set flush into the floor of the wide valley up which they were moving.

"That's the Theater where . . . *ouch!*" the Leewit said. She fell silent then but turned to give Maleen a resentful look.

"Something strangers shouldn't be told about, eh?" the captain said tolerantly. Goth glanced at him from the side.

"We've got rules," she said.

He let the ship down a little as they passed over "the Theater where—" It was a sort of large, circular arena with numerous steep tiers of seats running up around it. But all was bare and deserted now.

On Maleen's direction, they took the next valley fork to the right and dropped lower still. He had his first look at Karres animal life then. A flock of large creamy-white birds, remarkably terrestrial in appearance, flapped by just below them, apparently unconcerned about the ship. The forest underneath had opened out into a long stretch of lush meadow land, with small creeks winding down into its center. Here a herd of several hundred head of beasts was grazing—beasts of mastodonic size and build, with hairless, shiny black hides. The mouths of their long, heavy heads were twisted into sardonic crocodilian grins as they blinked up at the passing *Venture*.

"Black Bollems," said Goth, apparently enjoying the captain's expression. "Lots of them around; they're tame. But the gray mountain ones are good hunting."

"Good eating, too!" the Leewit said. She licked her lips daintily. "Breakfast—!" she sighed, her thoughts diverted to a familiar track. "And we ought to be just in time!"

"There's the field!" Maleen cried, pointing. "Set her down there, Captain!"

The "field" was simply a flat meadow of close-trimmed grass running smack against the mountainside to their left. One small vehicle, bright blue in color, was parked on it; and it was bordered on two sides by very tall blue-black trees.

That was all.

The captain shook his head. Then he set her down.

The town of Karres was a surprise to him in a good many ways. For one thing there was much more of it than one would have thought possible after flying over the area. It stretched for miles through the forest, up the flanks of the mountain and across the valley—little clusters of houses or individual ones, each group screened from all the others and from the sky overhead by the trees.

They liked color on Karres; but then they hid it away! The houses were bright as flowers, red and white, apple-green, golden brown—all spick and span, scrubbed and polished and aired with that brisk green forest-smell. At various times of the day there was also the smell of remarkably good things to eat. There were brooks and pools and a great number of shaded vegetable gardens in the town. There were risky-looking treetop playgrounds, and treetop platforms and galleries which seemed to have no particular purpose. On the ground was mainly an enormously confusing maze of paths—narrow trails of sandy soil snaking about among great brown tree roots and chunks of gray mountain rock, and half covered with fallen needle leaves. The first few times the captain set out unaccompanied, he lost his way hopelessly within minutes and had to be guided back out of the forest.

But the most hidden of all were the people. About four thousand of them were supposed to live currently in the town, with as many more scattered about the planet. But you never saw more than three or four at any one time—except when now and then a pack of children, who seemed to the captain to be uniformly of the Leewit's size, burst suddenly out of the undergrowth across a path before you and vanished again.

As for the others, you did hear someone singing occasionally, or there might be a whole muted concert going on all about, on a large variety of wooden musical instruments which they seemed to enjoy tootling with, gently.

But it wasn't a real town at all, the captain thought. They didn't live like people, these witches of Karres—it was more like a flock of strange forest birds that happened to be nesting in the same general area. Another thing: they appeared to be busy enough—but what was their business?

He discovered he was reluctant to ask Toll too many questions about it. Toll was the mother of his three witches, but only Goth really resembled her. It was difficult to picture Goth becoming smoothly matured and pleasantly rounded, but that was Toll. She had the same murmuring voice, the same air of sideways observation and secret reflection. She answered all the captain's questions with apparent frankness, but he never seemed to get much real information out of what she said.

It was odd, too! Because he was spending several hours a

day in her company, or in one of the next rooms at any rate, while she went about her housework. Toll's daughters had taken him home when they landed; and he was installed in the room that belonged to their father—busy just now, the captain gathered, with some sort of geological research elsewhere on Karres. The arrangement worried him a little at first, particularly since Toll and he were mostly alone in the house. Maleen was going to some kind of school; she left early in the morning and came back late in the afternoon. And Goth and the Leewit were plain running wild! They usually got in long after the captain had gone to bed and were off again before he turned out for breakfast.

It hardly seemed like the right way to raise them. One afternoon, he found the Leewit curled up and asleep in the chair he usually occupied on the porch before the house. She slept there for four solid hours, while the captain sat nearby and leafed gradually through a thick book with illuminated pictures called "Histories of Ancient Yarthe." Now and then he sipped at a cool green, faintly intoxicating drink Toll had placed quietly beside him some while before, or sucked an aromatic smoke from the enormous pipe with a floor rest, which he understood was a favorite of Toll's husband.

Then the Leewit woke up suddenly, uncoiled, gave him a look between a scowl and a friendly grin, slipped off the porch and vanished among the trees.

He couldn't quite figure that look! It might have meant nothing at all in particular, but—

The captain laid down his book then and worried a little more. It was true, of course, that nobody seemed in the least concerned about his presence. All of Karres appeared to know about him, and he'd met quite a number of people by now in a casual way. But nobody came around to interview him or so much as dropped in for a visit. However, Toll's husband presumably would be returning presently and—

How long had he been here, anyway?

Great Patham, he thought, shocked. He'd lost count of the days!

Or was it weeks?

He went in to find Toll.

"It's been a wonderful visit," he said, "but I'll have to be leaving, I guess. Tomorrow morning, early . . . ."

Toll put some fancy sewing she was working on back in a glass basket, laid her strong, slim witch's hands in her lap, and smiled up at him.

"We thought you'd be thinking that," she said, "and so we . . . you know, Captain, it was quite difficult to decide on the best way to reward you for bringing back the children."

"It was?" said the captain, suddenly realizing he'd also clean forgotten he was broke! And now the wrath of Onswud lay close ahead.

"However," Toll went on, "we've all been talking about it in the town, and so we've loaded a lot of things aboard your ship that we think you can sell at a fine profit!"

"Well, now," the captain said gratefully, "that's fine of—"

"There are furs," said Toll, "the very best furs we could fix up—two thousand of them!"

"Oh!" said the captain, bravely keeping his smile. "Well, that's wonderful!"

"And the Kell Peak essences of perfume," said Toll. "Everyone brought one bottle, so that's eight thousand three hundred and twenty-three bottles of perfume essences!"

"Perfume!" exclaimed the captain. "Fine, fine—but you really shouldn't—"

"And the rest of it," Toll concluded happily, "is the green Lepti liquor you like so much and the Wintenberry jellies. I forget just how many jugs and jars, but there were a lot. It's all loaded now." She smiled. "Do you think you'll be able to sell all that?"

"I certainly can!" the captain said stoutly. "It's wonderful stuff, and I've never come across anything like it before."

The last was very true. They wouldn't have considered miffel fur for lining on Karres. But if he'd been alone he would have felt like bursting into tears.

The witches couldn't have picked more completely unsalable items if they'd tried! Furs, cosmetics, food, and liquor—he'd be shot on sight if he got caught trying to run that kind of merchandise into the Empire. For the same reason it was barred on Nikkeldepain—they were that scared of contamination by goods that came from uncleared worlds!

He breakfasted alone next morning. Toll had left a note beside his plate which explained in a large rambling script that she had to run off and catch the Leewit, and that if he was gone before she got back she was wishing him good-by and good luck.

He smeared two more buns with Wintenberry jelly, drank a large mug of cone-seed coffee, finished every scrap of the omelet of swan hawk eggs and then, in a state of pleasant repletion, toyed around with his slice of roasted Bollem liver. Boy, what food! He must have put on fifteen pounds since he landed on Karres.

He wondered how Toll kept that slim figure.

Regretfully, he pushed himself away from the table, pocketed her note for a souvenir and went out on the porch. There a tear-stained Maleen hurled herself into his arms.

"Oh, Captain!" she sobbed. "You're leaving—"

"Now, now!" murmured the captain, touched and surprised by the lovely child's grief. He patted her shoulders soothingly. "I'll be back," he said rashly.

"Oh, yes, do come back!" cried Maleen. She hesitated and added, "I become marriageable two years from now—Karres time."

"Well, well," said the captain, dazed. "Well, now—"

He set off down the path a few minutes later, a strange melody tinkling in his head. Around the first curve, it changed abruptly to a shrill keening which seemed to originate from a spot some two hundred feet before him. Around the next curve, he entered a small, rocky clearing full of pale, misty, early-morning sunlight and what looked like a slow motion fountain of gleaming rainbow globes. These turned out to be clusters of large, varihued soap bubbles which floated up steadily from a wooden tub full of hot water, soap, and the Leewit. Toll was bent over the tub; and the Leewit was objecting to a morning bath with only that minimum of interruptions required to keep her lungs pumped full of a fresh supply of air.

As the captain paused beside the little family group, her red, wrathful face came up over the rim of the tub and looked at him.

"Well, Ugly," she squealed, in a renewed outburst of rage, "who you staring at?" Then a sudden determination came into her eyes. She pursed her lips.

Toll upended her promptly and smacked her bottom.

"She was going to make some sort of a whistle at you," she explained hurriedly. "Perhaps you'd better get out of range while I can keep her head under. . . . And good luck, Captain!"

Karres seemed even more deserted than usual this morning. Of course it was quite early. Great banks of fog lay here and there among the huge dark trees and the small bright houses. A breeze sighed sadly far overhead. Faint, mournful bird-cries came from still higher up—it might have been swan hawks reproaching him for the omelet.

Somewhere in the distance somebody tootled on a wood instrument, very gently.

He had gone halfway up the path to the landing field when something buzzed past him like an enormous wasp and went CLUNK! into the bole of a tree just before him.

It was a long, thin, wicked-looking arrow. On its shaft was a white card, and on the card was printed in red letters:

STOP, MAN OF NIKKELDEPAIN!

The captain stopped and looked around cautiously. There was no one in sight. What did it mean?

He had a sudden feeling as if all of Karres were rising up silently in one stupendous cool, foggy trap about him. His skin began to crawl. What was going to happen?

"Ha-ha!" said Goth, suddenly visible on a rock twelve feet to his left and eight feet above him. "You did stop!"

The captain let his breath out slowly.

"What did you think I'd do?" he inquired. He felt a little faint.

She slid down from the rock like a lizard and stood before him. "Wanted to say good-by!" she told him.

Thin and brown, in jacket, breeches, boots, and cap of gray-green rock lichen color, Goth looked very much in her element. The brown eyes looked up at him steadily; the mouth smiled faintly; but there was no real expression on her face at all. There was a quiverful of those enormous arrows slung over her shoulder, and some arrow-shooting device—not a bow—in her left hand.

She followed his glance.

"Bollem hunting up the mountain," she explained. "The wild ones. They're better meat."

The captain reflected a moment. That's right, he recalled; they kept the tame Bollem herds mostly for milk, butter, and cheese. He'd learned a lot of important things about Karres, all right!

"Well," he said, "good-by, Goth!"

They shook hands gravely. Goth was the real Witch of Karres, he decided. More so than her sisters, more so even than Toll. But he hadn't actually learned a single thing about any of them.

Peculiar people!

He walked on, rather glumly.

"Captain!" Goth called after him. He turned.

"Better watch those take-offs," Goth called, "or you'll kill yourself yet!"

The captain cussed softly all the way up to the *Venture*.

And the take-off was terrible! A few swan hawks were watching but, he hoped, no one else.

There was, of course, no possibility of resuming direct trade in the Empire with the cargo they'd loaded for him. But the more he thought about it, the less likely it seemed that Councilor Onswud would let a genuine fortune slip through his hands because of technical embargoes. Nikkeldepain knew all the tricks of interstellar merchandising, and the councilor was undoubtedly the slickest unskinned miffel in the Republic. It was even possible that some sort of trade might be made to develop eventually between Karres and Nikkeldepain.

Now and then he also thought of Maleen growing marriageable two years hence, Karres time. A handful of witch-notes went tinkling through his head whenever that idle reflection occurred.

The calendric chronometer informed him he'd spent three weeks there. He couldn't remember how their year compared with the standard one.

He discovered presently that he was growing remarkably restless on this homeward run. The ship seemed unnaturally quiet—that was part of the trouble. The captain's cabin in particular and the passage leading past it to the *Venture's* old crew quarters had become as dismal as a tomb. He made a few attempts to resume his sessions of small talk with Illyla via her picture; but the picture remained aloof.

He couldn't quite put his finger on what was wrong. Leaving Karres was involved in it, of course; but he wouldn't have wanted to stay on that world indefinitely, among its hospitable but secretive people. He'd had a very agreeable, restful interlude there; but then it clearly had been time to move on. Karres wasn't where he belonged.

Nikkeldepain . . . ?

He found himself doing a good deal of brooding about Nikkeldepain, and realized one day, without much surprise, that if it weren't for Illyla he simply wouldn't be going back there now. But where he would be going instead, he didn't know.

It was puzzling. He must have been changing gradually these months, though he hadn't become too aware of it before. There was a vague, nagging feeling that somewhere was something he should be doing and wanted to be doing. Something of which he seemed to have caught momentary glimpses of late, but without recognizing it for what it was. Returning to Nikkeldepain, at any rate, seemed suddenly like walking back into a narrow, musty cage in which he had spent too much of his life . . . .

Well, he thought, he'd have to walk back into it for a while anyway. Once he'd found a way to discharge his obligations there, he and Illyla could start looking for that mysterious something else together.

The days went on and he learned for the first time that space travel could become nothing much more than a large hollow period of boredom. At long last, Nikkeldepain II swam up in the screens ahead. The captain put the *Venture 7333* on orbit, and broadcast the ship's identification number. Half an hour later Landing Control called him. He repeated the identification number, added the ship's name, owner's name, his name, place of origin, and nature of cargo.

The cargo had to be described in detail. It would be attached, of course; but at that point he could pass the ball to Onswud and Onswud's many connections.

"Assume Landing Orbit 21,203 on your instruments," Landing Control instructed him curtly. "A customs ship will come out to inspect."

He went on the assigned orbit and gazed moodily from

the vision ports at the flat continents and oceans of Nikkeldepain II as they drifted by below. A sense of equally flat
depression overcame him suddenly. He shook it off and
remembered Illyla.

Three hours later a ship ran up next to him, and he shut
off the orbital drive. The communicator began buzzing. He
switched it on.

"Vision, please!" said an official-sounding voice. The captain frowned, located the vision stud of the communicator
screen and pushed it down. Four faces appeared in the screen,
looking at him.

"Illyla!" the captain said.

"At least," young Councilor Rapport said unpleasantly, "he's
brought back the ship, Father Onswud!"

"Illyla!" said the captain.

Councilor Onswud said nothing. Neither did Illyla. Both
continued to stare at him, but the screen wasn't good enough
to let him make out their expressions in detail.

The fourth face, an unfamiliar one above a uniform collar,
was the one with the official-sounding voice.

"You are instructed to open the forward lock, Captain
Pausert," it said, "for an official investigation."

It wasn't until he was about to release the outer lock to the
control room that the captain realized it wasn't Customs who
had sent a boat out to him but the Police of the Republic.

However, he hesitated only a moment. Then the outer lock
gaped wide.

He tried to explain. They wouldn't listen. They had come
on board in contamination-proof repulsor suits, all four of
them; and they discussed the captain as if he weren't there.
Illyla looked pale and angry and beautiful, and avoided looking at him.

However, he didn't want to speak to her in front of the
others anyway.

They strolled back through the ship to the storage and gave the Karres cargo a casual glance.

"Damaged his lifeboat, too!" Councilor Rapport remarked.

They brushed past him up the narrow passage and went back to the control room. The policeman asked to see the log and commercial records. The captain produced them.

The three men studied them briefly. Illyla gazed stonily out at Nikkeldepain II.

"Not too carefully kept!" the policeman pointed out.

"Surprising he bothered to keep them at all!" said Councilor Rapport.

"But it's all clear enough!" said Councilor Onswud.

They straightened up then and faced him in a line. Councilor Onswud folded his arms and projected his craggy chin. Councilor Rapport stood at ease, smiling faintly. The policeman became officially rigid.

"Captain Pausert," the policeman said, "the following charges—substantiated in part by this preliminary examination—are made against you—"

"Charges?" said the captain.

"Silence, please!" rumbled Councilor Onswud.

"First, material theft of a quarter-million value of maels of jewels and jeweled items from a citizen of the Imperial Planet of Porlumma—"

"They were returned!" the captain said indignantly.

"Restitution, particularly when inspired by fear of retribution, does not affect the validity of the original charge," Councilor Rapport quoted, gazing at the ceiling.

"Second," continued the policeman. "Purchase of human slaves, permitted under Imperial law but prohibited by penalty of ten years to lifetime penal servitude by the laws of the Republic of Nikkeldepain—"

"I was just taking them back where they belonged!" said the captain.

"We shall get to that point presently," the policeman replied.

"Third, material theft of sundry items in the value of one hundred and eighty thousand maels from a ship of the Imperial Planet of Lepper, accompanied by threats of violence to the ship's personnel—"

"I might add in explanation of the significance of this particular charge," added Councilor Rapport, looking at the floor, "that the Regency of Sirius, containing Lepper, is allied to the Republic of Nikkeldepain by commercial and military treaties of considerable value. The Regency has taken the trouble to point out that such hostile conduct by a citizen of the Republic against citizens of the Regency is likely to have an adverse effect on the duration of the treaties. The charge thereby becomes compounded by the additional charge of a treasonable act against the Republic."

He glanced at the captain. "I believe we can forestall the accused's plea that these pilfered goods also were restored. They were, in the face of superior force!"

"Fourth," the policeman went on patiently, "depraved and licentious conduct while acting as commercial agent, to the detriment of your employer's business and reputation—"

"WHAT?" choked the captain.

"—involving three of the notorious Witches of the Prohibited Planet of Karres—"

"Just like his great-uncle Threbus!" nodded Councilor Onswud gloomily. "It's in the blood, I always say!"

"—and a justifiable suspicion of a prolonged stay on said Prohibited Planet of Karres—"

"I never heard of that place before this trip!" shouted the captain.

"Why don't you read your Instructions and Regulations then?" shouted Councilor Rapport. "It's all there!"

"Silence, please!" shouted Councilor Onswud.

"Fifth," said the policeman quietly, "general willful and negligent actions resulting in material damage and loss to your employer to the value of eighty-two thousand maels."

"I still have fifty-five thousand. And the stuff in the storage," the captain said, also quietly, "is worth a quarter of a million, at least!"

"Contraband and hence legally valueless!" the policeman said.

Councilor Onswud cleared his throat.

"It will be impounded, of course," he said. "Should a method of resale present itself, the profits, if any, will be applied to the cancellation of your just debts. To some extent that might reduce your sentence." He paused. "There is another matter—"

"The sixth charge," the policeman announced, "is the development *and* public demonstration of a new type of space drive, which should have been brought promptly and secretly to the attention of the Republic of Nikkeldepain."

They all stared at him—alertly and quite greedily.

So *that* was it—the Sheewash Drive!

"Your sentence may be greatly reduced, Pausert," Councilor Onswud said wheedlingly, "if you decide to be reasonable now. What have you discovered?"

"Look out, father!" Illyla said sharply.

"Pausert," Councilor Onswud inquired in a fading voice, "what is that in your hand?"

"A Blythe gun," the captain said, boiling.

There was a frozen stillness for an instant. Then the policeman's right hand made a convulsive motion.

"Uh-uh!" said the captain warningly.

Councilor Rapport started a slow step backwards.

"Stay where you are," said the captain.

"Pausert!" Councilor Onswud and Illyla cried out together.

"Shut up!" said the captain.

There was another stillness.

"If you'd looked on your way over here," the captain told them, in an almost normal voice, "You'd have seen I was getting the nova gun turrets out. They're fixed on that boat of yours. The boat's lying still and keeping its yap shut. You do the same."

He pointed a finger at the policeman. "You open the lock," he said. "Start your suit repulsors and squirt yourself back to your boat!"

The lock groaned open. Warm air left the ship in a long, lazy wave, scattering the sheets of the *Venture's* log and commercial records over the floor. The thin, cold upper atmosphere of Nikkeldepain II came eddying in.

"You next, Onswud!" the captain said.

And a moment later: "Rapport, you just turn around—"

Young Councilor Rapport went out through the lock at a higher velocity than could be attributed reasonably to his repulsor units. The captain winced and rubbed his foot. But it had been worth it.

"Pausert," said Illyla in justifiable apprehension, "you are stark, staring mad!"

"Not at all, my dear," the captain said cheerfully. "You and I are now going to take off and embark on a life of crime together."

"But, Pausert—"

"You'll get used to it," the captain assured her, "just like I did. It's got Nikkeldepain beat every which way."

"You can't escape," Illyla said, white-faced. "We told them to bring up space destroyers and revolt ships . . ."

"We'll blow them out through the stratosphere," the captain said belligerently, reaching for the lock-control switch. He added, "But they won't shoot anyway while I've got you on board."

Illyla shook her head. "You just don't understand," she said desperately. "You can't make me stay!"

"Why not?" asked the captain.

"Pausert," said Illyla, "I am Madame Councilor Rapport."

"Oh!" said the captain. There was a silence. He added, crestfallen, "Since when?"

"Five months ago, yesterday," said Illyla.

"Great Patham!" cried the captain, with some indignation. "I'd hardly got off Nikkeldepain then! We were engaged!"

"Secretly . . . and I guess," said Illyla, with a return of spirit, "that I had a right to change my mind!"

There was another silence.

"Guess you had, at that," the captain agreed. "All right. The lock's still open, and your husband's waiting in the boat. Beat it!"

He was alone. He let the locks slam shut and banged down the oxygen release switch. The air had become a little thin.

He cussed.

The communicator began rattling for attention. He turned it on.

"Pausert!" Councilor Onswud was calling in a friendly but shaking voice. "May we not depart, Pausert? Your nova guns are still fixed on this boat!"

"Oh, that . . ." said the captain. He deflected the turrets a trifle. "They won't go off now. Scram!"

The police boat vanished.

There was other company coming, though. Far below him but climbing steadily, a trio of atmospheric revolt ships darted past on the screen, swung around and came back for the next turn of their spiral. They'd have to get closer before they started shooting, but they'd stay between him and the surface of Nikkeldepain while space destroyers closed in from above. Between them then, they'd knock out the *Venture* and bring her down in a net of paramagnetic grapples, if he didn't surrender.

He sat a moment, reflecting. The revolt ships went by once more. The captain punched in the *Venture's* secondary drives, turned her nose towards the planet, and let her go. There were some scattered white puffs around as he cut through the revolt ships' plane of flight. Then he was below them, and the *Venture* groaned as he took her out of the dive. The revolt ships were already scattering and nosing over for a countermaneuver. He picked the nearest one and swung the nova guns toward it.

"—and ram them in the middle!" he muttered between his teeth.

SSS-whoosh!

It was the Sheewash Drive—but like a nightmare now, it kept on and on . . . .

"Maleen!" the captain bawled, pounding at the locked door of the captain's cabin. "Maleen, shut it off! Cut it off! You'll kill yourself. Maleen!"

The *Venture* quivered suddenly throughout her length, then shuddered more violently, jumped and coughed, and commenced sailing along on her secondary drives again.

"Maleen!" he yelled, wondering briefly how many light-years from everything they were by now. "Are you all right?"

There was a faint *thump-thump* inside the cabin, and silence. He lost nearly two minutes finding the right cutting tool in the storage and getting it back to the cabin. A few seconds later a section of steel door panel sagged inwards; he caught it by one edge and came tumbling into the cabin with it.

He had the briefest glimpse of a ball of orange-colored fire swirling uncertainly over a cone of oddly bent wires. Then the fire vanished and the wires collapsed with a loose rattling to the table top.

The crumpled small shape lay behind the table, which was why he didn't discover it at once. He sagged to the floor beside it, all the strength running out of his knees.

Brown eyes opened and blinked at him blearily.

"Sure takes it out of you!" Goth muttered. "Am I hungry!"

"I'll whale the holy howling tar out of you again," the captain roared, "if you ever—"

"Quit your yelling!" snarled Goth. "I got to eat."

She ate for fifteen minutes straight before she sank back in her chair and sighed.

"Have some more Wintenberry jelly," the captain offered anxiously. She looked pretty pale.

Goth shook her head. "Couldn't . . . and that's about the first thing you've said since you fell through the door, howling for Maleen. Ha-ha! Maleen's *got* a boy friend!"

"Button your lip, child," the captain said. "I was thinking." He added, after a moment, "Has she really?"

Goth nodded. "Picked him out last year. Nice boy from the town. They get married as soon as she's marriageable. She just told you to come back because she was upset about you. Maleen had a premonition you were headed for awful trouble!"

"She was quite right, little chum," the captain said nastily.

"What were you thinking about?" Goth inquired.

"I was thinking," said the captain, "that as soon as we're sure you're going to be all right, I'm taking you straight back to Karres."

"I'll be all right now," Goth said. "Except, likely, for a stomach-ache. But you can't take me back to Karres."

"Who will stop me, may I ask?" the captain asked.

"Karres is gone," Goth said.

"Gone?" the captain repeated blankly, with a sensation of not quite definable horror bubbling up in him.

"Not blown up or anything," Goth reassured him. "They just moved it. The Imperials got their hair up about us again. This time they were sending a fleet with the big bombs and stuff, so everybody was called home. And right after you'd left . . . *we'd* left, I mean . . . they moved it."

"Where?"

"Great Patham!" Goth shrugged. "How'd I know? There's lots of places!"

There probably were, the captain agreed silently. A scene came suddenly before his eyes—that lime-white, arenalike bowl in the valley, with the steep tiers of seats around it, just before they'd reached the town of Karres. The "Theater where—"

But now there was unnatural night-darkness all over and about that world; and the eight-thousand-some witches of Karres sat in circles around the Theater, their heads turned towards one point in the center where orange fire washed hugely about the peak of a cone of curiously twisted girders.

And a world went racing off at the speeds of the Sheewash Drive! There'd be lots of places, all right. What peculiar people!

"Aren't they going to be worried about you?" he asked.

"Not very much. We don't get hurt often."

Once could be too often. But anyway, she was here for now . . . The captain stretched his legs out under the table, inquired, "Was it the Sheewash Drive they used to move Karres with?"

Goth wrinkled her nose doubtfully. "Sort of like it." She added, "I can't tell you much about those things till you've started to be one yourself."

"Started to be what myself?" he asked.

"A witch like us. We got our rules. And that likely won't be for a while. Couple of years maybe, Karres time."

"Couple of years, eh?" the captain repeated thoughtfully. "You were planning on staying around that long?"

Goth frowned at the jar of Wintenberry jelly, pulled it towards her and inspected it carefully. "Longer, really," she acknowledged. "Be a bit before *I'm* marriageable age!"

The captain blinked at her. "Well, yes, it would be . . ."

"So I got it all fixed," Goth told the jelly, "as soon as they started saying they ought to pick out a wife for you on Karres. I said it was me, right away; and everyone else said finally that was all right then—even Maleen, because she had this boy friend."

"You mean," said the captain, startled, "your parents knew you were stowing away on the *Venture*?"

"Uh-huh." Goth pushed the jelly back where it had been

standing and glanced up at him again. "It was my father who told us you'd be breaking up with the people on Nikkeldepain pretty soon. He said it was in the blood."

"What was in the blood?" the captain asked patiently.

"That you'd break up with them . . . That's Threbus, my father. You met him a couple of times in the town. Big man with a blond beard. Maleen and the Leewit take after him. He looks a lot like you."

"You wouldn't mean my great-uncle Threbus?" the captain inquired. He was in a state of strange calm by now.

"That's right," said Goth.

"It's a small galaxy," the captain said philosophically. "So that's where Threbus wound up! I'd like to meet him again some day."

"You're going to," said Goth. "But probably not very soon." She hesitated, added, "Guess there's something big going on. That's why they moved Karres. So we likely won't run into any of them again till it's over."

"Something big in what way?" asked the captain.

Goth shrugged. "Politics. Secret stuff. . . . I was going along with you, so they didn't tell me."

"Can't spill what you don't know, eh?"

"Uh-huh."

Interstellar politics involving Karres and the Empire? He pondered it a few seconds, then gave up. He couldn't imagine what it might be and there was no sense worrying about it.

"Well," he sighed, "seeing we've turned out to be distant relatives, I suppose it is all right if I adopt you meanwhile."

"Sure," said Goth. She studied his face. "You still want to pay the money you owe back to those people?"

He nodded. "A debt's a debt."

"Well," Goth informed him, "I've got some ideas."

"None of those witch tricks now!" the captain said warningly. "We'll earn our money the fair way."

Goth blinked not-so-innocent brown eyes at him. "This'll be fair! But we'll get rich." She shook her head, yawned slowly. "Tired," she announced, standing up.

"Better hit the bunk a while now."

"Good idea," the captain agreed. "We can talk again later."

At the passage door Goth paused, looking back at him.

"About all I could tell you about us right now," she said, "you can read in those Regulations, like the one man said. The one you kicked off the ship. There's a lot about Karres in there. Lots of lies, too, though!"

"And when did you find out about the intercom between here and the captain's cabin?" the captain inquired.

Goth grinned. "A while back. The others never noticed."

"All right," the captain said. "Good night, witch—if you get a stomach-ache, yell and I'll bring the medicine."

"Good night," Goth yawned. "I might, I think."

"And wash behind your ears!" the captain added, trying to remember the bedtime instructions he'd overheard Maleen giving the junior witches.

"All right," said Goth sleepily. The passage door closed behind her—but half a minute later it was briskly opened again. The captain looked up startled from the voluminous stack of *General Instructions and Space Regulations of the Republic of Nikkeldepain* he'd just discovered in the back of one of the drawers of the control desk. Goth stood in the doorway, scowling and wide-awake.

"And you wash behind yours!" she said.

"Huh?" said the captain. He reflected a moment. "All right," he said. "We both will, then."

"Right," said Goth, satisfied.

The door closed once more.

The captain began to run his finger down the lengthy index of K's—could it be under W?

Chapter THREE

The key word was PROHIBITED . . . .

Under that heading the Space Regulations had in fact devoted a full page of rather fine print to the Prohibited Planet of Karres. Most of it, however, was conjecture. Nikkeldepain seemed unable to make up its mind whether the witches had developed an alarmingly high level of secret technology or whether there was something downright supernatural about them. But it made it very clear it did not want ordinary citizens to have anything to do with Karres. There was grave danger of spiritual contamination. Hence such contacts could not be regarded as being in the best interests of the Republic and were strictly forbidden.

Various authorities in the Empire held similar opinions. The Regulations included a number of quotes from such sources:

" . . . their women gifted with an evil allure . . . Hiding under the cloak of the so-called klatha magic—"

Klatha? The word seemed familiar. Frowning, the captain dug up a number of memory scraps. Klatha was a metaphysical concept—a cosmic energy, something not quite of this universe.

Some people supposedly could tune in on it, use it for various purposes.

He grunted. Possibly that gave a name to what the witches were doing. But it didn't explain anything.

No mention was made of the Sheewash Drive. It might be a recent development, at least for individual spaceships. In fact, the behavior of Councilor Onswud and the others suggested that reports they'd received of the *Venture's* unorthodox behavior under hot pursuit was the first they'd heard of a superdrive possessed by Karres.

Naturally they'd been itching to get their hands on it.

And naturally, the captain told himself, the Empire, having heard the same reports, wanted the Sheewash Drive just as badly! The *Venture* had become a marked ship . . . and he'd better find out just where she was at present.

The viewscreens, mass detectors, and communicators had been switched on while he was going over the Regulations. The communicators had produced only an uninterrupted, quiet humming—a clear indication there were no civilized worlds within a day's travel. Occasional ships might be passing at much closer range; but interstellar travel must be very light or the communicators would have picked up at least a few garbled fragments of ship messages.

The screens had no immediately useful information to add. An odd-shaped cloud of purple luminance lay dead ahead, at an indicated distance of just under nine light-years. It would have been a definite landmark if the captain had ever heard of it before; but he hadn't. Stars filled the screens in all directions, crowded pinpoints of hard brilliance and hazy clusters. Here and there swam dark pools of cosmic dust. On the right was a familiar spectacle but one which offered no clues—the gleaming cascades of ice-fire of the Milky Way. One would have had approximately the same view from many widely scattered points of the galaxy. In this forest of light, all routes looked equal to the eye. But there was, of course, a standard way of getting a location fix.

The captain dug his official chart of navigational beacon indicators out of the desk and dialed the communicators up to space beacon frequencies. Identifying three or four of the strongest signals obtainable here should give him their position.

Within a minute a signal beeped in. Very faint, but it had the general configuration of an Imperial beacon. Its weakness implied they were far outside the Empire's borders. The captain pushed a transcription button on the beacon attachment, pulled out the symbol card it produced, and slid it into the chart to be matched and identified.

The chart immediately rejected the symbol as unrecognizable.

He hesitated, transcribed the signal again, fed the new card to the chart. It, too, was rejected. The symbols on the two cards were identical, so the transcription equipment seemed to be in working order. For some reason this beacon signal simply was not recorded in his chart.

He frowned, eased the detector knobs back and forth, picked up a new signal. Again an Imperial pattern.

Again the chart rejected the symbol.

A minute later it rejected a third one. This had been the weakest symbol of the three—barely transcribable. And evidently it was the last one within the *Venture's* present communicator range . . . .

The captain leaned back in the chair, reflecting. Of course the navigational beacon charts made available by Nikkeldepain to its commercial vessels didn't cover the entire Empire. Business houses dealt with the central Imperium and some of the western and northern provinces. It was a practical limitation. Extending shipping runs with any ordinary cargo beyond that vast area simply couldn't be profitable enough to be taken into consideration.

Goth hadn't worked the Sheewash Drive much more than

two minutes before it knocked her out. But that apparently had
been enough to take them clear outside the range covered by
the official beacon charts!

He grunted incredulously, shook his head, got out of the
chair. Back in a locked section of the storage was a chest filled
with old ship papers, dating back to the period before the
Venture's pirate-hunting days when she'd been a long-range
exploration ship and brand-new. He'd got into the section one
day, rummaged around curiously in the chest. There were thick
stacks of star maps covering all sorts of unlikely areas in there,
along with old style beacon charts. And maybe . . . .

It was a good hunch. The chart mechanisms weren't the kind
with which he was familiar but they were operable. The third
one he tried at random gave a positive response to the three
beacon signals he'd picked up. When he located the correspond-
ing star maps they told him within a light-day where the ship
had to be at present.

In spite of everything else that had happened, he simply
didn't believe it at first. It was impossible! He went through
the checking procedure again. And then there was no more
doubt.

There were civilized worlds indicated on those maps of
which he had never heard. There were other names he did
know—names of worlds which had played a role, sometimes
grandly, sometimes terribly, in galactic history. The ancient
names of worlds so remote from Nikkeldepain's present sphere
of commercial interest that to him they seemed like dim legend. Goth's run on the Sheewash Drive had not simply moved
them along the Imperial borders beyond the area of the official charts. It had taken them back into the Empire, then all
the way through it and out the other side—to Galactic East
of the farthest eastern provinces. They were in a territory where,
as far as the captain knew, no ship from Nikkeldepain had
come cruising in over a century.

He stood looking out the viewscreens a while at the

unfamiliar crowded stars, his blood racing as excitement continued to grow in him. Here he was, he thought, nearly as far from the stodginess of present-day Nikkeldepain as if he had, in fact, slipped back through the dark centuries to come out among lost worlds of history, his only companion the enigmatic witch-child sleeping off exhaustion in the captain's cabin . . . .

About him he could almost sense the old ship, returned to the space roads of her youth and seemingly grown aware of it, rise from the miasma of brooding gloom which had settled on her after they left Karres, shaking herself awake, restored to adventurous life—ready and eager for anything.

It was like coming home to something that had been lost a long while but never really forgotten.

Something eerie, colorful, full of the promise of the unexpected and unforeseen and somehow dead right for him!

He sucked in air, turned from the screens to take the unused star maps and other materials back to the storage. His gaze swung over to the communicators. A small portable lamp stood on the closer of the two, its beam fixed on the worktable below it.

The captain gave the lamp a long, puzzled stare. Then he scowled and started towards it, walking a little edgily, hair bristling, head thrust forward—something like a terrier who comes suddenly on a new sort of vermin which may or may not be a dangerous opponent.

There was nothing wrong or alarming about the lamp's appearance. It was a perfectly ordinary utility device, atomic-powered, with a flexible and extensible neck, adjustable beam, and a base which, on contact, adhered firmly to bulkhead, deck, machine, or desk, and could be effortlessly plucked away again. During the months he'd been traveling about on the *Venture* he'd found many uses for it. In time it had seemed to develop a helpful and friendly personality of its own, like a small, unobtrusive servant.

At the moment its light shone exactly where he'd needed

it while he was studying the maps at the worktable. And *that* was what was wrong! Because he was as certain as he could be that he hadn't put the lamp on the communicator. When he'd noticed it last, before going to the storage, it was standing at the side of the control desk in its usual place. He hadn't come near the desk since.

Was Goth playing a prank on him? It didn't seem quite the sort of thing she'd do. . . . And now he remembered—something like twenty minutes before, he was sitting at the table, trying to make out a half-faded notation inked into the margin of one of the old maps. The thought came to him to get the lamp so he'd have better light. But he'd been too absorbed in what he was doing and the impulse simply faded again.

Then, some time between that moment and this, the better light he'd wanted was produced for him—strengthening so gently and gradually that, sitting there at the table, he didn't even become aware it was happening.

He stared a moment longer at the lamp. Then he picked it up, and went down the passage to the captain's cabin, carrying it with him.

Goth lay curled on her side in the big bunk, covers drawn up almost to her ears. She breathed slowly and quietly, forehead furrowed into a frown as if she dreamed about something of which she didn't entirely approve. Studying her face by the dimmed light of the lamp, the captain became convinced she wasn't faking sleep. Minor deceptions of that sort weren't Goth's way in any case. She was a very direct sort of small person . . . .

He glanced about. Her clothes hung neatly across the back of a chair, her boots were placed beside it. He dimmed the light further and withdrew from the cabin without disturbing her, making a mental note to replace the ruined door after she woke up. Back in the control room he switched off the lamp, set it on the desk, and stood knuckling his chin abstractedly.

It hadn't been a lapse of memory; and if Goth had done

it, she hadn't done it deliberately. Perhaps this klatha force could shift into independent action when a person who normally controlled it was asleep. There might be unpleasant possibilities in that. When Goth came awake he'd ask her what—

The sharp, irregular buzzing which rose suddenly from a bank of control instruments beside him made him jump four inches. His hand shot out, threw the main drive feed to the off position. The buzzing subsided, but a set of telltales continued to flicker bright red . . . .

There was nothing supernatural about *this* problem, he decided a few minutes later. But it was a problem, and not a small one. What the trouble indicators had registered was a developing pattern of malfunction in the main drive engines. It was no real surprise; when he'd left Nikkeldepain half a year before, it had looked like an even bet whether he could make it back without stopping for major repairs. But the drives had performed faultlessly—until now.

They might have picked a more convenient time and place to go haywire. But there was no reason to regard it as a disaster just yet.

He found tools, headed to the storage and on down to the engine deck from there, and went to work. Within half an hour he'd confirmed that their predicament wasn't too serious, if nothing else happened. A minor breakdown at one point in the main engines had shifted stresses, immediately creating a dozen other trouble spots. But it wasn't a question of the engines going out completely and making it necessary to crawl through space, perhaps for months, on their secondaries before they reached a port. Handled with care, the main drive should be good for another three or four weeks, at least. But the general deterioration clearly had gone beyond the point of repair. The antiquated engines would have to be replaced as soon as possible, and meanwhile he should change the drive settings manually, holding the engines down to half their normal output to reduce strain on them. If somebody came around with hostile intentions, an emergency override on the control desk would still allow occasional spurts at full thrust. From what he'd been told of the side effects of the Sheewash Drive, it wasn't likely Goth would be able to do much to help in that department . . . .

In a port of civilization, with repair station facilities on hand and the drive hauled clear of the ship, the adjustments he had to make might have been completed and tested in a matter of minutes. But for one man, working by the manual in the confined area of the *Venture's* engine room, it was a lengthy, awkward job. At last, stretched in a precarious sprawl a third down the side of the drive shaft, the captain squinted wearily at the final setting he had to change. It was in a shadowed recess of the shaft below him, barely in reach of his tools.

He wished he had a better light on it—

His breath caught in his throat. There was a feeling as if the universe had stopped for an instant; then a shock of alarm. His scalp began prickling as if an icy, soundless wind had come astir above his head.

He knew somehow exactly what was going to happen next— and that there was no use trying to revoke his wish. Some klatha machinery already was in motion now and couldn't be stopped . . . .

A second or two went past. Then an oval of light appeared quietly about the recess, illuminating the setting within. It grew strong and clear. The captain realized it came from above, past his shoulder. Cautiously, he looked up.

And there the little monster was, suspended by its base from the upper deck. Its slender neck reached down in a serpentine curve to place a beam of light precisely where he'd wanted to have it. His skin kept crawling as if he were staring at some nightmare image—

But this was only klatha, he told himself. And after the

Sheewash Drive and other matters, a lamp which began to move around mysteriously was nothing to get shaky about. Ignore it, he thought; finish up the job . . . .

He reached down with the tools, laboriously adjusted the thrust setting, tested it twice to make sure it was adjusted right. And that wound up his work in the engine room. He hadn't glanced at the lamp again, but its light still shone steadily on the shaft. The captain collapsed the tools, stowed them into his pockets, balanced himself on the curving surface of the drive shaft, and reached up for it.

It came free of the overhead deck at his touch. He climbed down from the shaft, holding the lamp away from him by the neck as if it were a helpful basilisk which might suddenly get a notion to bite. In the control room he placed it back on the desk, and gave it no further attention for the next twenty minutes while he ran the throttled engines through a complete instrument check. They registered satisfactorily. He switched the main drive back on, tested the emergency override. Everything seemed in working condition; the *Venture* was operational again . . . within prudent limits. He turned the ship on a course which would hold it roughly parallel to the Empire's eastern borders, locked it in, then went to the electric butler for a cup of coffee.

He came back with the coffee, finally stood looking at the lamp again. Since he'd put it down in its usual place, it had done nothing except sit there quietly, casting a pool of light on the desk before it.

The captain put the cup aside, moved back a few steps.

"Well," he said aloud, "Let's test this thing out!"

He paused while his voice went echoing faintly away through the *Venture's* passages. Then he pointed a finger at the lamp, and swung the finger commandingly towards the worktable beside the communicator stand.

"Move over to that table!" he told the lamp.

The whole ship grew very still. Even the distant hum of the

drive seemed to dim. The captain's scalp was crawling again, kept on crawling as the seconds went by. But the lamp didn't move.

Instead, its light abruptly went out.

"No," Goth said. "It wasn't me. I don't think it was you either—exactly."

The captain looked at her. He'd grabbed off a few hours sleep on the couch and by the time he woke up, Goth was up and around, energies apparently restored.

She'd been doing some looking around, too, and wanted to know why the *Venture* was running on half power. The captain explained. "If we happen to get into a jam," he concluded, "would you be able to use the Sheewash Drive at present?"

"Short hops," the witch nodded reassuringly. "No real runs for a while, though!"

"Short hops should be good enough." He reflected. "I read that item in the Regulations. They right about the klatha part?"

"Pretty much," Goth acknowledged, a trifle warily.

"Well . . ." He'd related his experiences with the lamp then, and she'd listened with obvious interest but no indications of surprise.

"What do you mean, it wasn't me—exactly?" he said. "I was wondering for a while, but I'm dead sure now I don't have klatha ability."

Goth wrinkled her nose, hesitant, said suddenly, "You got it, captain. Told you you'd be a witch, too. You got a lot of it! That was part of the trouble."

"Trouble?" The captain leaned back in his chair. "Mind explaining?"

Goth reflected worriedly again. "I got to be careful now," she told him. "The way klatha, is, people *oughtn't* to know much more about it than they can work with. Or it's likely never going to work right for them. That's one reason we got rules. You see?"

He frowned. "Not quite."

Goth tossed her head, a flick of impatience. "It wasn't me who ported the lamp. So if you didn't have klatha, it wouldn't have *got* ported."

"But you said . . ."

"Trying to explain, Captain. You ought to get told more now. Not too much, though. . . . On Karres they all knew you had it. Patham! You put it out so heavy the grown-ups were all messed up! It's that learned stuff they work with. That's tricky. I don't know much about it yet . . . ."

"You mean I was, uh, producing klatha energy?"

But he gathered one didn't *produce* klatha. If one had the talent—inborn to a considerable extent—one attracted it to oneself. Being around others who used it stimulated the attraction. His own tendencies in that direction hadn't developed much before he got to Karres. There he'd turned promptly into an unwitting focal point of the klatha energies being manipulated around him—to the consternation of the adult witches who found their highly evolved and delicately balanced klatha controls thrown out of kilter by his presence.

A light dawned. "That's why they waited until I was off Karres again before they moved it!"

"Sure," said Goth. "They couldn't risk that with you there—they didn't know what would happen . . . ." He had been the subject of much conversation and debate during his stay on Karres. So as not to disturb whatever was coming awake in him, the witches couldn't even let him know he was doing anything unusual. But only the younger children, using klatha in a very direct and basic, almost instinctive manner, weren't bothered by it. Adolescents at around Maleen's age level had been affected to some extent, though not nearly as much as their parents.

"You just don't know how to use it, that's all," Goth said. "You're going to, though."

"What makes you think that?"

Her lashes flickered. "They said it was like that with Threbus. He started late, too. Took him a couple of years to catch on— but he's a whizdang now!"

The captain grunted skeptically. "Well, we'll see.... You're a kind of a whizdang yourself, for my money."

"Guess I am," Goth agreed. "Aren't many grown-ups could jump us as far as this."

"Meaning you know where we went?"

"Uh-huh."

"I . . . no, let's get back to that lamp first. I can see that after your big Sheewash push we might have had plenty of klatha stirred up around the *Venture*. But you say I'm not able to use it. So . . ."

"Looks like you pulled in a vatch," Goth told him.

She explained that then. It appeared a vatch was a sort of personification of klatha, or a klatha entity. Vatches didn't hang around this universe much but were sometimes drawn into it by human klatha activities, and if they were amused or intrigued by what they found going on they might stay and start producing klatha phenomena themselves. They seemed to be under the impression that their experiences of the human universe were something they were dreaming. They could be helpful to the person who caught their attention but tended to be quite irresponsible and mischievous. The witches preferred to have nothing at all to do with a vatch.

"So now we've got something like *that* on board!" the captain remarked nervously.

Goth shook her head. "No, not since I woke up. I'd rell him if he were around."

"You'd rell him?"

She grinned.

"Another of the things I can't understand till I can do it?" the captain asked.

"Uh-huh. Anyway, you got rid of that vatch for good, I think."

"I did? How?"

"When you ordered the lamp to move. Vatch would figure you were telling him what to do. They don't like that at all. I figure he got mad and left."

"After switching the lamp off to show me, eh? Think he might be back?"

"They don't usually. Anyway, I'll spot him if he does."

"Yes . . . ." The captain scratched his chin. "So what made you decide to bring us out east of the Empire?"

Goth, it turned out, had had a number of reasons. Some of them sounded startling at first.

"One thing, here's Uldune!" Her fingertip traced over the star map between them, stopped. "Be just about a week away, on half-power."

The captain gave her a surprised look. Uldune was one of the worlds around here which were featured in Nikkeldepain's history books; and it was not featured at all favorably. Under the leadership of its Daal, Sedmon the Grim, and various successors of the same name, it had been the headquarters of a ferocious pirate confederacy which had trampled over half the Empire on a number of occasions, and raided far and wide beyond it. And that particular section of history, as he recalled it, wasn't very far in the past.

"What's good about being that close to Uldune?" he inquired. "From what I've heard of them, that's as bloodthirsty a bunch of cutthroats as ever infested space!"

"Guess they were pretty bad," Goth acknowledged. "But that's a time back. They're sort of reformed now."

"*Sort* of reformed?"

She shrugged. "Well, they're still a bunch of crooks, Captain. But we can do business with them."

"Business!"

She seemed to know what she was talking about, though. The witches were familiar with this section of galactic space—

Karres, in fact, had been shifted from a point east of the Empire
to its recent station in the Iverdahl System not much more than
eighty years ago. And while Goth was Karres-born, she'd done
a good deal of traveling around here with her parents and
sisters. Not very surprising, of course. With the Sheewash Drive
available to give their ship a boost when they felt like it, a witch
family should be able to go pretty well where it chose.

She'd never been on Uldune but it was a frequent stopover
point for Karres people. Uldune's reform, initiated by its previous Daal, Sedmon the Fifth, and continued under his successor,
had been a matter of simple expediency—the Empire's expanding space power was making wholesale piracy too unprofitable
and risky a form of enterprise. Sedmon the Sixth was an able
politician who maintained mutually satisfactory relations with
the Empire and other space neighbors, while deriving much of
his revenue by catering to the requirements of people who
operated outside the laws of any government. Uldune today was
banker, fence, haven, trading center, outfitter, supplier, broker,
and middleman to all comers who could afford its services. It
never asked embarrassing questions. Outright pirates—successful
ones, at any rate—were still perfectly welcome. So was anybody
who merely wanted to transact some form of business unham-
pered by standard legal technicalities.

"I'm beginning to get it!" the captain acknowledged. "But
what makes you think we won't get robbed blind there?"

"They're not crooks that way—at least not often. The Daal
goes for the skinning alive thing," Goth explained. "You get
robbed, you squawk. Then somebody gets skinned. It's pretty
safe!"

It did sound like the Daal had hit on a dependable method
to give his planet a reputation for solid integrity in business
deals. "So we sell the cargo there," the captain mused. "They
take their cut—probably a big one—"

"Uh-huh. Runs around forty per."

"Of the assessed value?"

"Uh-huh."

"Steep! But if they've got to see the stuff gets smuggled to buyers in the Empire or somewhere else, they're taking the risks. And, allowing for what the new drive engines will cost us, we'll be on Uldune then with what should still be a very good chunk of money. . . . Hmm!" He settled back in his chair. "What were those other ideas?"

The first half of the week-long run to Uldune passed uneventfully. They turned around the plans Goth had been nourishing, amended them here and there. But basically the captain couldn't detect many flaws in them. He didn't tell her so, but it struck him that if Goth hadn't happened to be born a witch she might have made out pretty well on Nikkeldepain. She seemed to have a natural bent for the more devious business angles. As one of their first transactions on the reformed pirate planet, they would pick up fictitious identities. The Daal maintained a special department which handled nothing else and documented its work so impeccably that it would stand up under the most thorough investigation. It was a costly matter, but the proceeds of the cargo sale would cover the additional expense. If the search for the *Venture* and her crew spread east of the Empire, established aliases might be very necessary.

In that respect the Sheewash Drive had turned into a liability. Used judiciously, however, it should be an important asset to the independent trader the *Venture* was to become. This was an untamed area of space; there were sections where even the Empire's heavily armed patrols did not attempt to go in less than squadron strength. And other sections which nobody tried to patrol at all . . . .

"The Sea of Light, f'rinstance," Goth said, nodding at the twisted purple cosmic cloud glow the captain had observed on his first look out of the screens. It had drifted meanwhile over to the *Venture's* port side. "That's a *hairy* place! You get too close to that, you've had it! Every time."

She didn't know exactly what happened when one got too close to the cloud. Neither did anyone else. It had been a long while since anybody had tried to find out.

The Drive wouldn't exactly allow them to go wherever they chose, even if Goth had been able to make regular and unlimited use of it. But as an invisible and unsuspected part of the ship's emergency equipment it would let them take on assignments not many others would care to consider.

There should be money in that, the captain thought. Plenty of money. Once they were launched, they shouldn't have much to worry about on that score. But it meant having the *Venture* rebuilt very completely before they took her out again.

The prospects for the next few years looked good all around. Goth evidently wasn't at all disturbed by the fact that it might be at least that long before she saw her people again. The witches seemed to look at such things a little differently. Well, he thought, the two of them should see and learn a lot while making their fortune as traders; and he'd take care of Goth as best he could. Though from Goth's point of view, it had occurred to him, it might seem more that she was taking care of Captain Pausert.

He couldn't quite imagine himself developing witch powers. He'd tried to pump Goth about that a little and was told in effect not to worry—he'd know when it began to happen and meanwhile there was no way to hurry it up. Just what would happen couldn't be predicted. The type of talents that developed and the sequence in which they appeared varied widely among Karres children and the relatively few adults in whom something brought klatha into sudden activity. Goth was a teleporting specialist and had, perhaps because of that, caught on to the Sheewash Drive very quickly and mastered it like a grown-up. So far she'd done little else. The Leewit, besides being the possessor of a variety of devastating whistles, which she used with considerable restraint under most circumstances, was a klatha linguist. Give her a few words of a language she'd never heard before, and something in her swept out, encompassed it all; and she'd soon be chattering away in it happily as if she'd spoken nothing else in all her young life.

Maleen was simply a very good all-around junior witch who'd recently been taken into advanced training three or four years earlier than was the rule.

Goth clearly didn't think he should be given much more information than that at present; and he didn't press her for it. As long as he didn't attract any more vatches he'd be satisfied. He retained mixed feelings about klatha. Useful it was, no doubt, if one knew how to handle it. But it was uncanny stuff.

There were enough practical matters on hand to keep them fully occupied. He gave Goth a condensed course in the navigation of the *Venture*; and she told him more of what had been going on east of the Empire than he'd ever learned out of history books. It confirmed his first impression that life around here should be varied and interesting . . . .

One interesting variation came their way shortly after the calendric chronometer had recorded the beginning of the fourth day since they'd turned on course for Uldune. It was the middle of the captain's sleep period. He woke up to find Goth violently shaking his shoulder.

"Uh, what is it?" he mumbled.

"You awake?" Her voice was sharp, almost a hiss. "Better get to the controls!"

That aroused him as instantly and completely as a bucketful of ice-cold water . . . .

There was a very strange-looking ship high in the rear viewscreen, at an indicated distance of not many light-minutes away. Its magnified image was like that of a flattened ugly dark bug striding through space after them on a dozen spiky legs set around its edges. The instruments registered a mass about twice that of the *Venture*. It was an unsettling object to find coming up behind one.

"Know who they are?" he asked.

Goth shook her head. The ship had been on the screens for about ten minutes, had kept its distance at first, then swung in and begun to pull up to them. She'd put out a number of short-range query blasts on the communicators, but there'd been no response.

It looked like trouble. "How about the Drive?" he asked.

Goth indicated the open passage door. "Ready right out there!"

"Fine. But wait with it." They didn't intend to start advertising the Sheewash Drive around here if they could avoid it. "Try the communicators again," he said. "They could be on some off-frequency."

He hadn't thrown the override switch on the throttled main drive engines yet. It might have been the *Venture's* relatively slow progress which had attracted the creepy vessel's interest, giving whoever was aboard the idea that here was a possibility of easy prey which should be investigated. But if they set off at speed now and the stranger followed, it could turn into a long chase . . . and one long chase could finish his engines.

If they didn't run, the thing would move into weapons range within less than five minutes.

"Captain!"

He turned. Goth was indicating the communicator screen. A green-streaked darkness flickered on and off in it.

"Getting them, I think!" she murmured.

He watched as she slowly fingered a pair of dials, eyes intent on the screen. There was a loud burst of croaking and whistling noises from one of the communicators. Then, for a second or two, the screen held a picture.

The captain's hair didn't exactly stand on end, but it tried to. There was a sullen green light in the screen, lanky gray shapes moving through it; then a face was suddenly looking out at them. Its red eyes widened. An instant later the screen went blank, and the communicator racket ended.

"Saw us—cut us off!" Goth said, mouth wrinkling briefly in distaste.

The captain cleared his throat. "You know what those are?"

She nodded. "Think so! Saw a picture of a dead one once."

"They're, uh, unfriendly?"

"They catch us, they'll eat us," Goth told him. "That's Megair Cannibals."

The name seemed as unpleasant as the appearance of their pursuers. The captain, heart hammering, reflected a moment, eyes on the grotesque ship in the rear screens. It was considerably closer, seemed to have put on speed.

"Let's see if we can scare them off first," he said suddenly. "If that doesn't work, you better hit the Drive!"

Goth's expression indicated approval. The captain turned, settled himself in the control chair, tripped the override switch, fed the *Venture* power, and set her into a tight vertical turn as the engine hum rose to a roar. His hand shifted to the nova gun mechanisms. The image of the pursuing ship flicked through the overhead screens, settled into the forward ones, spun right side up and was dead ahead, coming towards them. The gun turrets completed their lift through the *Venture's* hull and clicked into position. The small sighting screen lit up; its cross-hairs slid around and locked on the scuttling bug shape.

He snapped in the manual fire control relays. They still had a good deal of space to cover before they came within reasonable range of each other; and if he could help it they wouldn't get within reasonable range. He'd done well enough in gunnery training during his duty tour on a space destroyer of the Nikkeldepain navy, but the Megair Cannibals might be considerably better at games of that kind. However, it was possible they could be bluffed out of pressing their attack. He edged the *Venture* up to full speed, noted the suggestion of raggedness that crept into the engines' thunder, put his thumb on the firing stud, pressed down.

The nova guns let go together. Reaching for the ship rushing towards them and falling far short of it, their charge shattered space into shuddering blue sheets of fire.

It was an impressive display, but the Megair ship kept coming. Something hot and primitive, surprisingly pleasurable, began to roil in the captain as he counted off thirty seconds, pressed the firing stud again. Blue sheet lightning shivered and crashed. The scuttling thing beyond held its course. Answering fire suddenly speckled space with a cluster of red and black explosions.

"Aa-aa-ah!" breathed the captain, head thrust forwards, eyes riveted on the sighting screen. Something about those explosions . . . .

Why, he thought joyfully, we've got the range on them!

He slapped the nova guns on automatic, locked on target, rode the *Venture's* thunder in a dead straight line ahead in the wake of the guns' trail of blue lightning. Red and black fire appeared suddenly on *this* side of the lightning, rolling towards them—

Then it vanished.

There was something like the high-pitched yowl of a small jungle cat in the captain's ears. A firm young fist pounded his shoulder delightedly. "They're running! *They're running!*"

He cut the guns. The sighting screen was empty. His eyes followed Goth's pointing finger to another screen. Far under their present course, turning away on a steep escape curve, went the Megair Cannibals' ship, scuttling its best, dipping, weaving, dwindling . . . .

As they drew closer to Uldune, other ships appeared with increasing frequency in the *Venture's* detection range. But these evidently were going about their own business and inclined to keep out of the path of strange spacecraft. None came close enough to be picked up in the viewscreens.

While still half a day away from the one-time pirate planet, the *Venture's* communicators signaled a pick-up. They switched on the instruments and found themselves listening to a general broadcast from Uldune, addressed to all ships entering this area of space.

If they were headed for Uldune on business, they were invited to shift to a frequency which would put them in contact with a landing station off-planet. Uldune was anxious to see to it that their visit was made as pleasant and profitable as possible and would facilitate matters to that end in every way. Detailed information would be made available by direct-beam contact from the landing station.

It was the most cordial reception ever extended to the captain on a planetary approach. They switched in the station, were welcomed warmly to Uldune. Business arrangements then began immediately. Before another hour was up Uldune knew in general what they wanted and what they had to offer, had provided a list of qualified shipbuilders, scheduled immediate appointments with identity specialists, official assessors who would place a minimum value on their cargo, and a representative of the Daal's Bank, who would assist them in deciding what other steps to take to achieve their goals to best effect on Uldune.

Helpful as the pirate planet was to its clients, it was also clear that it took no unnecessary chances with them. Visitors arriving with their own spacecraft had the choice of leaving them berthed at the landing stations and using a shuttle to have themselves and their goods transported down to a spaceport, or of allowing foolproof seals to be attached to offensive armament for the duration of the ship's stay on Uldune. A brief, but presumably quite effective, contamination check of the interior of the ship and of its cargo was also carried out at the landing station. Otherwise, aside from an evident but no-comment interest aroused by the nova guns in the armament specialists engaged in securing them, the Daal's officials at the station displayed a careful lack of curiosity about the *Venture,* her crew, her cargo, and her origin. An escort boat presently guided them down to a spaceport and their interview at the adjoining Office of Identities.

Chapter FOUR

CAPTAIN ARON, of the extremely remote world of Mulm, and his young niece Dani took up residence late that evening in a rented house in an old quarter of Uldune's port city of Zergandol. It had been a strenuous though satisfactory day for both of them. Much business had begun to roll.

Goth, visibly struggling for the past half hour to keep her eyelids open wide enough to be able to look out, muttered good-night to the captain as soon as they'd located two bedrooms on the third floor of the house, and closed the door to one of them behind her. The captain felt bone-weary himself but his brain still buzzed with the events of the day and he knew he wouldn't be able to sleep for a while. He brewed a pot of coffee in the kitchen and took it up to a dark, narrow fourth-story balcony which encircled the house, where he sipped it from a mug, looking around at the sprawling, inadequately lit city.

Zergandol, from what he had seen of it, was a rather dilapidated town, though it had one neatly modern district. One might have called it quaint, but most of the streets and buildings were worn, cracked, and rather grimy; and the architecture seemed a centuries-old mixture of conflicting styles. The house they were in looked like a weathered layer cake, four round sections containing two rooms each placed on top of one another, connected by a narrow circular stairway. Inside and out, it was old. But the rent was moderate—he wasn't sure yet where they would stand financially by the time they were done with Uldune and Uldune was done with them; and the house was less than a mile up a winding street from the edge of the spaceport and the shipyards of the firm of Sunnat, Bazim & Filish where, during the following weeks, the *Venture* would be rebuilt.

The extent to which the ship would be rebuilt wasn't settled yet. So far there'd been time for only a brief preliminary discussion with the partners. And the day had brought an unexpected development which would make it possible to go a great deal farther with that than they'd planned. It was one of the things the captain was debating now. The Daal's appraiser, with whom they'd gotten together immediately after being equipped with new identities, hadn't seemed quite able to believe in the Karres cargo:

"Wintenberry jelly *and* Lepti liquor?" he'd repeated, lifting his eyebrows, when the captain named the first two of the items the witches: had loaded on the *Venture.* "These are, uh, the *genuine* article?"

Surprised, the captain glanced at Goth, who nodded. "That's right," he said.

"Most unusual!" declared the appraiser interestedly. "What quantity of them do you have?"

The captain told him and got a startled look. from the official. "Something wrong?" he asked, puzzled.

The appraiser shook his head. "Oh, no! No, not at all." He cleared his throat. "You're certain . . . well, you must be, of course!" He made some notes, cleared his throat again. "Now— you've indicated you also have peltries to sell—"

"Yes, we do," said the captain. "Very fine stuff!"

"Hundred and twenty-five tozzami," Goth put in from her end of the table. She sounded as if she were enjoying herself. "Fifty gold-tipped lelaundel—all prime adults."

The appraiser looked at her, then at the captain.

"That is correct, sir?" he asked expressionlessly.

The captain assured him it was. It hadn't occurred to him to ask Goth about the names of the creatures that had grown the magnificent furs in the storage; but "tozzami" and "gold-tipped lelaundel" evidently were familiar terms to this expert. His reactions had indicated he also knew about the green Lepti liquor and the jellies. Possibly Karres exported such articles as a regular thing.

"That perfume I put down," the captain went on. "I don't know if you've heard of Kell Peak essences—"

The appraiser bared his teeth in a strained smile.

"Indeed, I have, sir!" he said softly. "Indeed, I have!" He looked down at his list. "Eight thousand three hundred and twenty-three *half-pints* of Kell Peak essences. . . . In my twenty-two years of professional experience, Captain Aron, I have never had the opportunity to evaluate an incoming cargo of this nature. I don't know what you've done, but allow me to congratulate you."

He left with samples of the cargo to have their genuineness and his appraisal notations confirmed by other specialists. The captain and Goth went off to have lunch in one of the space-port restaurants. "What was he so excited about?" the captain asked, intrigued.

Goth shrugged. "He figures we stole it all."

"Why?"

"Hard stuff to just *buy!*"

She explained while they ate. Tozzamis and lelaundels were indigenous to Karres, part of its mountain fauna; but very few people knew where the furs came from. They had high value, not only because of their quality, but because they were rarely available. From time to time, when the witches wanted money, they'd make up a shipment and distribute it quietly through various contacts.

It was a somewhat different matter with the other items, but it came out to much the same thing. The significant ingredients of the liquor, jellies, and perfume essences could be grown only in three limited areas of three different Empire planets, and in such limited quantities there that the finished products hardly ever appeared on the regular market. The witches didn't advertise the fact that they'd worked out ways to produce all three on Karres. Klatha apparently could also be used to assist a green thumb . . . .

"That might be worth a great deal more than we've calculated on, then!" the captain said hopefully.

"Might," Goth agreed. "Don't know what they'll pay for it here, though."

They found out during their next appointment, which was with a dignitary of the Daal's Bank. This gentleman already had the appraiser's report on hand and had opened an account for Captain Aron of Mulm on the strength of it. He went over their planned schedule on Uldune with them, added up the fees, licenses, and taxes that applied to such activities, threw in a figure to cover general expenses involved with getting the *Venture*—renamed *Evening Bird*, operating under a fictitious Mulm charter—established as a trading ship, and deducted the whole from the anticipated bid value of the cargo, which allowed for the customary forty per cent risk cut on the appraised real value. In this instance the bidding might run higher. What they'd have left in cash in any case came to slightly less than half a million Imperial maels, and they could begin drawing on the bank immediately for anything up to that sum.

He'd counted on reimbursing Councilor Onswud via a nontraceable subradio deposit for the estimated value of the *Venture*, the *Venture's* original Nikkeldepain cargo, and the miffel farm loan, plus interest. And on investing up to a hundred and fifty thousand in having the *Venture* reequipped with what it took to make her dependably spaceworthy. It had looked as if they'd be living rather hand-to-mouth after that until they'd put a couple of profitable trading runs behind them.

Now, leaving themselves only a reasonable margin in case general expenses ran higher than the bank's estimate, they could, if they chose, sink nearly four hundred thousand into the *Venture*. That should be enough to modernize her from stem to stern, turn her into a ship that carried passengers in comfort as well as cargo—a ship furthermore equal to the best in her class for speed, security, and navigational equipment, capable of running rings around the average bandit or slipping away if necessary from a nosy Imperial patrol. All that without having to fall back on the Sheewash Drive, which still would be available to them when required.

There hadn't been a good opportunity today to discuss that notion with Goth. But Goth would like it. As for himself . . . .

The captain shook his head, realizing he'd already made up his mind. He smiled out over the balcony railing at dark Zergandol. After all, what better use could they make of the money? Tomorrow they'd get down to business with Sunnat, Bazim & Filish!

He placed the empty coffee mug on a window ledge beside the chair he'd settled himself in and stretched out his legs. There was a chill in the air now and it had begun to get through to him, but he still wasn't quite ready to turn in. If someone had told him even a month ago that he'd find himself one day on blood-stained old Uldune . . . .

They'd varnished over their evil now, but there was evil enough still here. As far as the Daal's Bank knew, he'd committed piracy and murder to get his hands on the rare cargo they'd taken on consignment from him. And if anything, they respected him for it.

In spite of the Daal's rigid limitations on what was allowable nowadays, they weren't really far away from the previous bad pirate period. In the big store where he and Goth had picked up supplies for the house, the floor manager earnestly advised them to invest in adequate spy-proofing equipment. The captain hadn't seen much point to it until Goth gave him the sign. The device they settled on then was small though expensive, looked like a pocket watch. Activated, it was guaranteed to make a twenty-foot sphere of space impervious to ordinary eavesdroppers, instrument snooping, hidden observers, and lip-readers. They checked it out with the store's most sophisticated espionage instruments and bought it. There'd be occasions enough at that when they'd want to be talking about things nobody here should know about; and apparently no one on the planet was really safe from prying eyes and ears unless they had such protection.

In the open space about Uldune, of course, the old wickedness flourished openly. During the day, he'd heard occasional references to a report that ships of a notorious modern-day pirate leader, called the Agandar, had cleaned out a platinum mining settlement on an asteroid chain close enough to Uldune to keep the Daal's space defense forces on red alert overnight . . . .

The captain's eyes shifted to the sky. Low over the western horizon hung the twisted purple glow of the Sea of Light, as familiar to him by now as any of the galactic landmarks in the night skies of Nikkeldepain. He watched it a few minutes. It was like a challenge, a cold threat; and something in him seemed to reply to it:

Wait till we're ready for you . . . .

About it lay the Chaladoor. Another ill-omened name out of history, out of legend . . . a vast expanse of space beginning some two days' travel beyond Uldune, with a reputation still as bad as it ever had been in the distant past. Very little shipping moved in that direction, although barely half a month away, on the far side of the Chaladoor, there were clusters of prosperous independent worlds wide open for profitable trade. They could be reached by circumnavigating the Chaladoor, but that trip took the better part of a year. The direct route, on the other hand, meant threading one's way through a maze of navigational hazards, hazards to an ordinary kind of ship such as to discourage all but the hardiest. Inimical beings, like the crew of the Megair highwayman which had stalked the *Venture* during the run to Uldune, were a part of the hazards. And other forces were at work there, disturbing and sometimes violently dangerous forces nobody professed to understand. Even the almost universally functioning subradio did not operate in that area.

Nevertheless there was a constant demand for commercial transportation through the Chaladoor, the time saved by using the direct route outweighing the risks. And the passage wasn't impossible. Certain routes were known to be relatively free of problems. Small, fast, well-armed ships stood the best chance of traversing the Chaladoor successfully along them—and one or two runs of that kind could net a ship owner as much as several years of ordinary trading.

More importantly, from the captain's and Goth's point of view, Karres ships, while they carefully avoided certain sections of the Chaladoor, crossed it as a matter of course whenever it lay along their route. Constant alertness was required. Then the Sheewash Drive simply took them out of any serious trouble they encountered . . . .

What it meant was that the remodeled, rejuvenated *Venture* also could make that run.

The captain settled deeper into the chair, blinking drowsily at the bubble of light over the spaceport, which seemed the one area still awake in Zergandol. Afterwards, he couldn't have said at what point his reflections turned into dream-thoughts. But he did begin to dream.

It was a vague, half-sleep dreaming, agreeable to start with.

Then, by imperceptible degrees, uneasiness came creeping into it, a dim apprehension which strengthened and ebbed but never quite faded. Later he recalled nothing more definite about that part of it, but considerable time must have passed in that way.

Then the vague, shifting dream imagery gathered, took on form and definite menace. He was aware of color at first, a spreading yellow glow—a sense of something far away but drawing closer. It became a fog of yellow light, growing towards him. A humming came from it.

Fear awoke in him. He didn't know of what until he discovered the fog wasn't empty. There were brighter ripplings and flashes within it, a seething of energies. These energies seemed to form linked networks inside the cloud. At the points where they crossed were bodies.

It would have been difficult to describe those bodies in any detail. They seemed made of light themselves, silhouettes of dim fire in the yellow haze of the cloud. They were like fat worms which moved with a slow writhing; and he had the impression that they were not only alive but aware and alert; also that in some manner they were manipulating the glowing fog and its energies.

What alarmed him was that this mysterious structure was moving steadily closer. If he didn't do something he would be engulfed by it.

He did something. He didn't know what. But suddenly he was elsewhere, sitting in chilled darkness. The foggy fire and its inhabitants were gone. He discovered he was shaking, and that in spite of the cold air his face was dripping with sweat. It was some seconds before he was able to grasp where he was—still on the fourth-story balcony of the old house they had rented that day in the city of Zergandol.

So he'd fallen asleep, had a nightmare, come awake from it. . . . And he might, he thought, have been sleeping for several hours because Zergandol looked almost completely blacked out now. Even the spaceport area showed only the dimmest reflection of light. And there wasn't a sound. Absolute silence enclosed the dark buildings of the old section of the city around him. To the left a swollen red moon disk hung just above the horizon. Zergandol might have become a city of the dead.

Chilled to the bone by the night air, shuddering under his clothes, the captain looked around. And then up.

Two narrow building spires loomed blackly against the night sky. Above and beyond them, eerily outlining their tips, was a yellowish haze, a thin, discolored glowing smear against the stars which shown through it. It was fading as the captain stared at it, already very faint. But it was so suggestive of the living light cloud of his dream that his heart began leaping all over again.

It dimmed further, was gone. Not a trace remained. And while he was still wondering what it all meant, the captain heard the sound of voices. They came from the street below the balcony—two or three people speaking rapidly, in hushed tones.

They might have been having a nervous argument about something, but it was the Uldunese language, so he wasn't sure. He heaved himself stiffly out of the chair, moved to the balcony railing and peered down through the gloom. A groundcar was parked in the street, two shadowy, gesticulating figures standing beside it. After some seconds they broke off their discussion and climbed into the car. He heard a metallic click as its door closed. The driving lights came on dimmed, and the car moved off slowly along the street. In the reflection of the lights he'd had a glimpse of markings on its side, which just might have been the pattern of bold squares that was the insignia of the Daal's police.

Here and there, as he gazed around now, other lights began coming on in Zergandol. But not too many. The city remained very quiet. Perhaps, he thought, there had been an attempted raid from space by the ships of that infamous pirate, the

Agandar, which had now been beaten off. But if there'd been some kind of alert which had darkened the city, he'd slept through the warning; and evidently so had Goth.

He had never heard of a weapon though which could have produced that odd yellow discoloring of a large section of the night sky. It was all very mysterious. For a moment the captain had the uneasy suspicion that he was still partly caught up in his nightmare and that what he'd thought he'd seen up there had been nothing more real than a lingering reflection of his musings about the ancient evil of Uldune and the space about it.

Confused and dog-tired, he left the balcony, carefully locking its door behind him, found his bedroom and was soon asleep.

He didn't tell Goth about his experiences next day. He'd intended to, but when they woke up there was barely time for a quick breakfast before they hurried off to keep an early appointment with Sunnat, Bazim & Filish. The partners made no mention of unusual occurrences during the night, and neither did anybody else they met during the course of the crowded day. The captain presently became uncertain whether he hadn't in fact dreamed up the whole odd business. By evening he was rather sure he had. There was no reason to bore Goth with the account of a dream.

Within a few days, with so much going on connected with the rebuilding of the *Venture* and their other plans, he forgot the episode completely. It was several weeks then before he remembered it again. What brought it to mind was a conversation he happened to overhear between Vezzarn, the old Uldunese spacedog they'd hired on as purser, bookkeeper, and general crewhand for the *Venture*, and one of Vezzarn's cronies who'd dropped in at the office for a visit. They were talking about something called Worm Weather . . . .

Meanwhile there'd been many developments, mostly of a favorable nature. Work on the *Venture* proceeded apace. The captain couldn't have complained about lack of interest on the side of his shipbuilders. After the first few days either Bazim or Filish seemed always around, supervising every detail of every operation. They were earnest, hardworking, middle-aged men—Bazim big, beefy, and sweaty, Filish lean, weathered, and dehydrated-looking—who appeared to know everything worth knowing about the construction and outfitting of spaceships. Sunnat, the third member of the firm and apparently the one who really ran things, was tall, red headed, strikingly handsome, and female. She could be no older than the captain, but he had the impression that Bazim and Filish were more than a little afraid of her.

His own feelings about Sunnat were mixed. During their first few meetings she'd been polite, obviously interested in an operation which should net the firm a large, heavy profit, but aloof. Her rare smiles remained cold and her gray-green eyes seemed constantly on the verge of going into a smoldering rage about something. She left the practical planning and work details to Bazim and Filish, while they deferred to her in the financial aspects.

That had suddenly changed, at least as far as the captain was concerned. From one day to another, Sunnat seemed to have thawed to him; whenever he appeared in the shipyard or at the partners' offices, she showed up, smiling, pleasant, and talkative. And when he stayed in the little office he'd rented to take care of other business, in a square of the spaceport administration area across from S., B. & F., she was likely to drop in several times a day.

It was flattering at first. Sunnat's sternly beautiful face and graceful, velvet skinned body would have quickened any man's pulses; the captain wasn't immune to their attractiveness. In public she wore a gray cloak which covered her from neck to ankles, but the outfit beneath it, varying from day to day, calculatingly exposed some sizable section or other of Sunnat's person—sculptured shoulders and back, the flat and pliable midriff, or a curving line of thigh. Her perfumes and hair-styling seemed to change as regularly as the costumes. It became a daily barrage, increasing in intensity, on the captain's senses; and on occasion his senses reeled. When Sunnat put her hand on his sleeve to emphasize a conversational point or brushed casually along his side as they clambered about together on the scaffoldings now lining the *Venture's* hull, he could feel his breath go short.

But there still was something wrong about it. He wasn't sure what except perhaps that when Goth came around he had the impression that Sunnat stiffened inside. She always spoke pleasantly to Goth on such occasions, and Goth replied as pleasantly, in a polite little-girl way, which wasn't much like her usual manner. Their voices made a gentle duet. But beneath them the captain seemed to catch faint, distant echoes of a duet of another kind—like the yowling of angry jungle cats.

It got to be embarrassing finally, and he found himself increasingly inclined to avoid Sunnat when he could. If he saw the tall, straight shape in the gray cloak heading across the square towards his office, he was as likely as not to slip quietly out the back door for lunch, leaving instructions with Vezzarn to report that he'd been called out on business elsewhere.

Vezzarn was a couple of decades beyond middle age but a spry and wiry little character, whose small gray eyes didn't seem to miss much. He was cheery and polite, very good with figures. Above all, he'd logged six passes through the Chaladoor and didn't mind making a few more—for the customary steep risk pay and with, as he put it, the right ship and the right skipper. The *Evening Bird*, building in the shipyard, plus Captain Aron of Mulm seemed to meet his requirements there.

The day the captain recalled the odd dream he'd had during their first night in Zergandol, a man named Tobul had dropped by at the office to talk to Vezzarn. They were distant relatives, and Tobul was a traveling salesman whose routes took him over most of Uldune. He'd been a spacer like Vezzarn in his younger days; and like most spacers, the two used Imperial Universum in preference to Uldunese when they talked together. So the captain kept catching scraps of the conversation in Vezzarn's cubicle.

He paid no attention to it until he heard Tobul inquire, "Safe to mention Worm Weather around here at the moment?"

Wondering what the fellow meant, the captain looked up from his paper work.

"Safe enough," replied Vezzarn. "Hasn't been a touch of it for a month now. You been running into any?"

"More'n I like, let me tell you! There was a bad bout of it in . . ." He gave the name of some Uldune locality which the captain didn't quite get. "Just before I got there. Very bad! Everywhere you went people were still going off into screaming fits. Didn't hang around there long, believe me!"

"Don't blame you."

"That evening after I left, I saw the sky starting to go yellow again behind me. I made tracks. . . . They could've got hit as bad again that night. Or worse! Course you never hear anything about it."

"No." There was a pause while the captain listened, straining his ears now. The sky going yellow? Suddenly and vividly he saw every detail of that ominous fiery dream-structure again, drifting towards him, and the yellow discoloration fading against the stars above Zergandol. . . . "Seems like it keeps moving farther west and south," Vezzarn went on thoughtfully. "Ten years ago nobody figured it ever would get to Uldune."

"Well, it's been all around the planet this time!" Tobul assured him. "Longest bout we ever had. And if—"

The captain lost the rest of it. He'd glanced out the window just then and spotted Sunnat coming across the square. It was a one-way window so she couldn't see him. He hesitated a moment to make sure she was headed for the office. Once before he'd ducked too hastily out the back entrance and run into her as she was coming through the adjoining building arcade. There was no reason to hurt her pride by letting her know he preferred to avoid her.

Today she was clearly on her way to see him. The captain picked up his cap, stopped for an instant at Vezzarn's cubicle.

"I've been gone for a couple of hours," he announced, "and may not be back for a few more."

"Right, sir!" said Vezzarn understandingly. "The chances are you're at the bank this very moment . . . ."

"Probably," the captain agreed, and left. Once outside, he recalled several matters he might as well be taking care of that afternoon; so it was, in fact, getting close to evening before he returned to the office. Tobul had left and Sunnat wasn't around; but Goth had showed up, and Vezzarn was entertaining her in the darkening office with horror tales of his experiences in the Chaladoor and elsewhere. He told a good story, apparently didn't exaggerate too much, and Goth, who no doubt could have topped his accounts by a good bit if she'd felt like it, always enjoyed listening to him.

The captain told him to go on, and sat down. When Vezzarn reached the end of his yarn, he asked, "By the way, just what is that Worm Weather business you and Tobul were talking about today?"

He got a quick look from Goth and Vezzarn both. Vezzarn appeared puzzled.

"Just what? I'm not sure I understand, sir," he said. "We've had a good bit of it around Uldune for the past couple of months, and that's very unusual for these longitudes, of course. But—"

"I meant," explained the captain, "what is it?"

Vezzarn now looked startled. He glanced at Goth, back at the captain.

"You're serious? Why, you're *really* a long way from home!"

he exclaimed. Then he caught himself. "Uh—no offense, sir! No offense, little lady! Where you're from is none of my foolish business, and that's the truth. . . . But you've never heard of Worm Weather? The Nuris? Manaret, the Worm World? . . . Moander Who Speaks with a Thousand Voices?"

"I don't know a thing about any of them," the captain admitted. Goth very likely did, now that he thought of it; but she said nothing.

"Hm!" Vezzarn scratched the grizzled bristles on his scalp, and grimaced. "Hm!" he repeated dubiously. He got up behind his desk, went to the window, glanced out at the clear evening sky and sat down on the sill.

"I'm not particularly superstitious," he remarked. "But if you don't mind, sir, I'll stay here where I can keep an eye out while I'm on that subject. You'll know why when I'm done . . . ."

If Vezzarn had been more able to resist telling a good story to someone who hadn't heard it before, it is likely the captain would not have learned much about Worm Weather from him. The little spaceman became increasingly nervous as he talked on and the world beyond the window continued to darken; his eyes swung about to search the sky every minute or so. But whatever apprehensions he felt didn't stop him.

Where was the Worm World, dread Manaret? None knew. Some thought it was concealed near the heart of the Chaladoor, in the Sea of Light. Some believed it lay so far to Galactic East that no exploring ship had ever come on it—or if one had, it had been destroyed too swiftly to send back word of its awesome find. Some argued it might be anywhere—a burning world, or a glittering ice sphere sheathed in mile-thick layers of solidified poisonous gas. Any of those guesses could be true, because almost all that was known of Manaret was of its tunneled, splendidly ornamented interior.

Vezzarn inclined to the theory it was to be found, if one cared to search for it, at some vast distance among the star swarms to Far Galactic East. Year after year, decade after decade, as long as civilized memory went back, the glowing plague of Worm Weather had seemed to come drifting farther westward to harass the worlds of humanity.

And what was Worm Weather? Eh, said Vezzarn, the vehicles, the fireships of the Nuri worms of Manaret! Hadn't they been seen riding their webs of force in the yellow-burning clouds, tinging the upper air of the planets they touched with their reflections? He himself was one of the few who had encountered Worm Weather in deep space and lived to tell of it. Two months east of Uldune it had been. There in space it was apparent that the clouds formed globes, drifting as swiftly as the swiftest ships.

"In the screens we could see the Nuris, those dreadful worms," Vezzarn said hoarsely, hunched like a dark gnome on the window sill against the dimming city. "And who knows, perhaps they saw us! But we turned and ran and they didn't follow. It was a bold band of boys who crewed that ship; but of the twelve of us, three went mad during the next few hours and never recovered. And the rest couldn't bring ourselves to slow the ship until we had eaten up almost all our power—so we barely came crawling back to port at last!"

The captain pushed his palm over his forehead, wiping clammy sweat. "But what are they?" he asked. "What do they want?"

"What are they? They are the Nuris. . . . What do they want?" Vezzarn shook his head. "Worm Weather comes! Perhaps only a lick of fire in the sky at night. Perhaps nothing else happens . . . ." He paused. "But when they send out their thoughts, sir—then it can be bad! Then it can be very bad!"

People slept, and woke screaming. Or walked in fear of

something for which they had no name. Or saw the glorious and terrible caverns of Manaret opening before them in broad daylight. . . . Some believed they had been taken there, and somehow returned.

People did vanish when Worm Weather came. People who never were seen again. That was well established. It did not happen always, but it had happened too often . . . .

Perhaps it wasn't even the thoughts of the Nuris that poured into a human world at such times, but the thoughts of Moander. Moander the monster, the god, who crouched on the surface of Manaret . . . who spoke in a thousand voices, in a thousand tongues. Some said the Nuris themselves were no more than Moander's thoughts drifting out and away endlessly through the universe.

It had been worse, it seemed, in the old days. There were ancient stories of worlds whose populations had been swept by storms of panic and such wildly destructive insanity that only mindless remnants were later found still huddling in the gutted cities. And worlds where hundreds of thousands of inhabitants had tracelessly disappeared overnight. But those events had been back in the period of the Great Eastern Wars when planets enough died in gigantic battlings among men. What role Manaret had played in that could no longer be said with any certainty.

"One thing is true though, sir," Vezzarn concluded earnestly. "I've been telling you this because you asked, and because you should know there's danger in it. But it's a bad business otherwise to talk much about Worm Weather or what it means— even to think about it too long. That's been known a long time. Where there's loose talk about Worm Weather, there Worm Weather will go finally. It's as if they can feel the talk and don't like it. So nobody wants to say much about it. It's safer to take no more interest in them than you can help. Though it's hard to keep from thinking about the devil-things when you see the sky turning yellow above your head!

"Now I'll wish you good-night, Dani and Captain Aron. It's time and past for supper and a nightcap for old Vezzarn—who talks a deal more than he should, I think."

"Didn't know the Worm stuff had been around here," Goth remarked thoughtfully as they turned away from the groundcab that had brought them back up to their house.

"You already knew about that, eh?" The captain nodded. "I had the impression you did. Got something to tell you—but we'd better wait till we're private."

"Uh-huh!"

She went up the winding stairway to the living room while the captain took the groceries they'd picked up in the port shopping area to the kitchen. When he followed her upstairs he saw an opaque cloudy shimmering just beyond the living room door, showing she'd switched on their spy-proofing gadget. The captain stepped into the shimmering and it cleared away before him. The watch-shaped device lay on the table in the center of the room, and Goth was warming her hands at the fireplace. She looked around.

"Well," he said, "now we can talk. Did Vezzarn have his story straight?"

Goth nodded. "Pretty straight. That Worm World isn't really a world at all, though."

"No? What is it?"

"Ship," Goth told him. "Sort of a spaceship. Big one! Big as Uldune or Karres. . . . Better tell me first what you were going to."

"Well—" The captain hesitated. "It's that description Vezzarn gave of the Nuris . . . ." He reported his dream, the feelings it had aroused in him, and what had been going on when he woke up. "Apparently there really was Worm Weather over Zergandol that night," he concluded.

"Uh-huh!" Goth's teeth briefly indented her lower lip. Her eyes remained reflectively on his face.

"But I don't have any explanation for the dream," the captain said. "Unless it was the kind of thing Vezzarn was talking about."

"Wasn't exactly a dream, captain. Nuris have a sort of klatha. You were seeing them that way. Likely, they knew it."

"What makes you think that?" he asked, startled.

"Nuris hunt witches," Goth explained.

"Hunt them? Why?"

She shrugged. "They've figured out too much about the Manaret business on Karres. . . . Other reasons, too!"

Now he became alarmed. "But then you're in danger while we're on Uldune!"

"*I'm* not," Goth said. "You were in danger. You'd be again if we got Worm Weather anywhere near Zergandol."

"But . . ."

"You got klatha. Nuris'd figure you for a witch. We'll fix that now!"

She moved out before him, facing him, lifted a finger, held it up in front of his eyes, a few feet away. Her face grew dead serious, intent. "Watch the way it moves!"

He followed the fingertip as it drew a fleeting, wavy line through the air. Goth's hand stopped, closed quickly to a fist as if cutting off the line behind it. "You do it now," she said. "In your head."

"Draw the same kind of line, you mean?"

"Uh-huh."

She waited while the captain went through some difficult mental maneuverings.

"Got it!" he announced at last, with satisfaction.

Goth's finger came up again. "Now this one . . . ."

Three further linear patterns were traced in the air for him, each quite different from the others. Practicing them mentally, the captain felt himself grow warm, perspiry, vaguely wondered why. When he was able to say he'd mastered the fourth one, Goth nodded.

"Now you do them together, Captain . . . one after the other, the way I showed you quick as you can!"

"Together, eh?" He loosened his collar. He wasn't just perspiring now; he was dripping wet. A distinct feeling of internal heat building up . . . some witch trick she was showing him. He might have felt more skeptical about it if it weren't for the heat. "This helps against Nuris?"

"Uh-huh. A lock." Goth didn't smile; she was disregarding his appearance, and her small brown face was still very intent. "Hurry up! You mustn't forget any of it."

He grunted, closed his eyes, concentrated.

Pattern One—easy! Pattern Two . . . Pattern Three—

His mind wavered an instant, groping. Internal heat suddenly surged up. Startled, he remembered:

Four!

A blurred pinwheel of blue brilliance appeared, spun momentarily inside his skull, collapsed to a diamond-bright point, was gone. As it went, there was a snapping sensation, also inside his skull—an almost audible snap. Then everything was relaxing, went quiet. The heat magically ebbed away while he drew a breath. He opened his eyes, somewhat shaken.

Goth was grinning. "Knew you could do it, Captain!"

"What *did* I do?" he asked.

"Built a good lock! You'll have to practice a little still. That'll be easy. The Nuris come around then, you switch the lock on. They won't know you're there!"

"Well, that's fine!" said the captain weakly. He looked about for a cloth, mopped at his face. He'd have to change his clothes, he decided. "Where'd that heat come from?"

"Klatha heat. It's a hot pattern, all right—that's why it's so good. . . . Don't show those moves to somebody who can't do them right. Not unless you don't mind about them."

"Oh? Why not?"

"Because they'll burn right up—flames and smoke—if they

try to do them and don't stop fast enough," Goth said. "Never seen someone do it, but it's happened."

She might have thought he was nervous if he hadn't repeated the experiment right away to get in the practice she felt he needed. So he did. It was surprisingly easy then. On the first run through, the line patterns seemed to flicker into existence almost as his thoughts turned to one after another of them. On the second, he could barely keep up with the overall pattern as it took shape and was blanked out again by the spinning blue blur. On the third, there was only an instant flash of brilliance and that odd semiaudible snap near the top of his skull. At that point he realized there had been no recurrence of the uncomfortable heat sensations.

"You got it now!" his mentor decided when he reported. "Won't matter if you're asleep either. The locks know their business."

"Incidentally, how did you know I could do it?" the captain inquired.

"You picked up the Nuris," Goth said. "That's good, so early . . . ." Over dinner she filled out his picture of the Worm World and its unpleasant inhabitants. Manaret and the witches had been at odds for a considerable time—around a hundred and fifty years, Karres time, Goth said; though she wasn't sure of the exact period. The baleful effect of the Worm World on human civilizations was more widespread and more subtle than anyone like Vezzarn could guess, and not limited to the Nuri raids. There were powerful and malignant minds there which could act across vast reaches of space and created much mischief in human affairs.

Telepathic adepts among the people of Karres set out to trace these troubles to their source and presently discovered facts about Manaret no one had suspected. It was not a world at all, they found, but a ship of unheard-of size that had come out of an alien universe which had no normal connections to the universe known to humanity. Several centuries ago, some vast cataclysm had temporarily disabled the titanic ship and hurled it and its crew into this galaxy; and the disaster was followed by a mutiny led by Moander, the entity who "spoke in a thousand voices." Moander, the witches learned, was a monstrous robot-brain which had taken almost complete control of the great ship, forcing the race which had built Manaret and been its masters to retreat to a heavily defended interior section where Moander's adherents could not reach them.

Karres telepaths contacted these people, who called themselves the Lyrd-Hyrier, gaining information from them but no promise of help against Moander. Moander was holding the ship in this universe with the apparent purpose of gaining control of human civilizations here and establishing itself as ultimate ruler. The Nuris, whose disagreeable physical appearance gained Manaret the name of Worm World, were a servant race which in the mutiny had switched allegiance from the Lyrd-Hyrier to Moander.

"So then," Goth said, "Moander found out Karres was spying on him. That's when the Nuris started hunting witches . . . ."

The discovery also slowed down Moander's plans of conquest. Karres, the megalomaniac monster evidently decided, must be found and destroyed before it could act freely. The witches at that time had no real defense against the Nuris' methods of attack and, some eighty years ago, had been obliged to shift their world beyond the western side of the Empire to avoid them. The Nuris were not only a mental menace. They had physical weapons of alien type at their disposal which could annihilate the life of a planet in very short order. There had been a great deal to learn and work out before the witches could consider confronting them openly.

"They've been coming along with that pretty well, I think," Goth said. "But it's about time, too. Manaret's been making a lot of trouble and it's getting worse."

"In what way?" The captain found himself much intrigued by all this.

The Worm World more recently had developed the tactics of turning selected individual human beings into its brainwashed tools. It was suspected the current Emperor and other persons high in his council were under the immediate influence of Moander's telepathic minions. "One of the reasons we don't get along very well with the Imperials," Goth explained, "is the Emperor's got orders out to find a way to knock out Karres for good. They haven't found one yet, though."

The captain reflected. "Think the reason your people moved Karres had to do with Manaret again?" he asked.

Goth shrugged. "Wouldn't have to," she said. "The Empire's politics go every which way, I guess. We help the Empress Hailie—she's the best of the lot. Maybe somebody got mad about that. I don't know. Anyway, they won't catch Karres that easy . . . ."

He reflected again. "Have they found out where the Worm World is? Vezzarn thought . . . ."

"That's strategy, Captain," Goth said, rather coldly.

"Eh?"

"If anyone on Karres knows where it is, they won't say so to anyone else who doesn't have to know they know. Supposing you and I got picked up by the Nuris tonight?"

"Hm!" he said. "I get it."

It sounded like the witches were involved in interesting maneuvers on a variety of levels. But he and Goth were out of all that. Privately, the captain regretted it a little.

Their own affairs on Uldune, however, continued to progress satisfactorily. Public notice had been posted that on completion of her outfitting by the firm of Sunnat, Bazim & Filish, the modernized trader *Evening Bird*, skippered by Captain Aron of Mulm, would embark on a direct run through the Chaladoor to the independent world of Emris. Expected duration of the voyage: sixteen days. Reservations for cargo and a limited number of passengers could be made immediately, at standard risk run rates payable with the reservations and not refundable. A listing of the *Evening Bird's* drive speeds, engine reserves, types of detection equipment, and defensive and offensive armament was added.

All things considered, the response had been surprising. Apparently competition in the risk run business was not heavy at present. True, only three passengers had signed up so far, while the *Venture's* former crew quarters had been remodeled into six comfortable staterooms and a combined dining room and lounge. But within a week the captain had been obliged to put a halt to the cargo reservations. He'd have to see how much space was left over after they'd stowed away the stuff he'd already committed himself to carry.

They were in business. And the outrageous risk run rates made it rather definitely big business.

Of the three passengers, one was a beautiful dark-eyed damsel, calling herself Hulik do Eldel, who wanted to get to Emris as soon as she possibly could, for unspecified personal reasons, and who had, she said, complete confidence that Captain Aron and his niece would see her there safely. The second was a plump, fidgety financier named Kambine, who perspired profusely at any mention of the Chaladoor but grew hot-eyed and eager when he spoke of an illegal fortune he stood to make if he could get to a certain address on Emris within the next eight weeks. The captain liked that part not at all when he heard of it. But penalties on cancellations of risk run reservations by the carrier were so heavy that he couldn't simply cross Kambine off the passenger list. They'd have to get him there; but he would give Emris authorities the word on the financier's underhanded plot immediately on arrival. That might be very poor form by Uldune's standards; but the captain couldn't care less.

The last of them was one Laes Yango, a big-boned, dour-faced businessman who stood a good head taller than the captain and had little to say about himself. He was shepherding some crates of extremely valuable hyperelectronic equipment through the Chaladoor, would transfer with them on Emris for a destination several weeks' travel beyond. Yango, the captain thought, should create no problems aboard. He wasn't so sure of the other two.

When it came to problems on Uldune, he still had a number to handle there. But they were business matters and would be resolved. Sunnat appeared to have realized at last she'd been making something of a nuisance of herself and was now behaving more sensibly. She was still very cordial to the captain whenever they met; and he trusted he hadn't given the tall redhead any offense.

Chapter FIVE

SEDMON THE SIXTH, the Daal of Uldune, was a lean, dark man, tall for the Uldunese strain, with pointed, foxy features and brooding, intelligent eyes. He was a busy ruler who had never been known to indulge in the frivolity of purely social engagements. Yet he always found time to grant an audience to Hulik do Eldel when she requested it. Hulik was a very beautiful young woman who, though native to Uldune, had spent more than half her life in the Empire. She had been an agent of Central Imperial Intelligence for several years; and she and the Daal had been acquainted for about the same length of time. Sometimes they worked together, sometimes at cross-purposes. In either situation, they often found it useful to pool their information, up to a point.

Hulik had arrived early that morning at the House of Thunders, the ancient and formidable castle of the Daals in the highlands south of Zergandol, and met Sedmon in his private suite in one of the upper levels of the castle.

"Do you know," asked Hulik, who could be very direct when she felt like it, "whether this rumored super spacedrive of Karres really exists?"

"I have no proof of it," the Daal admitted. "But I would not be surprised to discover it exists."

"And if you did, how badly would you want it?"

Sedmon shrugged.

"Not badly enough to do anything likely to antagonize Karres," he said.

"Or to antagonize the Empire?"

"Depending on the circumstances," the Daal said cautiously, "I might risk the anger of the Empire."

Hulik was silent a moment.

"The Imperium," she said then, "very much wants to have this drive. And it does not care in the least whether it antagonizes Karres, or anybody else, in the process of getting it."

Sedmon shrugged again. "Each to his taste," he said drily.

Hulik smiled. "Yes," she said, "and one thing at a time. To begin with then, do you believe a ship we have both shown interest in during the past weeks is the one equipped with this mysterious drive?"

The Daal scratched his neck.

"I'm inclined to believe the ship *was* equipped with the drive," he acknowledged. "I'm not sure it still is." He blinked at her. "What are you supposed to do?"

"Either obtain the drive or keep trace of the ship until other agents can obtain it," Hulik said promptly.

"No small order," said Sedmon.

"Perhaps. What do you know about the man and the girl? The information I have is that the man is a Captain Pausert, citizen of Nikkeldepain, and that the child evidently is one of three he picked up in the Empire shortly before the first use of the drive was observed and reported. A child of Karres."

"That is also the story as I know it," Sedmon told her. "Let's have a look at those two . . . ."

He went to a desk, pressed a switch. A picture of the captain and Goth appeared in a wall screen. They came walking towards the observer along one of the winding, hilly streets of Zergandol. When their figures filled the screen, the Daal stopped the motion, stood staring at them.

"To all appearances," he said, "this man is the citizen of Nikkeldepain described and shown in the reports. But there are still unanswered questions about him. I admit I find those questions disturbing."

"What are they?" Hulik asked, a trace of amusement in her voice.

"He may be officially the citizen of Nikkeldepain he is supposed to be, now masquerading with the assistance of my office as Captain Aron of Mulm—and still be a Karres agent and a witch. Or he may be a Karres witch who has taken on the appearance of Captain Pausert of Nikkeldepain. One simply never knows with these witches . . . ."

He paused, shaking his head irritably. After a moment Hulik said, "That's what is bothering you?"

"That is what is bothering me," Sedmon agreed. "If Captain Pausert, alias Captain Aron, is in fact a witch, I want no trouble with him or his ship."

"And if he isn't?"

"The girl almost certainly is of the witches," the Daal said. "But I might be inclined to take a chance with her. Even that I would not like too well, since Karres has ways of finding out about occurrences that are of interest to it."

"May I point out," said Hulik, "that the entire world of Karres was reliably reported to have disappeared about the time this Captain Pausert was last observed in the Nikkeldepain area? The official opinion in the Imperium is that the planet was accidentally destroyed when the witches tested some super-weapon of their devising, against the impending arrival of a punitive Imperial Fleet."

The Daal scratched his neck again.

"I have heard of that," he said. "And, in fact, I have received a report from one of my own men in the meanwhile, to the effect that Karres does seem to be gone from the Iverdahl

System. It is possible that it is destroyed. But I don't believe it."

"Why not?"

"I have had dealings with a good number of the witches, Hulik, and for many years I have made a study of Karres and its history. This is not the first time it was reported that world had disappeared. Nor, when it was observed again, was it necessarily within some months of ship travel of the point where it had been observed before."

"A super spacedrive which moves a world?" Hulik smiled. "Really Sedmon!"

"As to that, I will say nothing more," replied the Daal. "There are other possibilities. For all I know, Karres still is at present in the Iverdahl System but made invisible, indetectable, by the skills of the witches."

"That, too, seems rather improbable," Hulik remarked.

"It may seem that way," said Sedmon. "But I know it to be a fact that, before this, ships have gone to the Iverdahl System in search of the world of Karres and were unable to find it there."

He shrugged. "In any event, it seems much safer to me to assume that the world of Karres and the witches of Karres have not disappeared permanently . . . ."

He stared at the frozen figures in the screen, pursed his mouth in puzzled worriment. "And besides . . ."

"Well?" said Hulik as he hesitated.

The Daal waggled his finger at the screen. "I have the strangest feeling I have encountered that man before! Perhaps also the child . . . And yet I find no place for either of them in my memories."

Hulik glanced curiously at him. "That must be your imagination," she told him. "But your nervousness about the witches explains why you have been conducting your search for Captain Pausert's mystery drive in what I felt was an excessively roundabout manner."

The Daal grinned briefly.

"I have," he said, "great faith in the basic unscrupulousness of Sunnat, Bazim & Filish. And in the boldness of Sunnat. The story that came to her naturally did not mention the possibility that her clients were witches. But she and her partners are completely convinced the superdrive exists."

"And have been searching most industriously for it in the course of rebuilding the ship," Hulik added. "Sunnat also has attempted to bedazzle Captain Aron with her obvious physical assets . . . you, in the meanwhile, hovering above all this, hoping they would discover the drive for you."

"That in part," nodded the Daal.

"Yes. Sunnat has the greed and fury of a wild pig. I think she is not quite sane. She has not bedazzled Captain Aron, and nothing resembling concealed drive mechanisms has been found so far in the ship. Before the *Evening Bird* is ready to leave, you expect her then to resort to actions which will force this Captain Aron or Pausert to reveal whether or not he is a witch?"

"It will not surprise me if that occurs," Sedmon admitted. "If it be comes apparent that he is a witch, I simply will be through with the matter."

"And still be unimplicated," Hulik agreed. "Of course," she went on, "if he is *not* a witch and does *not* have a mystery drive to produce, even if strenuously urged, it's probable that he and the child will be murdered before Sunnat decides she may have made a mistake—"

Sedmon shifted his eyes from the wall screen to her, said slowly, "This drive, if I can get it—and have afterwards a little time to work in, undisturbed—will restore Uldune to its ancient place in the hierarchy of galactic power!"

"A point," said Hulik, "of which the Imperium is well aware."

He watched her, his face expressionless.

"We shall work in different ways," Hulik smiled. "If I get it, it may bring me great honor and rewards from the Imperium.

Or it may, which really seems at least as likely, bring me quick death, by decision of the Imperium." The smile became almost impish. "On Uldune, on the other hand ... well, I would be most interested in seeing that the House of Eldel is also restored to something approximating the place of power it once held here."

"An honorable ambition!" Sedmon nodded approvingly. "As for me—I am perhaps overly prudent and certainly not as young as I was—I could very well use a partner with youth, audacity, and intelligence, to help me direct the affairs of Uldune. In particular, of the greater Uldune that may be."

Hulik laughed. "Great dreams! But very well ... We shall work carefully. I have not yet made a report that the ship once named the *Venture* appears to be at present on Uldune."

The Daal's eyes lightened.

"But," Hulik went on, "I shall proceed exactly as if I had made that report. If, in spite of Sunnat's efforts and yours, the *Evening Bird* lifts from Uldune on schedule I'll be on board as passenger.... Now, I believe that little Vezzarn they've signed on for the ship is your man?"

"He is," Sedmon said. "Of course he doesn't know for whom he's working."

"Of course. I know Kambine's background. He's nothing."

"Nothing," the Daal agreed.

"Laes Yango?"

"A man to be reckoned with in his field."

"What specifically is his field? I've been able to get very little information on him."

"He deals. High-value, high-profit items only. He maintains his own cruiser, makes frequent space trips, uses other carriers for special purposes, as in this case. He banks a considerable amount of money at all times, makes and receives large payments at irregular intervals to and from undisclosed accounts by subradio. Some of his business seems to be legitimate."

"He should not become a problem then?" Hulik said.

"There is no reason to assume he would be, in this matter." The Dad looked at her curiously. "Am I to understand you intend to continue your efforts to obtain the drive, even if Captain Aron turns out to be what I suspect he is?"

"I do intend that," Hulik nodded. "I have my own theory about your Karres witches."

"What is that?"

"They are, among other things, skilled and purposeful bluffers. The disappearing world story, for example. Karres has been described to me as a primitive, forested planet showing no detectable signs of inhabitation. There are many such uninhabited worlds. Few are even indicated in standard star maps. It seems most probable to me that the witches, instead of moving Karres through space, themselves move by more conventional methods of travel from one world of that sort to a similar one elsewhere—and presently let it be known that 'Karres' was magically transported by them to a new galactic sector! I believe their purpose is to frighten everyone, including even the Imperium, into leaving them severely alone. That they are capable of a number of astonishing tricks seems true. It is even possible they have developed a superdrive to transport ordinary spaceships. But worlds?" She shook her head skeptically. "Pausert may be a Karres witch. If so, his mysterious powers have not revealed to him even the simple fact that Vezzarn was planted on him as a spy. . . . No, I'm not afraid of the witches!"

"You don't feel afraid of the Chaladoor either?" the Daal asked.

"A little," Hulik admitted. "But considerably more afraid of not getting the drive from Captain Pausert, if it should turn out later that there really was such a thing on his ship. When the stakes are high, the Imperium becomes a stringent employer!" She shrugged. "And since success in this might be as deadly to me as failure, you and Uldune can count on me . . . afterwards."

✧   ✧   ✧

A colored, soundless whirlwind was spinning slowly and steadily about the captain. He watched it bemusedly a while, then had his attention distracted by a puzzled awareness that he seemed to be sitting upright, none too comfortably, on something like a cold stone floor, his back touching something like a cold stone wall. He realized suddenly that he had his eyes closed, and decided he might as well open them.

He did. The giddily spinning colors faded from his vision; the world grew steady. But what place was this? . . . What was he doing here?

He glanced around. It seemed a big underground vault, wide and low, perhaps a hundred and fifty feet long. Thick stone pillars supported the curved ceiling sections. A number of glowing white globes in iron cages hung by chains from the ceiling, giving a vague general illumination to the place. Across the vault, the captain saw a narrow staircase leading up through the wall. It seemed the only exit.

On his right, some thirty feet away, was a fireplace . . . .

He gazed at the fireplace thoughtfully. It was built into the wall; in it was a large, hot coal fire. The individual coals glowed bright red, and continuous flickerings of heat ran over the piled mass. A poker shaped like a small slender spear stood at a slant, its tip in the coals, its handle resting on a bronze fire grate.

Some feet away from the fire was a marble-topped table. Beside it, a large wooden tub.

It was an odd-looking arrangement. And why should anyone build such a great fire on a warmish spring evening on Uldune? He could feel the waves of heat rolling out of it from here.

Warmish spring evening—the captain's memory suddenly awoke. This was the day they'd made a complete ground check of the *Evening Bird's* instrumentation. Everything was in fault-less working order; he and Goth had been delighted. Then Goth had gone back to the house. Sunnat, who'd attended the check-out with Filish, suggested sociably he buy them a drink as reward for the good job the firm had done so far. But Filish had excused himself.

He could see no harm in buying her a drink. There'd been a low-ceilinged, half dark, expensive bar off the spaceport. Somebody guided them around a couple of corners, left them at a table in a dim-lit niche by themselves. The drinks appeared—and right around then that rainbow-hued whirlwind seemed to have begun revolving around him. He couldn't recall another thing.

Well, no sense sitting here and pondering about it! He'd go upstairs, find someone to tell him where he was and what had happened to Sunnat. He gathered his legs under him, then made another discovery. This one was startling.

A narrow metal ring was closed around his right ankle. A slender chain was locked to the ring, and eight feet away the chain ended in a link protruding from the solid wall. He stared down at it in shocked outrage. Why, he was a prisoner here! Conflicting surmises tumbled in momentary confusion through his mind. The most likely thought seemed then that there'd been trouble of some kind in the bar and that as a result he'd wound up in one of the Daal's jails . . . but he still couldn't remember a thing about it.

The captain scrambled to his feet, the chain making mocking clanks along the floor beside him. "Hey!" he yelled angrily. "Hey! Somebody here?"

For a moment he thought he'd heard a low laugh somewhere. But there was no one in sight.

"*Hey!*"

"Why, what's the trouble, Captain Aron?"

He turned, saw Sunnat twenty feet off on his left, standing beside one of the thick pillars which supported the ceiling of the vault. She must have stepped out from behind it that very moment.

The captain stared at her. She was in one of her costumes. This one consisted of crimson trousers and slippers, a narrow strip of glittering green material wound tightly about her breasts, and a crimson turban which concealed her hair and had a great gleaming green stone set in the front of it above her forehead. She stood motionless, her face in shadow, watching him.

The costume didn't make her appear attractive or seductive. Standing in the big, silent vault, she looked spooky and menacing. Her head shifted slightly and there seemed to be a momentary glitter in the eyes of the shadowed face. The captain cleared his throat, twisted his mouth into a smile.

"You had me worried, Sunnat!" he admitted. "How did you do it? I really thought I was waking up in an Uldune prison!"

Sunnat didn't answer. She turned, started over towards the fireplace as if he hadn't spoken.

"How about getting me loose from the wall now?" the captain said coaxingly. "A joke's a joke . . . but there are really a number of things I should be taking care of. And I told, uh, Dani I'd be home in time for dinner."

Sunnat turned her head, eyes half shut, and gave him an odd, slow smile. It sent a chill down his spine. He wished he hadn't mentioned Goth.

"Come on, Sunnat!" He put a touch of annoyance into his voice. "We're grown ups, and this game's getting a little childish!"

Sunnat muttered something he didn't understand. She might have been talking to herself. She'd reached the fireplace, stood staring down at the poker a moment, then picked it out of the coals by its handle and came towards him with it, holding it lightly like a sword, the fiery tip weaving back and forth. The captain watched her. Her eyes were wide open now, fixed on him. The tall body swayed forward a little as she walked. She looked like some snake-thing about to strike.

He wasn't too alarmed. Sunnat might be drugged or drunk, or she might have gone out of her mind. And he didn't like the poker. This was trouble, perhaps bad trouble. But if she got close enough to use the poker, he'd jump her and get it from her . . . .

She didn't come that close. She stopped twelve feet away, well beyond his reach.

"Captain Aron," she said, "I think you already know this isn't really a joke! I want something you have, and you're going to give it to me. Now let me tell you a story . . . ."

It was the story, somewhat distorted and with many omissions, of his experiences with the Sheewash Drive on the far side of the Empire. It didn't mention Karres and didn't mention klatha. Neither did it mention that he'd picked up three witch children on Porlumma. Otherwise, it came uncomfortably close to the facts.

"I don't have any such drive mechanism on the ship," the captain repeated, staring at her, wondering how she could possibly have got that information. "Whoever told you I did was lying!"

Sunnat smiled unpleasantly. He knew by now that she wasn't drunk or drugged. Neither was she out of her mind, at least by her own standards. She was engaged in a matter of business, in the old Uldune style. And she looked the part. The poker was cooling but could be quickly reheated. She might have been some pirate chieftain's lady, who had volunteered to interrogate a stubborn prisoner.

"No, you're lying," she said. "Though it may be true that the drive mechanism is not on the ship at present. But you know where it is. And you'll tell me."

As the captain started to speak, she brought some small golden object from a pocket of her trousers, lifted it to her mouth. There was a short, Piercing whistle. Sunnat turned away from him, smiled back at him over her shoulder and returned to the fireplace, the poker dangling loosely from her hand. He heard sounds from the stairway, shuffling footsteps.

Filish and Bazim appeared, coming carefully down the stairs

side by side, carrying a chair between them. Goth was in the chair. There was a gag in her mouth; and even at that distance the captain could see her arms were fastened by the wrists to the sides of the chair.

"Over here!" Sunnat called to her partners. They started towards her with Goth. She put the poker back in the coals, its handle resting on the grate, and stood waiting for them. As they came up, she reached out and snatched the gag from Goth's mouth. Goth jerked forward, then settled back while the two men put the chair down beside the table, facing the fire. Sunnat tossed the gag into the coals.

"No need for that here, you see!" she informed the captain. "This is a very old place, Captain Aron, and there's been a great deal of strange noise made down here from time to time, which never disturbed anybody outside. It will cause no disturbance tonight."

"Now then, we have your brat. You're quite fond of her, I think. In a minute or two, I'll also have a very hot poker. If you don't wish to talk now, you needn't. On the other hand, you may tell me anything you wish—until I decide the poker is as hot as I want it to be. After that I'm afraid I'll be too busy to listen to what you have to say—if I'm able to hear you, which I doubt—for, well, perhaps ten minutes . . . ."

She swung to face him fully, jabbed a finger in his direction.

"And then, Captain Aron, when it's become quiet enough so you can speak to me again—then I'll be convinced that what you want to tell me is no lie but the truth. But that may be a little late for your Dani."

He felt like a chunk of ice. Goth had glanced over at him with her no-expression look, but only for an instant; she was watching Sunnat again now. The two men clearly didn't like this much—Bazim was sweating heavily and Filish's face showed a frozen nervous grimace. He could expect no interference from those two. Sunnat was running the show here, as she usually did in the firm. But perhaps he could gain a little time.

"Wait a moment, Sunnat," he said suddenly. "You don't have to hurt Dani—I'll tell you where the thing is!"

"Oh?" replied Sunnat. She'd pulled the poker out of the coals, was waving the glowing tip back and forth in the air, studying it. "Where?" she asked.

"It's partly disassembled," the captain improvised rapidly. "Part of it is still in the ship—very difficult to find, of course . . . ."

"Of course," Sunnat nodded. "And the rest?"

"One small piece is in the house. Everything else has been locked up in two different bank vaults. I had to be careful—"

"No doubt," she said. "Well, Captain Aron, you're still lying, I'm afraid! You're not frightened enough yet. . . . Bazim, get the water ready. Let's test this on the brat's sleeve, as a start."

Bazim reached into the wooden tub beside the table and brought out a dripping ladle of water. He moved behind Goth's chair, stood holding the ladle in a hand that shook noticeably. Water sloshed from it to the floor.

"Steady, now!" Sunnat laughed at him. "This won't even hurt the brat yet, if I'm careful. Ready?"

Bazim grunted. Sunnat's hand moved and the poker tip delicately touched the sleeve of Goth's jacket. The captain held his breath. Smoke curled from the jacket as the poker moved up along the cloth. There was a sudden flicker of fire.

Bazim reached over hastily. But his hand shook too hard— water spilled all over Goth's lap instead of on the sleeve. Sunnat stepped back, laughing. Bazim turned, dipped the ladle back into the tub, flung its contents almost blindly in Goth's direction.

It landed with a splat and a hiss exactly where it was needed. The line of fire vanished—and Sunnat let out a startled yell . . . .

The captain found he was breathing again. Crouched and

tense, he watched. Sunnat was behaving very strangely! Grasping the poker handle in both hands, she backed away from Goth and the others along the wall, holding the poker out and down, arms stiff and straight. The partners stared open-mouthed. The captain saw the muscles in Sunnat's arms strain as if it took all the strength she had to hold the poker. Her face was white and terrified.

"Quick!" she screamed suddenly. "Filish! Bazim! Your guns! Kill him—now! He's doing it. *He's pulling it away from me!* Ah—*no!*"

The last was a howl of despair as the poker twitched violently, spun out of Sunnat's hands and fell. It twisted on the flooring, its fiery tip darting back up towards her legs. She gave a shriek, leaped high and to one side, looked back, saw the poker rolling after her. She dodged away from it again, screaming, "*Shoot! Shoot!*"

But other things were happening. Bazim began to bellow wildly and went into a series of clumsy leaps, turns and twists, clutching his seat with both hands. Filish swung around towards the captain, reaching under his coat . . . and the captain felt something smack into the palm of his right hand. He wrapped his fingers around it before it could drop, saw with no surprise at all that it was a gun, lifted it to trigger a shot above Filish's head. But by then there was no need to shoot— Filish, too, was howling and gyrating about with Bazim. And Sunnat was sprinting towards the stairs while something clattered and smoked along the floor a yard behind her.

There were a couple of light clinks at the captain's feet. Another gun lay there, and a small key. There was a mighty splash not far away. He looked up, saw Bazim and Filish sitting side by side in the tub, their legs hanging over its edge, tears streaming down their faces. Sunnat had disappeared up the stairs. He couldn't see the poker.

Quite calmly, the captain went down on his left knee, fitted the key into the lock of the metal ring around his ankle and turned it. The ring snapped open. He put the other gun, which would be Bazim's, into a pocket, stood up and went over to Goth. The partners stared at him in wide-eyed horror, trying to crouch deeper into the tub.

"Thanks, Captain!" Goth said in a clear, unruffled voice as he came up. "Was wondering when you'd let those three monkeys have it!"

The captain couldn't think immediately of something appropriate to reply to that. He knew it hadn't been some vagrant vatch at work this time—it had been all Goth. So he only grunted as he began to loosen the cords around her wrists. Then he ran his finger along the burned streak on her jacket sleeve. "Get singed?" he asked.

"Uh-uh!" Goth smiled up at him. "Didn't even get warm!" She looked over at Bazim and Filish. "Served them right to get hot coals in their back pockets for that, though!"

"I thought so," the captain agreed.

"'Fraid that poker didn't catch up with Sunnat," Goth added. She'd got out of the chair, stood rubbing her wrists, looking around.

"No. I was rather busy, you know. . . . I doubt she'll get far." If Goth felt it was best to let Bazim and Filish believe he was the one who'd done the witching around here, he'd go along with it. He gave the two a look. They cringed anew. "Well, now . . ." he began.

"Somebody's coming, Captain!" Goth interrupted, cocking her head.

It seemed quite a number of people were coming. Boots clattered hurriedly on the staircase, descending towards them. Then a dozen or so men in the uniform of the Daal's Police boiled down the stairs into the vault, spread out, holding guns. The one in the lead caught sight of the captain and Goth, shouted, "Halt!" to the others and hurried towards them while his companions stayed where they were.

"Ah, Your Wisdoms!" the officer greeted them respectfully

as he approached. "You are unharmed, of course—but accept the Daal's profound apologies for this occurrence, extended for the moment through his unworthy servant. We learned of the plans these rascals were devising against you too late to spare you the annoyance of having to deal with them yourselves." He gave the partners a look of stern loathing. "I see you have been merciful—they live. But not for long, I feel! We captured the woman as she attempted to escape to the street. . . . Now if Your Wisdoms will permit me to speak to you privately while my men remove this scum from your presence—"

The captain found it difficult to get to sleep that night.

The policeman, a Major something-or-other—he hadn't caught the name—had transmitted an invitation to them from the Daal to attend the judging of the villainous partners at the Daal's Little Court in the House of Thunders next day. He'd accepted. A groundcar would come by two hours after sunrise to take them there.

Goth had explained the "Your Wisdoms" form of address after they returned to the house and switched on their spyscreen. "It's how they talk to a witch around here," she said, "when they want to be polite . . . and when they're supposed to know you're a witch."

Apparently it was regarded as good policy on Uldune to be polite to witches of Karres. And the Daal evidently had intended to let them know in this roundabout way that he knew they were witches.

He was only half right, of course . . . .

Did Sedmon the Sixth have something else in mind with the invitation? Goth figured he did but she didn't feel it was anything to worry about. "The Daal wants to get along with Karres—"

There shouldn't be any trouble with the overlord of Uldune in connection with the Sheewash Drive, of which he would hear from the prisoners tomorrow, if he didn't already know about it. But the captain's thoughts kept veering towards some probably very unpleasant aspects of their visit to the House of Thunders. He realized presently he was afraid to go to sleep because he probably would start dreaming about them.

He raised his head suddenly from the pillow. There was shimmering motion in the dim-lit hall beyond the open door of the room, a blurred suggestion of a small figure beyond it. The shimmering came into the room, advanced towards the bed, blotting out the room behind it, moved along the bed, passed over the captain's head, and went on into the wall. The room had become visible again and Goth, in her white sleep-pants, was now perched on the foot of the bed, legs crossed, looking at him. She had their spy-proofing device in one hand.

"What's the matter?" he asked.

"You're worrying about that pig getting skinned!" Goth told him.

"Hmm . . . Sunnat?"

"Who else?"

"Well, the others, too," said the captain. "It's a rather horrid practice, you know!"

"Uh-huh. You needn't worry, though."

"Why not?"

"Sedmon isn't having anyone skinned tomorrow, if we don't say so."

"Why should he care what we say?"

"We're witches, Your Wisdom!" Goth said. She chuckled gently.

"Well, but . . ."

"Threbus and Toll know Sedmon, Captain. They visited his place four, five times before I was born. They told me about him. He's got a sort of skullcap he uses that keeps klatha waves out of his mind. You can bet he'll wear it tomorrow! But he still doesn't want trouble with witches. He knows too much about them."

"That's why you got them to think I did those klatha tricks tonight?" the captain asked.

"Sure. If they found out we got the Drive here, they better think we can keep it. Far as Sedmon is concerned, you're a witch now."

"What kind of a fellow is he otherwise?" the captain asked. "I've heard stories . . ."

"I can tell you stories about Sedmon you won't believe," Goth said. "But not tonight. Just one thing. If we're alone with him—not if someone else is around—and it looks as if he's starting to wonder again if you're a witch, call him 'Sedmon of the Six Lives.' He'll snap to it then."

"Sedmon of the Six Lives, eh? What does that mean?"

"Don't know," Goth said. She yawned. "Threbus can tell you when we see him. But it'll work."

"I'll remember it," the captain said.

"Going to do any more worrying?" Goth asked.

"No. Night, witch!"

"Night, Your Wisdom!" She slipped down from the bed, clicking off the spy screen, and was gone from the room.

Impressive as the House of Thunders looked from a distance, it became apparent, as the military groundcar carrying Goth and the captain approached it up winding mountain roads, that its exterior was as weather-beaten and neglected as the streets of the old quarter of Zergandol. The Daal's penuriousness was proverbial on Uldune. Evidently it extended even to keeping up the appearance of the mighty edifice which was the central seat of his government.

The section of the structure through which they presently were escorted was battered, but filled with not particularly unobtrusive guards. Several openings and hallways revealed the metallic gleam of heavy armament, obviously in excellent repair. Dilapidated the House of Thunders might look, the captain thought, but for the practical purpose of planetary defense it should still be a fortress to be reckoned with. The escorting officers paused presently before an open door, bowed the visitors through it and drew the door quietly shut behind them.

This was a windowless room, well furnished, its walls concealed by the heavy ornamental hangings of another period. Sedmon stood here waiting for them. The captain saw a lean, middle-aged man, dark-skinned, with steady, watchful eyes. Uldune's lord wore a long black robe and a helmet-like cap of velvet green which covered half his forehead and enclosed his skull to the nape of his neck. The last must be the anti-klatha device Goth had mentioned.

He greeted them cordially, using the names with which they had been supplied by his Office of Identities, apologized for the outrage attempted against them by Sunnat, Bazim & Filish.

"My first impulse," he said, "was to have those wretches put to death without an hour's delay!"

"Well," said the captain uncomfortably, quickly blotting out another mental vision of the Daal's executioners peeling wicked Sunnat's skin from her squirming body, "it may not be necessary to be *quite* so severe with them!"

Sedmon nodded. "You are generous! But that was to be expected. In fact, in the cases of Bazim and Filish Your Wisdom appears to have inflicted on the spot the punishment you regarded as suitable to their offense—"

"It was what they deserved," the captain agreed.

The Daal coughed. "Also," he said, "I have considered that Bazim and Filish are, when in their senses, most valuable subjects. They claim they acted as they did solely out of their great fear of Sunnat's anger. If it is your wish then, I shall release them to conclude the work on your ship, as stipulated by contract—with this condition. They may not receive one Imperial mael from you in payment! Everything shall be done at their expense. Further, my inspectors will be looking over their shoulders; and if they, or you, should find cause for the slightest complaint, there will be additional penalties, and far

more drastic ones. . . . Does this meet with Your Wisdoms'
approval?"

The captain cleared his throat, assured him it did.

"There remains the matter of Sunnat," the Daal resumed.
"Your testimony against her is not required—her partners'
separate statements have made it clear enough that she was
the instigator of the plot. However, it would be well if Your
Wisdoms would accompany me to the Little Court now to see
that the judgment rendered against this pernicious woman is
also in accordance with your wishes . . ."

A handful of minor officials were arranged about the mir-
rored expanse of the Daal's Little Court when they entered.
Sedmon seated himself, and the visitors were shown to chairs
at the side of the bench. A moment later two soldiers brought
Sunnat in through a side door. She started violently when she
caught sight of the captain and Goth and avoided looking in
their direction again. Sunnat had clearly had a very bad night!
Her face was strained and drawn; her reddened eyes flickered
nervously as they glanced about. But frightened as she must
be, she soon showed she was still trying to squirm out of the
situation.

"Lies, all lies, Your Highness!" she exclaimed tearfully but
with a defiant toss of her head. "Never—*never!*—would I have
wished Their Wisdoms harm—or dared consider doing them
harm if I hadn't been forced to what I did by the cruel threats
of Bazim and Filish. They—"

It got her nowhere. The Daal pointed out quietly it was clear
she hadn't realized with whom she was dealing when she turned
on Captain Aron and his niece. Malice and greed had moti-
vated her. It was well known that her partners were fully under
her sway. Justice could not be delayed by such arguments.

No mention was made by either side of the mysterious
spacedrive Sunnat had tried to get in her possession. It seemed
she had been warned against saying anything about that in
court.

Sunnat was weeping wildly at that point. Sedmon glanced over at the captain, then looked steadily at Goth.

"Since the criminal's most serious offense was against the Young Wisdom," he said, "it seems fitting that the Young Wisdom should now decide what her punishment should be."

The Little Court became quiet. Goth remained seated for a moment, then stood up.

"It would be even more fitting, Sedmon," somebody beside the captain said, "if the Young Wisdom herself administered the punishment . . . ."

He started. The words had come from Goth—but that had not been Goth's voice! Everybody in the Little Court was staring silently at her. Then the Daal nodded.

"It shall be as Your Wisdom said . . . ."

Goth moved away from the captain, stopped a few yards from Sunnat. He couldn't see her face. But the air tingled with eeriness and he knew klatha was welling into the room. He had a glimpse of the Daal's face, tense and watchful; of Sunnat's, dazed with fear.

"Look in the mirror, Sunnat of Uldune!"

It *wasn't* her voice! What was happening? His skin shuddered and from moment to moment, now his vision seemed to blur, then clear again. The voice continued low, mellow, but somehow it was filling the room. Not Goth's voice but he felt he'd heard it before somewhere, sometime, and should know it. And his mind strained to understand what it said but seemed constantly to miss the significance of each word by the fraction of a second, as the quiet sentences rolled on with a weight of silent thunder in them. Sunnat faced one of the great mirrors in the room; he saw her back rigid and straight and thought she was frozen, unable to move. Sedmon's lean hands were clamped together, unconsciously knotting and twisting as he stared.

The voice rose on an admonitory note, ended abruptly in sharp command. It couldn't, the captain realized, actually have been speaking for more than twenty seconds. But it had seemed much longer. There was silence for an instant now. Then Sunnat screamed.

One couldn't blame her, he thought. Staring into the mirror, Sunnat had seen what everyone else in the Little Court could see by looking at her. Set on her shoulders instead of her own head was the bristled, red-eyed head of a wild pig, ugly jaws gaping and working, as screams continued to pour from them. There was a medley of frightened voices. The Daal shouted a command at Sunnat's white-faced guards, and the two grasped the writhing figure by the arms, hustled it from the Little Court. As they passed through the side door, it seemed to the captain that Sunnat's wails had begun to resemble a pig's frightened squealing much more than the cries of a young woman in terrible distress . . . .

"Toll!" the captain told Goth, rather shakily. "You were talking in Toll's voice! Your mother's voice!"

"Well, not really," Goth said. They were alone for the moment, in a small room of the House of Thunders, to which they had been conducted by a stunned looking official after the Daal, rather abruptly, concluded judicial proceedings in the Little Court following the Young Wisdom's demonstration. Sedmon was to rejoin them here in a few minutes—the captain guessed the Daal had felt it necessary to get settled down a little first. Their spy-screen snapped on the instant the room's door closed on the official, who seemed glad to be on his way.

"It's pretty much like Toll's voice," she agreed. "That was my Toll pattern."

"Your what?"

Goth rubbed her nose tip. "Guess I can tell you," she decided. "You won't get it all, though. I don't either . . . ."

Her Toll pattern was a klatha learning device. In fact, a nonmaterial partial replica of the personality of an adult witch whose basic individuality was similar to that of the witch child given the device. In this case, Toll's. "It's sort of with me in there," Goth said, tapping the side of her head. "Don't notice it much but it's helping. Now here—Sedmon was checking on how good I was. Don't know why exactly. I figured I ought to get fancy to show him but wasn't sure what I wanted to do. So the Toll pattern took over. It knew what to do. See?"

"Hmm . . . not entirely."

Goth pushed herself up on the edge of a gleaming, blue table and looked at him, dangling her legs. "Course you don't," she said. She considered. "Pattern can't do just anything. It has to be something I can almost do already so it only has to show me. Else it'd get me messed up, like I told you."

"Meaning you're almost able to plant a pig's head on somebody if you feel like it?" the captain asked.

"Wasn't a pig's head."

"Pretty good imitation then!"

"Bend light, bend color." Goth shrugged. "That's all. They'll stay that way as long as you want. When Sunnat puts her hands up to feel, she'll know she's got her own head. But she's going to look part pig for a time."

"Can't quite imagine you doing one of those incantations by yourself! That was impressive."

"Incant . . . oh, that! You don't need all that," Goth told him. "Toll pattern did it to scare everybody. Especially Sedmon."

"It worked, I think." He studied her curiously. "So when will you start bending light?"

Goth's face took on a bemused expression. There was a blur. Then a small round pig's head squinted at him from above her jacket collar, smirking unpleasantly.

"Oink!" it said in Goth's voice.

"Cut it out!" said the captain, startled.

The head blurred again, became Goth's. She grinned. "Told you I just had to be shown!"

"I believe you now. How long will Sunnat be stuck with the one she's got?"

"Didn't you hear what the pattern told her?"

He shook his head. "I heard it—it seemed to mean something. But somehow I wasn't really understanding a word. And I don't think anyone else there was."

"Sunnat understood it," Goth said. "It was talking to her. . . . She's got to quit wanting to do things like burning people and scaring people, like that fat old Bazim. The less she wants that, the less she'll look like a pig. She works at it, she could look pretty much like she was in about a month. And . . ."

Goth turned her head. There'd been a knock at the door. She put her hand in her pocket, snapped off the spy-screen, slid down from the table. The captain went over to the door to let in the Daal of Uldune.

"There are matters of such grave potential significance," the Daal said vaguely, "that it is difficult—extremely difficult—to decide to whom one may unburden oneself concerning them. I . . ."

His voice trailed off, not for the first time in this conversation. His gaze shifted across the shining blue table to the captain, to Goth—back to the captain. He shook his head again, bit at a knuckle with an expression of worried irritability.

The captain studied him with some puzzlement. Sedmon seemed itching to tell them something but unable to make up his mind to do it. What was the problem? He'd implied he had information of great importance to Karres. If so, they'd better get it.

The Daal glanced at Goth again, speculatively. "Perhaps Your Wisdom understands," he murmured.

"Uh-huh," said Goth brightly, in her little-girl voice.

He'd tell Goth if they were alone? The captain considered. There hadn't been many "Your Wisdoms" coming *his* way since that business in the Little Court! Possibly Sedmon had done some private reevaluating of the events in Sunnat's underground dungeon last night. It would take—as, in fact, it had taken—only one genuine witch on the team to account for that.

Not so good, perhaps. . . . He considered again.

"I really think," he heard himself say pleasantly, "it might be best if you did unburden yourself to us, Sedmon of the Six Lives."

The Daal's eyes flickered.

"So!" It was a small hiss. "I suspected . . . but it was a difficult thing to believe, even of such as you. Well, we all have our secrets, and our reasons for them . . . ." He stood up. "Come with me then—Captain Aron and Dani! You should know better what to make of what I have here than I do."

The captain hoped they would. He certainly did not know what to make of Sedmon the Sixth, and of the Six Lives, at the moment! But he seemed to have said the right thing at the right time, at that—

Sedmon led them swiftly, the hem of his black gown flapping about his heels, through a series of narrow passages and up stairways into another section of the House of Thunders. They met no one on the way. Three times the Daal stopped to unlock heavy doors with keys produced from a fold in the gown, locked them again behind them. He did not speak at all until they turned at last into a blind passage which showed only one door and that near the far end. There he slowed.

"Half the problem is here," he said, addressing them equally as they came up to the door. "When you've seen it, I'll tell you what else I know—which is little enough. There'll be another thing to show you later in another place."

He unlocked and opened the door. The room beyond was long and low, showed no furnishings. But something like a heavy, slowly rippling iron-gray curtain screened the far end.

"A guard field," said the Daal sourly. "I've done everything possible to keep the matter quiet. In that I think I've been successful. It was all I could do until I came in contact with a competent member of your people." He gave them a sideways glance. "No doubt you have your own problems—but for weeks I've been unable to learn where somebody who could act for Karres might be found!"

His manner had taken another turn. He was dropping all formality here, addressing them with some irritability as equals and including Goth as if she were another adult. And he was not concealing the fact that he felt he had reason for complaint—nor that he was a badly worried man. Reaching into his gown, he brought out a small device, glanced at it, pressed down with his thumb.

The guard field faded, and the far end of the room appeared beyond it. A couch stood there. On it, in an odd attitude of abruptly frozen motion, sat a man in spacer coveralls. He was strongly built, might have been ten years older than the captain. Goth's breath made a sharp sucking sound of surprise.

"You know this fellow?" the Daal asked.

"Yes," Goth said. "It's Olimy!"

"He's of Karres?"

"Yes."

She started forward, the captain moving with her, while the Daal stayed a few feet behind. Olimy gazed into the room with unblinking black eyes. He sat at the edge of the couch, legs stretched out to the floor, arms half lifted and reaching forwards, fingers curled as if closing on something. His expression was one of alertness and intense concentration. But the expression didn't change and Olimy didn't move.

"He was found like this, a month and a half ago, sitting before the controls of his ship," the Daal said. "Perhaps you understand his condition. I don't. He can be shifted out of the position you see him in, but when released he gradually returns to it. He can be lifted and carried about but can't actually be touched. There's a thin layer of force about him, unlike anything of which I've heard. It's detectable only by the fact that nothing can pass through it. He appears to be alive but—"

"He disminded himself." Goth's face and tone were

expressionless. She looked up at the captain. "We got to take him to Emris, I guess. They'll help him there."

"Uh-huh." Then she didn't know either how to contact other witches this side of the Chaladoor at present. "You mentioned his ship," the captain said to the Daal.

"Yes. It's three hours' flight from here, still at the point where it was discovered. He was the only one on board. How it approached Uldune and landed without registering on detection instruments isn't known." Sedmon's mouth grimaced. "He had an object with him which I ordered left on the ship. I won't try to describe it—you'll see it for yourselves. . . . Are there any measures you wish taken regarding this man before we go?"

Goth shook her head. The captain said, "There's nothing we can do for Olimy at the moment. He might as well stay here till we can take him off your hands."

Olimy's ship had come down in a nearly uninhabited section of Uldune's southern continent, and landed near the center of a windy plain, rock-littered and snow-streaked, encircled by misty mountains. It wasn't visible from the air, but its position was marked by what might have been a patch of gray mist half filling a hollow in the plain—a spy-screen had been set up to enclose the ship. On higher ground a mile away lay a larger bank of mist. The Daal's big aircar set down there first.

At ground level, the captain, sitting in a rear section of the car with Goth, could make out the vague outlines of four tents through the side of the screen. Two platoons of fur-coated soldiers and their commander had tumbled out and lined up. One of the Daal's men left the car, went over to the officer, and spoke briefly with him. He came back, nodded to the Daal, climbed in. The aircar lifted, turned and started towards Olimy's ship, skimming along the sloping ground.

There'd been no opportunity to speak privately with Goth. Perhaps she had an idea of what this affair of a Karres witch who had disminded himself was about, but her expression told nothing. Any question he asked the Daal might happen to be the wrong one, so he hadn't asked any.

The car settled down some fifty yards from the edge of the screening about Olimy's ship, and was promptly enveloped itself by a spy-screen somebody cut in. Sedmon, as he'd indicated, evidently took all possible precautions to avoid drawing attention to the area. The captain and Goth put on the warm coats which had been brought along for them and climbed out with the Daal, who had wrapped a long fur robe about himself. The rest of the party remained in the car. They walked over to the screen about the ship, through it, and saw the ship sitting on the ground.

It was a small one with excellent lines, built for speed. The Daal brought an instrument out from under his furs.

"This is the seal to the ship's lock," he said. "I'll leave it with you. The object your associate brought here with him is standing in a plastic wrapping beside the control console. When you're finished you'll find me waiting in the car."

The last was good news. If Sedmon had wanted to come into the ship with them, it might have complicated matters. The captain found the lock mechanism, unsealed it and pulled the OPEN lever. Above them, a lock opened. A narrow ladder ramp slid down.

They paused in the lock, looking back. The Daal already had vanished beyond the screening haze about the ship. "Just to be sure," the captain said, "better put up our own spy-screen. . . . Got any idea what this is about?"

Goth shook her head. "Olimy's a hot witch. Haven't seen him for a year—he goes around on work for Karres. Don't know what he was doing this trip."

"What's this disminding business?"

"Keeps things from getting to you. *Anything*. Sort of stasis. It's not so good though. Your mind's way off somewhere and can't get back. You have to be helped out. And that's not easy!"

Her small face was very serious.

"Hot witch in a fast ship!" the captain reflected aloud. "And he runs into something in space that scares him so badly he disminds to get away from it! Doesn't sound good, does it? Could he have homed the ship in on Uldune on purpose, first?"

Goth shrugged. "Might have. I don't know."

"Well, let's look around the ship a bit before we get at that object. Must be some reason the Daal didn't feel like talking about it . . . ."

They saw it in its wrappings as soon as they stepped into the tiny control cabin. The large, lumpy item, which could have been a four hundred pound boulder concealed under twisted, thick, opaque space plastic, stood next to the console. They let it stand there. The captain switched on the little ship's viewscreens, found them set for normal space conditions, turned them down until various angles of the windy Uldune plain appeared in sharp focus. The small patch of gray haze which masked the Daal's aircar showed on their port side.

They went through the little speedster's other sections. All they learned for their trouble was that Olimy had kept a very neat ship.

"Might as well look at the thing now," said the captain. "You figure, it's something pretty important to Karres, don't you?"

"Got to be," Goth told him. "They don't put Olimy on *little* jobs!"

"I see." Privately, the captain admitted to considerable reluctance as he poked gingerly around at the plastic. Whatever was inside seemed as hard and solid as the bulky rock he'd envisioned when he first saw the bundle. Taking hold of one strip of the space plastic at last, he pulled it back slowly. A patch of the surface of the item came to view. It looked, he thought, like dirty ice-pitted old glacier ice. He touched it with a finger. Slick and rather warm. Some kind of crystal?

He glanced at Goth. She lifted her shoulders. "Doesn't look

like much of anything!" he remarked. He peeled the plastic back farther until some two feet of the thing were exposed. It could be a mass of worn crystal, lumpish and shapeless as it had appeared under its wrapping.

Shapeless?

Studying it, the captain began to wonder. There were a multitude of tiny ridged whorls and knobby protrusions on its surface, and the longer he gazed at them the more he felt they weren't there by chance, but for a purpose, had been formed deliberately . . . that this was, in fact, some very curious sculptured pattern—

Within the cloudy gray of the crystal was a momentary flickering light, a shivering thread of fire, which seemed somehow immensely far away. He caught it again, again had a sense of enormous distances. And now came a feeling that the surface of the crystal was changing, flowing, expanding—that he was about to drop through, to be lost forever in the dim, fire-laced hugeness that was its other side. Terror surged up; for an instant he was paralyzed. Then he felt himself moving, pulling the plastic wrappings frantically back across its surface, Goth's hands helping him. He twisted the ends together, tightly, as they had been before.

Terror lost its edge in the same moment. It was as if something which had attacked them from without were now simply fading away. But he still felt uncomfortable enough.

He looked at Goth, drew in a long breath.

"Whew!" he said, shaken. "Was that klatha stuff?"

"Not klatha!" said Goth, face pale, eyes sharp and alert. "Don't know what it was! Never felt anything like it."

She broke off.

Inside the captain's head there was a tiny, purposeful click. Not quite audible. As if something had locked shut.

"Worm Worlders!" hissed Goth. They turned to the view-screens together.

A pale-yellow stain moved in the eastern sky above the

wintry plain outside, spread as it drifted swiftly up overhead, then faded in a sudden rush to the west.

"If we hadn't put it back when we did—" the captain said.

Some minutes had passed. Worm Weather hadn't reappeared above the plain, and now Goth reported that the klatha locks which had blocked the Nuri probes from their minds were relaxing. The yellow glow was a long distance away from them again.

"They'd have come here, all right!" Goth had her color back. He wasn't sure he had yet. That was a very special plastic Olimy had enclosed the lumpish crystal in! A wrapping which deflected the Worm World's sensor devices from what it covered—

But Manaret wanted the crystal. And Karres apparently wanted it as badly. Olimy had been carrying it in his ship, and for all his witch's tricks, he'd been harried by the Nuris into disminding himself to escape them. Since then Worm Weather had hung about Uldune, turning up here and there, searching . . . suspecting the crystal had reached the planet, but unable to locate it. . . . He said, "You'd think Sedmon would blow up half the countryside around here to get rid of that thing! It's what keeps the Nuris near Uldune."

Goth shook her head. "They'd come back sometime. Sedmon knows a lot! He doesn't have that cap of his just because of witches. He's scared of the Worm World. So he wants Karres to get that crystal thing."

"Should help against Manaret, eh?"

"Looks like Manaret thinks so!" Goth pointed out reasonably.

"Yes, it does . . . ." As important as that, then! The misty screen concealing the Daal's aircar on the plain was still there. The men inside it had seen the Worm Weather, too, had known better than to try to take off. The car would be buttoned tight now, armor plates snapped shut over the windows, doors locked, as it crouched like a frightened bird on the empty slope.

But in spite of his fears, Sedmon had come here with them today because he wanted Karres to get the crystal . . . .

The captain said, "If we can take it as far as Emris—"

Goth nodded. "Always somebody on Emris."

"They'd do the rest, eh?" He paused. "Well, no reason we can't. If we just take care it stays wrapped up in that stuff."

"Maybe we can," Goth said slowly. She didn't sound too sure of it.

"The Daal thinks we can make it," the captain told her, "or he wouldn't have showed it to us. And, as you say, he's a pretty knowing old bird!"

A grin flickered on her mouth. "Well, that's something else, Captain!"

"What is?"

"You look a lot like Threbus."

"I do?"

"Only younger," Goth said. "And I look a lot like Toll, only younger. Sedmon knows Threbus and Toll—and we got him thinking that's who we are. He figures we've done an age-shift."

"Age-shift?"

"Get younger, get older," explained Goth. "Either way. Some witches can. Threbus and Toll could, I guess."

"I see. Uh, well, still—"

"And Threbus and Toll," Goth concluded in a rather small voice, "are an almighty good pair of witches!"

For an instant, the barest instant then, and for the first time since he'd known her, Goth seemed a tiny, uncertain figure standing alone in a great and terrible universe.

Well, not exactly alone, the captain thought.

"Well," he said heartily, "I guess that means we're going to have to be an *almighty* good pair of witches now, too!"

She smiled up at him. "Guess we'd maybe *better* be, Captain!"

Chapter SIX

IT WAS SUPPOSED to be Vezzarn's sleep period, but for the past two hours he'd been sitting in his locked cabin on the *Evening Bird*, brooding. On this, the third ship day after their lift-off from Port Zergandol, Vezzarn had a number of things to brood about.

Working as undercover operator, for an employer known only as a colorless, quiet voice on a communicator, had its nervous moments; but over the years it had paid off for Vezzarn. There was a very nice sum of money tucked away under a code number in the Daal's Bank in Zergandol, money which was all his.

He hadn't liked various aspects of the Chaladoor assignment too well. Who would? But the bonus guaranteed him if he found what he was supposed to find on Captain Aron's ship was fantastic. He'd risked hide and sanity in the Chaladoor for a fraction of that before . . . .

Then, ten days before they were to take off, the colorless voice told him the assignment was canceled—in part. Vezzarn was to forget what he had been set to find, forget it completely. But he still was to accompany Captain Aron through the Chaladoor, use the experience he had gained on his previous runs through the area to help see the *Evening Bird* arrive safely at Emris.

And what would he get for it?

"I'll throw in a reasonable risk bonus," the communicator told him. "You're drawing risk pay from your skipper and your regular pay from me. That's it. Don't be a pig, Vezzarn."

Vezzarn had no wish to anger the voice. But straight risk money, even collected simultaneously from two employers, wasn't enough to make him want to buck the Chaladoor again. Not at his age. He mentioned the age factor, suggested a younger spacer with comparable experience but better reflexes might be of more value to Captain Aron on this trip.

The voice said it didn't agree. It was all it needed to say. Remembering things it had tonelessly ordered done on other occasions, Vezzarn shuddered. "If that's how you feel, sir," he said, "I'll be on board."

"That's sensible of you, Vezzarn," the communicator told him and went dead.

He smoldered for hours. Then the thought came that there was no reason why he shouldn't work for himself in this affair. The voice had connections beyond the Chaladoor, but it would be a while before word about Vezzarn arrived there. And if he'd got his hands on the secret superdrive Captain Aron was suspected of using occasionally, Vezzarn could be a long way off and a very rich man by then.

The decision made, his fears of the Chaladoor faded to the back of his mind. The chance looked worth taking once more. He got his money quietly out of the bank and had nothing to do then but wait and watch, listen and speculate, while he carried out his duties as Captain Aron's general assistant and handyman. His preparations for the original assignment had been complete; and the only change in it now would be that, if things worked out right, he'd have Captain Aron's spacedrive for himself.

Then, after he'd watched and listened a day or two, he started
to worry again. His alertness had become sharpened, and minor
differences in these final stages of preparing the *Evening Bird*
for space that he hadn't noticed before caught his attention.
Attitudes had shifted. The skipper was more tense and quiet.
Even young Dani didn't seem quite the same. Bazim and Filish
worked with silent, intent purpose as if the only thing they
wanted was to get the *Evening Bird* out of their yard and off
the planet. Oddly enough, both of them appeared to have
acquired painful limps! The Sunnat character didn't show up
at all. Casual inquiry brought Vezzarn the information that the
firm's third partner was supposed to be recovering in the
countryside from some very serious illness.

He scratched his head frequently. Something had happened—but what? Daalmen began coming around the shipyard and the ship at all hours of the day. Inspectors, evidently.
They didn't advertise their identity, but he knew the type.
Captain Aron, reasonably prudent about cash outlays until now,
suddenly was spending money like water. The system of detection and warning devices installed on the ship two weeks before
was the kind of first-class equipment any trader would want
and not many could afford. Vezzarn, interested in his personal
safety while on the *Evening Bird*, had looked it over carefully.
One morning, it was all hauled out like so much junk, and
replaced by instruments impossibly expensive for a ship of that
class. Vezzarn didn't get to see the voucher. Later in the day
the skipper was back with a man he said was an armaments
expert, who was to do something about the touchiness of the
reinstalled nova guns.

Vezzarn happened to recognize the expert. It was the chief
armorer of the great firm which designed and produced the
offensive weapons of Uldune's war fleet. They could have had
the *Evening Bird* bristling with battle turrets for the price of
the three hours the chief armorer put in working over the
ancient nova guns! Vezzarn didn't see that voucher either, but

he didn't have to. And it didn't seem to bother the skipper in the least.

What was the purpose? It looked as if the ship were being prepared for some desperate enterprise, of significance far beyond that of an ordinary risk run. Vezzarn couldn't fathom it, but it made him unhappy. He couldn't back out, however. Not and last long on Uldune. The voice would see to that.

One of their three passengers did back out—Kambine, the fat financier. He showed up at the office whining that his health wouldn't allow him to go through with the trip. Vezzarn wasn't surprised; he'd felt from the first it was even money whether Kambine's nerve would last till lift-off. What did surprise him was that the skipper instructed him then to refund two thirds of the deposited fare. You would have thought he was glad to lose a passenger!

The other two were on board and in their staterooms when the *Evening Bird* roared up from Zergandol Port at last and turned her needle nose towards the Chaladoor . . . .

Vezzarn got busy immediately. There might have been a faint hope that, if he could accomplish his purpose before they reached the Chaladoor, an opportunity would present itself to slip off undetected in the *Evening Bird's* lifeboat and get himself out of whatever perils lay ahead. If so, the hope soon faded. There was a group of ship-blips in the aft screens, apparently riding the same course.

The skipper told him not to worry. He'd heard a squadron of the Daal's destroyers was making a sweep to the Chaladoor fringes and back, on the lookout for the Agandar's pirates, and had obtained permission to move with them until they swung around. For the first two days, in effect, the *Evening Bird* would travel under armed escort.

That killed Vezzarn's notion. He'd be picked up instantly by the destroyers' instruments if he left while they were in the area. And he couldn't leave after they turned back—a man who'd voluntarily brave the Chaladoor in a lifeboat was a hopeless lunatic. He'd have to finish the trip with the rest of them. Nevertheless, he should establish as soon as he could where Captain Aron's drive was concealed. Knowing that, he could let further plans develop at leisure.

Vezzarn was a remarkably skilled burglar—one of the qualities which made him a valuable operator to the ungrateful voice. Now that they were in space, his duties had become routine and limited. He had plenty of time available and made good use of it.

There was a series of little surprises. He discovered that, except for the central passenger compartment and the control area in the bow, the ship had been competently bugged. Sections of it were very securely locked up. Vezzarn knew these precautions had been no part of the original remodeling design as set up by Sunnat, Bazim & Filish. Hence Captain Aron had arranged for them during the final construction period when other changes were made. Evidently he'd had a reason by then to make sure his passengers—and Vezzarn—didn't wander about the *Evening Bird* where they shouldn't.

Vezzarn wondered what the reason was. But the skipper's precautions didn't handicap him much. He had his own instruments to detect and nullify bugs without leaving a trace of what happened; and he knew, as any good burglar would, that the place to look for something of value was where locks were strongest. In about a day he felt reasonably certain the secret drive was installed in one of three places: the storage vault, or another rather small vault-like section newly added to the engine room, or a blocked-off area on the ship's upper level behind the passenger compartment and originally a part of it.

The engine room seemed the logical place. Next day Vezzarn slipped down there, unlocking and relocking various doors on his route. It was his sleep period and it was unlikely anyone would look for him for an hour or two. He reached the engine room without mishap. The locks to the special compartment took some study and cautious experimentation. Then Vezzarn had it open. At first glance it looked like a storage place for assorted engine room tools. But why keep them shut away so carefully?

He didn't hurry inside. His instruments were doing some preliminary snooping for him. They began to report there was other instrument activity in here—plenty of it! Almost all traces were being picked up from behind a large opaque bulge on a bulkhead across from the door. Vezzarn's hopes soared but he still didn't rush in. His devices kept probing about for traps. And presently they discovered a camera. It didn't look like one and it was sitting innocently among a variety of gadgets on one of the wall shelves. But it was set to record the actions of anyone who came in here and got interested in the bulge on the bulkhead.

Well, that could be handled! Vezzarn edged his way up to the camera without coming into its view range, opened it delicately from behind and unset it. Then he put his own recording devices up before the bulge which concealed so much intriguing instrument activity, and for the next ten minutes let them take down in a number of ways what was going on in there. When he thought they'd got enough, he reset the camera, locked up the little compartment and returned to the upper ship level and his cabin by the way he had come. There he started the recorders feeding what they had obtained into a device which presently would provide him with a three-dimensional blueprint derived from their combined reports. He locked the device into his cabin closet.

He had to wait until the next sleep period rolled around before he had a chance to study the results. The *Evening Bird* was edging into the Chaladoor by then. The destroyers had curved off and faded from the screens, and the skipper had announced certain precautionary measures which would remain in effect until the risk area lay behind them again. One of them was that for a number of periods during the ship-day Vezzarn would be on watch at a secondary set of viewscreens off the passenger lounge. The control section henceforth would be entered without special permission only by Captain Aron and his niece.

As soon as he reached his cabin and locked the door, Vezzarn brought his device back out of the closet. He placed it on the small cabin table, activated it, checked the door again, set the device in motion and looked down through an eyepiece at a magnified view of the miniature three-dimensional pattern the instrument had produced within itself.

It was a moving pattern, and it gave off faintly audible sounds. Vezzarn stared and listened, first with surprise, then in blank puzzlement, at last with growing consternation. The reproduced contrivance in there buzzed, clicked, hummed, twinkled, spun. It sent small impulses of assorted energy types shooting about through itself. It remained spectacularly, if erratically, busy. And within five minutes Vezzarn became completely convinced that it did, and could do, absolutely nothing that would serve any practical purpose.

Whatever it might be, it wasn't a spacedrive. Even the most unconventional of drives couldn't possibly resemble anything like that!

Then what was it? Presently it dawned on Vezzarn that he'd been tricked. That thing behind the bulge on the bulkhead had served a purpose! The entire little locked compartment in the engine room was set up to draw the interest of somebody who might be prowling about the *Evening Bird* in search of a hidden drive installation.

It was something of a shock! The skipper had impressed him as an open, forthright fellow. An act of such low cunning didn't fit the impression. Briefly, Vezzarn felt almost hurt. But at any rate he'd spotted the camera and hadn't got caught....

That was only one of the unsettling developments for Vezzarn that day. Since Captain Aron's precautionary measures might have been intended to keep tab on passengers rather than himself, he'd set up his own system of telltale bugs in various parts of the ship. They were considerably more efficient bugs than the ones which had been installed for Captain Aron; even a first-class professional would have to be very lucky to avoid them all. If Vezzarn had competitors on board in his quest for the secret drive, he wanted to know it.

It appeared now that he did. Running a check playback on the telltales, he discovered they'd been agitated by somebody's passage in several off-limit ship sections at times when the skipper, young Dani, and he himself had been up in the control compartment.

Which of the two was it? The Hulik do Eldel female, or that nattily dressed, big bruiser of a trader, Laes Yango?

Perhaps both of them, acting independently, Vezzarn thought worriedly. Two other agents looking for the same thing he was—that was all he needed on this trip!

Captain Aron, at about that hour, was doing some worrying on the same general subject. If he'd been able to arrange it, there would have been no passengers on the *Venture*—or *Evening Bird*—when she left Uldune. What they'd taken on board made the commercial aspects of the run to Emris completely insignificant. And not only that—their experience with Sunnat, Bazim & Filish raised the question of how many other groups on Uldune suspected the ship of containing the secrets of some new drive of stupendous power and incalculable value. Subradio had spread information about the *Venture* faster and farther than they'd foreseen. Almost anyone they ran into now could be nourishing private designs on the mystery drive.

One way to have stopped the plotting might have been to let word get out generally that they were Karres witches. Apparently few informed people here cared to cross the witches. But because of Olimy and his crystalloid item again, it was the last thing they could afford to do at present. The Worm World, from all accounts, had its own human agents about, enslaved and totally obedient minds; any such rumor was likely to draw the Nuris' attention immediately to them. They wanted to make the *Venture's* departure from Uldune as quiet a matter as possible.

So he'd been unable to leave Laes Yango and Hulik do Eldel behind. To do it against their wishes certainly would have started speculation. After Kambine canceled voluntarily, he'd invited the two to come to the office. The day before, a ship had limped into Zergandol Port after concluding a pass through the Chaladoor. The ship was in very bad shape, its crew in worse. It seemed, the captain said, that the Chaladoor's hazards had reached a peak at present. If they'd prefer to reconsider the trip for that reason, he would refund the entire fare.

The offer got him nowhere. Hulik do Eldel became tearfully insistent that she *must* rejoin her aging parents on Emris as soon as possible. And Yango stated politely that, if necessary, he would obtain an injunction to keep the *Evening Bird* from leaving without him. Some office of the Daal's no doubt would have quietly overruled the injunction; but meanwhile there would have been a great deal of loose talk. So the captain gave in.

"In case one of those two is after the Sheewash Drive," he told Goth, "we'd better do something about it."

"Do what?" asked Goth. It would have been convenient just now if her talents had included reading minds; but they didn't.

The captain had thought about it. "Set up a decoy drive."

Goth liked the idea. He'd almost forgotten what had happened to the leftovers of the cargo with which he had started out from Nikkeldepain—sometimes that day seemed to lie years in the past now—but he located them finally in storage at the spaceport. One of the crates contained the complicated, expensive, and somewhat explosive educational toys which probably were the property of Councilor Rapport and which had turned out to be unsalable in the Empire.

"There's a kind of gadget in there that could do the trick," he said to Goth. "Called the Totisystem Toy, I think."

He found a Totisystem Toy and demonstrated it for her. It had been designed to provide visual instruction in all forms of power systems known to Nikkeldepain, but something seemed to have gone wrong with the lot. When the toy was set in action, the systems all started to operate simultaneously. The result was a bewildering, constantly changing visual hash.

"Might not fool anybody who's got much sense for long," he admitted. "But all it has to do is let us know whether there's someone on board we have to watch. . . . Could have the ship bugged, too, come to think of it!"

They had the Totisystem Toy installed in the engine room, concealed but not so well concealed that a good snooper shouldn't be able to find it, and set up a camera designed for espionage work. The espionage supplies outfit which sold them the camera, and sent an expert to bug the *Venture* unobtrusively in the areas the captain wanted covered, acknowledged the devices couldn't be depended upon absolutely. Nothing in that class could. It was simply a matter of trying to keep a jump ahead of the competition.

"Spiders!" Goth remarked thoughtfully.

"Eh?" inquired the captain.

Spiders spun threads, she explained, and spiders got in everywhere. Even a very suspicious spy probably wouldn't give much attention to a spider thread or two even if he noticed them.

They brought a couple of well-nourished spiders aboard the ship and attached a few threads to the camouflaged camera in the engine room. Anyone doing anything at all to the camera was going to break a thread.

Vezzarn, of course, couldn't be completely counted out now as a potential spy. The old spacer's experience might make him very useful on the run; but if it could be made to seem that it was his own decision, they'd leave him on Uldune.

Vezzarn scratched his gray head.

"Sounds like the Chaladoor's acting up kind of bad right now, at that!" he agreed innocently. "But I'll come along anyway, skipper, if it's all right with you."

So Vezzarn also came along. If they'd discharged him just before starting on the trip for which he'd been hired, people would have been wondering again.

On the night before take-off, Daalmen in an unmarked van brought two sizable crates out to the *Evening Bird* and loaded them on the ship at the captain's directions. One crate went into a brand-new strongbox in the storage vault with a time lock on it. When it was inside, the captain set the lock to a date two weeks ahead. The other crate went into a stateroom recently sealed off from the rest of the passenger compartment. The first contained the crystalloid object which had been on Olimy's ship; and the other contained Olimy himself.

They'd completed all preparations as well as they could.

After they'd been aloft twelve hours, Goth went down to the engine room with one of the spiders in a box in her pocket, and looked into the locked compartment. The camera hadn't come into action, but the two almost imperceptible threads attached to it were broken. Someone had been there.

She had the spider attach fresh threads and came back up. None of their expensive bugs had been disturbed. The engine room prowler should be a spy of experience.

When they checked again next day, someone had been there again.

It didn't seem too likely it had been the same someone. The bugs still had recorded no movement. They had two veteran spies on board then—perhaps three. The Totisystem Toy might have had a third visitor before the spider threads were reattached to the camera. But the camera hadn't gone into action even once.

Short of putting all three suspects in chains, there wasn't much they could do about it at the moment. The closer they got to the Chaladoor, the less advisable it would be for either of them to be anywhere but in the control section or in their cabins, which opened directly on the control section, for any considerable length of time. The spies, whether two or three, might simply give up. After all, the only mystery drive to be found on the ship was a bundle of wires in a drawer of the bedside table in Goth's cabin. Plus Goth.

On the fourth ship-day something else occurred . . . .

The captain was in the control chair, on watch, while Goth napped in her cabin. The Chaladoor had opened up awesomely before them, and the *Venture* was boring through it at the peak thrust of her souped-up new drives. Their supersophisticated detection system registered occasional blips, but so far they'd been the merest flickers. The captain's gaze shifted frequently to the forward screens. A small, colorful star cluster hung there, a bit to port, enveloped in a haze of reddish-brown dust against the black of space. It was the first of their guideposts through the uncertainties of the Chaladoor, but one it was wise to give a wide berth to—the reputed lair, in fact, of his old acquaintances, the Megair Cannibals.

He tapped in a slight course modification. The cluster slid gradually farther to port. Then the small desk screen beside him, connected to the entrance to the control section, made a burring sound. He clicked it on and Vezzarn's face appeared.

"Yes?" said the captain.

Vezzarn's head shifted as he glanced back along the empty passage behind him. "Something going on you ought to know about, skipper!" he whispered hoarsely.

The captain simultaneously pressed the button which released the entrance door and the one which brought Goth awake in her cabin.

"Come in!" he said.

Vezzarn's face vanished. The captain slipped his Blythe gun out of a desk drawer and into his pocket, stood up as the little spaceman hastily entered the control room. "Well?" he asked.

"That NO ADMITTANCE door back of the passenger section, skipper! Looks like one of 'em's snooping around in there."

"Which one?" asked the captain as Goth appeared in the control room behind Vezzarn.

Vezzarn shrugged. "Don't know! No one in the lounge right now. I was coming by, saw the door open just a crack—"

"You didn't investigate?"

"No, sir!" Vezzarn declared virtuously. "Not me. Not without your permission, I wouldn't go in there! Thought I'd better tell you right away though."

"Come along," the captain told Goth. He snapped the control entrance door shut on lock behind the three of them, and they hurried along the passage to the lounge. Goth stayed there to keep an eye on the Chaladoor through the lounge screens. The captain and Vezzarn hastened on, stopped at the door to the sealed passage, at the far end of which Olimy sat unmoving in his dark stateroom.

"Closed now!" Vezzarn said.

The captain glanced at him, drawing the key to the passage from his pocket. "Sure you saw it open?" he asked.

Vezzarn looked hurt. "Sure as I'm standing here, skipper! Just a bit. But it was open!"

"All right." Whoever had been prowling about the ship before might have investigated the passage and the stateroom, discovered Olimy there—which should be a considerable shock to most people—and hurriedly left again. "You go wait with Dani in the lounge," he said. "I'll check."

The key turned in the lock. The captain twisted the handle. The door flew open, banging into him; and he caught Hulik do Eldel by the arm as she darted out. She twisted a dead-white face up to him, eyes staring. Then, before he could say anything, her mouth opened wide and she screamed piercingly.

✧   ✧   ✧

The scream brought Vezzarn back to the scene, Laes Yango lumbering behind him. Hulik was babbling her head off. The captain shoved the passage door shut, said curtly, "Let's get her to the lounge . . . ."

It was an awkward situation, but by the time they got to the lounge he had a story ready. The motionless figure Miss do Eldel had seen was simply another passenger and no cause for alarm. The man, whose name the captain was not at liberty to disclose, suffered from a form of paralysis for which a cure was to be sought on Emris. Some very important personages of Uldune were involved; and for reasons of planetary politics, the presence of the patient on board the *Evening Bird* was to have been a complete secret. It was unfortunate that Miss do Eldel had allowed her curiosity to take her into an off limits section of the ship and discover their fellow-passenger. He trusted, the captain concluded, that he could count on the discretion of those present to see that the story at least got no farther . . . .

Laes Yango, Vezzarn, and Hulik nodded earnestly. Whatever Hulik had thought when she turned on a light in Olimy's stateroom, she seemed to accept the captain's explanations. She was looking both relieved and very much embarrassed as he went off to relock the stateroom and passage doors . . . not that locking things up on the ship seemed to make much difference at present—

"If I could see you in the control section, Miss do Eldel," he said when he came back. "Vezzarn, you'd better stay at the viewscreens till Dani and I take over up front . . . ."

In the control room he asked Hulik to be seated. Goth already was at the console. But the detector system had remained reassuringly quiet, and the Megair Cluster was dropping behind them. The captain switched on the intercom, called Vezzarn off the lounge screens. Then he turned back to the passenger.

"I really must apologize, Captain Aron!" Hulik told him

contritely. "I don't know what possessed me. I assure you I don't make it a practice to pry into matters that are not my business."

"What I'd like to know," the captain said, "is how you were able to unlock the passage door and the one to the stateroom."

Hulik looked startled.

"But I didn't!" she said. "Neither door was locked and the one to the passage stood open. That's why it occurred to me to look inside. . . . Couldn't Vezzarn—no, you hadn't told Vezzarn about this either, had you?"

"No, I hadn't," said the captain.

"You're the only one who has keys to the door?"

He nodded. "Supposedly."

"Then I don't understand it. I swear I'm telling the truth!" Hulik's dark eyes gazed at him in candid puzzlement. Then their expression changed. "Or could the—the unfortunate person in there have revived enough to have opened the doors from within?" Her face said she didn't like that idea at all.

The captain told her he doubted it. And from what Goth knew of the disminded condition, it was in fact impossible that Olimy's shape could have moved by itself, let alone begun unlocking doors. Otherwise, it seemed the incident hadn't told them anything about the shipboard prowlers they didn't already know. Hulik do Eldel looked as though she were telling the truth. But then an experienced lady spy *would* look as if she were telling the truth, particularly when she was lying . . . .

He'd had an alarm device set up in the control desk which would go off if anyone tampered with the strongbox containing Olimy's crystalloid in the storage vault. He was glad now he had taken that precaution, though it still did seem almost unnecessary—the time lock on the strongbox was supposed to be tamper-proof; and the storage vault itself had been installed on the ship by the same firm of master craftsmen who'd designed the vaults for the Daal's Bank.

✧   ✧   ✧

Most of the next ship-day passed quietly—or in relative quiet. They did, in fact, have their first real attack alert, but it was not too serious a matter. A round dozen black needle-shapes registered suddenly in the screens against the purple glare of a star. Stellar radiation boiling through space outside had concealed the blips till then . . . and not by accident; it was a common attack gambit and they'd been on the watch for it whenever their course took them too near a sun. The black ships moved at high speed along an interception course with the *Venture*. They looked wicked and competent.

The buzzer roused Goth in her sleep cabin. Thirty seconds later one of the desk screens lit up and her face looked out at the captain. "Ready!" her voice told him. She raked sleep-tousled brown hair back from her forehead. "Now?"

"Not yet." Sneaking through the sun system, he hadn't pushed the *Venture*; they still had speed in reserve. "We might outrun them. We'll see. . . . Switch your screen to star-board—"

The ship's intercom pealed a signal. The passenger lounge. The captain cut it in. "Yes?" he said.

"Are you aware, sir," Laes Yango's voice inquired, "that we are about to be waylaid?"

The captain thanked him, told him he was, and that he was prepared to handle the situation. The trader switched off, apparently satisfied. He must have excellent nerves; the voice had sounded composed, no more than moderately interested. And sharp eyes, the captain thought—the lounge screens couldn't have picked up the black ships until almost the instant before Yango called.

It was too bad though that he was in the lounge at the moment. If the Sheewash Drive had to be used, the captain would slap an emergency button first, which, among other things, blanked out the lounge screens. Nevertheless, that in itself was likely to give Yango some food for thought . . . .

But perhaps it wouldn't be necessary. The captain watched

the calculated interception point in the instruments creep up. Still three minutes away. The black ships maintained an even speed. Four of them were turning off from the others, to cut in more sharply, come up again from behind. . . . He shoved the drive thrust regulator slowly flat to the desk. The drives howled monstrous thunder. A minute and a half later, they flashed through the interception point with a comfortably sixty seconds to spare. The black ships had poured on power at the last moment, too. but the *Venture* was simply faster.

His watch ended, and Goth's began. He slept, ate, came on watch again . . . .

Chapter SEVEN

IT WAS TIME to rouse Goth once more . . . past time by twenty minutes or so. But let her sleep a little longer, the captain thought. This alternate-watch arrangement would get to be a grind before the Chaladoor run was over! If he could only trust one of the others on board . . . .

Well, he couldn't.

He sniffed. For a moment he'd fancied a delicate suggestion of perfume in the air. Imagination. Hulik do Eldel used perfume, but it was over twenty-four hours since she'd been in the control room. Besides she didn't use this kind.

Something stirred in his memory. Who *did* use this kind of perfume? Wasn't it—

"Do you have a few minutes to spare for me, Captain Aron?" somebody purred throatily behind him. He started, spun about in the chair.

Red-headed Sunnat leaned with lazy, leggy grace against the far wall of the control room, eyes half shut, smiling at him. Her costume was the one which most of all had set the captain's pulses leaping rapidly, when she'd slid off her cloak and revealed it to him, back in Zergandol.

He started again, but less violently.

"Not bad!" he remarked. He cleared his throat. "You were off on the voice though and pretty far off, I'd say, on the perfume."

Sunnat stared at him a moment, smile fading. "Hm!" she said coldly. She turned, swayed into Goth's cabin. Goth came out a moment later, half frowning, half grinning.

"Thought I was her pretty good!" she stated. "Voice, too!"

"You were, really!" the captain admitted. "And just what, may I ask, was the idea?"

Goth hitched herself up on the communicator table and dangled her legs. "Got to practice," she explained. "There's a lot to it. Not easy to hold the whole thing together either!"

"Light waves, sound waves, and scents, eh? No, I imagine it wouldn't be. That's all you do?"

"Right now it's all," nodded Goth.

The captain reflected. "Another thing—if you saw *that* costume of hers, you were doing some underhanded snooping-around in Zergandol!"

"Looked like you might need help," Goth said darkly.

"Well, I didn't!"

"No." She grinned. "Couldn't know that, though. Want me to do Hulik? I got *her* down just right."

"Another time." The captain climbed out of the chair, adjusted the seat for her. "I'd better get some sleep. And you'd better forget about practicing and keep your eyes pinned to those screens! There've been a few flickers again."

"Don't worry!" She slipped down from the table, started over to him. Then they both froze.

There were short, screeching whistles, a flickering line of red on the console. An alarm—

"*Strongbox!*" hissed Goth.

They raced through the silent ship to the storage. The lounge was deserted, its lights dim. It had been ship-night for two hours.

The big storage door was shut, seemed locked, but swung open at the captain's touch. The automatic lighting inside was on—somebody there! Cargo packed the compartment to the ship's curved hull above. The captain brought out his gun as they went quickly down the one narrow aisle still open along the length of the storage, then came in sight of the vault at the far end to the left. The vault door—that massive, burglar-proof slab—stood half open.

Vezzarn lay face down in the door opening, legs within the vault as if he had stumbled and fallen in the act of emerging from it. He didn't move as they scrambled past him. The interior of the vault hummed like a hive of disturbed giant insects. The strongbox stood against one wall, its top section tilted up. A number of unfamiliar tools lay on the floor about it. The humming poured up out of the box.

It was like wading knee-deep through thick, sucking mud to get to it! The captain's head reeled in waves of dizziness. The humming deepened savagely. He heard Goth shout something behind him. Then he was bending over the opened box. Gray light glared out of it; cold fire stabbed—he seemed to be dropping forward, headlong into cold, gray distances, as his hands groped frantically about, found the tough, flexible plastic wrapping which had been pulled away from the crystal's surface, wrenched, tugged it back into place.

In seconds they had it covered again, the plastic ends twisted tightly together; they stood gasping and staring at each other as the angry humming subsided. It was as if something that had been coming awake had gone back to sleep.

"Just in time here—maybe!" panted the captain. "Let's hurry!"

They couldn't get the strongbox closed all the way, left it as it was—top pulled down, a gap showing beneath it. They hauled Vezzarn clear of the vault door, shoved the door shut, spun its triple locks till they clicked back into position. The captain wrestled Vezzarn up to his shoulder. The old spacer might be dead or merely unconscious; in any case, he was a loose, floppy weight, difficult to keep a grasp on.

They got the storage door locked. Then Goth was off, darting back to the control section, the captain hurrying and stumbling after her with Vezzarn. There was still no sign of the two passengers—but that didn't necessarily mean they were asleep in their staterooms.

He let Vezzarn slide to the control room floor and joined Goth at the instruments. The glittering dark of the Chaladoor swam about them but nothing of immediate importance was registering. Most particularly, nothing which suggested the far-off Worm World knew Olimy's crystal had been uncovered again on a ship thundering along its solitary course through space. They exchanged glances.

"Might have been lucky!" the captain said. "If there're no Nuris anywhere around here—" He drew in a long breath, looked back at Vezzarn. "Let's try to get that character awake!"

Spluttering, swallowing, coughing, Vezzarn woke up a few minutes later. The captain pulled back the flask of strong ship brandy he'd been holding to the little spacer's mouth, recapped it and set it on the floor. "Can you hear me, Vezzarn?" he asked loudly.

"Aaa-eeh," sighed Vezzarn. He looked around and his face seemed to crumple. He blinked up at the captain, started to lift a hand to wipe his tear-filled eyes, and discovered handcuffs on his wrists. "Ah?" he muttered, frightened, then tried to meet the captain's gaze again and failed. He cleared his throat. "Uh—what's happened, skipper?"

"You're going to tell us," said the captain coldly. "Look over there, Vezzarn!"

Vezzarn turned his head in the indicated direction, saw the inner port of the control section lock yawning open, looked back apprehensively at the captain.

"Dani," said the captain, nodding at Goth who sat sideways to them at the communicator table, an instrument case with dials on it before her, "is playing around with a little lie detector of ours over there! The detector is focused on you. Now—"

"I wouldn't lie to you, skipper!" Vezzarn interrupted earnestly. "I just wouldn't Anything you want to know I'll—"

"We'll see. If the detector says you're lying—" the captain jerked his thumb at the lock. "You go out, Vezzarn! That way. I won't listen to explanations. Out into the Chaladoor, as you are!" He moved back a step, put his hands on his hips, gave Vezzarn a glare for good measure. "Start talking!"

Vezzarn didn't wait to ask what he should talk about. Hurriedly he began spilling everything he could think of about what had been told him of Captain Aron's mystery drive, the voice who employed him, the change in assignment, his own plans, and events on the ship. "Now I've, uh, seen your drive, sir," he concluded, voice quivering reminiscently, "I wouldn't want the hellish thing! Not as a gift from you. I wouldn't want to come anywhere near it again. I'm playing it honest. I'm your man, sir, until we're through the Chaladoor and berthed safe on Emris. Believe me!"

The captain moved to the desk, turned down a switch. The lock sealed itself with a sharp snap. Vezzarn started, then exhaled in heavy relief.

"We seem to have a passenger on board who's interested in the same thing," the captain remarked. It wouldn't hurt if Vezzarn believed the crystalloid was the mystery drive. That he wasn't going near it again if he could help it was obvious. Apparently he'd fainted in sheer fright as he was trying to scramble out of the vault. "Which of them?"

"Both of them, I'd say," Vezzarn told him, speaking a little more easily. "Couldn't prove it—but they've both been moving around where they shouldn't be."

The captain studied him a moment. "I was assured," he said then, "that short of a beam that could melt battle-steel, nobody would be able to force a way into that vault or to open that box until the time lock opened it—"

Vezzarn cleared his throat, produced a small, modest smile.

"Well, sir," he said, "it's possible you could find two men on Uldune who're better safecrackers than I am. I'm not saying you would. It's possible. But I'll guarantee you couldn't find three. . . . I guess that explains it, sir!"

"I guess it does," the captain agreed. He considered. Hulik do Eldel and Laes Yango weren't at all likely to be in the same lofty safecracking class, but—"Could you fix the vault and the strongbox so *you* couldn't get in again?" he asked.

"Huh?" Vezzarn looked reflective for a moment. "Yeah," he said slowly, "that could be done . . . ."

"Fine," said the captain. "Get up. We'll go do it right now."

Vezzarn paled. "Skipper," he stated uncomfortably, "I'd really rather not go anywhere near . . ."

"The forward lock over there," warned the captain, "can be opened awfully quick again!"

Vezzarn climbed awkwardly out of the chair. "I'll go, sir," he said.

Worm Weather appeared in the screens seven hours later . . . .

It was very far away, but it was there—fuzzily rounded specks of yellowness drifting across the stars. They picked up five or six of the distant dots almost simultaneously, not grouped but scattered about the area. There seemed to be no pattern to their motion, either in relation to one another or to the *Venture*.

Within another half-hour there might have been nearly fifty in the screens at a time, to all sides of the ship. It was difficult to keep count. They moved with seeming aimlessness, dwindled unnaturally, were gone in distance. Others appeared. . . . Goth had set up the Drive, and came back to join the captain. The lounge screens had been cut off from the beginning. Laes Yango called on intercom to report the fact, was told of a malfunction which would presently be corrected.

And still the Nuri globes came no closer. The encounter might have been a coincidence, but the probability remained that Vezzarn's exposure of the crystal in the strongbox had drawn the swarms towards this area of space. They seemed to have no method of determining the *Venture's* moment-to-moment position more exactly. But sheer chance might bring one near enough to reveal the ship to them—

"You scared?" Goth inquired by and by in a subdued voice.

"Well, yes. . . . You?"

"Uh-huh. Bit."

"The Drive will get us out of it if necessary," he said.

"Uh-huh."

In another while there seemed fewer of the globes around. The captain waited some minutes to be sure, then commented on it. Goth had noticed it, too. Their number dwindled farther. At last only one or two doubtful specks remained in space, now far behind the ship. But neither of them felt like leaving the screens.

"Being a witch," sighed the captain, "can get to be quite a job!"

"Sometimes," Goth agreed.

He reflected. "Well, maybe things will quiet down for a spell. . . . Almost everything that could happen on board has happened by now!" He considered again, chuckled. "Unless one of those—what did you call them?—vatches joins the party!"

Goth cleared her throat carefully. "Well, about that, Captain—"

He gave her a quick, startled look.

"Can't say there's one around," Goth said. "Can't say there isn't though, either."

"*One around!* I thought you'd know!"

"They come close enough, I do. This one doesn't. If it's a vatch. Just get a feeling there's been something watching." She waved a hand at the Chaladoor in the screens. "From a ways off."

"It *could* be a vatch?"

"Could be," Goth acknowledged. "Wouldn't worry about it.

If it's your vatch, he's probably just been curious about what you were doing. They get curious about people."

The captain grunted. "Since when have you had that feeling?"

"Off and on," Goth said. "On the ship . . . once or twice in Zergandol."

He shook his head helplessly.

"Might fade off after a while," Goth concluded. "He starts making himself at home around here, I'll let you know."

"You do that, Goth!" the captain said.

Two watches farther along, it became apparent that not everything that could happen on the *Venture* had happened so far. What occurred wasn't vatch work, though for a moment the captain wasn't so sure. In fact, it was something for which nobody on board had any satisfactory explanation to offer.

Hulik do Eldel gave the alarm. The captain was on duty when the intercom rang. He switched it on, said, "Yes?"

"Captain Aron," Hulik told him in an unnaturally composed voice, "I'm locked in my stateroom and need immediate assistance! Knock before you try to enter, and identify yourself, or I'll shoot through the door."

The captain pressed Goth's buzzer. "Why would you shoot through the door?" he asked.

"Because," Hulik said, "there's some beast loose on the ship."

"Beast?" he repeated, startled. Goth's face appeared in her screen, pop-eyed, nodded at him, disappeared.

"Beast. Creature. Thing! *Monster!*" Hulik seemed to be speaking through hard clenched teeth. "I saw it. just now. In a passage off the lounge. Be careful on your way here! It's large, probably dangerous."

"I'll be there at once!" the captain promised.

"Bring your gun," Hulik told him, still in the flat, dead tone of choked-down hysteria. "Several, if you have them . . . ." She switched off as Goth came trotting out of her cabin, buttoning up her jacket. "Vatch?" the captain asked hurriedly.

Goth shook her head. "Not a whiff of one around! She couldn't see a vatch anyway, if there was one around." She looked puzzled and interested.

"Could something else have got on the ship—out of space? Something material?"

"Don't know," Goth said hesitantly. "Course you hear stories about the Chaladoor like that."

"The do Eldel's no doubt heard them, too!" commented the captain. He slid his gun into a pocket, felt his nerves tightening up again. "We'll hope it's her imagination! Come on."

They emerged from the control section, moved along the passage to the lounge, wary and listening. Nothing stirred. The lounge was dim, and the captain flipped the lights up to full strength as they entered. They went down a side passage, turned into another, stopped at a closed stateroom door.

"Let's stand aside a bit," the captain whispered. "The way she was talking, she *might* shoot through the door if she's startled!" He rapped cautiously on the panel, pressed the door speaker.

"Who's there?" Hulik's voice inquired sharply.

"Captain Aron," announced the captain. "Dani's with me."

There were two clicks. The door swung open a few inches and Hulik gazed out at them over a small but practical-looking gun. Her delicate face was drawn and pale, and there was a nervous flickering to the dark eyes that made the captain very uneasy. She glanced along the passage, hissed, "Come in! Quickly!" and opened the door wider.

" . . . I didn't get too good a look at it," she was telling them in the stateroom a few seconds later, still holding the gun. "It was in the passage leading back from the lounge, about thirty feet away and in shadow. A dark shape, moving up the passage towards me." She shivered quickly. "It was an animal of some kind—quite large!"

"How large?" the captain asked.

She considered. "The body might have been as big as that of a horse. It seemed lumpy, rounded. It was close to the floor—I had the impression it was crouching! The head—big, round, something like tusks or fangs below it." Hulik's finger lifted, made five quick, stabbing motions in the air. "Eyes!" she said. "Five eyes in a row along the upper part of the head. Rather small, bright yellow."

Everyone—with the exception of Olimy—was gathered in the control section; and except for Goth, all of them carried a gun. Hulik's story couldn't simply be ignored. It was clear she believed she had seen what she'd described. Vezzarn evidently believed it, too. His face was as pale as the do Eldel's. Laes Yango was more skeptical.

"I've heard tales of ships being boarded by creatures from space in the Chaladoor," he observed. "I have never felt there was reason to give much credence to them. Overwrought nerves can—"

"My nerves are as good as yours, sir!" Hulik interrupted hotly. "If they weren't, I would hardly have looked for passage through the Chaladoor in the first place. I know what I saw!"

Yango shrugged, indicated the viewscreens. "We're all aware there are very realistic dangers out there," he said. "Of many kinds. No one can foretell when one or the other of them will be next encountered. Are you proposing that we perhaps leave this child on guard to warn us of whatever may occur, while the rest spend upward of an hour searching every nook of the ship to locate an apparition?"

Hulik said sharply, "Dani can't remain here by herself, of course! We must all stay together. And, yes, I say we should search the ship immediately, as a group. We must find that creature and either kill it or drive it back into space." She looked at the captain. "For all we know, that unfortunate paralyzed person is in imminent danger at this very moment!"

The captain hesitated. To leave the control room unguarded for a considerable length of time certainly was not desirable. On the other hand, the Chaladoor looked as open and placid at the moment as one could wish. No stars, dust clouds, planetary bodies, or asteroid flows which might provide ambush points lay along the immediate course stretch ahead; the detectors had remained immobile for hours . . . .

It shouldn't, he pointed out to the others, take them an hour to conduct a search of the ship which would be adequate for the purpose. There were few hiding places for a creature of the size described by Miss do Eldel. Further, if the thing was aggressive, there was no reason to expect it would remain hidden. He'd turn on the ship's automatic alarm system now which would blast a warning over every intercom speaker on board if suspicious objects came within detector range. They'd keep together, move as a group through each compartment of the ship in turn. That could be done in less than twenty minutes. If they encountered nothing, they'd assume there were no lurking monsters here to be feared.

"After all," he concluded, "this creature, whatever it was, may have come aboard, looked about, and simply left again shortly after Miss do Eldel saw it . . . ."

Nobody appeared really satisfied with this solution, but they set off from the control section a few minutes later. The *Venture's* interior gradually came ablaze with lights as the search party went through the passenger area first, worked on to the back of the ship and the storage, finally checked out the lower deck. But no ungainly beast was flushed to view; nor could they find the slightest traces such a creature might have left, even in the passage where Hulik declared she had seen it. Hulik remained unconvinced.

"What the rest of you do is your own affair!" she stated. "But I intend to go on no-sleep for the next several ship-days and remain in my stateroom with the door locked. Vezzarn can bring me my meals. If nothing happens in that time, I shall be satisfied the thing is no longer on board. Meanwhile I advise all of you to take what precautions you can . . . ."

The captain felt Hulik was not being too realistic about the situation. A creature capable of transferring itself through the hull of an armored trader into the interior of the ship presumably would also be capable of transferring itself into any stateroom it selected. Perhaps Hulik simply did not want to admit that to herself. At any rate, no one mentioned the possibility.

As he sat at the control desk near the end of his next watch, Goth whispered suddenly from behind his shoulder, "Captain!"

He started. These had been rather unsettling days in one way and another, and he hadn't heard her come up. He half turned. "Yes?"

"Got any of the intercoms on?" her whisper inquired. She sounded excited about something.

"No. What do—" He checked abruptly. He'd swung all the way around in the chair to look at her.

And nobody was standing there.

"Goth!" he said loudly, startled.

"Huh?" inquired the voice. It seemed to come out of thin air not three feet from him. "Oh!" A giggle. "Forgot! I—*hey*, watch it!"

He'd reached out towards the voice without thinking, touched something. Then Goth suddenly stood there, two feet farther away, rubbing her forehead and frowning.

"Near put out my eye with your thumb!" she announced indignantly.

"But what . . . since when—"

"Oh, no-shape! Special kind of shape-change, that's all. just learned it this sleep period so I forgot to switch off when I came in. I was . . . ." She put her hands on her hips. "Captain, I found out where that thing Hulik saw is hiding!"

"*Huh?*" The captain came out of the chair, hand darting to the desk drawer where he kept the gun. "It *is* on the ship?"

Goth nodded, eyes gleaming. "In Yango's cabin!"

"Great Patham! Was Yango—"

"Don't worry about *him*. He was in there with it just now. Talking to it. I was listening at the door." Goth glanced down at herself, patted her flanks. "No-shape's pretty handy once you get used to not seeing you around anywhere!"

"Now wait," said the captain helplessly. "Did you just say Yango was talking to the creature?"

"And it to Yango," Goth nodded. "Snarly sort of thing! No kind of talk I know. Yango knows it, though."

He stared at her. "Goth, you're *sure* he has that animal in his stateroom with him?"

"Well, sure I'm sure! He opened the door a crack once to look out." Goth put her hands out on either side of her. "I was *that* far from him."

"That was dangerous! The creature might have caught your scent."

"No-shape, no-sound, no-scent!" Goth said complacently. "Had them all going, Captain. I wasn't *there*. Got a look through the door at a bit of the thing. Big, and brown fur. Saw part of a leg, too. Odd sort of leg—"

"Odd?"

"Kind of like a bug's leg. Got that shaggy fur all over it, though. Couldn't really see much." She looked at him. "What are we going to do?"

"If Laes Yango's talking to it, he's got some kind of control over it. We'd better handle this by ourselves and right now, while we know the thing's still in the stateroom."

"It won't go out by the door for a while," Goth said.

"Why not?"

"Doorlock won't turn till we get there. Pulled a bit of steel inside it. So it's stuck."

"Very good!" When Laes Yango's shipment of hyperelectronic equipment had been brought on board, he'd insisted on having one very large crate of particularly valuable items placed in his stateroom instead of the storage. "Remember that big box he has in there.?" the captain asked.

Goth looked dubious. "Don't think it's big enough for that thing to climb into!"

"Something with a body as large as that of a horse's—no, I guess not. It was just a thought." He pocketed the gun. "Let's go find out what it is and what Yango thinks he's doing with it." He looked down at her. "This might get rough. We'll sort of play it by ear."

Goth nodded, grinned briefly.

"And I go no-shape, eh"

"Plus the rest of it," said the captain. "But don't do anything to make Laes Yango think he's arguing with a witch—unless it looks absolutely necessary."

"Saving that up." Goth nodded.

"Exactly. We might still have to pull a few real surprises of our own before this trip's over. You'll clear the doorlock as soon as we get there—"

"Right," said Goth and vanished. He kept his ears cocked for any indication of her presence on the way to Laes Yango's stateroom, but caught nothing. The no sound effect seemed as complete as the visual blankout. As he came quietly up to the door, her fingers gave the side of his hand a quick ghostly squeeze and were gone.

He stood listening, ear close to the panel. He heard no voice sounds, but there were other faint sounds. Footsteps crossed the stateroom twice from different directions—brisk human footsteps, not some animal tread. Yango was moving about. Then came a moderately heavy thump, a metallic clank. After a few moments, two more thumps. . . . Then everything remained still.

The captain waited a minute, activated the door speaker.

He'd expected either a dead silence or some indication of startled, stealthy activity from the stateroom after the buzzer sounded. Instead, Laes Yango's voice inquired calmly, "Yes? Who is it?"

"Captain Aron," replied the captain. "May I come in, Mr. Yango?"

"Certainly, sir. . . . One moment, please. I believe the door is locked."

Footsteps crossed the stateroom again, approaching the door. Yango hadn't sounded in the least like a man who had something to hide. Those thumps? Thoughtfully, the captain moved back a little, slid a hand into his gun pocket, left it there.

The door swung open, showing enough of the stateroom to make it immediately clear that no large, strange beast stood waiting inside. The trader smiled a small, cold smile at him from beyond the door. "Come in, sir. Come in!"

The captain went in, drew the door shut behind him. A light was on over a table against the wall on the left; various papers lay about the table. The big packing crate rather crowded the far end of the room, but nothing approaching the bulk of a horse could possibly have been concealed in that. "I trust I'm not disturbing you," the captain said.

"Not at all, Captain Aron." Laes Yango, nodded at the table, smiled deprecatingly. "Paper work! . . . It seems a businessman never quite catches up with that. What was on your mind, sir?"

"A matter of ship security," the captain told him, casually drawing the gun from his pocket, holding it pointed at the floor between them. The trader's gaze shifted to the gun, then up to the captain's face. He looked mildly puzzled, perhaps a little startled.

"Ship security?" he repeated.

"Yes," said the captain. He lifted the gun muzzle an inch or two. "Would you hand me your gun, Mr. Yango? Carefully, please!"

The trader stared at him a moment. Then his smile returned. "Ah, well," he said softly. "You have the advantage of me, sir! The gun—of course, if you feel that's necessary!" His hand went slowly under his jacket, slowly brought out a gun, barrel held between thumb and finger, extended it to the captain. "Here you are, sir!"

The captain placed the gun in his left coat pocket.

"Thank you," he said. He indicated the packing crate. "You told me, I believe, Mr. Yango, that you had some very valuable and delicate hyperelectronic equipment in that box."

"That's correct, sir."

"I see you have it locked," said the captain. "I'll have to take a look inside. Would you unlock it, please?"

Laes Yango chewed his lip thoughtfully.

"You insist on that?" he inquired.

"I'm afraid I do," said the captain.

"Very well, sir. I know the law—on a risk run any question of ship security overrides all other considerations, at the captain's discretion. I shall open the lock, though not without protest against this invasion of my business privacy."

"I'm sorry," said the captain. "Open it, please."

He waited while the trader produced two sizable keys, inserted them in turn into a lock on the case, twisted them back and forth in a practiced series of motions and withdrew them. Then Yango stepped back from the case. Its top section was swinging slowly open, snapped into position, leaving the interior of the case exposed. The captain moved up, half his attention on the trader, until he could glance into it . . . .

It looked like a big, folded robe made of animal fur—long, coarse brown fur, streaked here and there with black tiger markings. The captain reached cautiously into the case, poked the fur, then grasped the hide through it and lifted. It came up with a kind of heavy, resilient looseness. He let it down again. The whole box might be filled with the stuff.

"*This*," he asked Yango, "is valuable hyperelectronic equipment?"

Yango nodded. "Indeed it is, sir! Indeed, it is! Extremely valuable—almost priceless. Very old and in perfect condition.

A disassembled Sheem robot. . . . The great artist who created it died over three hundred years ago."

"A disassembled Sheem robot," said the captain. "I see. . . . Have you had it assembled recently, Mr. Yango?"

"That is possible," Yango said stiffly.

The captain took hold of one end of the thick fold of furred material, drew it back—

The head lay just beneath it, bedded in more brown fur.

It didn't appear to be a head so much as the flattened-out bristly mask of one. But the eyes looked alive. Hulik do Eldel had described them accurately—a row of five smallish, round eyes of fiery yellow. They stared up out of the case at the ceiling of the stateroom. Near the other end of the head was a wide dark mouth-slit. A double pair of curved black tusks was thrust out at the sides of the mouth. It was a big head—big enough to go with a horse-sized body. And a thoroughly hideous one.

The captain pulled the folded fur back across it again.

"The Sheem Spider!" Laes Yango said. "A unique item, Captain Aron. The Sheem Robots were modeled after living animals of various worlds, and the Spider is considered to have been the most perfect creation of them all. This is the last specimen still in existence. You asked whether I had assembled it recently. . . . Yes, I have. It's a most simple process. With your permission—"

The captain swung the gun up, pointed it at Yango's chest.

"What are you hiding in your left hand?" he asked.

"Why, the activating mechanism." Yango frowned puzzledly. "I understood you wished to see it assembled. You see, the Sheem Robots assemble themselves when the signal to do it is registered by them."

The captain glanced aside into the case. The folded fur in there was shifting, sliding aside, beginning to heave up towards the top of the case.

"You have," he said, his voice fairly steady, "two seconds to deactivate it again! Then I'll shoot—and not for the shoulder."

There was the faintest of clicks from Laes Yango's closed left fist. The stirring mass in the case settled slowly back down into it, lay quiet. "It is deactivated, sir!" Yango said, eyeing the gun.

"Then I'll take that device," the captain told him. "And after you've locked up the case, I'll take the keys. . . . And then perhaps you'll let me know what this Sheem Robot is for, where you're taking it—and why you had it assembled and walking around on this ship without warning anybody about it."

Yango's expression had become surly but he offered no further protest. He relocked the case, turned over the keys and the activating mechanism. He'd been commissioned, he said, to obtain the Sheem Robot for the prince consort of Swancee, a world to Galactic North of Emris. Wuesselen was the possessor of a fabulous mechanical menagerie, and the standing price he'd offered for a Sheem Spider was fabulous in keeping. How or where Yango had obtained the robot he declined to say; that was a business secret. Above and beyond the price, he'd been promised a bonus if he could deliver it in time to have it exhibited by Wuesselen at the next summer festivals of northern Swancee; and the bonus was large enough to have made it seem worthwhile to take his chances with the Chaladoor passage.

"For obvious reasons," he said, "I have not wanted any of this to become known. I do not intend to have my throat cut before I can reach Swancee with the Spider!"

"Why did you assemble it here on the ship?" asked the captain.

"I've guaranteed to deliver it in good operating condition. These Robots must be tested—exercised, you might say—at least every few weeks to prevent deterioration. I regret very much that my action caused an alarm on board, but I didn't wish to reveal the facts of the matter. And no one was in danger. The Sheem Robots are perfectly harmless. They are simply enormously expensive toys!"

The captain grunted. "How can you get as big a thing as that into your case when it's disassembled?"

Yango looked at him. "Because these robots are hyper-electronic, sir! Assembled, they consist in considerable part of an interacting pattern of energy fields, many of which manifest as solid matter. As they disassemble, those fields collapse. The remaining material sections take up relatively little space."

"I see," nodded the captain. "Well, Mr. Yango, I feel you owe Miss do Eldel an explanation and an apology for the fright you gave her. After that's done, I'll bring the ship's crane up here and we'll move the robot's case into the storage vault. It should have had all the exercise it needs on this trip, and it will be safe enough there to satisfy you...."

Hulik do Eldel had to see the robot before she would believe what the two men were telling her. However, one glance at the great fanged head in the case was enough. "That's it!" she agreed, paling. She shuddered delicately. "Close it up again, please—quickly!"

When the case was locked, Laes Yango offered his apologies. Hulik looked at him a moment.

"I pride myself on being a lady," she said evenly then, "so I accept the apology, Mr. Yango. I will also blow your head off if you try another trick of any kind before we reach Emris!"

Bad blood among the passengers couldn't ordinarily be considered one of the more auspicious conditions for a space voyage. In this instance though, the captain reflected, some feuding between Laes Yango and the do Eldel might do no harm. It could help keep both of them out of his hair and generally hamper whatever sneaky maneuverings they'd be up to individually. He wondered whether Hulik would carry out her threat to blow off Laes Yango's head, if things came to that point. She might, he decided. Yango, according to the reports he'd had from Goth, was prudently keeping to his stateroom most of the time now. Of course, the big trader was at a disadvantage... the captain had retained custody of his gun, on general suspicion.

Neither Goth nor Vezzarn ever had heard anything at all of the antique Sheem Robots. Perhaps Yango's hyperelectronic spider monster was as harmless as he claimed, but it was staying right there in its locked-up crate in the vault until the *Venture* was ready to discharge her cargo in port There'd been robots built that were far from harmless . . . .

About time for Hulik to create a tense situation on the ship next!

Well, the trip to Emris wouldn't take forever! They were nearly halfway through the Chaladoor by now—

SMALL PERSON, said the vatch, YOU ARE MOST DIVERTING! I AM INCREASINGLY PLEASED TO HAVE FOUND YOU AMONG MY THOUGHTS.

Eh? What was *that*? Surprised, the captain groped around mentally, paused. Out of nowhere that vast voice came booming and whirling about him again, like great, formlessly shifting gusts of wind.

WHAT TROUBLES! WHAT PROBLEMS! exclaimed the vatch. HOW COMICALLY YOU STRUGGLE AMONG YOUR FELLOW-PHANTOMS! TINY CREATURE OF MY MIND, ARE YOU WORTHY OF CLOSER ATTENTION?

Impression, suddenly, of a mountain of wavy, unstable blackness before him. From some point near its peak, two huge, green, slitted eyes stared down.

SHALL WE MAKE THE GAME MORE INTERESTING, SMALL PERSON? SHOULD YOU BE TESTED FOR A GREATER ROLE? PERHAPS YOU WILL! . . . PERHAPS YOU WILL—

The captain jerked upright, found himself sitting in the control chair. There was only the familiar room and its equipment about, with the Chaladoor gazing in through the viewscreens.

Fallen asleep, he thought. Fallen asleep to dream of a preposterous vatch-thing, which had the notion it was dreaming *him!* His eyes went guiltily to the console chronometer. He'd nodded off for only a minute or two, apparently. But that was bad! It was still the early part of his watch.

He got coffee, lit a cigarette, sat down again and sighed heavily. It had occurred to him that he might ask Miss do Eldel if she could spare some of her stay-awake pills, but he'd given up the thought at once. Accepting drugs of any kind from a suspected spy wouldn't be the cleverest thing to do. He'd use all his next scheduled sleep period for sleep and nothing else, he promised himself. Standing watch half the time wasn't the problem—if Goth could do it with no indications of droopiness, he could. But the complications created by the others, and the need to be alert for more trouble from them, had cut heavily into the time he should have kept free for rest. The sensible move might be to lock all three of them up in their respective cabins.

And if there were *any* renewed indications of mischief, he decided, he'd do just that . . . .

Chapter EIGHT

FOR A WHILE, the passengers and the one-man crew seemed to be on their best behavior. The Chaladoor, however, was not. There were several abrupt alerts, and one hard run from something which blurred the detectors and appeared in the viewscreens' visual magnification as a cloud of brown dust. It displayed extraordinary mobility for a dust cloud. An electric-blue charge crackled and snapped about the *Venture's* hull for minutes as they raced ahead of it; then, gradually, they'd pulled away. Another encounter—when a great pale sphere of a ship came edging in swiftly on their course—was averted by warning snarls from the nova guns. The sphere remained parallel for a time, well beyond range, then swung off and departed.

And finally there was Worm Weather in the viewscreens again . . .

It was nothing like the previous occasion. One had to be alertly observant to catch them; and hours might pass without any sign at all. Then a tiny hazy glow would be there for a minute or two, moving distantly among the stars, and disappearing in the unexplained fashion of the Nuri globes. The lounge screens remained off—the captain had let it be known that the temporary malfunction was now permanent—so neither Vezzarn nor the passengers became aware of that particular phenomenon. But for the two responsible for the *Venture's* safety, and for matters which might be unthinkably more important, it was a nerve-stretching thing. Sleep periods were cut short again.

The captain, therefore, wasn't too surprised when he discovered himself waking up in the control chair during a watch period once more. Nor—at the moment—was he too concerned. He'd rigged up a private alarm device guaranteed to jar him out of deepest slumber, which he left standing on the desk throughout his watches. It had to be reset manually every three minutes to keep it silent, and, even in the Chaladoor, there were few stretches where anything very serious was likely to develop without previous warning in three minutes. At the first suggestion of drowsiness he turned it on.

But then came a disturbing recollection. This time he had not turned it on. He remembered a wave of heavy sleepiness, which had seemed to roll down on him suddenly, and must have literally blanked him out in an instant. It had been preceded by a momentary sense of something changing, something subtly wrong on the ship. He hadn't had time to analyze that . . . .

For an instant, his thoughts stopped in shock. Automatically, as he grew aware there'd been a lapse in wakefulness, he'd glanced over the detector system, found it inert, shifted attention to the ship's screens.

There was something very wrong there!

The appearance of the route pattern ahead of the *Venture* had changed completely. Off to the left by a few degrees, hung a blue-white sundisk the size of his thumb nail, a patch of furious incandescence which certainly hadn't been in view before! How long had he—

Three hours plus, the console chronometer told him silently.

A good three hours and twenty minutes! He flicked on Goth's intercom buzzer, held it down, eyes still rapidly searching the screens for anything of significance the detectors had left unregistered. A dozen times over, in those three hours, some Chaladoor raider could have swept down on them and knocked them out of space.... "Goth?"

The intercom screen remained blank. No answer.

Now fright surged through the captain. He half rose from the chair, felt sudden leaden pain buckling his left leg under him, and fell back heavily as Laes Yango's sardonic voice said from somewhere behind him, "Don't excite yourself, sir! The child hasn't been hurt. In fact, she's here in the room with us."

Hulik do Eldel and Vezzarn were also in the control room with them. Goth sat on the couch between the two, leaning slumped against Hulik, head drooping. All three looked as if they had fallen asleep and settled into the limply flexed poses of complete relaxation. "What did you do?" the captain asked.

Yango shrugged. "Traces of a mind drug in the ventilation system. If I named it, you wouldn't know it. Quite harmless. But unless the antidote is given, it remains effective for twelve to fourteen hours. Which will be twice the time required here."

"Required for what?" Yango had put a small gun-like object on the armrest of the chair in which he sat as he was speaking. A paralysis-producing object, and the captain could testify to its effectiveness. He was barely able to feel his left leg now, let alone use it.

"Well, let's take matters in order, sir," the trader replied. "I can hardly have your full attention until you've accepted the fact that there's nothing you can do to change the situation to your advantage. To start with then, I have your gun and the personal weapons of your companions. Your leg will regain its normal sensations within minutes, but let me assure you that you won't be able to leave that chair until I permit it." He tapped the paralyzer-producer. "You've experienced its light-est effect. That should be enough.

"Another thing you must remember, sir, is that I don't need you. Not in the least. You live by my indulgence. If it appears that you're going to be troublesome, you'll die. I can handle this ship well enough.

"Now the explanation. I am a collector of sorts. Of items of value. Which might on occasion be ships, or people . . ." Yango's left hand made an expansive gesture. "Money I obtain where I can, naturally. And information. I am an avid collec-tor of information. I've established what I believe to be one of the most efficient, farthest-ranging information systems presently in existence.

"One curious item of information that came to me some time ago concerned a certain Captain Pausert who has been until recently a citizen in good standing of the independent trans-Empire Republic of Nikkeldepain. This Captain Pausert was reported to have purchased three enslaved children on the Empire planet of Porlumma and to have taken them away with him on his ship.

"These children, three sisters, were believed to be natives of the witch world Karres and, in the emphatic opinion of vari-ous citizens of Porlumma, already accomplished sorceresses. Subsequently there were several reports that reliable witnesses had seen Captain Pausert's ship vanish instantly when threat-ened with attack by other spacecraft. It was concluded that by purchasing the Karres children he had gained control of a spacedrive of unknown type, perhaps magical in nature, which permitted him to take short-cuts through unknown dimen-sions of the universe and reappear in space at a point far removed from the one where he had been last observed.

"This, sir, was an interesting little story, particularly when considered in the light of other stories which have long been current regarding the strange world of Karres. It became far more interesting to me when, some while later, I received other information suggesting strongly that Captain Pausert, his ship, and one of the three witch children he had picked up on Porlumma were now at my present base of operations, Uldune. I initiated an immediate, very comprehensive investigation.

"It became evident that I was not the only one interested in the matter. Several versions, variously distorted, of the original story had reached Uldune. One of them implied that Captain Pausert was not a native of Nikkeldepain, but himself a Karres witch. Another made no mention of Karres or witchcraft at all but spoke only of a new spacedrive mechanism, a technological marvel which made possible the instantaneous transmission of an entire ship over interstellar distances.

"I proceeded cautiously. If you were Captain Pausert, it seemed that you must indeed control such a drive. There was no other good examination for the fact that you had arrived on Uldune so shortly after having been reported from several points west of the Empire. This was no trifling concern. There were competitors for this secret, and I arranged matters so that, whatever might happen, I should still eventually become its possessor. During your stay on Uldune, a full half of the Agandar's fleet of buccaneer ships were drawn into the vicinity of the planet, under orders to launch a planned, all-out attack on it if given the word. Not an easy operation, but I was determined that if the Daal obtained the drive from you—for a time there seemed reason to believe that those were Sedmon's intentions—it would be taken in turn from him."

The captain cleared his throat. "You're working with the pirates of the Agandar?" he asked.

"Well, sir, not exactly that," Laes Yango told him. "I *am* the Agandar, and my pirates work for me. As do others. As, if you so decide—and you have little real choice in the matter—will you. This was too important an undertaking to entrust to another, and too important to be brought to a hurried conclusion. If a mistake was made, everything might be lost.

"There were questions. If you had the drive, why the elaborate restructuring of your ship for risk run work? With such a device any tub capable of holding out space could go anywhere. Unless there were limitations on its use . . . Then what would the nature of such limitations be? How far was the nonmaterial science apparently developed by Karres involved? And of the two of you, who was the true witch? I needed the answers to those questions and others before I could act to best advantage.

"So I accompanied you into the Chaladoor. I watched and listened, not only by my body's eyes and ears. I am reasonably certain the drive has not been used since I came on this ship. Therefore there are limitations on it. It is not used casually or in ordinary circumstances. But there are indications enough that it was ready for use when it was needed. You, sir, are, if I may say so, an excellent ship-handler. But you are not a witch. That story, whatever its source, was unfounded. When a situation arises which threatens to turn into more than you and your ship between you might be able to meet, you call on the child. The witch child. She remains ready to do then, at the last moment, whatever will need doing to escape.

"So then, I think, we have the principal answers. You do not control the drive as was reported, except as the child does what you wish. For the witch is the drive, and the drive is the witch. That is the essential fact here. To me it means that to control the drive I, too, must learn to control the witch. And the witch is young, relatively inexperienced, relatively defenseless. I think it will be possible to control her."

"She has a large number of friends who are less inexperienced," the captain pointed out carefully.

"Perhaps. But Karres, whatever has happened to it, is at present very far out of the picture. Time is what I need now, and the circumstances are giving it to me. Consider the situation. This ship will not reappear from the Chaladoor—a fact disappointing to the owners of her cargo but not really surprising to anyone. If they learn of it eventually, even the girl's witch friends will not know where to begin to search for her here. And, of course, she will not be here."

"Where will she be?" asked the captain.

"On my flagship, sir. A ship which will have developed a very special capacity—one that will be most useful if never advertised . . . ."

"I see. Meanwhile it might be a good idea if you gave the witch the same antidote you gave me."

Laes Yango shook his head slightly. "Why should I do that?"

"Because," said the captain, nodding at the console, "the detectors have begun to register a couple of blips! We may need her help in a few minutes."

"Oh, come now, sir!" The Agandar picked up the paralysis gun, stood up and came striding over towards the desk. However, he stopped a good twelve feet away, eyes searching the screens. "Yes, I see them! Take the controls, Captain Pausert. The ship is yours again for now. Step up speed but remain on course—unless we presently have sufficient reason to change it."

"It isn't the course we were on," the captain observed. His leg felt all right again, but unless the Agandar came a good deal closer that wasn't much help. What else could he do? This incredible man had worked out almost everything about the Sheewash Drive, and wasn't at all likely to fall into traps. If Goth were awake, they'd handle him quickly between them. But apparently he suspected they might.

"I'm afraid I took it on myself to set up a new course," the Agandar agreed mildly. "I shall explain that in a moment." He nodded at the screen. "It seems our presence has been noted!"

The pair of blips had shifted direction, were angling towards them. Detector instruments of some kind over there, probably of extremely alien type, had also come awake. Distance still too great to afford other suggestions of the prospective visitors' nature . . . Would it do any good to tell this pirate chieftain something about Olimy and the strongbox in the vault? Probably not. Too early for a move of that sort, anyway—

"The Chaladoor holds terrors no man can hope to withstand," the Agandar remarked, watching the screen. "But they are rare—and whether one draws their attention or not becomes a matter of good sense as much as of fortune. For the common run of its vermin, such as we can take those two to be, audacity and a dependable ship are an even match or better. As you've demonstrated repeatedly these days, Captain Pausert."

The captain glanced over at him. Under rather different circumstances, he thought, he might have liked Laes Yango— some ten thousand cold-blooded murders back! But there was something no longer quite human about this living symbol of fear which had turned itself into the dreaded Agandar.

"Already they begin to hesitate!" the pirate went on. The blips were veering once more to take up a parallel course. "They will follow for some minutes now, then, finding themselves ignored, decide this is not a day for valor . . . ." He looked at the captain, returned to the chair, settled himself into it. "Remain on course, sir. No need to disturb your young friend over a matter like this!"

"Perhaps not. But some four hours ago," the captain said, "there was Worm Weather in the screens."

The Agandar's face became very thoughtful. "It has been a long time since that was last reported in these areas," he stated presently. "I'm not sure I believe you, sir."

"It was not at all close," said the captain, "but we had the Drive ready. Are you certain you could get her awake in time if we see it again—and it happens to see us?"

"Nothing is certain about the phenomenon you've mentioned," Yango told him. "The witch can be brought awake very quickly. But I will not awaken her without absolute need before we reach our present destination. That will be in approximately six hours. Meanwhile we shall keep close watch on the screens."

"And what's our destination?" asked the captain.

"My flagship. I've been in contact with it through a shielded transmitter. Preparations are being made aboard which will dissuade the witch from attempting to become a problem while she is being coaxed into full cooperation." Yango's tone did not change in any describable manner; nevertheless the last was said chillingly. "For the rest of you, places will be found suited to your abilities. I don't waste good human material. Are you aware Miss do Eldel is an intelligence agent for the Imperium?"

"Nobody told me she was," said the captain. There were several ways in which letting the Agandar know there might be a reason why Worm Weather was quartering the Chaladoor along the *Venture's* general route could make matters immediately worse instead of better; he decided again to keep quiet. "I've suspected she might be something of the sort," he added.

"I've been informed she's very capable," Yango said. "Once she's experienced the discipline of my organization, Miss do Eldel should reorient her loyalties promptly. Vezzarn has been doing odd jobs for an unpublicized branch of the Daal's services; we can put him back to work with her. And I can always use a good ship-handler . . . ." Yango smiled briefly. "You see, sir, while you have no real choice, as I said, the future is not too dark for any of you here. My flagship is a magnificent machine—few of the Chaladoor's inhabitants she has encountered so far have cared to cross her, and none of those survived to cross her twice. You are a man who appreciates a fine ship; you should like her. And you'll find I make good service rewarding."

As the captain started to reply, the detector warning system shrieked imminent attack.

"Get Goth awake, *fast!* She may get us out of this yet—"

He'd flicked one horrified look about the screens, slapped the yammering detectors into silence, spun in the chair to face Yango.

Then he checked. Yango was watching him alertly, unmoving, the paralysis gun half raised.

"Don't try to trick me, sir!" The Agandar's voice was deadly quiet.

"Trick you! Great *Patham!*" bellowed the captain. "Can't you see for yourself!"

The gun came full up, pointing at his chest. The Agandar's eyes shifted quickly about the screens, came back to the captain. "What am I supposed to see?" he asked, with contempt.

The captain stared at him. "You didn't hear the detectors either!" he said suddenly.

"The detectors?" Now there was an oddly puzzled look about Yango's eyes, almost as if he were struggling to remember something. "No," he said slowly then. The puzzled look faded. "I didn't hear the detectors. Because the detectors have made no sound. And there is nothing in the screens. Nothing at all! If you are pretending insanity, Captain Pausert, you are doing it too well. I have no room in my organization for a lunatic."

The captain looked again, for an instant only, at the screens. There was no need to study them to see what they contained. All about the ship swam the great glowing globes of Manaret, moving with them, preceding them, following them. Above his own ragged breathing there was a small, momentary near-sound, a click not quite heard.

Then he knew there was only one thing left to do. And almost no time in which to do it.

"I was wrong!" he said loudly, beginning to rise from the chair. "There *is* nothing there—" The entire port screen was filling with yellow fire now, reflecting its glare down into the room, staining the air, the walls, the Agandar's motionless figure, the steadily held gun. But if he could get, even for an instant, within four or five feet of the man— "I'm in no shape to handle the ship, Mr. Yango!" he shouted desperately at the figure. "You'll have to take over!"

"Stay in that chair!" Yango told him in a flat, strained voice.

"And be quiet! Be absolutely quiet. Don't speak. Don't move. If you do either, I pull this trigger a trifle farther and your heart, sir, stops in that instant. . . . I must listen and think!"

The captain checked all motion. The gun remained rock-steady; and Yango, with the yellow glare from the globe just beyond the port side of the ship still gradually strengthening about them, also sat motionless and silent while some seconds went by.

Then Yango said, "No, you were not wrong, sir. You were right. I see the Worm Weather now, too. But it makes no difference."

The gun muzzle still pointed unswervingly at the captain's chest. The captain suggested, very carefully, "If you'll wake up Goth, or give me the antidote—then—"

"No. You don't understand," Yango told him. "We are all going to die unless, within the next fifteen or twenty minutes, you can think of a way to get us out of it in spite of anything I may do to stop you."

He nodded at the screens. "Now *I* have no choice left! I found they have complete control of me. I can do only what they wish. They have tried to control you, but something prevents it. That makes no difference either. There is an object on this ship they fear and must destroy. I do not know what the nature of this object is, but it seems you know about it. The Worms are under a compulsion which prohibits them from harming it by their own actions. It is impossible for them to come closer to the ship than they are now."

"So they have selected a new destination for us—that star you see almost dead ahead! The blue giant. You are to put the ship on full drive and turn towards it. They want the situation here to remain exactly as it is in all other respects until the ship and everything it contains plunges into the star and is annihilated. They believe that some witch stratagem may be employed to evade them if they relax their present control over

us even for an instant. If you refuse to follow my orders, I am
to kill you and guide the ship to the star in your stead." Yango's
face twisted in a slow, agonized grimace. "And I will do it! I
have no more wish to die in that manner than you have,
Captain Pausert. But I *cannot* disobey the Worms—and die in
that star we shall unless, between this moment and the instant
before we arrive there, you have found a way of escape! *There
may be such a way!* These beings seem hampered and confused
by the proximity of the object concealed on the ship. I have
the impression it blinds them mentally. . . . You have only a few
seconds left to make up your mind—"

OHO! exclaimed the vatch. WHAT A FASCINATING PRE-
DICAMENT! BUT TO AVOID A PREMATURE END TO THIS
GAME, LET US SHUFFLE THE PIECES A LITTLE . . . .

Storm-bellowing around the ship and within it. Darkness
closed in as the control room deck heaved up sharply. The
captain felt himself flung forwards against the desk, then back
away from it. Every light in the section had gone out and the
Venture seemed to be tumbling through pitch blackness. Pieces
of equipment or furnishing smashed here and there against the
walls about him. Then the ship appeared to slew around and
ride steady. Light simultaneously returned to the screens—dim,
reddish brown light.

The captain had no time to notice other details just then.
He was scrambling up on hands and knees when something
slammed hard and painfully against his thigh. He heard Laes
Yango curse savagely above him, and ducked forward in time
to let the next boot heel coming down scrape past the back
of his head. He caught the big man's other leg, pulled sharply
up on it. Yango came down on him like a sack of rocks.

They went rolling over the floor, into obstacles and away
from them. The captain hit every section of Yango in reach
from moment to moment, suspected rapidly he was not getting the best of this. Then he had one of Yango's arms twisted

under him. Yango's other hand came up promptly and closed on his throat.

It was a large muscular hand. It seemed to tighten as inexorably as a motor-drive wrench. The captain, head swimming, let go the pirate's other arm, heaved himself sideways on the floor, knocked his wrist against something solidly metallic, picked it up and struck where Yango's head should be.

The head was there. Yango grunted and the iron grip on the captain's throat went slack. He struggled out from under the heavy body, came swaying to his feet in the semi-dark room, eyes shifting to the screens. No Nuri globes in sight, anyway! Otherwise the view out there was not particularly inviting. But that could wait.

"Goth!" he called hoarsely, which sent assorted pains stabbing through his mauled throat Then he remembered that Goth couldn't hear him.

He found her lying beside the couch which had skidded halfway to the end of the room and turned over. He righted it, pushed it back against the wall. Goth made small muttering noises as he picked her up carefully and placed her back on the couch; but they were noises of sleepy irritability, not of pain. She didn't seem to have been damaged in whatever upheaval had hit the *Venture*. The captain discovered Hulik and Vezzarn lying nearby and let them lie for the moment. As he started back to the control desk the room's lights came on. Some self-repair relay had closed.

There still wasn't time to start pondering about exactly what had happened. First things had to come first, and he had a number of almost simultaneous first things on hand. The felled Agandar was breathing; so were the other two. Yango had an ugly swelling bruise on the right side of his forehead just below the hairline, where the captain's lucky swing had landed. He got Yango's wrists secured behind him with the ship's single pair of emergency handcuffs, then went quickly through the man's pockets. In one of them was a wallet-like affair designed to hold five small hypodermics, of which three were left. That almost had to be the antidote. The captain hesitated, but only for a moment. He badly wanted to wake up Goth but he wasn't going to try to do it with something which, considering Yango's purpose on the *Venture*, might have been a killing device.

There was nothing else on Yango's person that seemed of immediate significance. The captain turned his attention to the ship and her surroundings. The *Venture* appeared to have gone on orbital drive automatically as soon as the unexplained tumult which had brought her to this section of space subsided—the reason was that she had found herself then within orbiting range of a planetary body.

At first consideration it was not a prepossessing planet, but that might have been because its light came from a swollen, dull-red glowing coal of a sun which filled most of the starboard screen. The captain turned up screen magnification on the port side for a brief closer look. Through the hazy reddish twilight below, which was this world's midday illumination, he got an impression of a landscape consisting mostly of desert and low, jagged mountain ranges. He went on to test the instruments and drives, finally switched in the communicators. The *Venture* was in working condition; the detectors registered no hostile presence about, and the communicators indicated that nobody around here wanted to talk to them at the moment. So far, not bad.

And now—how had they got here?

Not through Goth this time, he told himself. Not via the Sheewash Drive. During the first moments of that spinning black confusion which plucked the ship out of the cluster of Nuri globes herding them towards fire-death in a terrible star, he'd been sure it was the Drive . . . that a surge of klatha magic had brought Goth awake in this emergency and she'd slipped unnoticed into her cabin.

But even before the ship began to settle out again, he'd known it couldn't have been that. He'd seen Goth on the couch, slumped loosely against Hulik, moments before the blackness rushed and roared in on them. Something quite other than the Drive had picked them up, swung them roughly through space, dropped them at this spot—

That great, booming voice in his mind, the one he'd assumed was a product of dream—imagination—throwing out thought impressions that came to one like the twisting shifts of a gale. . . . In the instant before the *Venture* was swept away from the Worm World trap, he had seemed to hear it again, though he could bring up only a hazy half-memory now of what he'd felt it was saying.

It had to be the vatch.

Not a dream-vatch! A real one. Goth had believed there'd been something watching again lately.

Well, he thought, they'd been lucky, extremely lucky, that something *had* been watching . . . and decided to take a hand for a moment in what was going on. A rough, careless giant hand; but it had brought them here alive.

The captain cleared his throat.

"Thank you," he said aloud, keeping his voice as steady as he could. "Thank you, vatch! Thank you very much!"

It seemed the least he could do. There was an impression of the words rolling away from him as he uttered them, fading quickly into vast distance. He waited a moment, half afraid he'd get a response. But the control room remained quite still.

He broke out the bottle of ship brandy, stuck it in his jacket pocket, and half carried, half dragged Laes Yango back through the ship and into the storage. It took a minute or two to get the big man hauled up to the top of one of the less hard bales of cargo; and Yango was beginning to groan and stir about while the captain wired his ankles together and to the bale. That and the handcuffs should keep him secure, and he'd be out of the way here.

He turned the Agandar on his back, opened the brandy bottle and trickled a little into the side of the man's mouth.

Yango coughed, spluttered, opened bloodshot eyes, and glared silently at the captain.

The captain brought out the little container which held three needles of what should be the antidote to the drug Yango had released in the ventilation system. "Is this the antidote?" he asked.

Yango snarled a few unpleasantries, added, "How could the witch use the drive?"

"I don't know," said the captain. "Be glad she did. Is it the antidote?"

"Yes, it is. Where are we now?"

The captain told him he'd be trying to find out, and locked the storage up again behind him. He left the lighting turned on. Not that it would make Yango much happier. His skull was intact, but his head would be throbbing a while.

The pirate probably had told the truth about the antidote and, in any case, everything would be stalled here until Goth came alert again. The captain made a brief mental apology to Vezzarn—somebody had to be first—and jabbed one of the needles into the little man's arm. Under half-shut lids, Vezzarn's eyes began rolling alarmingly; then his hands fluttered. Suddenly he coughed and sat up on the couch, looking around.

"What's happened?" he whispered in fright when he discovered where he was and saw Goth and Hulik unconscious on the couch beside him.

The captain told him there'd been a problem, caused by Laes Yango, but that the ship seemed to be safe now and that Goth and Miss do Eldel should be all right. "Let's get them awake . . . ."

Hulik do Eldel received the contents of the second needle. She showed none of Vezzarn's reactions. Two or three minutes went by; then she quietly opened her eyes.

Confidently, the captain gave Goth the third shot. While he waited for it to take effect, he began filling in the other two sketchily but almost truthfully on recent events. They were still potential trouble makers, and they might as well realize at once that this was a serious situation, in which it would be healthy for all involved to cooperate. The role played by the item in the strongbox naturally was not mentioned in his account. Neither did he refer to entities termed vatches, or attempt to explain exactly how they had arrived where they were. If Hulik and Vezzarn wanted to do some private speculating about mystery drives which might be less than reliable, he didn't care.

He failed to note that the eyes of his two listeners grew very round before he'd much more than gotten started on his story. Neither of them said a word. And the captain's attention was mainly on Goth. Like Hulik, she was showing no immediate response to the drug . . . .

Then a full six minutes had passed, and Goth still wasn't awake!

There seemed to be no cause for actual alarm. Goth's breathing and pulse were normal, and when he shook her by the shoulder he got small, sleepy growls in response. But she simply wouldn't wake up. From what Yango had said, the drug would wear off by itself in something like another eight or nine hours. However, the captain didn't like the looks of the neighborhood revealed in the viewscreens too well; and his companions evidently liked it less. Loitering around here did not seem a good idea—and setting off blindly through an unknown section of space to get themselves oriented, without having Goth and the Drive in reserve, might be no better.

He switched on the intercom to the storage, stepped up the reception amplification, and said, "Mr. Yango?"

There was a brief, odd, unpleasant sound. Then the pirate's voice replied, clearly and rather hurriedly, "Yes? I hear you. Go ahead . . . ."

"I've used the antidote," the captain told him. "Miss do Eldel and Vezzarn have come awake. Dani hasn't."

"That doesn't surprise me," Yango said, after a moment.

"Why not?" asked the captain.

"I had a particular concern about your niece, sir. As you know." Laes Yango, after his lapse from character, had gone back to being polite. "When she became unconscious with the rest of you, I drugged her again with a different preparation. I was making sure that any unusual resistance she might show would not bring her back to her senses before I intended her to regain them."

"Then there's an antidote to that around?"

"I have one. It isn't easy to find."

"What do you want?" the captain asked.

"Perhaps we can reach an agreement, sir. I am not very comfortable here."

"Perhaps we can," the captain said.

He flicked off the intercom. The other two were watching him.

"He probably does have it," he remarked. "I searched him but I'm not in your line of business. He could have it hidden somewhere. The logical thing would be to haul him up here and search him again."

"It looks to me," said Vezzarn thoughtfully, "that that's what he wants, skipper."

"Uh-huh."

Hulik said, "Just before that man spoke, I heard a noise."

"So did I," said the captain. "What did you make of it?"

"I'm not certain."

"Neither am I." It might, thought the captain, have been the short, angry half-snarl, half-whine of some large animal-shape, startled when his voice had sounded suddenly in the storage.... A snarly sort of thing, Goth had said. But the Sheem robot's locked case stood inside the locked door of that almost impregnable vault—

Hulik do Eldel's frightened eyes told him she was turning over the same kind of thoughts. "We can get a look down into the storage from here," he said.

There was a screen at the end of the instrument console,

used to check loading and unloading operations on the ship from the control room. Its pick-up area was the ceiling of the storage compartment. The captain hurriedly switched it on. "We're wondering whether Yango's robot is in the storage," he told Vezzarn.

Vezzarn shook his head. "It can't be there, skipper! There's no way Yango could have got into the vault without your keys. I guarantee that!"

And there was no way Yango should have been able to get out of his handcuffs, the captain thought. He'd checked the vault before he left the storage. It was still securely locked then and the keys to it were here, in a locked desk drawer.

"We'll see," he said.

The screen lit up—for a second or two. Then it was dark again. The screen was still on. The light in the storage compartment had been cut off.

But they'd seen the robot for the moments it was visible. The great dark spider shape crouched near the storage entry. Its unfettered master stood a dozen feet from it. Yango had looked up quickly as the screen view appeared, startled comprehension in his face, before his hand darted to the lighting switches beside the entry door. Cargo cases throughout the compartment had been shifted and tumbled about as though the bulky robot had forced a passage for itself through them . . . .

That wasn't the worst of it.

"You saw what happened to the side of the vault?" the captain asked unsteadily.

They'd seen it. "Burned out!" Vezzarn said, white-faced. "High intensity—a combat beam! It'd take that. It's an old war robot he's got with him, skipper. You can't stop a thing like that. . . . What do we do now?" The last was a frightened squeal.

Laes Yango suggested, via intercom from the storage, that surrender was the logical move.

"Perhaps you don't fully understand the nature of my pet," he told the captain. "It's been in my possession for fifteen years. It killed over eighty of my men while we were taking the ship it guarded, and would have killed me if I had not cut one of the devices that controlled it from the hand of the lordling whose property it had been. It knew then who its new master was. It's a killing machine, sir! It was made to be one. The Sheem Assassin. Your hand weapons can't harm it. And it has long since learned to obey my voice as well as its guiding instruments . . . ."

The captain didn't reply. The last of the war robots were supposed to have been destroyed centuries before, and the deadly art of their construction lost. But Vezzarn had been right. The thing that beamed its way out of the vault must be such a machine. None of them doubted what Yango was telling them.

They had some time left. No more time than the Agandar could help—and the robot undoubtedly was burning out the storage door while he'd been speaking to them. The door was massive but not designed to stand up under the kind of assault that had ruptured the vault from within. The two would be out of the storage quickly enough.

But they couldn't reach the control section immediately then. The ship's full emergency circuits had flashed into action seconds after Vezzarn's frantic question—layers of overlapping battle-steel slid into position, sealing the Venture's interior into ten air-tight compartments. At least four of those multiple layers of the toughest workable material known lay between the control room and the storage along any approach Yango might choose to take. They probably wouldn't stop a war robot indefinitely; but neither would they melt at the first lick of high intensity energy beams. And the captain had opened the intercom system all over the ship. That should give them some audible warning of the degree of progress the robot was making.

Otherwise there seemed to be little he could do. The activating device he'd taken from Yango when the robot was stored in the vault was not where he'd locked it away. So the Agandar had discovered it on looking around after he'd knocked the four of them out. When the captain searched him, it wasn't on his person. But he hadn't needed it. There was a ring on his forefinger he'd been able to reach in spite of the handcuffs; and the ring was another control instrument. The Assassin had come awake in the vault and done the rest, including burning off its master's bonds.

It made no difference now where the other device was stored away on the ship. They couldn't leave the section to look for it without opening the emergency walls.

And if they had it, the captain thought, it wasn't likely they'd be able to wrest control of the robot away from the Agandar. Yango, at any rate, did not appear to be worrying about the possibility . . . .

SMALL PERSON, announced the vatch, THIS IS THE TEST—THE SITUATION THAT WILL DETERMINE YOUR QUALITY! THERE IS A WAY TO SURVIVE. IF YOU DO NOT FIND IT, MY INTEREST AND YOUR DREAM EXISTENCE END TOGETHER—

The captain looked quickly over at Vezzarn and Hulik. But their faces showed they'd heard nothing of what that great, ghostly wind-voice had seemed to be saying. Of course—it was meant for him.

He'd switched off the intercom connection with Yango moments before. "Any ideas?" he asked now.

"Skipper," Vezzarn told him, jaw quivering, "I think we'd better surrender—while he'll still let us!"

Hulik was shaking her head. "That man is the Agandar!" she said. "If we do surrender, we don't live long. Except for Dani. He'll squeeze from us whatever we can tell him, and stop when he has nothing left to work on."

"We'd have a chance!" Vezzarn argued shakily. "A chance.

What else can we do? We can't stop a war robot—and there's nowhere to run from it!"

Hulik said to the captain, "I was told you might be a Karres witch. Are you?"

"No," said the captain.

"I thought not. But that child is?"

"Yes."

"And she's asleep and we can't wake her up!" Hulik shrugged resignedly. Her face was strained and white. "It would take something like magic to save us now, I think!"

The captain grunted, reached over the desk and eased in the atmosphere drive. "Perhaps not," he said. "We may have to abandon ship. I'm going down."

The *Venture* went sliding out of orbit, turning towards the reddish dusk of the silent planet.

Vezzarn had all the veteran spacer's ingrained horror of exchanging the life-giving enclosure of his ship for anything but the equally familiar security of a civilized port or a spacesuit. He began arguing again, torn between terrors; and there was no time to argue. The captain took out his gun, placed it on the desk beside him.

"Vezzarn!" he said; and Vezzarn subsided. "If you want to surrender," the captain told him, "you'll get the chance. We'll lock you in one of those cabins over there and leave you for Yango and the robot to find."

"Well—" Vezzarn began unhappily.

"If you don't want that," the captain continued, "start following orders."

"I'll follow orders, skipper," Vezzarn decided with hardly a pause.

"Then remember one thing . . ." The captain tapped the gun casually. "If Yango starts talking to us again, I'm the only one who answers!"

"Right, Sir!" Vezzarn said, eying the gun.

"Good. Get busy on the surface analyzers and see if you can find out anything worth knowing about this place. Miss do Eldel, you've got good hearing, I think—"

"Excellent hearing, Captain!" Hulik assured him.

"The intercom is yours. Make sure reception amplification stays at peak. Compartment E is the storage. Anything you hear from there is good news. D is bad news—they'll be through one emergency wall and on their way here. Then we'll know we have to get out and how much time we have to do it. G is drive section of the engine room. Don't know why Yango should want to go down there, but he could. The other compartments don't count at the moment. You have that?"

Hulik acknowledged she did. The captain returned his attention to the *Venture* and the world she was approaching. Vezzarn hadn't let out any immediate howls at the analyzers, so at least they weren't dropping into the pit of cold poison the surface might have been from its appearance. The lifeboat blister was in the storage compartment; so was the ship's single work spacesuit. Not a chance to get to either of those . . . The planetary atmosphere below appeared almost cloudless. Red half-light, black shadows along the ranges, lengthening as the meridian moved away behind them . . . .

How far could he trust the vatch? Not at all, he thought. He should act as if he'd heard none of that spooky background commentary. But the vatch, capricious, unpredictable, immensely powerful—not sane by this universe's standards—would remain a potential factor here. Which might aid or destroy them.

Let nothing surprise you, he warned himself. The immediate range of choice was very narrow. If the compartment walls didn't hold, they had to leave the ship. If the walls held, they'd remain here, at emergency readiness, until Goth awoke. But the Agandar's frustrated fury would matter no more than his monster then—unless Yango's attention turned on the strongbox in the vault. No telling what might happen . . . but that was borrowing trouble! Another factor, in any case, was that while Goth remained unconscious, Yango would want her to stay alive. All the pirate's hopes were based on that now. It should limit his actions to some extent . . . .

"Skipper?" Vezzarn muttered, hunched over the analyzers.
"Yes?"

Vezzarn looked up, chewing his lip. "Looks like we *could* live down there a while," he announced grudgingly. "But these things don't tell you everything—"

"No." The *Venture* wasn't equipped with an exploration ship's minutely detailing analysis instruments. Nevertheless, there'd been a sudden note of hope in Vezzarn's voice. "You're sure you're coming along if we have to get out?" the captain asked.

The spacer gave him a wry, half-ashamed grin. "You can count on me, sir! Panicked a moment, I guess."

The captain slid open a desk drawer. "Here's your gun then," he said. "Yours, too, Miss do Eldel. Yango collected them and I took them back from him."

They almost pounced on the weapons. Hulik broke her gun open, gave a sharp exclamation of dismay.

"Zero charge! That devil cleaned them out!"

The captain was taking a box from the drawer. "So he did," he said. "But he didn't find my spare pellets. Standard Empire military charge—hope you can use them!"

They could, and promptly replenished their guns. The captain looked at the console chronometer. Just over nine minutes since he'd broken intercom contact with Yango. The lack of any indication of what the pirate was doing hadn't helped anybody's nerves here; but at least he hadn't got out of the storage compartment yet. The captain set Vezzarn to detaching and gathering up various articles—keys and firing switches to the nova gun turrets, the main control release to the lifeboat blister, the keys to the main and orbital drives . . . .

There were mountains just below now, and the shallow bowls of plains. The dull red furnace glare of the giant sun bathed the world in tinted twilight. The *Venture* continued to spiral down towards a maze of narrow valleys and gorges winding back into the mountains . . . .

They flinched together as the intercom hurled the sounds of a hard metallic crashing into the control room. It was repeated a few seconds later.

"Compartment D!" whispered Hulik, nodding at the intercom panel. "They're through the first wall—"

A dim, heavy snarling came from the intercom, then a blurred impression of Yango's voice. Both faded again.

"Shut them off," the captain said quietly. "We're through listening." Eleven and a half minutes . . . and it might have been a minute or so before Yango set the Assassin to work on the wall.

Hulik switched off the intercom system, said, a little breathlessly, "If Yango, realizes we've landed . . . ."

"I'm going to try to keep him from realizing it," the captain told her. The ship was racing down smoothly towards the mouth of a steep-walled valley he'd selected as the most promising landing point barely a minute before.

"But if he does," Hulik said, "and orders the robot to beam a hole directly through the side of the ship—how long would it be before they could get outside that way?"

Vezzarn interjected, without looking up from his work, "About an hour. Don't worry about that, Miss do Eldel! He won't try the cargo lock or blister either. He knows ships and knows they're as tough as the rest of it and can't be opened except from the desk. He'll keep coming to the control room— and he'll be here fast enough!"

"We've got up to thirty minutes," the captain said. "And we can be out in three if we don't waste time! You're finished, Vezzarn?"

"Yes, sir."

"Wrap it up—don't bother to be neat! Any kind of package I can shove into my pocket—"

The red sun vanished abruptly as the *Venture* settled into the valley. On their right was a great sloping cliff-face, ragged with crumbling rock, following the turn of the valley into the mountains. The captain brought the ship down on her under-drives, landed without a jar on a reasonably level piece of ground, as near the cliffs as he'd been able to get. Beside him, Hulik gave a small gasp as the control section lock opened with two hard metallic clicks.

"Out as fast as you can get out!" The captain stood up, twisted the last set of drive keys from their sockets, dropped them into his jacket pocket, jammed the package Vezzarn was holding out to him in on top of them, zipped the pocket shut, and started over to the couch to pick up Goth. "*Move!*"

Faces looked rather pale all around, including, he suspected, his own. But everybody was moving . . . .

Chapter NINE

THE CAPTAIN USED the ground-level mechanism to close the lock behind them, sealed the mechanism, and added the key to the seal to the assortment of minor gadgetry in his jacket pocket. Then, while Hulik stood looking about the valley, her gun in her hand, he got Goth up on his back and Vezzarn deftly roped her into position there, legs fastened about the captain's waist, arms around his neck. It wasn't too awkward an arrangement and, in any case, the best arrangement they could make. Goth wasn't limp, seemed at moments more than half awake; there were numerous drowsy grumblings, and before Vezzarn had finished she was definitely hanging on of her own.

"Been thinking, skipper," Vezzarn said quietly, fingers flying, testing slack, tightening knots. "He ought to be able to spot us in the screens—"

"Uh-huh. Off and on. But I doubt he'll waste time with that."

"Eh? Yes, a killer robot'd be a good tracking machine, wouldn't it?" Vezzarn said glumly. "You want to pull Yango away from the ship, then angle back to it?"

"That's the idea."

"Desperate business!" muttered Vezzarn. "But I guess it's a desperate spot. And he wants Dani—never'd have figured her for one of the Wisdoms! . . . There! Finished, sir! She'll be all right now—"

As he stepped back, Hulik said in a low, startled voice, "Captain!" They turned towards her quickly and edgily. She was staring up the valley between the crowding mountain slopes.

"I thought I saw something move," she said. "I'm not sure . . . ."

"Animal?" asked Vezzarn.

"No . . . Bigger. Farther away . . . A shadow. A puff of dust. If there were a wind—" She shook her head.

The air was still. No large shadows moved anywhere they looked. This land was less barren than it had appeared from even a few miles up. The dry, sandy soil was cluttered with rock debris; and from among the rocks sprouted growth—spiky, thorny, feathery stuff, clustering into thickets here and there, never rising to more than fifteen or twenty feet. "Let's go!" said the captain. "There probably are animals around. We'll keep our eyes open—"

As they headed towards the ragged cliffs to the right of the ship, the valley's animal life promptly began to give indications of its presence. What type of life it might be wasn't easy to determine. Small things skittered out of their path with shadowy quickness. Then, from a thicket they were passing, there burst a sound like the hissing of ten thousand serpents, so immediately menacing that they spun together to face it, guns leveled. The hissing didn't abate but drew back through the thicket, away from them, and on to the left. The uncanny thing was that though their ears told them the sound was receding across open ground, towards the center of the valley, they could not see a trace of the creature producing it.

They hurried on, rather shaken by the encounter. Though

it might have been, the captain thought, nothing more ominous than the equivalent of a great swarm of harmless insects. A minute or two later Hulik said sharply, "Something's watching us!"

They could see only the eyes. Two brightly luminous yellow eyes peering across the top of a boulder at them. The boulder wasn't too large; the creature hidden back of it couldn't be more than about half human size. It made a high giggling noise behind them after they were past. Other sets of the same sort of eyes began peering at them from around or above other boulders. They seemed to be moving through quite a community of these creatures. But they did nothing but stare at the intruders as they went by, then giggle thinly among themselves.

The ground grew steeper rapidly. Goth's weight wasn't significant; the captain had carried knapsacks a good deal heavier in mountaineering sport and during his period of military training. His lungs began to labor a little; then he had his second wind and knew he was good for a long haul at this clip before he'd begin to tire. Vezzarn and Hulik were keeping up with no apparent effort. Hulik, for all her slender elegance, moved with an easy sureness which indicated she was remarkably quick and strong, and Vezzarn scrambled along with them like an agile, tough little monkey.

The ground leveled out. They waded through low tangled growth which caught at their ankles, abruptly found a steep ravine before them, running parallel to the cliffs. Beyond it was a higher rocky rise.

"Have to find a place to cross!" panted the captain.

Vezzarn looked back at the long shadow-shape of the *Venture* in the valley below and behind them. "If we climb down there, sir," he argued, "we can't see them when they come out! We won't have any warning."

"They won't be out for a while," Hulik told him. "We've been walking only ten minutes so far."

They turned left along the edge of the ravine. Perhaps half

a mile ahead was a great rent in the side of the mountain, glowing with the dim light of the red sun. Cross a few more such rises, the captain thought, then turn right to a point from where they could still see Yango, when he came tracking them with the robot. As soon as their pursuers had followed the trail down into this maze of ravines, they'd have their long headstart back to the ship . . . .

They came to a place where they could get down into the ravine, hanging on to hard, springy ropes of a thick vine-like growth for support. They scrambled along its floor for a couple of hundred yards before they reached a point where the walls were less steep and they could climb out on the other side. Level ground again, overlooking the valley; they began glancing back frequently at the dim outline of the ship. Something followed them for a stretch, uttering short, deep hoots, but kept out of sight among the rocks. Then another ravine cutting across their path. As they paused at its edge, glancing up and down for a point of descent, Vezzarn exclaimed suddenly, "He's opened the lock!"

They looked back. A small sharp circle of light had appeared near the *Venture's* bow. They hurried on. The light glowed steadily in the hazy dimness of the valley for about two minutes. Then it vanished. "Could he have found a way to seal the lock against us?" Hulik's tone was frightened.

"No. Not from outside," the captain said. "I have the only key that will do that. I think he's cut off the light in the control section before leaving—doesn't want to attract too much attention to the ship . . . ."

Hulik was staring down at the *Venture*. "I think I see something there!"

The others saw it, too, then. A small, pale green spark on the ground this side of the ship. It appeared to be moving along the route they had taken.

"That could be that robot!" Vezzarn said, awe in his voice.

It might have been. Or some searchlight Yango was

carrying. But there wasn't much doubt now that they were being tracked.

As they turned away, Hulik exclaimed, "What was *that?*"

They listened. It had been a sound, a distant heavy sound such as might have been uttered, miles up the valley, by some great, deep-voiced bell or gong. It seemed a very strange thing to hear in a place like this. It died slowly. Then, after moments, from a point still farther off in the mountains, came a faint echo of the same sound. And once more, still more remote, barely audible.

They were down in the next ravine minutes later, and had worked almost up to the point where spilling dim sunlight flushed a wide cleft in the mountain's flank before they again reached a level from where they could look into the valley. Nothing showed in the sections they could see; and they began doubling back in the shadow of the cliffs to reach a point to the right of their line of approach. Lungs and legs were tiring now, but they moved hurriedly because it seemed possible Yango and his killing machine already had entered the area of broken sloping ground between them and the valley and were coming along their trail through one of the lower ravines.

And then, lifting over a rocky ridge much closer than the ones they'd been watching for it, was a pale green shimmer of light and the spider robot came striding into view. The captain saw it first, stopped the others with a low, sharp word. They stood frozen, staring at it. It was a considerable distance below them but in all not more than three hundred yards away.

It had come to a halt now, too, half turned in their direction; and for a moment they couldn't know whether it had discovered them or not. The green light came from the sides of the heavy segmented body, so that it stood in its own glow. Yango became visible behind it suddenly, came up close to its side. The robot crouched, remained in that position a few seconds, then swung about and went striding along the ridge, the great jointed legs carrying it quickly, smoothly, and with an air of almost dainty lightness in spite of its heavy build. Just before it vanished beyond an outcropping of rock, they could see the man was riding it.

It explained how the pair had followed their trail so swiftly. But now—

"Skipper," Vezzarn's voice said hoarsely from fifteen feet away, "don't move, sir! I'm pointing my gun at you, and if you move, I'll fire. You stand still, too, for a moment, Miss do Eldel. I'm doing this for both of us but don't interfere.

"Skipper, I don't want to do this. But the Agandar is after you and the little Wisdom. He doesn't care about Miss do Eldel or myself. . . . Miss do Eldel, I'm throwing you my knife. Cut the ropes from Dani and put her down. Then tie the skipper's hands behind him. Skipper, if you make a wrong move or don't let her tie your hands, I'll blast you on the spot. I swear it!"

"What good will that do?" Hulik's voice asked tightly from behind the captain.

"You saw them!" There was a brief clatter on the rocky ground to the right as Vezzarn's knife landed there. "You saw how fast it is. The thing's tracking us so it's moving off again. But it will reach this spot in maybe five, six minutes. And the Agandar will see the skipper and Dani lying here. We'll be gone and he won't bother with us. Why should he? All he'll want is to get away with the two of them again—"

The captain spun suddenly, crouching down and jerking the gun from his pocket. He didn't really expect to gain anything from it except to hear the snarl of Vezzarn's blaster—and perhaps that of Hulik's. Instead there came a great strange cry from the air above them, and a whipping swirl of wind. They saw a descending shadow, an odd round horned head on a long neck reaching out behind Vezzarn. The three guns went off together, and the flying creature veered up and away in a sweep that carried it almost beyond sight in an instant. Its wild voice drifted back briefly as it sped on into the hazy upper reaches of the valley—and Vezzarn, turning quickly again, saw two guns pointed at him, let out a strangled squawk, bounded sideways and scrambled and slid away down the rocky slope. He ducked out of view behind a thicket. In a moment, they heard his retreat continue rapidly, farther on from there.

"Well," Hulik said, lowering her gun, "Old Horny really broke up the mutiny! What do we do now? Do you have any ideas— except to run on until the Spider comes walking up behind us?" She nodded down the slope. "Unless, of course, Vezzarn's done us a favor and it turns off after him here. Happy thought!"

The captain shook his head. "It won't," he said, rather breathlessly. "Yango talks to it. He'll know the trail has split and can work out who went where . . . ." Goth was squirming around uncomfortably on his back; he got her adjusted a little until she clung firmly to him again, with a grip as instinctive as a sleeping young monkey's. If Yango had heard the commotion and turned his Sheem Assassin up towards it, they might have less than five minutes before the robot overtook them. But no one had screamed, and blasters weren't audible at any great distance. It should have sounded like simply another manifestation of local life—one to be avoided rather than investigated.

In which case Vezzarn, in his terror, had overrated the Spider's pace. It should be close to fifteen minutes, rather than five or six, before it approached again, striding with mechanical smoothness along their trail. Even so, it was reducing the distance between them much too quickly to make it possible to get back to the *Venture* before it caught up.

"There is something else we can do," he said. "And I guess we'll have to try it now. I was hoping we wouldn't. It'll be a risky thing."

"What isn't, here?" Hulik said reasonably. "And anything's better than running and looking back to see if that Sheem horror is about to tap us on the shoulder!"

"Let's move on while I tell you, then," the captain said.

"Vezzarn's right, of course, about Yango not caring too much about you two. He wants Dani. And he wants what I've got here." He tapped the pocket containing the package of small but indispensable items they'd removed from the *Venture* just before leaving. "He can't use the ship without it. And he'll figure I'm hanging on to that. And to Dani."

"Right," Hulik nodded. The captain pulled the package from his pocket.

"So if the trail splits again here," he said, "I'm the one the Spider will follow."

Hulik looked down at the package. "And what will I do?"

"You'll get down to the ship with this. There are a few separate pieces I'll give you—you'll need them all. Get them fitted back in and get the ship aloft. We'll have Yango pinned then. With the nova guns—"

Something occurred to him. "Uh, you *can* handle spaceguns, can't you?"

"Unfortunately," Hulik said, "I can *not* handle spaceguns. Neither can I get a ship like that aloft, much less maneuver it in atmosphere. I doubt I could even fit all those little pieces you're offering me back in where they belong."

The captain was silent.

"Too bad Vezzarn panicked," she told him. "He probably could do all that. But, of course, the Spider would kill you, and Yango would have Dani, anyway, before Vezzarn even reached the ship."

"No, not necessarily," the captain said. "I've got something in mind there, too. . . . Miss do Eldel, you could at least get into the ship and close it up until—"

"Until Yango and the robot come back and burn out the lock? No, thanks! And it isn't just those two. You know something else has followed us up here, don't you?"

The captain grunted. He'd known the slopes had remained unquiet throughout, and in a very odd way. After the first few encounters, nothing much seemed astir immediately around them. But, beginning perhaps a hundred yards off—above, below, on both sides—there'd been, as they climbed higher and threaded their way along the ravines, almost constant indications of covert activity. A suggestion of muted animal voices, the brief clattering of a dislodged stone, momentary shadowy motion. Not knowing whether his companions were aware of it or not, he'd kept quiet. A Sheem Spider seemed enough for anyone to be worrying about . . . .

"Little noises?" he asked. "Things in the thickets?"

"Little noises," Hulik nodded. "Things in the thickets. This and that. We're being followed and watched. So is Yango. He's had more than one reason, I think, for staying on the back of his Assassin most of the time."

"Whatever those creatures are, they've kept their distance," the captain said. "They don't seem to have been bothering Yango either."

"Almost anything *would* keep its distance from the Spider!" Hulik remarked. "And perhaps it's your little witch who's been holding them away from us. I wouldn't know. But I'm sticking close to you two while I can, that's all. . . . So what do you have in mind to do about Yango?"

The captain chewed his lip. "If it doesn't work," he said, "the Spider will have us."

"I should think so," Hulik agreed.

He glanced at her, said, "Let's turn back then. We're going in the wrong direction for that."

"Back along our trail?" Hulik said as they swung around.

"A couple of hundred yards. I noticed a place that looked about right. Just before we saw the robot." He indicated the cliffs looming over them. "It'll take pretty steep climbing, I'm afraid!"

"Up there? You're not counting on outclimbing the Spider, are you?"

"No. It should be able to go anywhere we can, faster."

"But you've thought of a way to stop it."

"Not directly", said the captain. "But we might make Yango stop it—or stop Yango."

There'd been a time when something had nested or laired on the big rock ledge jutting out from the cliff face and half overhung by it. Its cupped surface still held a litter of withered vegetation and splintered old bones, along with the musty smell of dried animal droppings. A narrow shelf zigzagging away to the right along the cliff might have been the occupant's means of access.

Winded and shaking, stretched out full length in the ancient filth, the captain hoped so. Almost any way down from here—except dangling from the jaws or a taloned leg of the Sheem Spider—must be better than the way they had come up. Peering over one corner of the ledge, he stared back along that route. About a hundred and twenty yards of ascent. From here it looked almost straight down and he wondered briefly again how they'd made it. In a kind of panicky rush, he decided, scrabbling for handholds and toeholds, steadying each other for an instant now and then when a solid-looking point crumbled and powdered as human weight came on it, not daring to hesitate or stop to think—to think, in particular, of the distance growing between them and the foot of the cliff below. And then he'd given the do Eldel's smallish, firm rear a final desperate boost, come scrambling up over the corner of the ledge behind her, and collapsed on the mess half filling the wide, shallow, wonderfully horizontal rock cup.

They unroped Goth from him then, and laid her down against the cliff under the sloping roof of the ledge. She scowled and murmured something, then abruptly turned over on her side, drew her knees up to her chin, and was gone and lost again, child face smoothing into placidity, in the dream worlds of Yango's special drug. He and Hulik stretched out face down, one at each corner of the big stone lip, holding their guns, peering from behind a screen of the former occupant's litter at the shadowy thickets and boulders below.

They had come past there with Vezzarn, not many minutes before, along a shoulder of rock, scanning the lower slopes for any signs of pursuit. And there, in not many more minutes, Yango and the Spider must also appear. The robot might discover the trail was doubling back at that point and swerve with its rider directly towards the cliff. Or stride on and return. In either case the Agandar soon would know his quarry had gone up the rock.

If he rode the robot up after them, they would have him. That was the plan. They'd let him get good and high. Their guns couldn't harm the Sheem machine, but at four yards' range they would tear the Agandar's head from his shoulders if he didn't make the right moves. Nothing more than the guns would be showing. The war robot's beam would have only the ponderous ledge overhanging it and its master for a target.

With a gun staring at him from either corner of the ledge, caught above a hundred yard drop, Yango wasn't likely to argue. He'd toss up his control devices. They'd let the Spider take him back to the foot of the cliff then before they gave the gadgets the twist that deactivated and collapsed it . . . .

"And if," Hulik had asked, "he does *not* come riding up on the thing? He might get ideas about this ledge and wait below while it climbs up without him to see if we're hiding here or have gone on."

"Then we shoot Yango."

"That part will be a pleasure," the do Eldel remarked. "But what will the robot do then?"

They didn't know that, but there was some reason to think the Sheem Spider would be no menace to them afterwards. It must have instructions not to kill in this situation—at least not to kill indiscriminately—until the Agandar had Goth safe. The instructions might hold it in check when they shot down Yango. Or they might not.

✧ ✧ ✧

Something like a short, hard cannon-crack tore the air high above the valley, startled them both into lifting their heads. They looked at each other.

"Thunder," the captain said quietly. "I've been hearing some off and on. The sound came again as he spoke, more distantly and from another angle, far off in the mountains."

"No," Hulik said, "it's them. They're looking for us."

He glanced at her uneasily. She nodded towards the valley. "It goes with the great, deep sound we heard down there— and other things. They've been moving around us. Circling. They're looking for us and they're coming closer."

"Who's looking for us?" asked the captain.

"The owners of this world. We've disturbed them and they don't like visitors. The things that've been following us are their spies. Old Horny was a spy—he flew off to tell about us. A while ago a shadow was moving along the other side of the valley. I thought they'd discovered us then but it went away again. It's because we're so small, I think. They don't know what they're looking for, and so far they haven't been able to find us. But they're getting close."

Her voice was low and even, her face quite calm. "We may stop Yango here, but I don't think we'll be able to get away from this world again. It's too late for that! So it doesn't really matter so much about the Spider." She nodded towards the captain's right. "It's coming now, Captain!"

He dropped his head back behind the tangle of dusty, withered stuff he'd arranged before him, watching the thickets below on the right through it. For a moment, half screened by the growth, a pale green glimmer moved among the rocks, then disappeared again. Still perhaps two hundred yards away! He glanced briefly back at Hulik. She'd flattened down, too, gun hand next to her chin, head lifted just enough to let her peer out from the left side of the ledge. Whatever fearful and fantastic thoughts she'd developed about this red-shadowed world, she evidently didn't intend to let them interfere with concluding their business with the Agandar. If anything, her notions seemed to be steadying her as far as the Sheem Assassin was concerned—as if that were now an insignificant terror. She might, he thought uncomfortably, be not too far from a state of lunatic indifference to what happened next.

No time to worry about it now. The green glow reappeared from around an outcropping; and with a smooth shifting of great jointed legs, the Spider moved into view, Yango riding it, gripping the narrow connecting section of the segmented body between his knees. The Spider's head swung from side to side in a steady searching motion which seemed to keep time with the flowing walk; the paired jaws opened and closed. Seen at this small distance, it was difficult to think of it as a machine and not the awesome hunting animal which had been its model. But the machine was more deadly than the animal could ever have been . . . .

There was the faintest of rustling noises to the captain's left. He turned his head, very cautiously because the Sheem Spider and its rider were moving across the rock shoulder directly in front of them now, saw with a start of dismay that Hulik had lifted her gun, was easing it forward through the concealing pile of litter before her, head tilted as she sighted along it. If she triggered the blaster now—

But she didn't. Whether she decided it was too long a shot in this dim air or remembered in time that only if they failed to trap Yango and his machine on the cliff were they to try to finish off the man, the captain couldn't guess. But the robot's long, gliding stride carried it on beyond a dense thicket at the left of the ledge, and it and the Agandar were out of sight again. Hulik slowly drew back her gun, remained motionless, peering down.

There was silence for perhaps a minute. Not complete silence. The captain grew aware of whisperings of sound, shadow motion, stealthy stirrings, back along the stretch the Agandar had come. Yango had brought an escort up from the valley with him, as they had. . . . Then, off on the left, some distance away, he heard the heavy singsong snarl of the Sheem Spider.

Hulik twisted her head towards him, lips silently shaping the word "Vezzarn." He nodded. The pursuit seemed checked for the moment at the point where Vezzarn's trail had turned away from theirs.

The snarls subsided. Silence again . . . and after some seconds he knew Yango was on his way back, because the minor rustlings below ended. The unseen escort was falling back as the robot approached. Perhaps another minute passed. He glanced over at Hulik, saw a new tension in her. But there was nothing visible as yet from his side of the ledge. The massively curved jut of the rock cut off part of his view.

Then, over a hundred yards down, on the sloping ground at the foot of the cliff, the Sheem Spider came partly out from under the ledge. Two of the thick, bristling legs appeared first, followed by the head and a forward section of the body. It moved with stealthy deliberation, stopped again and stood dead still, head turned up, the double jaws continuing a slow chewing motion. He could make out the line of small, bright-yellow eyes across the upper part of the big head, but there was not enough of the thing in sight to tell him whether Yango was still on its back. Hulik knew, of course. The robot must have come gliding quietly through the thickets on their left and emerged almost directly below her.

Shifting very cautiously—the thing seemed to be staring straight up at him—the captain turned his head behind his flimsy barricade, looked over at Hulik. She had her gun ready again, was sighting down along it, unmoving. The gun wasn't aimed at the Spider; the angle wasn't steep enough for that. So Yango—

The captain's eyes searched the part of the thickets he could see behind the robot. Something moved slightly there, moved again, stopped. A half-crouched figure interested in keeping as much screening vegetation as it could between itself and possible observers from above. The Agandar.

The Spider still hadn't stirred. The captain inched his gun forwards, brought it to bear on the center of the crouching man-shape. Not too good a target in that tangle, if it came to shooting! But perhaps it wouldn't. If the robot's sensor equipment couldn't detect them here, if they made no incautious move, Yango still might decide they weren't in the immediate neighborhood and remount the thing before it began its ascent along their trail . . . .

That thought ended abruptly.

The robot reared, front sets of legs spread, swung in towards the cliff face and, with that, passed again beyond the captain's limited range of vision. He didn't see the clawed leg tips reach up, test the rough rock for holds and settle in; but he could hear them. Then there were momentary glimpses of the thing's shaggy back, as it drew itself off the ground and came clambering up towards the ledge.

Heart thudding, he took up the slack on the trigger, held the gun pointed as steadily as he could at Yango's half hidden shape. When he heard Hulik's blaster, he'd fire, too, at once. But otherwise wait—a few seconds longer; wait, in fact, as long as he possibly could! For Yango might move, present a better target, or he might discover some reason to check the robot's ascent before it reached the ledge. If they fired now and missed—

Sudden rattle and thud of dislodged rock below! The section of the robot's back he could see at the moment jerked sharply. The thing had lost a hold, evidently found another at once for it was steady again—and startlingly close! Already it seemed to have covered more than half the distance to the ledge.

And down in the thickets, apprehensive over the robot's near-slip, Yango was coming to his feet—instantly recognizing his mistake and ducking again as Hulik's blaster spat. The captain shot, too, but at a figure flattened down, twisting sideways through dense cover, then gone. He stopped shooting.

From below the ledge came a noise somewhere between the robot's usual snarl and the hiss of escaping steam. Hulik was still firing, methodically shredding the thicket about the point where the Agandar had last been in view. The captain came up on hands and knees, leaned forward, looked down at the robot.

The thing had slewed halfway around on the cliff, head twisted at a grotesque angle as it stared at the whipping thicket. The hissing rose to giant shrieks. It swung back to its previous position. From between the black jaws protruded a thick gray tube, pointed up at the ledge. The captain threw himself sideways, caught Hulik's ankle, dragged her back through the lair litter to the cliff wall with him, pulled her around beside Goth.

The ledge shuddered in earthquake throes as the Sheem robot's war-beam slammed into it from below. It was thick, solid rock, and many tons of it, but it wasn't battle-steel. It lasted for perhaps two seconds; then most of it separated into four great chunks and dropped. Halfway down, the falling mineral mass scraped the robot from the cliff and took it along. Through the thunderous crash of impact on the slope below the cliff came sharper explosive sounds which might have been force fields collapsing. When the captain and Hulik peered down from what was left of the ledge a moment later, they could make out a few scraps of what looked like shaggy brown fur lying about in the wreckage of rocks. The Spider hadn't lasted either . . . .

The captain sucked in a deep lungful of air, looked at Goth's face. She was smiling a little, might have been peacefully asleep in her own bed. Some drug! "Better move!" he remarked unsteadily. He fished rope from his pocket, shoved his gun back into the pocket. "Think you hit Yango?"

Hulik didn't answer. She was sitting on her heels, face turned towards the dim red sky above the valley, lips parted, eyes remote. As if listening to something. "Hulik!" he said sharply.

The do Eldel blinked, looked at him. "Yango? Yes . . . I got him twice, at least. He's dead, I suppose." Her voice was absent, indifferent.

"Help me get Dani back up! We—"

Thunderclap! Monstrously loud—the captain had the impression it had ripped the air no more than four hundred yards above them. Then a series of the same sounds, still deafening but receding quickly as if spaced along a straight line in the sky towards the mouth of the valley and beyond. There were no accompanying flashes of light. As the racket faded, a secondary commotion was erupting on the slopes about the foot of the cliff—hooting, howling, yapping voices, a flapping of wings, shadowy shapes gliding up into the air. And all that, too, moved rapidly away, subsided again.

"Dear me!" Hulik giggled. "We *really* have them upset now." She reached for the rope in the captain's hand. "Lift the little witch up and I'll get her fastened. It doesn't matter though. We won't make it back to the ship."

But they did make it back to the ship. Afterwards, the captain couldn't remember too much of the hike down along the slope. He remembered that it had seemed endless, that his legs had turned into wobbly rubber from time to time, while Goth's small body seemed leaden on his back. The do Eldel walked and clambered beside or behind him. Now and then she laughed. For a while she'd hummed a strange, wild little tune that made him think of distant drum-dances. Later she was silent. Perhaps he'd told her to shut up. He couldn't remember that.

He remembered fear. Not of things following on the ground or of some flying monster that might come swooping down again. As far as he could tell, they had lost their escort; the gorges, ravines, the thicket-studded slopes, seemed almost swept clean of life. Nothing stirred or called. It was as if instead of drawing attention now, they were being carefully avoided.

The fear had no real form. There were oppressive feelings of hugeness and menace gathering gradually about. There was an occasional suspicion that the red sky had darkened for moments as if shadows too big to be made out as shadows had just passed through it. The staccato thunder, which had no lightning to explain it, reverberated now and then above the mountains; but that disturbance never came nearly as close again as it had done at the cliff. When they reached the edge of the ravine where, on the way up, they'd stopped to listen to something like a series of deep, giant bells, far off in the valley, he thought he heard a dim echoing of the same sound again. No matter, he told himself—the *Venture* still lay undisturbed below and ahead of them in the valley, not many more minutes away . . . .

"They're waiting for us at the ship," Hulik said from behind him. She laughed.

He didn't reply. The do Eldel had been a good companion when it came to facing the Agandar and his killing machine. But this creepy shadow world simply had become too much for her.

Then, on the final stretch down, Hulik faltered at last, started weaving and stumbling. The captain helped her twice to her feet, then clamped an arm around her and plodded on. He began to do some stumbling himself, got the notion that the ground was shifting, lifting and settling underfoot, like the swell of an uneasy sea. When he looked up once more to see how much farther it was, he came to a sudden stop. The bow of the *Venture* loomed above them; the ramp was a dozen steps away. He glanced at the dark open lock above it, steered Hulik to the foot of the ramp, shook her shoulder.

"We're there!" he said loudly as she raised her head and gave him a dazed look. "Back at the ship! Up you go—up the ramp! Wake up!"

"They're here, too," Hulik giggled. "Can't you feel it?" But she did start up the ramp, the captain following close behind in case she fell again.

He felt something, at that. A cold electric tingling seemed to trickle all through his body, as if he'd stepped into the path of a current of energy. And looking up past the ship's bow he'd seen something he was certain hadn't been in view only minutes before—a great dark cloud mass boiling up over the cliffs on the far side of the valley.

So a storm was coming, he told himself.

He hustled Hulik through the lock, slammed it shut behind them before he switched on the control section lights, pulled out a knife on his way over to the couch and cut the ropes which held Goth fastened to him. He slid her down on the couch. When he looked back for Hulik, she had crumpled to the floor in the center of the control room.

The captain let her lie, pulled the package of wrapped gadgetry from his pocket and dumped it on the control desk. He began moving hurriedly about. Getting the *Venture* readied for action again seemed to take a long time, but it might have taken three minutes in fact. The electric tingling was becoming uncomfortably pronounced when he finally settled himself in the control chair. He fed the underdrives a warm-up jolt, held one hand on the thrust regulator as he checked the gun turrets, finally switched on the viewscreens.

A black cloud wall was rising above the cliffs on either side, and the screens showed it also surging up from distant upper stretches of the valley . . . and from the plain beyond the valley mouth behind the ship. A turbulent, awesomely towering bank of darkness encircling this area—yes, past high time to be away from here! The captain started to shove the thrust regulator forwards, then checked the motion with a grunt of astonishment.

The starboard screen showed a tiny man-shape running

towards the ship, arms pumping. The captain stepped up the screen magnification. Vezzarn—

He swore savagely, flicked over the desk's forward lock controls, heard the lock open—then a new rumbling roar from the world outside the lock. Vezzarn, at least, hadn't much more than two hundred yards to cover, and was sprinting hard. His head came up for an instant—he'd seen the sudden blaze of light from the lock.

The captain waited, mangling his lip with his teeth. Each second, the surrounding giant cloud banks were changing appearance, lifting higher . . . and now they seemed also to slant inwards like dark waves cresting—about to come thundering down from every direction to engulf the ship! Vezzarn passed beyond the screen's inner range. More seconds went by. The roaring racket beyond the lock grew louder. Those monster clouds *were* leaning in towards the *Venture!* Then a clatter of boots on the ramp. The captain glanced back as Vezzarn flung himself headlong through the lock, rolled over, gasping, on the floor. The thrust regulator went flat to the desk in that instant.

They leaped five hundred feet from the ground while the lock was clicking shut. The *Venture's* nose lifted high as they cleared the cliffs and the atmosphere drive hurled her upwards. Three quarters of the sky above seemed a churning blackness now. The ship turned towards the center of the remaining open patch. At the earliest possible moment the captain cut in the main drive—

The roiling elemental furies dwindled to utter insignificance beneath them as they hurtled off the world of red twilight like a wrong-way meteor, blazing from stem to stem. Space quenched the flames seconds later. The bloated giant sun and its satellite appeared in the rear screens. Cooling, the *Venture* thundered on.

"Whooo-oof!" breathed the captain, slumping back in the

chair. He closed his eyes then, but opened them again at once . . . .

It was something like smelling a grumble, or hearing dark green, or catching a glimpse of a musky scent. As Goth had suggested, it was not to be described in any terms that made sense. But it was quite unmistakable. He knew exactly what he was doing—he was relling a vatch.

The vatch. Big Wind Voice. Old Windy—

CONGRATULATIONS! cried the vatch. THE TEST IS OVER. AGAIN YOU SURPRISE AND DELIGHT ME, SMALL PERSON! NOW THE GLORY OF A GREATER DREAM GAME IS TRULY EARNED. LET US SPEAK AT ONCE TO ANOTHER OF ITS PLAYERS . . . .

With that, the control room blurred and was gone. He, too, the captain decided a stunned moment later, had blurred and was gone, at least in most respects. Beneath him still hung a kind of pale, shifting luminance which might bear some resemblance to his familiar body in its outlines. He seemed to be moving swiftly with it through a sea of insubstantial grayness . . . .

A greater dream game! What was that vatch monster getting him into—and what would happen to Goth and the *Venture*? He couldn't—

PATIENCE, SMALL PERSON! PATIENCE! Old Windy boomed good-humoredly from the grayness. THE GAME IS ONE IN WHICH YOU HAVE AN INTEREST. YOUR PHANTOM COMPANIONS WILL BE SAFE UNTIL YOU RETURN.

The last, at least, was somewhat reassuring. . . . A game in which he had an interest?

WORM WORLD! bellowed the vatch-voice delightedly, rolling and tumbling and swooping about him. WORM WORLD . . . WORM WORLD . . . WORM WORLD—

Chapter TEN

HE DID HAVE, the captain acknowledged cautiously, a very strong interest in the Worm World. Where was it?

For a moment he received the impression of a puzzled lack of comprehension in the vatch. WHERE IS IT? the great voice rumbled then, surprised. IT IS WHERE IT IS, SMALL PERSON!

So the captain realized that instruments like stellar maps meant nothing to this klatha entity, that it had in fact no real understanding of location as the human mind understood it. But it didn't need such understanding. The universe of humanity seemed a product of vatch dream-imagination to the vatch. It roamed about here as freely as a man might roam among creations of his imagination. If it wanted to be somewhere, it simply was there.

With the exception of the Worm World. The Worm World, the vatch explained, was an enigma. A tantalizing enigma. Having picked up reports of Manaret and its terrors here and there in its prowling, it had decided to take a look at it.

It discovered it was unable to approach Manaret. Something

barred it—something blocked it. Its essence was held at a distance by the Worm World. That shouldn't have been possible, but it was so.

It made the Worm World a challenge. The vatch investigated further, began to fit together a picture of what was known about Manaret. There was the dire monster Moander which ruled it and commanded the worm globes that terrorized human worlds wherever they went. The vatch learned that Manaret was in fact a ship—a tremendous ship designed along planetary dimensions. Confined within a section of the ship was a race of proud and powerful beings, who had built it and originally had been its masters, but who were now the prisoners of Moander. These were known as the Lyrd-Hyrier to humans who had gained contact with them in seeking the means to resist Moander and his Nuris. If there was anything the Lyrd-Hyrier could do to overthrow Moander and regain possession of Manaret, they would do it. And that would end at the same time the oppressive and constantly growing threat Moander presented to humanity.

The vatch was intrigued by the situation and had watched the captain become involved in the game against the Worm World. It thought now he could be developed into the player who would bring about Moander's downfall.

What could he do, the captain asked.

Information was needed first, the vatch-voice told him. The means to act against the monster might be at hand, if they understood how to use it. And information could be obtained best from those who had most to tell about Moander—the Lyrd Hyrier confined in Manaret. The vatch could not reach them, and nothing material could be sent through the barriers maintained by Moander. But in his present form the captain lacked all material substance and could be projected directly into the one section of Manaret still held and defended by the Lyrd-Hyrier. There, by following the vatch's instructions, he would learn what he needed to know . . . .

✧   ✧   ✧

There were advantages to being a ghost—a temporary ghost, the captain hoped.

Fire from concealed energy guns had blazed through and about him the instant he arrived in the private chamber of the Lord Cheel, Prince of the Lyrd-Hyrier, the Great People, in a central section of Manaret. The guns hadn't caused the captain any discomfort. When, at some unseen signal, the firing ended, he was still there insubstantial but intact. The hostile reception was no surprise. Knowing nothing of vatch powers, the Lyrd-Hyrier would regard any intrusion here as being an attempted attack by Moander.

So the captain was thinking expressions of polite greeting and friendly purpose at the Lord Cheel as he drifted down closer towards him. This was in line with the vatch's instructions.

There was no immediate response to his greetings from Cheel, who was sitting up in a nest of rich robes on a wide couch near the center of the chamber, watching the approach of the wraith which had invaded his privacy, and apparently disturbed his slumber, with large, unblinking golden-green eyes. The vatch had told the captain that the Lyrd-Hyrier lord had a mind of great power, and that if he formulated his thoughts carefully and clearly, Cheel would understand them and think back at him. The captain began to wonder how well the plan was going to work. What the robes allowed to be seen of Cheel's person might have been sections of a purple-scaled reptile cast into very tall, attenuated human form. The neck was snaky. But the large round head at the end of it did suggest that it bulged with capable brains; and Cheel's whole attitude, at a moment which must have been rather startling to him, was that of a bold, arrogant, and resourceful being.

About a third of the way down to the couch—the chamber had the dimensions of a spaceship hangar and the jeweled magnificence of a royal audience room—the captain encountered a highly charged force field. He realized what it was: any material object or inimical energy encountering that barrier should have been spattered against the walls. But the only feeling he had was one of moving, for a moment, through something rather sticky and resistive. Then he was past the force field. Cheel gave up on defensive measures. His long purple arm moved under the robes; and his thoughts now touched the captain's mind.

"The inner barriers are turned off," they said. "It appears you are not Moander's tool. Are you then one of the friendly witch people?"

The captain formulated the thought that he was an associate of the witch people and Moander's foe as they were, that he might be in a position to give assistance against the machine, and that he was in need of information to show him what he could do. Cheel seemed to understand all this well enough. "Ask your questions!" he responded. "Without aid, our situation here will soon be hopeless—"

The exchange continued with only occasional difficulties. Manaret, at the time it appeared in the home-universe of humanity, had been under the control of a director machine called a synergizer, an all-important instrument unit which actuated and coordinated the many independent power systems required to maintain and drive the ship. The same near-disaster which hurled Manaret and the Lyrd-Hyrier out of their dimensional pattern of existence into this one also had temporarily incapacitated the synergizer. Moander, an emergency director of comparatively limited function, had become active in the synergizer's stead, as it was designed to do. Manaret was an experiment, a new type of Lyrd-Hyrier warship. There had been no previous opportunity to test out Moander under actual emergency conditions.

Now it appeared there had been mistakes made in planning it. Alerted to substitute for the synergizer only until that unit resumed functioning, the emergency director had taken action to perpetuate the emergency which left it in charge. The synergizer was very nearly indestructible. But Moander had placed it in a torpedolike vehicle and set the vehicle on a course which should plunge it into a great star near the point where the giant ship had emerged here. Free of its more powerful rival, Moander could not be controlled by any method available to the Lyrd-Hyrier.

"We know the synergizer was not destroyed at that time," Cheel's thoughts told the captain. "Apparently the vehicle was deflected from its course towards the star, presumably by the synergizer's own action. But it has not returned and we have never found out where it went. Recently, there was a report—"

The thought halted. The captain was producing a mental image of Olimy's mysterious crystalloid . . . .

"*That is it!*" Cheel's recognition of the object came almost as a shriek. "Where have you seen it?"

His excitement jumbled communication briefly; then he steadied. The Lyrd Hyrier had received reports through a spy system they'd been able to maintain in various sections of Manaret that Moander's Nuris had picked up the long-lost trail of the synergizer. Only hours old was the information that a witch ship transporting the instrument had eluded an attempt to force it and its cargo into a sun, and had disappeared.

The captain acknowledged the ship was his own. Temporarily the synergizer was safe.

The alien golden-green eyes were smoky with agitation. A view of a great dim hall, walls tapestried with massed instrument banks, appeared in the captain's mind. "The central instrument room—it is under our control still. Once there, in its own place, the synergizer is all-powerful! Away from it, it can do little . . . ." The picture flicked out. Cheel's thoughts hurried on. A long time ago they had picked up fragmentary messages directed at Manaret by others of their kind from the dimensions of reality out of which they had been thrown. A vast machinery had been constructed there which would pluck the giant ship back from wherever it had gone the instant it was restored to operational condition under the synergizer's direction. All problems would be solved in that moment!

But there was no method known to the Lyrd-Hyrier, Cheel admitted, of bringing a material object through Moander's outer defenses of Manaret. The synergizer was many things more than it appeared to be, but it was in part material. And Manaret's defenses were being strengthened constantly. "The Nuris again are weaving new patterns of energy among the dead suns which surround us here on all sides . . . ." Of late, Moander evidently had found means of disrupting mental exchanges between the Lyrd-Hyrier and some telepathic witches of Karres. They had recently become unable to establish contact with Karres.

It seemed a large "But . . ." "Any chance your friends eventually might send something like a relief ship here which could handle Moander?" the captain inquired.

"Impossible!" View of madly spinning blurs of energies, knotting and exploding . . . "There is no dimensional interface between us—there is a twisting plunge through chaos! We were there; we were here. In a million lifetimes that precise moment of whirling shift could not be deliberately duplicated. *They* cannot come here! They must draw the ship back *there* . . . and they can do that only when its total pattern of forces is intact and matches the pattern they have powered to attract it."

Which required the synergizer . . .

If they could get it to Karres—

"How vulnerable is Moander to an outside attack?"

"Its defenses are those of Manaret." Cheel, formidable individual though he appeared to be, was allowing discouragement to tinge his thoughts, now that his excitement had abated somewhat. "Additionally . . ."

View of a massive structure with down-sloping sides affixed to a flat surface of similarly massive look. "Moander's stronghold on the outer shell of Manaret," Cheel's thought said. "Every defense known both to the science of the Great People and to the science of your kind on the worlds the Nuris have studied appears incorporated in it. And deep within it is Moander. The monster, for all its powers, is wary. All active operating controls of the ship are linked through the stronghold, and from it Moander scans your universe through its Nuris."

"It has us in a death-grip, and is preparing to close its grip on your kind. If we—and you—are to escape, then haste is very necessary! For the Nuris have built new breeding vats and are entering them in great numbers. It is their time . . . ."

"Breeding vats?" interjected the captain.

The Nuris—pliable and expendable slaves of whoever or whatever was in a position to command them—were bred at long intervals in the quantities required by their masters. Such a period had begun, and it was evident that Moander planned now to multiply the Nuri hordes at his disposal a hundred-fold.

"In themselves the Worm People are nothing," said Cheel's thought. "But they are Moander's instruments. As the swarms grow, so grows the enemy's power. If Moander is not defeated before the worms have bred, our defenses will be overwhelmed . . . and your worlds, too, will die in a great Nuri plague to come."

"Restore the synergizer to its place in the central instrument room, or break Moander's stronghold and Moander—those are the only solutions now. And we cannot tell you how to do either—"

The thought-flow was cut off as Cheel and the great chamber suddenly blurred and vanished. The captain's wraith-shape drifted again in featureless grayness.

He relled vatch, faintly at first, then definitely.

I HEARD ALL, the vatch-voice came roaring about him out of the grayness. A MOST BEAUTIFUL PROBLEM! . . . WAIT HERE A LITTLE NOW, GREAT PLAYER OF GREAT GAMES!

Its presence faded. At least there was nothing to rell any more. The captain drifted, or the grayness drifted.

A beautiful problem! Something new to entertain the vatch, from the vatch's point of view. . . . But a very terrible and urgent problem for everyone else concerned, if the Cheel creature had told the truth.

What could he do about it? Nothing, of course, until the vatch returned to get him out of this whatever-it-was, and back into his body and the rest of it.

And there probably would be very little he actually could do then, the captain thought. Because whatever he tried, the vatch would be looking over his shoulder, and the vatch definitely would want the game played its way. Which might happen to be a very bad way again for everyone else involved. There was no counting on the vatch.

How could you act independently of an entity which not only was able to turn you inside out when it felt like it but was also continuously reading your mind? He thought of the Nuri lock Goth had taught him to construct . . . .

If there were something like a vatch lock now—

The thought checked. In the grayness before him there'd appeared a spark of bright fire. It stayed still for an instant, then quiveringly began to move, horizontally from left to right. It left a trail behind it—a twisted, flickering line of fire as bright as itself. It was—

Awful fright shot through him. *Stop that!* he thought.

The spark stopped. The line of fire remained where it was, quivering and brilliant. It looked very much like one of the linear sections of the patterns that had turned into the Nuri lock.

But this was a far heavier line—not a line at all really but a bar of living fire! Klatha fire, he thought . . . It had stopped where it was only because he'd checked it.

He hesitated then. If this, too, was part of a potential lock pattern, then that lock must be an enormously more powerful klatha device than the one which had shut the Nuris out of his mind!

Well—

"Are you certain," something inside him seemed to ask very earnestly, "that you want to try it?"

He was, he decided. It seemed necessary.

He did something he couldn't have described, even to himself. It released the klatha spark. The line of fire marched on. From above, a second line came trickling down on it—a third zigzagged up from below . . . .

It was awesomely hot stuff! There was a moment when the universe seemed to stretch very tight. But the fire lines crossed, meshed, froze; there was a flash of silent light, and that was it. The pattern had completed itself and instantly disappeared. The ominous tightness went with it.

It was not, the captain decided, the kind of pattern that needed to be practiced. It had to be done right once, or it would not be done at all. And it had been done right.

He waited. After a while he relled vatch. That strengthened presently, grew fainter again, almost faded away. Then suddenly it became very strong. Old Windy was with him, close by.

And silent for the moment! Possibly puzzled, the captain thought.

Then the wind voice spoke. But not in its usual tumultuous fashion and not addressing him. The vatch seemed to be muttering to itself. He made out some of it.

Hmmm? . . . BUT WHAT *IS* THIS? . . . MOST UNUSUAL . . . IT APPEARS UNDAMAGED, BUT—

SMALL PERSON, the familiar bellowing came suddenly then, CAN YOU HEAR ME?

"Yes!" the captain thought at it.

HMMM? . . . COMPLETE BLOCK! BUT NO MATTER, the vatch decided. A MINOR HANDICAP! LET THE GAME GO ON—

A momentary sense of rumbling through icy blackness, of vast distances collapsing to nothing ahead of him. Then the captain found himself lying face down on something cool, hard, and prickly. He opened his eyes, lifted his head. He had eyes to open and a head to lift again! He had everything back! He rolled over on rocky ground, sat up in a patch of withered brown grass, looked around in bright sunlight. A general awareness of windy autumn scenery, timbered hills about and snowcapped mountain ranges beyond them, came with the much more important discovery of the *Venture* standing some four hundred feet away, bow slanted towards him, forward lock open and ramp out. He scrambled to his feet, started towards it.

"*Captain!*"

He swung about, saw Goth running down the slope of the shallow depression in which he and the ship stood, shouted something and ran to meet her, relief so huge he seemed to be soaring over dips in the ground. Goth took off in a jump from eight feet away and landed on his chest, growling. The captain hugged her, kissed her, rumpled her hair, set her on her feet, and gave her a happy swat.

"*Pat*ham!" gasped Goth. "Am I glad to see you! Where you *been?*"

"Worm World," said the captain, grinning fatuously down at her.

"Worm—HUH?"

"That's right. Say, that crystal thing of Olimy's—it's still on the ship, isn't it?"

"How'd I know?" Goth said. "*Worm* World!" She looked stunned. She shook her head, added, "Ship came just now, with you."

"Just now?"

"Minute ago. I was headed back to camp—"

"Camp? Well, skip that. Hulik and Vezzarn are with you?"

"Both. Not Olimy. I relled a vatch. *Giant*-vatch—you don't do things small, Captain! Turned around, and there the *Venture* was. Then you stood up—"

"Come along," he said. "We've got to make sure it's on board! I know what it is now. Ever hear of a synergizer in connection with Manaret?"

"Syner . . . no," said Goth, trotting beside him. "Important, huh?"

"The most!" the captain assured her. "The most! Tell you later."

They scrambled up the ramp and through the lock. The control section lighting was on, the heating system going full blast. The bulkheads felt icy to the touch. They took a moment to check the control desk, found everything but the general emergency switch and the automatic systems in off position, left things as they were and headed for the back of the ship. They paused briefly again at the first emergency wall. The Sheem Spider hadn't exactly burned out a hole in it; it had cut out a section big enough to let it through endwise along with its master and knocked the loose chunk of battle-steel into the next compartment, shattering fifteen feet of deck.

"One tough robot!" remarked Goth, impressed, "Kind of sorry I slept through all that!"

"So were we, child," the captain told her. "Come on . . . ."

The lost synergizer of Manaret was in the strongbox in the vault, in its wrappings. They picked their way back out of the shattered vault, opened Olimy's locked stateroom next and saw him imprisoned but safe in his eternal disminded moment there, locked up the room and left the ship by the ramp.

"Let's sit," said Goth. She settled down cross-legged in the grass. "The others are all right. What happened to you? How'd you get to the Worm World? What's that synergizer thing?"

She listened without interrupting, face intent, as he related his experience up to the point where he'd decided to take a fling at constructing a vatch lock. For various reasons it didn't seem advisable to mention that at the moment. "The vatch seemed to say something about going on with the game," he concluded. "Next thing I knew I was here."

Goth sighed. "That vatch!" she muttered. She rubbed her nose tip. "Looks sort of bad, doesn't it?"

"Not too good at present," the captain admitted. "But we have the synergizer safe here. That's something. . . . We don't know what the vatch intends to do next, of course."

"No."

"But if it leaves us alone for a while . . . any idea of where we are here?"

"Know exactly where we are," Goth told him. "Can't see that'll help much, though!" She patted the ground beside her. "This is Karres."

"*What!*" He came to his feet. "But then—"

"No," Goth said. "It's not that simple. This isn't Karres-now. It's Karres-then."

"Huh?"

She indicated the big yellow sun disk above the mountains. "Double star," she said. "Squint your eyes, you can see just a little bit of white sticking out behind it on the left. That's its twin. This is the Talsoe System where Karres was when witches found it—its own system. There's nobody here yet but us."

"How do you . . . You think that vatch sent us back in *time?*"

"Long way back in time!" Goth nodded.

"How can you be sure? Now you've mentioned it, this could be Karres by its looks! But a lot of worlds—"

"Uh-uh!" Her forefinger pointed at a shining white mountain peak beyond the rise. "I ought to know *that* mountain, Captain! That's where I was born . . . or where I'm going to be born, thirty miles from here. Town's going to be in the valley north of it." Goth's hand swept about. "I know all this country—it's Karres!"

"All right But they could have moved it to the Talsoe System the last time, couldn't they? Let's get in the ship and . . ."

Goth shook her head. "Not a bit of klatha around except ours and the vatch. There're no witches here yet, believe me!

And won't be for another three hundred thousand years any-way—"

"*Three hundred thou . . . !*" the captain half shouted. He checked himself. "How do you know *that?*"

"Got a little moon here. You'll see it tonight. Karres had one early, but then it smacked down around the north pole and messed things up pretty bad for a while. They figured that must have been a bit more than three hundred thousand years back . . . so we're back before *that!* Besides, there's the animals. A lot of them aren't so much different from what they're going to be. But they're different. You see?"

"Yeah, I guess I do!" the captain admitted. He cleared his throat. "It startled me for a moment."

"Pretty odd, isn't it?" Goth agreed. "No Empire at all yet, no Uldune! Patham—*no starships even!* Everybody that's there is still back on old Yarthe!" Her head tilted up quickly. "Umm!" she murmured, eyes narrowing a little.

The captain had caught it, too. Vatch sign! Old Windy was somewhere around. Not too close, but definitely present . . . They remained quiet for a minute or two. The impression seemed to grow no stronger in that time. Suddenly it was gone again.

"Giant-vatch, all right!" Goth remarked a few seconds later. "Brother! You picked yourself a big one, Captain!"

"They're not all the same then, eh?"

"Come in all sizes. Bigger they are, the more they can do. That's mostly make trouble, of course! This one's a whale of a vatch!" She frowned. "I don't know . . . ."

"They can read our minds—human minds, can't they?" asked the captain.

"Lot of them can."

"Can they do it from farther away than we can rell them?"

"Not supposed to be able to do it," said Goth. "But I don't know."

"Hmm—is there such a thing as a klatha lock that will keep vatches from poking around in your thoughts?"

"Uh-huh. Takes awfully heavy stuff, though! I don't know how to do that one. There's only three, four people I know that use a vatch lock."

"Oh?" said the captain, somewhat startled. Goth looked up at him questioningly, then with sudden speculation. "Ummm," she said slowly. She considered a moment again, remarked, "Now there's something I do that works about as good as a lock against vatches. Can't tell you how to do that either, though."

"Why not?" he asked.

Goth shrugged. "Don't know how I do it. Born with it, I guess. Takes just a little low intensity klatha. Dab of it on anything particular I don't want anybody to know I'm thinking about, and that's it! Somebody sneaks a look into my mind then, he just can't see it."

"You sure?" the captain asked thoughtfully.

"Ought to be! Some real high-powered mind-readers tried it. Wanted to study out how it was done so others could use it. They never did figure that out—but it works just fine! They couldn't even tell there'd been anything blurred."

"That will be a help now," the captain said.

"Uh-huh! Vatch isn't going to find out anything from me he shouldn't know about." She cocked her head, looking up at him. "*Did* you make yourself a vatch lock, Captain?"

"I think so." He gave her a general description of the process. Goth listened, eyes first round with apprehension, then shining. "Even when I thought directly at it," he concluded, "it didn't seem able to read me."

"That is a vatch lock then. A *vatch lock!*" Goth repeated softly. "You're going to be a hot witch, Captain—you wait!"

"Think so?" He felt pleased but there was too much to worry about at present for the feeling to linger. "Well, let's assume that when we can't rell the vatch, we can talk freely," he said.

"And that when we do rell it, we'd better keep shut up about anything important but needn't worry about what we're thinking. . . . But now, what can we do? We've got the *Venture* but there's no sense in flying around space three hundred thousand years from our time. There's nowhere to go. Is there any possible klatha way you know of we might use to get back?"

Goth shook her head. Some witches had done some experimentation with moving back in time, but she hadn't heard of anyone going back farther than their own life span. The vatch must have used klatha in bringing them here; but then it *was* a giant-vatch, with immense powers.

It looked as if they'd have to depend on the vatch to get them back, too. It was not a reassuring conclusion. The klatha entity was playing a game and regarded them at present as being among its pieces. It had heard that there seemed to be no way to overcome Moander in his stronghold on Manaret and was out to prove it could be done. At best it would consider them expendable pieces. It might also simply decide it had no further use for them and leave them where they were. But as long as the synergizer remained in their custody, they could assume they were still included in the vatch's plans.

It wasn't a good situation. But at the moment there seemed to be nothing they could do to change it.

"Olimy found the synergizer and should have been on his way to Karres with it when the Nuris nearly caught him," the captain observed reflectively. "About the same time it was reported the Empire was launching an attack on Karres, and Karres disappeared. There was no word it had showed up again anywhere else before we left Uldune."

Goth nodded. "Looks like they knew Olimy was coming with the thing and went to meet him."

"Yes . . . at some previously arranged rendezvous point. Now, you once told me," the captain said, "that Karres was developing klatha weapons to handle the Nuris and was pretty far along with the program."

"Uh-huh. They might have been all set that way when we left," Goth agreed. "I wasn't told. They weren't far from it."

"Then the synergizer actually could have been the one thing they were waiting to get before tackling the Worm World. They'd know from their contacts with the Lyrd-Hyrier it wouldn't be long before Moander had so many more Nuris to fight for him that reaching him would become practically impossible . . . ."

Goth nodded again. "Guess they'll hit Manaret whether they get the synergizer or not!" she remarked. "Looks like they have to. But if they were waiting for it they got a way to use it—and they'd still want it bad, and fast!"

The captain scowled frustratedly.

"Even if we were back in our time," he said, "and on our own—meaning no vatch around—the best we could do about it would be to get the thing to Emris! We don't know where Karres is. And we don't know where Manaret is . . . even though I've been there now, in a way."

"Well, I'm not sure," Goth told him. "Maybe we do know where they are, Captain."

"Huh? What do you mean?"

"You said Cheel told you the Nuris were putting up new space barriers between the dead suns all around Manaret—"

The captain nodded. "So he did."

"Never heard of but one place where you'd see dead suns all around," Goth said. "And that's in the Chaladoor—the Tark Nembi Cluster. There're people who call it the Dead Suns Cluster. It's another spot everyone keeps away from because when you don't, you don't come back. So the Worm World could have been sitting inside it all the time. . . . And if it's there," Goth concluded, "we ought to be able to find Karres about one jump from Tark Nembi right now."

The captain grunted. "I bet you're right—and that could be

our solution! If we get back and can make a break for the Cluster on the Sheewash Drive without being stopped by the vatch, we'll give it a try!"

"Right," said Goth. "Looks like the vatch will have to move first, though."

"So it does," agreed the captain. "Well—" He sighed. "You say you set up camp with Vezzarn and Hulik around here?"

Goth came to her feet. "Just a bit behind the rise," she said. "Quarter-mile. Let's go get them—easier than moving the ship."

Halfway up the slope they turned aside to pick up some items she'd dropped when she caught sight of the captain— a sturdy handmade bow and a long quiver of tree bark out of which protruded the feathered shafts of arrows. Beside these articles lay a pair of freshly killed furry white-and-brown animals tied together by their hind legs. The captain lifted them while Goth slung bow and quiver over her shoulders. "Dinner, eh?" he said. "Didn't take you long to get set up for the pioneering life!"

"Forgot to tell you about that," said Goth. "Can't quite figure it, but while you were having a talk with the Cheel-thing we've been here eight days...."

The captain couldn't quite figure it either. Goth filled him in as they went on towards the camp. Neither Hulik do Eldel nor Vezzarn remembered anything between the crash take-off from the planet of the red sun and their awakening in a chill, misty dawn on Karres. Goth had come awake first, by half an hour or so, had known immediately on what world she was, and deduced the rest when the Talsoe Twins lifted above the mountains and the mists thinned enough to show her a small moon still floating in the northern sky. She hadn't informed her companions of their whereabouts in space and time—both were upset enough as it was for a while. Hulik's impulse, when she awoke and discovered Vezzarn stretched out unconscious beside her, was to blast him for a filthy traitor as he lay there. "Couldn't find her gun though—or his—till she'd cooled down

again," Goth said with a grin. "Then Vezzarn came to—and
he bawled like a baby for an hour."

"What about?"

"Because you waited to let him get aboard before you took
off. So then he was going to shoot himself rather than face
you when you got back. Couldn't find his gun either, though."

"Looks like you've had your hands full with the two!"

"Oh, they settled down pretty quick. Hulik's even speaking
to Vezzarn again. She's not the worst, that Hulik."

"No, she isn't," agreed the captain, remembering the bad
moments on the ledge of the cliff. "What do they make of the
situation?"

Both seemed to have decided they'd gotten themselves
involved in some very heavy witch business and the less they
heard about it, the better, Goth said. They hadn't asked questions. She'd told them Captain Aron would be rejoining them,
but she didn't know when, and they'd better settle down here
for a perhaps lengthy stay.

She glanced up at him. "Didn't know *if* you'd show up, really!
Specially when it got to be four, five days. Figured it must be
the vatch, of course . . . and you never can tell with vatches!"

But that was a private distress. Outwardly they'd had no
problems. Vezzarn, doing what he could to make up for an
enormity committed in panic, had a shipshape little camp set
up for them on the banks of a creek before evening of the first
day, kept it tidy and improved on it daily thereafter, fashioned
Goth's hunting gear for her though not without misgivings,
tended to the cooking, and was dissuaded with difficulty from
charging forth, waving his blaster, whenever sizable specimens
of Karres fauna came close enough to be regarded by him as
a potential menace to the ladies. Hulik stayed tightened up for
some twenty-four hours, keeping a nervous eye on the mountain horizons as if momentarily expecting vast, nameless
menaces to begin manifesting there. But on the second day,
the autumn warmth of the Talsoe suns seemed to soak what

was left of those tensions out of her, and she'd been reasonably relaxed and at ease since.

"Any idea, by the way," asked the captain, "what we ran into on that world? It does look as if something besides the robot was deliberately out to get us—and nearly made it finally."

Goth nodded. "Guess something was, Captain! From what Vezzarn and Hulik say, it sounds like you got a bunch of planetaries stirred up when you landed. And some of them can get mighty mean."

It appeared planetaries were a type of klatha entity native to this universe and bound to the worlds of their origin. They varied widely in every way. Most worlds had some, Goth thought. Karres definitely did; but they were mild, retiring beings who rarely gave indications of their presence. Sometimes they'd been helpful. The world of the red sun evidently harbored a high-powered and aggressive breed which did not tolerate trespassers on what it considered its exclusive domain.

The arrival at camp was made briefly embarrassing by Vezzarn who began weeping at sight of the captain, then knelt and tried to kiss his hand. Not until the captain announced formally that everybody had forgiven him, this time, would Vezzarn get to his feet again.

"I'm a rat, sir!" he told the captain earnestly then. "But I'm a grateful rat. You'll see . . . ."

They left the camp standing as it was, returned to the *Venture* together. Goth and Vezzarn went off to see what could be done about tidying up the trail of destruction left by the Sheem robot, Hulik following them. The captain closed the lock and settled down at the control desk for a routine engine check.

It turned out to be non-routine. There was no indication of malfunction of any kind, except for one thing. The engine systems were not delivering power to any of the drives.

He chewed his lip. Vatch, he thought. It had to be that. Thrust was being developed—smooth, even, heavy thrust. By all physical laws, there was nowhere for it to go except into one of the drives. But it wasn't reaching them.

He shut the engines down again, reopened the lock. The vatch had made sure they'd stay here until it came for them. There was nothing wrong with the ship—they were merely being prevented from leaving with it. He decided it didn't matter too much. In this time, there was no place they'd want to go in the *Venture* anyway.

When he looked around, Hulik do Eldel stood in the entry to the control room, watching him.

"Come in and sit down," the captain said. "I'm afraid I never really got around to thanking you for helping out with the Agandar!"

She smiled and came in. After the eight days she'd spent camping out on Karres, Hulik looked perhaps better than she ever had. And she'd looked extremely good in a delicate-featured, elegant way since the first time the captain had seen her. For a moment it became a bit difficult to believe those warm, dark eyes had been sighting down the gun which blasted death at last into the legendary Agandar.

"I was helping myself out, too, you know!" she remarked. She added, "I heard the engines just now and wondered whether we were leaving."

"No, probably not for a while," the captain said. He hesitated. "The fact is I don't know when we'll be leaving or where we'll go when we do. We're still in something of a jam, you see. I can't tell you what it's about but I hope things will work out all right. And I'm sorry you're in it with us, but there's nothing I can do about that."

Hulik was silent a moment. "Did you know I'm an Imperial agent?" she asked.

"Yango mentioned it."

"Well, he told the truth for once. I signed up for passage on the Chaladoor run in order to steal the secret drive you were supposed to have on this ship."

"Hmm, yes!" nodded the captain. "I gathered that. . . . It isn't something that would be of any use to you or the people you work for."

"I," Hulik said, "had gathered that some two ship-days before the trouble with Yango began. At any rate, if I'm in a jam with you and our little witch, it's because I've worked myself into that position. I suspect I can't be of much further assistance in getting us out of it. If I can, let me know. Otherwise I'll simply try to keep out of the way. I'm considered a capable person, but Karres matters have turned out to be above my head."

The captain didn't tell her he'd entertained similar feelings off and on. He hoped that when this was over the do Eldel would be among the survivors, if any. But her future looked at least as uncertain as Goth's and his own.

That evening they had their supper outside the ship, camp-style, which was Hulik's suggestion. She'd grown fond of this world, she said, felt more comfortable and at home here after a week than she could remember feeling anywhere else. Goth looked pleased in a mildly proprietary way; and Karres came through with a magnificently blazing sunset above the western ranges as the Talsoe Twins sank from sight. The wind died gradually and they sat around a while, talking about inconsequential things carefully remote from the present and themselves. The sky was almost cloudless now. The captain watched a dainty, clean-etched little moon appear, and tried again to think of something he might do besides waiting for the vatch to show its hand. The disconcerting fact still seemed to be, however, that they had to wait for the vatch to act. Goth might have shifted them and the *Venture* light-years away from here; but literally and figuratively that could get them nowhere that counted. . . . He realized suddenly he'd just heard Goth suggest they all bunk out beside the ship for the night.

He gave her a quick look. The troops obviously liked the idea at once; after everything that had happened, their cabins in the *Venture's* passenger compartment might look somewhat lonely and isolated to be passing a sleep period in. But to detach themselves from the ship overnight didn't seem a good notion. Depending on the vatch's whims, they could awaken to find it permanently gone.

Goth acknowledged his look with no more than a flicker of her lashes, but it was an acknowledgment. So she had something in mind besides reassuring their companions . . . but what?

Then he felt his hackles lifting and knew the vatch had returned.

It wasn't close by; he could barely retain a sense of its presence. But it remained around. Goth had grown aware of it before he did—that much was clear. He still didn't see what it had to do with moving out of the ship for the night.

He waited while the others cleared away supper dishes and utensils, began hauling out bedding, and went back for more. The vatch came closer, lingered, drew back—

There was a sense of a sudden further darkening of the evening air. Thunder pealed, far overhead. As the captain looked up, startled, into the sky, rain crashed down, on and about him, with the abruptness of an upended gigantic bucket of water.

He scrambled around, hauling up the drenched bedding, swearing incoherently. It was an impossible downpour. Water spattered up from the rocks, doused him with dirt from instantly formed puddles and hurrying rivulets. Thunder cracked and snarled, lightning flickered, eerily festooning the thick, dark, churning mass of storm clouds which now almost filled what had been a serene, clear sky above the *Venture* less than a minute before. Vezzarn came sliding down the ramp to help him. Vatch-laughter rolled through the thunder, howling in delight as they slipped and fell in the mud, struggled back up with the sodden bedding in their arms, shoved it at last into the lock, scrambled in and through themselves. The lock slammed shut and the rain drummed its mindless fury on the *Venture's* unheeding back.

Chapter ELEVEN

"WELL, WE'VE LEARNED one thing," the captain remarked grumpily. "The vatch evidently prefers us to stay in the ship . . . ."

Goth said that wasn't all. "Never knew there *were* that many cuss words!"

He grunted. He was dry again but still more than a little fed up with the unmannerly ways of vatches. "You just forget what you heard!" he said. He looked at the desk chronometer. It was over an hour since the downpour outside had begun, and it was still going on, not with its original violence but as a steady, heavy rain. The ship's audio pickups registered intermittent rumbles of thunder; and the screens showed the *Venture's* immediate vicinity transformed to a shallow lake. The captain's nostrils wrinkled briefly as if trying to catch an elusive scent.

"You're sure you can't get even a trace of the thing?" he asked.

Goth shook her head. "Far as I can make out, it's been gone pretty near an hour. Think you're relling something now?"

The captain hesitated. "No," he said at last. "Not really. I just keep having a feeling— Look, witch, it's getting late! Better run and get your sleep so you'll stay fresh. I'll sit up for another smoke. If that self-inflated cosmic clown does show up again, I'll let you know."

"Self-inflated cosmic . . . pretty good!" Goth said admiringly, and slipped off to her cabin. The captain took out a cigarette and lit it, scowling absently at the screens. The door between the control room and the rest of the section was closed—Hulik and Vezzarn had chosen to bunk up front on the floor tonight. What with the vatch's startling thunderstorm trick coming on top of everything else they'd experienced lately, he hadn't felt like suggesting they'd be more comfortable in their staterooms. On the other hand, the night still might provide events it would be better they didn't witness, if it could be avoided. He'd brought the strongbox enclosing the Manaret synergizer out of the vault with the ship's crane and set it down against the wall in the control room—an act which probably had done nothing to help Vezzarn's peace of mind.

There was something vatchy around. That was the word for it. Not the vatch but something that seemed to go with the vatch. He wasn't relling it. Goth figured his contacts with the vatch might have begun to develop some other perception. At any rate, he was receiving impressions of another kind here; and the impressions had kept getting more definite. The best description he could have given of them now would have been to say he was aware of a speck of blackness which seemed to be in a constant blur of internal motion.

The muted growl of thunder came through the pickups again, and the captain reached over and shut them off, then extended the screens' horizontal focus outward by twenty miles. Except for fleecy wisps to the east, the skies of Karres were clear all about tonight—once one had moved five or six miles away from the *Venture.* The inexhaustible bank of rain clouds the vatch had produced for them stayed centered directly overhead . . . .

The vatchy speck of blackness had begun to seem connected with that. The captain laid the cigarette aside, shifted the overhead screen to a point a little above the cloud level. . . . Around here?

And there it was, he thought. Something he was neither seeing—it couldn't be seen—nor imagining, because it was there and quite real. It came closest to being a visual impression of a patch of blackness, irregular in outline and inwardly a swirling rush of multitudinous motion.

Vatch stuff, left planted in the Karres sky after the vatch itself had gone. Not enough of it to excite the relling sensation. And what it was doing up there, of course, was to keep the rain clouds massed above the drenched *Venture.* . . . The captain found himself reaching towards it.

That again seemed the only description for a basically indescribable action. It was a reaching-towards in which nothing moved. He stopped short of touching it. A sense of furious heat came from the swirling blackness. Power, he thought. Vatch power; plenty of it. Living klatha . . . .

He put pressure against the side of the living klatha. *Move,* he thought.

It began to move sideways, gliding ahead of the pressure. The pressure kept up with it—

The captain licked his lips, turned the horizontal screens back to close focus around the ship, picked up the cigarette and settled back in the chair, watching the steady, dark, downward rush of rain about them in the screens. The vatch device continued moving southwards. Now and then the captain glanced at the chronometer. After some nine minutes the rain suddenly lessened. Then it stopped. The night was clear and cloudless above the ship. But a quarter-mile away to the south, rain still poured on the slopes.

He put out the cigarette and eased off the pressure on the vatch device. *Stop there,* he thought. . . . While it was drifting away from the ship he'd become aware of a second one around.

There would be, of course. A much smaller one . . . it would be that, too, for the comparatively minor purpose it was serving—

It took a couple of minutes to get it pinpointed—down in the *Venture's* engine room, a speck of unseeable blackness swirling silently and energetically above the thrust generators, ready to make sure that the *Venture* didn't go anywhere at present.

A rock hung suspended in the clear night air of Karres, spinning and wobbling slowly like a top running down. It was a sizable rock—the *Venture* could have been fitted comfortably into the hole it had left in the planet's surface when it soared up from it a minute or two before. And it was a sizable distance above that surface. About a mile and a half, the captain calculated, watching it in the screen.

He let it turn end for end twice, bob up and down a little, then leap up another instant half-mile.

There was a soft hiss of surprise from behind his shoulder.

"What you *doing?*" Goth whispered.

"Using some loose vatch energy I found hanging around," the captain said negligently. "The vatch left it here to keep us pinned under that rainstorm . . . ." He added, "Don't know how I'm doing it, but it works just fine! Like the rock to try anything in particular?"

"Loop the loop," suggested Goth, staring fascinatedly into the screen.

The rock flashed up and around in a smooth, majestic three-mile loop and stood steady in midair again—steady as a rock.

"Anything else?" he offered.

"Can you do *anything* with it?"

"Anything I've tried so far. Ask for a tough one!"

Goth considered, glanced up at the little moon, high in the northern sky by now. "How about putting it on the other side of the moon?"

"All right," said the captain. He clicked his tongue. "Wait a minute. We'd better *not* try that!"

"Why not?"

He glanced at her. "Because we don't know just what the vatch stuff can do—and because the moon's scheduled to come crashing down on the pole some time in the future here. I'd hate to have it turn out that we were the ones who accidentally knocked it down!"

"Pa*tham!*" exclaimed Goth, startled. "You're right! Give the rock a boost straight out into space then!"

And the rock simply disappeared. "Guess it's out there and traveling," the captain said after a few seconds. "Plenty of power there, all right!" He chewed his lip, frowning. "Now I'll try something else . . . ."

Goth didn't inquire what. She looked on, eyes watchful, as he shifted the view back to the area immediately about the ship. A big tree stood on the rim of the rise to the north. He brought it into as sharp a focus as he could, sensed the vatch device move close to the tree as he did it. The device remained poised there, ready to act.

He gave it a silent command, waited.

But nothing happened. After half a minute he turned his attention to a small shrub not far from the tree. The patch of blackness slid promptly over to the shrub. As he began to repeat the command, the shrub vanished.

Goth made a small exclamation beside him. "*Time* move?" she asked.

"Yes," said the captain, not at all surprised she'd guessed his intention. He cleared his throat. "I'm very much afraid that won't do us any good, though."

"Why *not?* Patham, if—"

"Tried to move the big tree into the future first, and it didn't go. Just not enough power for that, I guess. . . . Let's try that medium-sized one nearer to us—"

There wasn't enough vatch power around to move the

medium-sized tree into the future either. The black patch did what it could. As the captain formulated the mental command, the tree was ripped from the ground. As it toppled over then, they could see the upper third of its crown had disappeared.

The vatch device was of no use to them that way. Adding the speck on guard in the engine room to it would make no significant difference—apparently shifting objects through time required vastly more power than moving the same objects about in space. What level of energy it would take to carry the *Venture* and her crew back to their own time was difficult to imagine . . . .

"Something might have gone wrong anyway," the captain said, not quite able to keep disappointment out of his voice. "We don't know enough about those things. . . . Better quit playing around now. I want to have everything back as it was before the vatch shows up again."

He brought the unit of vatch energy as close to the ship as the viewscreens permitted first. At that distance both of them relled it. Goth's face became very intent for perhaps half a minute; he guessed she had all her klatha antennae out, probing for other indications. Then she shook her head. "Can't spot it!" she said. "Know it's there because it rells, that's all."

Neither was there anything in her current equipment which would let her direct the energy about as the captain had been doing. That might require the ability to recognize it clearly as a prior condition. She hadn't heard of witches who did either, but that didn't mean there weren't any.

The captain described its pseudo-appearance. Goth said the vatches themselves were supposed to be put together in much the same way. "Thought of anything else you can do with it yet?"

He hadn't. "Somewhere along the line it might come in handy to know the stuff can be manipulated," he said. "Especially if the vatch doesn't suspect it." He shifted the screens, added, "Right now we'd better use it to get that cloud pack back before it drifts apart!"

The thunderstorm, left to itself, had turned gradually on an easterly course; but the vatch device checked it and drew it back towards the *Venture*. Some minutes later they saw the wall of rain advancing on them in the viewscreen and shortly the ship was again enveloped in a steady downpour.

It was an hour or so before dawn when the captain was aroused from an uneasy half-sleep on the couch by Goth's buzzer signaling an alert from the control desk. He relled vatch at once, glanced over at the open door to her cabin and coughed meaningfully. The buzzer sound stopped. He laid his head back on the cushions and tried to relax. It wasn't too easy. The vatch indications weren't strong, but the next moments might bring some unpredictable new shift in their situation.

However, nothing happened immediately. The impressions remained faint, seemed to strengthen a trifle, then faded almost to the limits of perceptibility. Goth stayed quiet. The captain began to wonder whether he was still sensing the creature at all. Then suddenly it came close, seemed to move in a circle about them, drew away again. There was a brief, distant rumble of the wind-voice.

It went on a while. The klatha entity hung around, moved off, returned again. The captain waited, puzzled and speculating. There was something undecided in its behavior, he thought presently. And perhaps a suggestion of querulous dissatisfaction in the occasional mutterings he picked up.

He cleared his throat cautiously. The vatch hadn't addressed him directly since it realized something was preventing it from sensing his thoughts. It might suspect it was something he had done or assume there was a block of unknown type between them which also would keep him from understanding it. Possibly—if it hadn't been able to work out a solution to the Worm World problem, which seemed indicated by the way it was acting—it would be useful to reopen communication with it. But he'd have to try to avoid offending the monster, which apparently was easy enough to do with vatches. Under the circumstances, that probably would be disastrous now.

He cleared his throat again. It seemed fairly close at the moment.

"Vatch?" he said aloud.

He had an impression that the vatch paused.

"Vatch, can you hear me?"

A vague faint rumble—it might have been surprise or suspicion rather than a response to the question. Then gradually the vatch grew closer . . . very close, so that it seemed to loom like a mountain of formless blackness in the night above the ship, the rain washing through it. Once again the captain had the impression that from some point near the peak of that mountain two great, green, slitted eyes stared at him. And he became aware of something else . . . Goth's comment about the probable makeup of vatches was true. This gigantic thing seemed to consist of swirling torrents of black energy, pouring up and down through it, curved and intermingled as they slid past and about each other in tight patterns of endlessly changing intricacy. The scraps of vatch power it had left here on Karres to hold them secure during its absence might have been simply flecks of itself.

"There is a way Moander can be destroyed," the captain told the looming blackness.

The rumbling came again—perhaps a stirring of annoyance, perhaps a muttered question.

"You need only take us and this ship and the synergizer to the other Karres," the captain said. "To the Karres of Moander's time . . ."

The vatch was silent now, staring. He went on. The witches on the other Karres had a way to break the power of the Worm World's ruler if they were given the synergizer. They had abilities and knowledge neither he nor anyone else on the ship at present possessed—and that was what was required to beat

Moander. Transferring them to that Karres would be the winning move, the way to end the long game—

The blackness stirred. Vatch laughter exploded deafeningly about the captain, rolled and pealed. The ship shook with it. Then a great wind-rush, fading swiftly. The vatch was gone . . . .

Goth slipped out of her cabin as the captain swung around and stood up from the couch. "Don't know what good that did!" he said, rather breathlessly. "But we might see some action now!" He switched on the room lighting.

Goth nodded, eyes big and dark. "Vatch is going to do something," she agreed. "Like to know what, though!"

"So would I." He'd already made sure the Manaret synergizer's strongbox was still standing in its place against the wall. It had occurred to him he might have sold the vatch on the importance of getting that potent device to the Karres of their time without giving it enough reason to take them and the *Venture* along with the synergizer.

Another thought came suddenly. "Say, we'd better look inside that box!"

But when he opened the box, the synergizer was there. He locked it up again. Goth suggested, "Vatch might have gone to Karres-now first to figure out what they'd do with it if they got it!"

"Yeah." The captain scratched his head. He hadn't much liked that wild gust of laughter with which the thing departed. Some vatchy notion had come to it while he was talking—and about half its notions at least spelled big trouble! He checked the time, said, "We'll just have to wait and see. Night's about over . . . ."

They sat before the screens, watched the air lighten gradually through the steady rainfall, waited for the vatch to return and speculated about what it might be up to. "There've been times just recently, child," the captain observed, "when I've wished you were safely back on Karres with your parents and Maleen and the Leewit! May not be long now before we're all there."

"Uh-huh. And if they're set to jump the Worm World, may not be so safe there either!" Goth remarked.

"There's that."

"Anyway," she said, "if I weren't keeping an eye on you, you'd likely as not be getting into trouble."

"Might, I suppose," the captain agreed. He looked at the chronometer. "Getting hungry? Sitting here won't hurry up anything, and it's pretty close to breakfast time."

"Could eat," Goth admitted and got out of her chair.

They found their passenger and the crewman wrapped up in their blankets on the floor of the outer section of the control compartment, soundly asleep. Before settling down for the night, the do Eldel had brought sleep pills from her stateroom; and Vezzarn had asked for and received a portion. The captain felt the two might as well slumber on as long as they could, but they came groggily awake while he was preparing breakfast and accepted his invitation to come to table.

They were halfway through breakfast when the Leewit arrived on the *Venture . . . .*

The captain and Goth had a few seconds' warning. He'd been wondering what he could say to their companions to prepare them for the moment when things suddenly would start happening again. It wasn't easy since he had no idea himself of just what might happen. They were both basically hardy souls though, and, with their backgrounds, must have been in sufficiently appalling situations before. Like Hulik, Vezzarn now appeared to be facing up stoically to the fact that he was caught in a witchcraft tangle where his usual skills couldn't help him much, which he couldn't really understand, and from which he might or might not emerge safely. The probability was that Vezzarn, as he'd sworn, wouldn't panic another time. He gave the captain a determinedly undaunted grin over his coffee, remarked that the viewscreens indicated the day would remain rainy, and asked what the skipper would like him to be doing around the ship the next few hours.

As the captain was about to reply, he became aware of a sound. It seemed very far off and was a kind of droning, heavy sound, a steady humming, with bursts of other noises mixed in, which could barely be made out in the humming, but which made him think at once of the vatch. This commotion, whatever it was, was moving towards him with incredible speed. A glance at the faces of Hulik and Vezzarn, who sat at the table across from him, told the captain it was not the sort of sound physical ears could pick up; their expressions didn't change.

He did not have time to look around at Goth, who'd left the table for a moment, and was somewhere in the room behind him. As distant as it seemed when he first caught it, the droning swelled enormously in an instant approaching the *Venture's* control compartment in such a dead straight line that the captain felt himself duck involuntarily, as if to dodge something which couldn't possibly be dodged. The accompanying racket, increasing equally in volume, certainly was the vatch's bellowing wind-voice but with an odd quality the captain had never heard before. The notion flashed through his mind that the vatch sounded like a nearly spent runner, advancing in great leaps to keep ahead of some dire menace pressing close on his heels, while he gasped out his astonishment at being so pursued.

Then the droning reached the control compartment—and stopped, was wiped out, as it reached it. An icy pitch-blackness swept through the room and was gone. For a moment the captain had relled vatch overwhelmingly. But that was gone, too. Then he realized he could still hear the monster's agitated voice, now receding into distance as swiftly as it had approached. In an instant it faded completely away.

As it faded, Goth said, "Captain!" from across the room behind him, and Hulik made a small, brief, squealing noise.

Twisting about, half out of his chair, the captain froze again, staring at the Leewit.

Toll's youngest daughter was on the floor in the center of the room, turning over and coming up on hands and knees. She stayed that way, blond hair tangled wildly, gray eyes glaring like those of a small, fierce animal, as her head turned quickly, first towards the captain, then towards Goth, hurrying towards her.

"Touch-talk! Quick!" the Leewit's high child-voice said sharply, and Goth dropped to her knees next to her. The captain heard the scrape of chairs, quick footsteps, glanced back and saw Vezzarn and Hulik hastily leaving the compartment section, returned his attention to the witch sisters. Goth had pulled the Leewit around and was holding her against herself, right palm laid along the side of the Leewit's head, her other hand pressing the Leewit's palm against her own temple. They stayed that way for perhaps a minute. Then the Leewit's small shape seemed to sag. Goth let her down to the floor, drew a long breath, stood up.

"Where did . . . is she going to be all right?" the captain inquired hoarsely.

"Huh? Sure! That was Toll," Goth told him, blinking absently at the Leewit.

"Toll?"

"Holding on and talking through the Leewit." Goth tapped the side of her head. "Touch-talk! Told me a lot before she had to go back to Karres-now . . . ." She glanced about, went to the stack of folded blankets used by Hulik and Vezzarn during the night, hauled them out of the corner and started pulling them apart. "Better help me get the Leewit wrapped in five, six of these before she comes to, Captain!"

Joining her, the captain glanced at the Leewit. She was lying on one side now, eyes closed, knees drawn up. "Why wrap her in blankets?" he asked.

"Spread them out like so. . . . Vatch took her over the Egger

Route. She'll throw three fits when she first wakes up—most everyone does! Route's pretty awful! Won't last long, but she'll be hard to hang on to if we don't have her wrapped."

They laid the Leewit on the blankets, began rolling her up tightly in them. "Cover her head good!" Goth cautioned.

"She won't be able to breathe—"

"She isn't breathing now," Goth told him, with appalling unconcern. "Go ahead—that's the way to do it!"

By the time they were done, the bundled-up non-breathing Leewit looked unnervingly like a small mummy laid away for a thousand-year rest. They knelt on the floor at either end of her, Goth holding her shoulders, the captain gripping her wrapped ankles. "Can cut loose any time now!" Goth said, satisfied.

"While we're waiting," said the captain, "what happened?"

Goth shook her head. "First off, what's *going* to happen. The Leewit mustn't hear that because she can't block a vatch. They're coming for us. Don't know when they'll make it, but they'll be here."

"Who's coming?"

"Toll and the others. Whoever they can spare. Can't spare too many though, because they're already fighting the Worm Worlders. They're at the Tark Nembi place—the Dead Suns Cluster, where I thought it might be—trying to work through to Manaret. Right now Karres is stuck in a force-web tangle, with so many Nuri globes around you can't look into space from there—"

It sounded like an alarming situation, but Goth said the witches had their new weapons going and figured they could make it. They'd had a plan to use the Manaret synergizer, which would have made their undertaking much less difficult; but time was running out, and they'd given up waiting for Olimy to arrive with the device or report his whereabouts. They had to assume he'd been trapped and was lost. But now that they knew what had happened, they were throwing everyone available on the problem of tracing out the Egger Route section the vatch had broken into the distant past. Toll still had a line on the Leewit, though a tenuous one, so they'd know exactly to what point to go. When they arrived, they'd reverse and take the *Venture* with everyone and everything on it back to Karres-now.

"They can move the whole ship over the Route?"

"Sure. Don't worry about that! You could move a sun over the Route except it'd nova before it got anywhere. If they get to us quick enough, that'll be it."

"The vatch . . . ."

"Looks to me," Goth said, "like the vatch got the idea backwards. You said get the synergizer to the other Karres, to the witches that can use it. So instead it brought a Karres witch back to the synergizer."

"The *Leewit?*" said the captain, astonished.

"Can't figure that either yet!" Goth admitted. "Well, it's a vatch—"

"What was the humming noise?"

"That's the Route. Vatch punched it straight into the ship so it could drop the Leewit in with us."

He grunted. "How did Toll do, uh, whatever she did?"

Goth said no one had realized a giant-vatch was hanging around Karres-now until it scooped up the Leewit. With all the klatha forces boiling on and about the planet at the moment, the area was swarming with lesser vatches, attracted to the commotion; among them the giant remained unnoticed. But when the Leewit disappeared, Toll spotted it and instantly went after it. She'd got a hook into the vatch and a line on her daughter and was rapidly overhauling the vatch when it managed to jerk free.

"I see," nodded the captain. Another time might be better to inquire what esoteric processes were involved in getting a hook into a giant-vatch and a line through time on one's daughter.

"Toll didn't have enough hold on the Leewit then to do much good right away," Goth continued. "There was just time for the touch-talk before she got sucked back to Karres-now."

"I suppose touch-talk's a kind of thought-swapping?"

"Sort of, but—"

The small blanket-wrapped form between them uttered a yowl that put the captain's hair on end. The next moment he was jerked forward almost on his face as the Leewit doubled up sharply, and he nearly lost his grip on her ankles. Then he found himself on his side on the floor, hanging on to something which twisted, wrenched, kicked, and rotated with incredible rapidity and vigor. The vocal din bursting from the blankets was no less incredible. Goth, lying across the Leewit with her arms locked around her, was being dragged about on the deck.

Then the bundle suddenly went limp. There was still a good deal of noise coming from it; but those were the Leewit's normal shrieks of wrath, much muffled now.

"Woo-ooof!" gasped Goth, relaxing her hold somewhat. "Rough one! She's all right now, though—you can let go—"

"Hope she hasn't hurt herself!" The captain was a little out of breath, too, more with surprise and apprehension than because of the effort he'd put out.

Goth grinned. "Take more than that bit of bouncing around to hurt her, Captain!" She gave the blankets a big-sisterly hug, put her mouth down close to them, yelled "Quit your screeching—it's me! I'm letting you out—"

The captain found Vezzarn and Hulik in the passenger lounge, spoke soothingly if vaguely of new developments which might get them all out of trouble shortly, and returned to the control section hoping he'd left the two with the impression that the Leewit's mode of arrival and the subsequent uproar were events normal enough in his area of experience and nothing for them to worry about. They'd agreed very readily to remain in the lounge area for the time being.

Goth and the Leewit were swapping recent experiences at a rapid-fire rate when he came back into the room. They still sat on the floor, surrounded by scattered blankets. "They got a klatha pool there now like you never saw before!" the Leewit was exclaiming. "They—" She caught sight of the captain and abruptly checked herself.

"Don't have to watch it with him any more!" Goth assured her. "Captain knows all about that stuff now."

"Huh!" When they'd loosened the blankets and the Leewit came eeling out, red faced and scowling, and discovered the captain there, her immediate inclination apparently had been to blame him for her experience, though she hadn't been aware of Toll's touch-talk conversation with Goth, in which Toll simply had used her as a handy medium—switching her on for the purpose about like switching on a ship intercom, the captain had gathered. The Leewit, in fact, remembered nothing clearly since the moment she'd relled a giant-vatch and simultaneously felt the vast entity sweeping her away from Karres. She recalled, shudderingly, that she'd been over the Egger Route. She knew it had been a horrifying trip. But she could only guess uneasily now at what had made it so horrifying. That blurring of details was a frequent experience of those who came over the Route and one of its most disturbing features. Since it was the captain who'd directed the vatch's attention to Karres in the first place, the Leewit wasn't so far off, of course, in feeling he was responsible for her kidnapping. However, nobody mentioned that to her.

The look she gave him as he squatted down on his heels beside the sisters might have been short of full approval, but she remarked only, "Learned mighty quick if you know all about it!"

"Not *all* about it, midget," the captain said soothingly. "But it looks like I've started to learn. One thing I can't figure at the moment is that vatch."

"What about the vatch?" asked Goth.

"Well, I had the impression that after it dropped the Leewit here, it took off at top speed—as if it were scared Toll might catch up with it."

The Leewit gave him a surprised stare.

"It *was* scared Toll would catch up with it!" she said.

"But it's a giant-vatch!" said the captain.

The Leewit appeared puzzled. Goth rubbed the tip of her nose and remarked, "Captain, if *I* were a giant-vatch and Toll got mad at me, I'd be going somewhere fast, too!"

"Sure would!" the Leewit agreed. "No telling what'd happen! She'd short out its innards, likely!"

"Pull it inside out by chunks!" added Goth.

"Oh?" said the captain, startled. "I didn't realize that, uh, sort of thing could be done."

"Well, not by many," Goth acknowledged. "Toll sure can do it!"

"Got a fast way with vatches when her temper's up!" the Leewit nodded.

"Hmm," said the captain. He reflected. "Then maybe we're rid of the thing, eh?"

Goth looked doubtful. "Wouldn't say that, Captain. They're mighty stubborn. Likely it'll come sneaking back pretty soon to see if Toll's still around. Could be too nervous about it to do much for a while though."

She regarded the Leewit's snarled blond mop critically. "Let's go get your hair combed out," she said. "You're kind of a mess!"

They went into Goth's cabin. The captain wandered back towards the screens, settled into the control chair, rubbed his jaw, relled experimentally. Nothing in range—but they probably hadn't lost the vatch yet. He'd been wondering about the urgent haste with which it had seemed to pass here when pursued by only one angry witch mother. Klatha hooks . . . shorting out vatch innards. . . . He shook his head. Well, Toll was a redoubtable sorceress even among her peers, from all he'd heard.

Klatha hooks—

The captain knuckled his jaw some more. No way of knowing when the Egger Route would come droning awesomely up again, this time bringing a troop of witches to transport the Manaret synergizer, the *Venture* and themselves to the embattled Karres of more than three hundred thousand years in the future. It might be minutes, hours, or days, apparently. There was no way of knowing either when the vatch would start to get over being nervous and discover there was no hot-tempered witch mother around at present—

The captain grunted, shifted attention mentally down to the *Venture's* engine room, to the thrust generators. Almost immediately an awareness came of the tiny, swirling speck of blackness there which couldn't be seen with physical eyes . . . the minute scrap of vatch stuff that carried enough energy in itself to hold the ship's drives paralyzed.

What immaterial manner of thing, he thought, would be a klatha hook shaped to snag that immaterial fragment of vatch?

Brief wash of heat. . . . The speck jumped, stood still again, its insides whirling agitatedly. The captain pulled in some fashion, felt something tighten between them like the finest of threads, grow taut.

So *that* was a klatha hook! . . . He let out his breath, drew on the hook, brought the speck in steadily with it until it was swirling above the control desk a few feet away from him.

Stay there, he thought, and released the hook. The speck stayed where it was. As close to it as this, he could rell its vatch essence, though faintly. He flicked another klatha snag to it, drew it closer, released it again . . . .

Hooks, it seemed, he could do. He might also find he was able to short out the speck's innards if he made the attempt. But there was no immediate point in that. The speck was a tool with powers and limitations, a working device, a miniature vatch machine. He'd already discovered some of the ways such a machine could be made to operate. What else could it do that might be useful to know . . . perhaps might become very necessary to know about?

The captain stared at the speck in scowling concentration, half aware Goth and the Leewit had left the cabin. He could hear them talking in the outer control section, voices lowered and intent. . . . Turn it inside out, in chunks? That might wreck it as a device. But since it was non-material vatch stuff, it might not.

There was a pipe in one of the drawers in his cabin, an old favorite of more leisurely days, though he hadn't smoked it much since the beginning of the Chaladoor trip. He brought an image of it now before his mind, pictured it lying on the control desk before him, turned his attention back to the vatch speck.

Just enough of you to do the job! . . . Get it!

Out of the speck, with the thought, popped a lesser speck, so tiny it could produce no impression at all except an awareness that it was there. It hung beside the other for an instant, then was gone, and was back. The pipe lay on the desk.

So they could be taken apart in chunks and the chunks still put to work! Now—

" . . . not *sure!*" The Leewit's young voice trilled suddenly through his abstraction. "Yes, I do, just barely. . . . Stinkin' *thing!*"

The captain glanced around hastily at the open door. Were they relling the vatch speck in here? It would do no harm, of course, if Goth knew about his new line of experimentation. But the Leewit—

Then he stiffened. *Together!* he thought at the two specks. The lesser one flicked back inside the other. *Back down where you*—but the reassembled vatch speck was swirling again above the thrust generators in the engine room before the thought was completed. He drew his attention quickly away from it.

"Captain?" Goth called from the outer room.

"Yes—I'm getting it, Goth!" His voice hadn't been too steady. The giant-vatch was barely in range, the relling sensation so distantly faint it had been overlapped by the one produced by the vatch-speck immediately before him. The entity had returned, might be prowling around cautiously as Goth had expected, to avoid another encounter with Toll and with klatha hooks of an order to match its own hugeness. But he had been careless—it wouldn't do at all to have the vatch surprise him while he was tinkering with the devices it had stationed here.

It drew closer gradually. The witch sisters remained silent. So did the captain. He began to get impressions of vatch-muttering, indistinct and intermittent. It did seem to be trying to size up the situation here now, might grow bolder as it became convinced it had lost its pursuer—

Why had it brought the Leewit through time to the *Venture*? She was a capable witch-moppet when it came to producing whistles that shattered shatterable objects to instant dust. From what Goth had said, she also had blasts in her armory with an effect approximating a knock-out punch delivered by a mighty fist. Neither, however, seemed very useful in getting the Manaret synergizer back to Manaret, past Moander, the Nuris, and the dense tangles of energy barriers that guarded the Worm World.

The Leewit's other main talent then was a linguistic one, as the witches understood linguistics—a built-in klatha ability to comprehend any spoken language she heard and translate and use it without effort or thought. And Moander, the monster-god of the Worm World legends, who was really a great robot, reputedly "spoke in a thousand tongues." Nobody seemed to know just what that meant; but conceivably the vatch knew. So conceivably the Leewit's linguistic talent was the vatch's reason for deciding to fit her into its plans to overthrow Moander through the captain.

There was no way of trying to calculate the nature of those schemes or of the Leewit's role in them more specifically. The manner in which the vatch played its games seemed to be to manipulate its players into a critical situation which they could solve with a winning move if they used their resources and made no serious mistakes . . . and weren't too unlucky. But it gave them no clues to what must be done. If they failed, they were lost, and the vatch picked up other players. And since it was a capricious creature, one couldn't be sure it wouldn't on occasion deliberately maneuver players into a situation which couldn't possibly be solved, enjoying the drama of their desperate efforts to escape a foreseeable doom.

The captain realized suddenly that he wasn't relling the vatch any more—then that the control room was spinning slowly about him, turning misty and gray. He made an attempt to climb out of the chair and shout a warning to Goth; but by then the chair and the control room were no longer there and he was swirling away, faster and faster, turning and rolling helplessly through endless grayness, while rollicking vatch laughter seemed to echo distantly about him.

That faded, too, and for a while there was nothing—

"Try to listen carefully!" the closer and somewhat larger of the two creatures was telling him. There was sharp urgency in its tone. "We've dropped through a time warp together, so you're feeling confused and *you've forgotten everything!* But I'll tell you who you are and who we are—then you'll remember it all again."

The captain blinked down at it. He did feel a trifle confused at the moment. But that was simply because just now, with no warning at all, he'd suddenly found himself standing with these two unfamiliar-looking creatures inside something like a globular hollow in thick, shifting fog. His footing felt solid enough, but he saw nothing that looked solid below him. In the distance, off in the fog, there seemed to be considerable noisy shouting going on here and there, though he couldn't make out any words.

But he didn't feel so confused that he couldn't remember who he was—or that, just a few moments ago, some vatch trick again had plucked him from the control room of the *Venture*, standing on a rainy, rocky slope of the Karres of over three hundred thousand years in the past.

Further, since the creature had addressed him in what was undisguisedly Goth's voice, he could conclude without difficulty that it was, in fact, Goth who had pulled a shape-change on herself. It didn't look at all like her; but then it wouldn't. And, by deduction, while the smaller, chunky, dog-like creature standing silently on four legs just beyond her looked even less like the Leewit, it very probably was the Leewit.

However, Goth evidently had warned him he'd better act bewildered, and she must have a reason for it.

"Umm. . . . yes!" the captain mumbled, lifting one hand and pressing his palm to his forehead. "I do feel rather . . . who . . . what . . . where am I? Who . . . ." He'd noticed something dark wagging below his chin as he was speaking, and the arm he lifted seemed clothed in a rich-textured light blue sleeve he'd never seen before, with a pattern of small precious stones worked into it. When he glanced down along his nose at the dark thing, he glimpsed part of a gleaming black beard. So he, too, had been shape-changed!

"You," the Goth-creature was saying hurriedly, "are Captain Mung of the Capital Guard of the Emperor Koloth the Great. My name's Hantis. I'm a Nartheby Sprite and you've known me a long time. That"—it indicated the other creature—"is a grik-dog. It's called Pul. It—"

"Grik-dogs," interrupted the grik-dog grumpily in the Leewit's voice, "can talk as good as anybody! Ought to tell him that so—"

"Yes," Goth-Hantis cut in. "They can speak, of course—shut up, Pul. So you'd bought it for the Empress at the Emperor's orders and we are taking it back to the capital when all this suddenly happened . . . ."

He'd been staring at her while she spoke. Goth might have gone on practicing her shape-changing on the quiet because this was a perfect, first-class job! Even from a distance of less than three feet, he couldn't detect the slightest indication that the Nartheby Sprite wasn't the real thing. He remembered vaguely that galactic legend mentioned such creatures. It looked like a small, very slender, brown-skinned woman, no bigger than Goth, dressed skimpily in scattered patches of some green material. The cheekbones were set higher and the chin was more pointed than a human woman's would have been; with the exception of the mouth, the rest of the face and head did not look human at all. The slender ridge of the nose was barely indicated on the skin but ended in a delicate tip and small, flaring nostrils. The eyes had grass green pupils which showed more white around them than human ones would; they seemed alert, wise eyes. The brows were broad tufts of soft red fur. A round, tousled mane of the same type of fur framed the face, and through it pro- truded pointed, mobile foxy ears. The grik-dog might be no less an achievement. The image was that of a solidly built, pale-yellow animal which would have been about the Leewit's weight, with a large round head and a dark, pushed-in, tru- culent, slightly toothy face. The gray eyes could almost have been those of the Leewit; and they stared up at the captain with much of the coldly calculating expression which was the Leewit's when things began to look a little tight.

"What, uh, did happen, Hantis?" the captain asked. "I seem almost to remember that I . . . but—"

The Sprite image shrugged.

"We're not really sure, Captain Mung. One moment we were on your ship, the next we were in this place! It's the place of a great being called Moander. We haven't seen him but he's talked to us. He's upset because nothing was supposed to be able to get in here—and now we've come in, through time! It must have been a warp. But Moander won't believe yet it was an accident."

"He'd better believe it!" snorted the captain haughtily, playing his part. "When Koloth the Great learns how his couriers have been welcomed here—"

"Moander says, sir," Goth-Hantis interrupted, "that in *his* time the Emperor Koloth the Great has been dead more'n three hundred years! Moander thinks we're perhaps spies of his enemies. He's setting this place up now so nobody else can get in the same way. Then we'll go to his laboratory so he can talk to us. He—"

"GRAZEEM!" a great voice shouted deafeningly in the fog above them. "*Grazeem!* Grazeem! . . . Grazeem . . ." The word seemed to echo away into the distance. Then there was more shouting all around them by the same mighty voice.

"What's the yelling about?" the captain asked in what he felt would be Captain Mung's impatient manner.

"Moander talking to the other machines," said the grik-dog. "Got a different language for each of them—don't know why. *It's* just a big, dumb machine, like they said."

"Pul, you—"

"S'all right, Goth," the grik-dog told the Sprite. "'Grazeem' means 'all units.' Moander's talking to all of them now. Machine that was listening to us won't till Moander stops again. You got something to say, better say it!"

"Guess she's right, Captain!" Goth-Hantis said hurriedly. "Vatch got us into Moander's place on the Worm World, our time. Haven't relled it, so it's not here. Got any ideas?"

"Not yet. You?"

"Uh-uh. Just been here a few minutes."

"The vatch figures there's something we can do if we're smart enough to spot it," the captain said. "Keep your minds ticking! If somebody sees something and we can't talk, say, uh—"

"Starkle?" suggested the grik-dog.

"Eh? All right, starkle. That will mean 'attention!' or 'notice that!' or 'get ready!' or 'be careful!' and . . ."

"*Starkle!*" said the grik-dog. "All-units talk's stopping!"

The captain couldn't tell much difference in the giant shouting, but again they probably could trust the Leewit in that. Whatever machine had been listening to them had begun to listen again. Goth-Hantis was glancing about, the image's big, pointed, furry ears twitching realistically.

"Looks like we've started to move," she announced. "Probably going to Moander's laboratory, like he said . . . ."

The fog substance enveloping the spherical hollow which contained them—and which must be the interior of a globular force field—was streaming past with increasing swiftness. There was no sensation of motion, but the appearance of it was that the globe was rushing on an upward slant through the gigantic structure on the surface of Manaret, Moander's massive stronghold, which the captain had glimpsed in a screen view during his talk with Cheel the Lyrd-Hyrier. The fog darkened and lightened successively about them, giving the impression that they were being passed without pause through one section of the interior after another. Sounds came now and then, presumably those of working machine units; and mingling with them, now distant, now from somewhere nearby, the shouted commands of Moander resounded and dropped away behind them.

Then, suddenly, there was utter silence . . . the vast, empty, icy kind of silence an audio pickup brings in from space. There were blurs of shifting color in the fog substance ahead and on all sides; and the fog no longer was rushing past but clinging densely about the globe, barely stirring. Evidently they had hurtled out of the stronghold and were in space above Manaret—and if Moander chose to deactivate the field about them now, the captain thought, neither the vatch's planning nor any witch tricks his companions knew could keep their lives from being torn from them by the unpleasantly abrupt violence of the void.

It seemed a wrong moment to move or speak, and Goth and the Leewit appeared to feel that, too. They stood still together, waiting in the cold, dark stillness of space while time went by—a minute, or perhaps two or three minutes. The vague colors in the fog which clung about the force field shifted and changed slowly. What the meaning of that was the captain couldn't imagine. There was nothing to tell them here whether the globe was still in motion or not.

But then a blackness spread out swiftly ahead and the globe clearly was moving towards it. The blackness engulfed them and they remained surrounded by it for what might have been a minute again, certainly no longer, before the globe slid out into light. After a moment then, the captain discovered that the fog was thinning quickly about them. He began to make out objects through it and saw that the force field had stopped moving.

They were within a structure, perhaps a large ship, which must be stationed in space above the surface of Manaret. The force globe was completely transparent, and as the last wisps of fog stuff steamed away, they saw it had stopped near the center of a long, high room. The only way the captain could tell they were still enclosed by it was that they were not standing on the flooring of the room but perhaps half an inch above it, on the solid transparency of a force field.

Almost as he realized this, the field went out of existence. There was the small jolt of dropping to the floor. Then he was in the room, with the images of a Nartheby Sprite and a grik-dog standing beside him.

The room, which was a very large one, had occupants. From their appearance and immobility, these might have been metal statues, many of them modeled after various living beings; but the captain's immediate feeling was that they were something other than statues. The largest sat on a throne-like arrangement filling the end of the room towards which he, Goth, and the Leewit faced. It could have been an obese old idol, such as primitive humanity might have worshipped; the broad, cruel face was molded in the pattern of human features, with pale blank disks for eyes which seemed to stare down at the three visitors. It was huge, towering almost to the room's ceiling, which must have been at least seventy feet overhead. Except for the eye-disks, the shape seemed constructed of the same metal as the throne on which it sat—rough-surfaced metal of a dark-bronze hue which gave the impression of great age and perhaps was intended to do so.

A round black table, raised six feet from the floor, stood much closer to the center of the room; in fact, not more than twenty feet from the captain. On it another bronze shape sat cross-legged. This one was small, barely half the size of a man. It was crudely finished, looked something like an eyeless monkey. In its raised right hand it held a bundle of tubes, which might have been intended to represent a musical instrument, like a set of pipes. The blind head was turned towards this device.

The remaining figures, some thirty or forty of them and no two alike, stood or squatted in two rows along the wall on either side of the captain and the witch sisters, spaced a few feet apart. Most of these were of more than human size; almost all were black, often with the exception of the eyes. Several, including a menacing, stern-faced warrior holding a gun, seemed modeled after humanity; and across from the warrior stood a black-scaled image which might have been that of Cheel, the Lyrd-Hyrier lord of Manaret. None of the others were recognizable as beings of which the captain had heard. The majority were shapes of nightmare to human eyes.

This was Moander's laboratory? Except for its disquieting assembly of figures, the great room seemed to hold nothing. The captain glanced up towards the ceiling. Much of that was a window, or a screen which served as a window. Through it one looked into space. And space was alive with the colors they had seen vaguely through the fog enclosing the force globe. Here they blazed brilliantly and savagely, and he could guess at once what they were—reflections of the great network of energy barriers Moander and his Nuris had constructed about the Worm World between the dead suns of the Tark Nembi Cluster. As he gazed, something edged into view at one side of the screen, blotting out the fiery spectacle. It was the metallic surface of Manaret. The structure of which this room was a part appeared to be rotating, turning the viewscreen now towards space, now to the Worm World far below it.

The witch children stood quietly beside him in their concealing shapes, glancing about with wary caution. Then came a softly hissed whisper:

"Starkle!"

The head of the great black warrior figure against the right wall turned slowly until the sullen face seemed to stare at them. The arm holding the gun lifted, swung the weapon around, and pointed it in their direction. Then the figure was still again—but there was no question that the weapon was a real weapon, the warrior a piece of destructive machinery perhaps as dangerous as the Sheem Robot. Nor was it alone in covering them. Across from it, beside the black Lyrd Hyrier image, a figure which seemed part beaked and long-necked bird, part many-legged insect, had moved at the same time, drawing back its head and turning the spear-tip of the beak towards them— a second weapon swiveled into position to bear on Moander's uninvited visitors.

"Starkle!" muttered the grik-dog. "*Double* starkle!"

The Leewit didn't mean the warrior and the bird-thing with that because the grik dog was staring straight ahead at the bronze monkey-figure which sat cross legged on the black table. At first the captain could see no change there; then he realized the monkey's mouth had begun to move and that faint sounds were coming from it . . . *Double*-starkle? Perhaps something familiar about those sounds . . . .

Yes, he thought suddenly, that was Moander's voice the monkey was producing—a miniaturized version of the brazen shouting which had followed the force-globe through the stronghold, the robot issuing its multilingual commands to the submachines . . . .

"I am Moander!" a giant voice said slowly above them.

They looked up together. The voice had come from the direction of the head of the big idol shape. As they stared at it, the eye disks in the idol head turned red.

"I am Moander!" stated a shape at the far end of the row along the wall on the right.

"I am Moander!" said the shape beside it.

"I am Moander . . . I am Moander . . . I am Moander . . . ," each of the shapes along the wall declared in turn, the phrase continuing to the end of the room, then shifting to the left wall and returning along it until it wound up with the shape which stood nearest the enthroned idol on that side. Then the monkey-shape, which had sat silent while this went on, turned its eyeless head around to the captain.

"I am Moander and the voice of Moander!" the tiny voice told him and the witch sisters, and the blind head swung back towards the bundle of pipes the shape held in one hand.

"Yes," said the big idol voice. "I am Moander, and each of these is Moander. But things are not as they seem, witch people! Look up—straight up!"

They looked. A section of Manaret's surface showed in the great screen on the ceiling again, and on it, seen at an angle from here, stood Moander's stronghold. Even at such a distance it looked huge and massively heavy, the sloping sides giving the impression that it was an outcropping of the ship-planet's hull.

"The abode of Moander the God. A holy place," said the idol's voice. "Deep within it lies *Moander*. About you are Moander's thoughts, Moander's voice, the god shapes which Moander in his time will place on a thousand worlds so that a thousand mortal breeds may show respect to a shape of Moander. . . . But *Moander* is not here.

"Do not move. Do not speak. Do not force me to destroy

you. I know what you are. I sensed the alien klatha evil you carry when you came out of time. I sensed your appearance was not your shape. I sensed your minds blocked against me, and by that alone I would know you, witch people!

"I listened to your story. If you were the innocent mortals you pretended to be, you would not have been taken here. You would have gone to the breeding vats in Manaret to feed my faithful Nuris, who always hunger for more mortal flesh.

"My enemies are taken here. Many have stood where you stand before the shape of Moander. Some attempted resistance, as you are attempting it. But in the end they yielded and all was well. Their selves became part of the greatness of Moander, and what they knew I now know."

The voice checked abruptly. The monkey-shape on the black table, which again had been sitting silently and unmoving while the idol spoke, at once resumed its tiny chatter. And now it was clear that the device in its hand was a speaker through which Moander's instructions were transmitted to the stronghold, to be amplified there into the ringing verbal commands which controlled the stronghold's machinery. The small shape went on for perhaps forty seconds, then stopped, and the voice which came from the great idol figure resumed in turn, "But I cannot spare you my full attention now. In their folly and disrespect, your witch kind is attacking Tark Nembi in force. I believe you were sent through time to distract me. I will not be distracted. My Nuris need my guidance in accomplishing the destruction of the world I have cursed. Their messages press on me."

It checked again. The small shape spoke rapidly again, paused.

" . . . press on me," the idol's voice continued. "My control units need my guidance or all would lapse into confusion. The barriers must be maintained. Manaret's energies must be fed the Nuris to hold high the attack on Karres the Accursed.

"I cannot give you much attention, witch people. You are

not significant enough. Open your minds to me now and your selves will be absorbed into Moander and share Moander's glory. Refuse and you die quickly and terribly—"

For the third time, it broke off. The monkey-shape instantly piped Moander's all units signal, "*Grazeem! Grazeem! Grazeem!*," at the device it held and rattled on. Holding his breath, the captain darted a sideways glance at his witches, found them staring intently at him. The Sprite nodded, very slightly. The grik-dog crouched. The captain reached for it as it sprang up at him, noticed it dissolved back into the Leewit as he caught it. He didn't notice much else because he was sprinting headlong towards the black table and the talkative monkey-shape with the Leewit by then. But there were metallic crashings to right and left, along with explosive noises . . . .

The monkey had stopped talking before he reached the table, sat there cross legged and motionless. Its metal jaw hung down, twisted sideways; the arm which held the transmission device had come away from the rest of it and dropped to the table top. There was renewed crashing farther down the room—Goth was still at work. The captain swung the Leewit up on the table, grasped the detached metal arm and held the transmitter before her. She clamped both hands about it and sucked in her breath—

It wasn't exactly a sound then. It was more like having an ice-cold dagger plunge slowly in through each eardrum. The pair of daggers met in the captain's brain and stayed there, trilling. The trilling grew and grew.

Until there was a noise nearby like smashing glass. The hideous sensation in his head stopped. The Leewit, sitting on the table beside the frozen, slack-jawed monkey-shape, scowled at the shattered halves of the transmitting instrument in her hands.

"Knew it!" she exclaimed.

The captain glanced around dizzily as Goth came trotting up, in her own shape. The rows of figures along the wall were in considerable disarray—machines simply weren't much good after a few small but essential parts had suddenly vanished from them. The black warrior's face stared sternly from a pile of the figure's other components. The bird-insect's head dangled beak down from a limp neck section, liquid fire trickling slowly like tears along the beak and splashing off the floor. The big idol's eye disks had disappeared and smoke poured out through the holes they'd left and wreathed about the thing's head.

The ceiling screen wasn't showing Moander's stronghold at the moment, but a section of Manaret's surface was sliding past. The structure should soon be in view. The captain looked at the Leewit. She must have held that horrid whistle of hers for a good ten seconds before the transmitting device gave up! For ten seconds, gigantically amplified, destructive non-sound had poured through every section of the stronghold below.

And every single simple-minded machine unit down there had been tuned in and listening—

"There it comes!" murmured Goth, pointing.

Faces turned up, they watched the stronghold edge into sight on the screen. A stronghold no longer—jagged cracks marked its surface, and puffs of flaming substance were flying out of the cracks. Farther down, its outlines seemed shifting, flowing, disintegrating. Slowly, undramatically, as it moved through the screen, the titanic construction was crumbling down to a mountainous pile of rubble.

The Leewit giggled. "Sure messed up his holy place!" Then her head tilted to the side; her small nostrils wrinkled fastidiously.

"And here comes you-know-who!" she added.

Yes, here came Big Wind-Voice, boiling up out of nothing as Manaret's barrier systems wavered. A gamboling invisible blackness . . . peals of rolling vatch laughter—

OH, BRAVE AND CLEVER PLAYER! NOW THE MIGHTY OPPONENT LIES STRICKEN! NOW YOU AND YOUR

PHANTOM FRIENDS SHALL SEE WHAT REWARD YOU
HAVE EARNED!

This time there was no blurring, no tumbling through grayness. The captain simply discovered he stood in a vast dim hall,
with Goth and the Leewit standing on his right. The transi-
tion had been instantaneous. Row on row of instruments lined
the walls to either side, rising from the blank black floor to
a barely discernible arched ceiling. He had looked at that scene
only once before and then as a picture projected briefly into
his mind by Cheel, the Lyrd-Hyrier prince, but he recognized
it immediately. It was the central instrument room of Manaret,
the working quarters of the lost synergizer.

And it was clear that all was not well here. The instrument
room was a bedlam of mechanical discord, a mounting, jar-
ring confusion. The controls of Manaret's operating systems
had been centered by Moander in his fortress; and with the
fall of that fortress the pattern was disrupted. But the Lyrd-
Hyrier must have been prepared long since to handle this
situation whenever it should arise—

They relled the vatch; it was not far away. Otherwise, except
for the raving instruments, the three of them seemed alone
in this place for several seconds following their arrival. Then
suddenly they had company.

A globe of cold gray brilliance appeared above and to the
left of them some thirty feet away. Fear poured out from
it like an almost tangible force; and only by the impact of
that fear was the captain able to tell that this thing of
sternly blazing glory was the lumpy crystalloid mass of the
Manaret synergizer, returned to its own place and transformed in it. An instant later a great viewscreen flashed into
sight halfway down the hall, showing the hugely enlarged
purple-scaled head of a Lyrd-Hyrier. The golden-green eyes
stared at the synergizer, shifted quickly to the three human
figures near it. The captain was certain it was Cheel even
before the familiar thought-flow came.

"Do not move, witch friends!" Cheel's thought told them. "This is for your protection—"

Something settled sluggishly about them, like a heavy thickening of the air. Motion seemed impossible at once. And layer on layer of heaviness still was coming down, though the air remained transparently clear. At the edge of the captain's vision was a momentary bright flashing as the synergizer rose towards the arched ceiling of the hall. He couldn't see where it went then or what it did, but a pale glow spread through the upper sections of the hall and the chattering din of instruments gone insane changed in seconds to a pulsing deep hum of controlled power.

Now the vatch shifted closer, turned into a looming mountainous blackness in which dark energies poured and coiled, superimposed on the hall, not blotting it out but visible in its own way along with the hall and extending up beyond it into the body of the ship-planet.

And the vatch was shaking with giant merriment . . . .

Chapter TWELVE

"WITCH FRIEND," Cheel's thought told the captain, "you and your associates have served your purpose . . . and now you will never leave in life the medium which has enclosed you. The synergizer is restored to its place, and its controls reach wherever Moander's did. Our Nuris are again ours, and Manaret is again a ship—a ship of conquest. It has weapons such as your universe has never seen. Their existence was concealed from Moander, and it could not have used them if it had known of them. But the synergizer can use them, and shall!

"Witch friend, we are not allowing Manaret to be restored to our native dimensional pattern. We are the Great People. Conquest is our destiny and we have adopted Moander's basic plan of conquest against your kind. At the moment our Nuris are hard pressed by your world of Karres and have been forced back among the cold suns. But Manaret is moving out to gather the globes about it again and destroy Karres. Then—"

It wasn't so much a thought as the briefest impulse. A lock took shape and closed in the same beat of time, and the connection to Cheel's mind was abruptly sliced off. What Cheel still had to say could be of no importance. What he already had said was abominable, but no great surprise. There'd simply been no way to determine in advance how trustworthy the Lyrd-Hyrier would be after they were relieved of their mutinous robot director. Since that must have been considered on Karres, too, it might be Cheel would not find Karres as easy to destroy now as he believed . . . .

But one couldn't count on that. And in any case, something would have to be done quickly. That there was death of some kind in this paralyzing heaviness which had closed down on him and his witches, the captain didn't doubt. He didn't know what it would be, but he could sense it being prepared.

And that made it a very bad moment. Because he was not at all sure that what could be done on a small scale, and experimentally, might also be done on an enormously larger scale under the pressures of emergency. Or that he was the one to do it. But there wasn't much choice—

OH, I KNEW IT! I FORESAW IT! the vatch-voice was bellowing delightedly. OH, WHAT A JEWEL-LIKE MIND HAS THIS PRINCE OF THE GREAT PEOPLE! WHAT A DEVAS-TATING MOVE HE HAS MADE! . . . WHAT NOW, SMALL PERSON, WHAT NOW?

Carefully, the captain shaped up a mind-image of the grid of a starmap. And perhaps—perhaps—it was a klatha sort of starmap, and that tiny dot on it was then not simply a dot but in real truth the living world of Emris, north of the Chaladoor, goal of the *Venture's* voyage. Now another dot on it which should be in empty space some two hours' flight from Emris—yes, *there!*

Then a mental view, a memory composite, of the *Venture* herself, combined with one of the *Venture's* control cabin. That part was easy.

And a third view of Goth and the Leewit, as they stood beside him unmoving in the death-loaded, transparent heaviness still settling silently on them all from above. . . . Easier still.

He couldn't move his head now; but physical motion wasn't needed to look up at the shifting, unstable mountain of vatch-blackness only he saw here, the monstrous torrents of black energy rushing, turning and coiling in endlessly changing patterns. Slitted green vatch-eyes stared at him from the blackness; vatch-laughter thundered:

YOU DID WELL, SMALL PERSON! VERY WELL! YOU'VE PLAYED YOUR PART IN THE GAME, BUT NO PLAYER LASTS FOREVER. NOW YOU'VE BEEN BEAUTIFULLY TRICKED; AND WE SHALL SEE THE END!

What manner of klatha hooks, the captain thought carefully, were needed to nail down a giant-vatch?

Flash of heat like the lick of a sun . . . The vatch-voice howled in shock. The blackness churned in tornado convulsions—

Not one hook, or three or four, the captain thought. Something like fifty! Great rigid lines of force, clamped on every section of the blackness, tight and unyielding! Big Windy, for all the stupendous racket he was producing, had been nailed down.

The captain glanced at his three prepared mind-pictures, looked into the seething vatch-blackness. *As much as we need for this! Put them together!*

YAAAAH! MONSTER! MONSTER—

A swirling thundercloud of black energy shot from the vatch's mass, hung spinning beside it an instant, was gone. Gone, too, in that instant were the two small witch figures who'd stood at the captain's right.

And now Manaret, that great evil ship—

We don't want it here . . . .

Black thunderbolts pouring from the vatch-mass, crashing throughout Manaret. Horrified shrieks from the vatch. The ship-planet shuddered and shook. Then it seemed to go spinning and blurring away from the captain, sliding gradually off into *something* for which he would never find a suitable description—except that the brief, partial glimpse he got of it was hideously confusing. But he remembered the impression he'd received from Cheel of the whirling chaos which raged between the dimension patterns, and knew the synergizer was taking the only course left open to save Manaret from being pounded apart internally by the detached sections of vatch energy released in it. And in another instant the Worm World had plunged back into the chaos out of which it had emerged centuries before and was gone.

As for the captain, he found himself floating again in the formless grayness which presumably was a special vatch medium, and which by now was beginning to seem almost a natural place for him to be from time to time. The vatch was there, not because it wanted to be there, but because he was still firmly tacked to it by the klatha hooks. It was a much reduced vatch. Over half its substance was gone—most of it dispersed in the process of demolishing Manaret, with which it had disappeared. The captain became aware of slitted green eyes peering at him fearfully from the diminished mass.

DREAM MONSTER, muttered a shaky wind-voice, RELEASE ME BEFORE YOU DESTROY ME! WHAT HORROR AM I EXPERIENCING HERE? LET ME AWAKE!

"One more job," the captain told it. "Then you can go—and you might be able to pick up a piece of what you've lost while you're doing the job."

WHAT IS THIS JOB?

"Return me to my ship . . . ."

He was plopped down with a solid thump on the center of the *Venture's* control room floor almost before he completed the order. The walls of the room swirled giddily around him—

"*Captain!*" Goth's voice was yelling from somewhere in the room. Then: "*He's here!*"

There was an excited squeal from the Leewit a little farther off; a sound of hurrying footsteps. And a wind-voice wailing, DREAM MONSTER . . . YOUR PROMISE!

Struggling up to a sitting position as the control room began to steady, the captain released the klatha hooks. He had a momentary impression of a wild, rising moan outside the ship which seemed to move off swiftly and fade in an instant into unimaginable distance.

As he came to his feet, helped up part way by Goth tugging with both hands at his arm, the Leewit arrived. Hulik do Eldel and Vezzarn appeared in the doorway behind her, stopped and stood staring at him. By then the walls of the room were back where they belonged. The feeling of giddiness was gone.

"All right, folks!" the captain said quickly and heartily, to get in ahead of questions he didn't want to answer just yet. "This has been rough, but I think we can relax . . . ." The viewscreens were a dark blur, which indicated the *Venture* was in space as she should be, while the screens were still set for close-up planetary scanning. The ship engines were silent. "Let's find out where we are. It should be north of the Chaladoor—"

"North of the Chaladoor—!" Vezzarn and Hulik chorused hoarsely.

"—around two hours from Emris." The captain slid into the control chair, flicked the screen settings to normal space-view. Stars appeared near and far. He turned up the detectors, got an immediate splattering of ship blips from medium to extreme range—a civilized area! "Vezzarn, pick me up some beacons here! I want a location check fastest!"

The spacer hurried towards the communicators, Hulik following. The captain cut in the main drive engines. They responded with a long, smooth roar and the *Venture* surged into flight. Before departing, the vatch appeared to have thriftily reabsorbed the speck of vatch-stuff it had left in the engine room to nullify drive energies . . . .

"Worm World?" Goth's urgent whisper demanded. The Leewit was pressed next to her against the chair, both staring intently at him.

"Went *pffttt!*" the captain muttered from the side of his mouth. "Tell you later—"

They gasped. "You *better!*" hissed the Leewit, gray eyes shining with a light of full approval the captain rarely had detected in them before. "What you *do?* That was the *scaredest* vatch I ever relled!"

"Emris beacons all around, skipper!" Vezzarn announced, voice quavvering with what might have been excitement or relief. "Have your location in a moment—"

The captain glanced at the witches. "Got a number we can call on Emris, to get in contact?" he asked quietly.

They nodded. "Sure do!" said Goth.

"We should be in range. Give it a try as soon as we have our course . . . ."

It seemed almost odd, a couple of minutes later, to be speaking to Toll by a method as unwitchy as ship-to-planet communicator contact. Hulik and Vezzarn had retired to the passenger section again when the captain told them there'd be Karres business coming up. The talk was brief. Toll had sheewashed to Emris from the Dead Suns Cluster just before their call came in, because someone she referred to as a probability calculator had decided the *Venture* and her crew should be showing up around there by about this time. Karres was still battling Nuri globes but winning handily in that conflict; and they'd realized something had happened to Manaret, but not what.

The captain explained as well as he could. Toll's eyes were shining much as the Leewit's as she blew him a kiss. "Now listen," she said, "all three of you. There's been more klatha simmering around the *Venture* lately than you'd normally find around Karres. Better let it cool off! We want to see you soonest but *don't* use the Drive to get here. Don't do anything but stay on course. . . . Captain, a couple of escort ships will meet you in about an hour to pilot you in. Children, we'll see you at the governor's spacefield in Green Galaine—oh, yes, and tell the captain what the arrangement is on Emris. . . . Now let's cut this line before someone taps it who shouldn't!"

"I just thought," the captain said to Goth and the Leewit as he switched off the communicator, "we'd better go make sure Olimy's all right! Come on . . . I'd like to hear about that Emris business then."

Olimy, unsurprisingly, was still in his stateroom, aloof and unaffected by the events which had thundered about him. On the way back they stopped to tell Hulik and Vezzarn they'd be making landfall on Emris in a couple of hours, and to find out what the experience of the two had been when they found themselves alone on the *Venture*. "There was this noise—" Hulik said. She and Vezzarn agreed it was an indescribable noise, though not a very loud one. "It was alarming!" said Hulik. It had come from the control section. They hadn't tried to investigate immediately, thinking it was some witch matter they shouldn't be prying into; but when the noise was followed by a complete silence from the forward part of the ship, they'd first tried to get a response from the control section by intercom, and when that failed they'd gone up front together. Except for the fact that there was no one present nothing had changed . . . the viewscreens showed the familiar rocky slope about them and the rain still pelting down steadily on the *Venture*. Not knowing what else to do, they'd sat down in the control section to wait . . . and they hadn't really known what they were waiting for.

"If you'll excuse me for saying so, skipper," said Vezzarn, "I wasn't so sure you three hadn't just gone off and left us for good! Miss do Eldel, she said, 'No, they'll be back.' But I wasn't so sure." He shook his grizzled head. "That part was bad!"

The captain explained there'd been no chance to warn them—didn't add there'd been a rather good chance, in fact, that no one ever would come back to the *Venture* again.

"Then the strongbox went!" reported Hulik. "I was looking at it, wondering what you had inside—and there was a puff of darkness about it, and that cleared, and the box was gone. Vezzarn hadn't seen it and didn't notice it, and I didn't tell him."

"If she'd told me, I'd've fainted dead!" Vezzarn muttered earnestly.

Then the blackness had come . . . Blackness about the ship and inside it and around them, lasting for perhaps a minute. When it cleared away suddenly, Goth and the Leewit were standing in the control room with them. Everyone had started looking around for the captain then until Goth suddenly announced his arrival from the control room a couple of minutes later . . . .

"Well, I'm sorry you were put through all that," the captain told the two. "It couldn't be helped. But you'll be safe down on Emris within another two hours. . . . Happen to remember just when it was you heard that strange noise?"

The do Eldel checked her timepiece. "It seems like several lifetimes," she said. "But as a matter of fact, it was an hour and fifteen minutes ago."

Which, the captain calculated on the way back to the control section, left about forty minutes as the period within which Moander had been buried under his mighty citadel, the Worm World pitched into chaos, and a giant-vatch taught an overdue and lasting lesson in manners. A rather good job, he couldn't help feeling, for that short a time!

The escort ships which hailed them something less than an hour later were patrol boats of the Emris navy. The purpose of the escort evidently was to whisk the *Venture* unchecked through the customary prelanding procedures here and guide her down directly to the private landing field of the governor of Green Galaine, one of the four major administrative provinces of Emris.

The captain wasn't surprised. From what Goth and the Leewit had told him, the Karres witches were on excellent terms with the authorities of this world; and the governor of Green

Galaine was an old friend of their parents. The patrol boats guided them in at a fast clip until they began to hit atmosphere, then braked. A great city, rolling up and down wooded hills, rose below; and he leveled the *Venture* out behind the naval vessels towards a small port lying within a magnificent cream-and-ivory building complex.

"Know this place?" he asked the Leewit, nodding at the semicircle of beautiful buildings.

"Governor's palace," she said. "Where we'll stay ...."

"Oh?" The captain studied the palace again. "Guess he's got room enough for guests, at that!" he remarked.

"Sure—lots!" said the Leewit.

"The tests," Threbus said, "show about what we expected. Of course, as I told you, these results reflect only your present extent of klatha control. They don't indicate in any way what you may be doing six months or a year from now."

"Yes, I understand that," the captain said.

"Let me look this over once more, Pausert, to make sure I haven't missed anything. Then I'll sum it up for you."

Threbus began to busy himself again with the notes he'd made on the klatha checks he'd been running the captain through, and the captain watched his great uncle silently. Threbus must be somewhere in his sixties if the captain's recollection of family records was correct, but he looked like a man of around forty and in fine shape for his age. Klatha presumably had something to do with that. During the captain's visit at Toll's house on Karres, he'd encountered Threbus a few times in the area and chatted with him, unaware that this affable witch was the father of Goth and her sisters or his own long-vanished kinsman. At the time Threbus had worn a beard, which he'd since removed. The captain could see that, without the beard and allowing for the difference in age, there was, as Goth had told him, considerable similarity between the two of them.

This was the morning of the third day since the *Venture* had landed on Emris. The night before, Threbus had suggested that he and the captain go for an off-planet run today to see how the captain would make out on the sort of standard klatha tests given witches at various stages of development. Off-planet, because they already knew he still had a decidedly disturbing effect on the klatha activities of most adult witches, simply by being anywhere near them; and it could be expected the effect would be considerably more pronounced when he was deliberately attempting to manipulate klatha energies.

Threbus folded his notes together, dropped them into the disposal box of the little ship which had brought the two of them out from Emris, and adjusted the automatic controls. He then leaned back in his chair.

"There are several positive indications," he said. "But they tell us little we didn't already know. You're very good on klatha locks. A valuable quality in many circumstances. Theoretically, you should be able to block out any type of mind reader I've encountered or heard about, assuming you become aware of his, her, or its intentions. You have very little left to learn in that area. It's largely a natural talent.

"Then, of course, you're a vatch-handler. A natural quality again, though a quite unusual one. Under the emergency conditions you encountered, you seem to have developed it close to its possible peak in a remarkably short time. A genuine klatha achievement, my friend, for which we can all be thankful!

"However, vatch-handling remains a talent with limited usefulness, particularly because it's practiced always at the risk of encountering the occasional vatch which cannot be handled. There is no way of distinguishing such entities from other vatches until the attempt to manipulate them is made—and when the attempt fails, the vatch will almost always destroy the unfortunate handler. So this ability is best kept in reserve, strictly as an emergency measure."

"Frankly," remarked the captain, "I'll be happiest if I never have to have anything to do with another vatch!"

"I can hardly blame you. And the chances are good—under ordinary conditions that it will be a long time before you have more than passing contacts with another one. You're sensitized now, of course, so you'll be aware of the occasional presence of a vatch as you couldn't have been formerly. But they rarely make more than a minor nuisance of themselves.

"Now I noticed various indications here that you tend to be a lucky gambler . . . ."

The captain nodded. "I usually win a bet," he said. "That comes natural, too, I suppose?"

"Yes, in this case. Quite generally, in fact, you have a good natural predisposition for klatha manipulation. And you are, as we already know, an exceptionally strong conductor of the energies. But aside from the two categories we've mentioned, you have as yet no significant conscious control of them. That's about the size of it at present . . . ."

The captain acknowledged it was also about what he'd expected. He had felt a minor isolated quiver or two of what might have been klatha force during the check run, but that was all.

Threbus nodded, cut out the auto controls, swung the little ship around towards Emris. "We might as well be getting back down," he said. "I understand from Goth, incidentally, that the two of you haven't yet made any definite arrangements for the *Venture*'s next enterprise."

The captain glanced quickly over at him. This was the first indication either of Goth's parents had given that they still had no objection to letting her travel about with him.

"No," he said. "The Chaladoor run set us up well enough— we can look around for the job we like best now." He cleared his throat. "I've been wondering though how you and Toll really felt about Goth's deciding to stay on the *Venture* with me."

"We're not opposing it," Goth's father told him, "for at least two very good reasons, aside from the opinion we have of you as a person. One of the reasons is that, even now, it would be extremely difficult to keep Goth from doing whatever she really wanted to do."

"Yes," nodded the captain. "I see that. But—"

"The other reason," continued Threbus, "is one Goth doesn't know about and shouldn't know about. Several of our most capable predictors agree she could have selected no more favorable course for herself than to remain in your company at present."

"At present?" asked the captain.

Threbus shrugged. "Let's say for approximately a year. Beyond that we don't know. It's very difficult for a predictor to be specific about individual destinies over a greater span of time— particularly when the individual in question is involved with klatha."

"I see," said the captain.

"No, not entirely, Pausert. Let me be frank about this. Goth's interest in you is a good thing for her. We know that, though we don't know precisely what part it is having in her development, in what way it will affect her future. However, you would find no probability calculator prepared to say it is a good thing for *you*. Your future—even of the next few months—is obscured by factors which cannot be understood. I'm not saying this means that Goth will bring you bad luck. But it might mean that. And it might be very bad luck."

"Well, I'll take a chance on it!" said the captain, relievedly. "The fact is I'd have missed Goth very much if she weren't going to be around the ship any more." He chuckled. "Of course I'm not taking her idea of getting married to me when she grows up too seriously!"

"Of course not," said Threbus. "No more, my purblind great-nephew, than I took Toll's ideas along those lines too seriously. Now, getting back to my original query about your plans—"

✧　　✧　　✧

"Uh, yes . . ." The captain hesitated. "Well, we cleared up the disposition of the last of the Uldune cargo yesterday, and the interior repairs on the *Venture* should be finished in another four days. Since I'm being a problem to you people in Green Galaine, I thought we might move the ship then to some other civilized world where we can make arrangements for new commercial runs. Until I can stop being a problem, it looks as if I'll simply have to keep away from Karres—or any place where witches are operating."

Threbus rubbed his chin. "There's a world named Karres," he remarked, "but Karres isn't that world. Neither is it an organization of witches. You might say it comes closest to being a set of attitudes, a frame of mind."

The captain looked at him. "I don't think I—"

"On Uldune," continued Threbus, "you discovered a bad and very dangerous situation. It was none of your business. Involving yourself in it would mean assuming the gravest sort of responsibility. It would also mean exposing yourself and Goth to the horrendous threat of the Nuris—"

"Well, yes," acknowledged the captain. "But we knew there was no one else around who could do it."

"No, there wasn't," Threbus agreed. "Now, in making the decision you did, you revealed yourself to be a member in good standing of the community of Karres, whether you were aware of the fact or not. It isn't a question of witchcraft. Witchcraft is a tool. There are other tools. And keeping away from a world of that name does not mean dissociating yourself from Karres. Whether you do dissociate yourself or not will again be your decision."

The captain considered him for some seconds. "What do you want me to do?" he asked.

"As I've indicated, it's a question of what you'll want to do," Threbus told him. "However, I might suggest various possibilities. I've admired your ship. It has speed, range, capacity, adequate armament. An almost perfect trader, freight and passenger carrier. You could turn it to nearly any purpose you chose."

The captain nodded. "That was the idea."

"Such a ship is a valuable tool," Threbus observed. "Particularly in combination with a skipper like yourself and the touch of audacious magic which is my daughter Goth. If you were operating in the Regency of Hailie, as a start, you would find profitable standard consignments coming your way almost automatically. Along with them would come nonstandard items, which must be taken from one place to another without attracting attention or at least without being intercepted. Sometimes these would be persons, sometimes documents or other materials."

"The *Venture* would be working on Karres business?" asked the captain.

"On the business of the Empress Hailie, which is also the business of Karres. You'd be a special courier, carrying the Seal of Hailie. Of course the Empire's internal politics is a game that's being played with considerable ferocity . . . you couldn't afford to get careless."

"No, I can see that. As a matter of fact," remarked the captain, "I'd intended avoiding the Empire for a while. Apparently a good many people are aware by now that the *Venture* has a special drive on board they feel would be worth acquiring. Changing her name and ours doesn't seem to have fooled them much."

"That part of it shouldn't be a problem much longer, Pausert. We're letting it become known that Karres has the Sheewash Drive and what it is. Simultaneously the word is spreading that Karres has destroyed the Worm World. We're borrowing your glory for a good purpose. The net effect will be that people informed enough to suspect the *Venture* possesses the Sheewash Drive will also be informed enough to feel no one in their senses would meddle with such a ship. . . . Well, great-nephew, what do you think?"

"I think, great-uncle," said the captain, "that the Empress has acquired a new special courier."

There had been a question of what should be done about the Nuri globes left behind after Manaret vanished from the universe. Many of the swarms which engaged Karres in the Tark Nembi cluster had been destroyed; but others slipped away into the Chaladoor, and the number of globes scattered about the galactic sector which had not been involved in the conflict was difficult to estimate. However, evidence came in within a few days that the problem was resolving itself in unexpected fashion. Globes had been observed here and there; and all drifted aimlessly through space, apparently in a process of rapid dissolution. In what manner they had drawn on the Worm World's energies to sustain them wherever they went never became known. But with Manaret gone the Nuri remnants died quickly. They might remain a frightful legend for centuries to come, but the last actual sighting of a globe was recorded a scant four days after the *Venture's* landing on Emris. It was a darkened, feebly flickering thing then, barely recognizable.

Satisfactory progress was being made, the captain heard, in establishing contact with Olimy in his disminded condition, though the Karres experts in such matters felt it still would be a lengthy, painstaking procedure to restore him fully to the here-and-now. Meanwhile, with the *Venture's* future role settled, and an early departure date indicated to get him out of the hair of his politely patient witch friends here, the captain had his time fully taken up with consultations, appointments, and supervision of assorted preparations involved with the lift-off. One day, coming through the lobby of a hotel off the province's main port, to which the *Venture* had been transferred after completion of the internal repair work, he found himself walking towards the slender elegance of Hulik do Eldel. They had a drink together for old times' sake, and Hulik told him she hadn't decided yet what her next move would be. Presently she inquired about Vezzarn. The captain said he'd paid off the old spacer, adding a bonus to the risk run money, and that Vezzarn had seemed reluctant to leave the *Venture*, which surprised the captain, considering the kind of trip they'd had.

"It was an unusual one," Hulik agreed. "But you brought us through in the end. How I'll never understand." She looked at him a moment. "And you told me you weren't a witch!"

"I'm not really," said the captain.

"Well, perhaps not. But Vezzarn may feel now you're a skipper the crew can depend on in any circumstances. For that matter, if you plan any more risk runs in a direction I might be interested in, be sure to let me know!"

The captain thanked her, said he wasn't planning any at present, and they parted pleasantly. He had another encounter, a rather curious one, some hours later. He was hurrying along one of the upper halls of the governor's palace, looking for an office Threbus maintained there. When the *Venture* left, two days from now, she would have two unlisted passengers on board to be carried secretly to the Regency of Hailie; and he was to be introduced to them in the office in a few minutes. So far he'd been unable to locate it. Deciding finally that he must have passed it in the maze of spacious hallways which made up the business section of the palace, he turned to retrace his steps. Coming up to a corner, he moved aside to let a small, slender lady wearing a huge hat and a lustrous fur jacket walk past, trailed by a stocky dog. The captain went on around the corner, then checked abruptly and came back to stare after the two.

What had caught his notice first was that the lady's jacket was made up of the fabulously expensive tozzami furs of Karres, of which he'd sold a hundred and twenty-five on Uldune. Then there'd been something familiar about that chunky, yellow, sour-faced dog—

Yes, of course! He hurried after them, grinning. "Just a moment!" he said as he came up.

They turned to look at him. The lady's face was concealed by a dark veil which hung from the brim of the hat, but the dog was giving him a cold, gray-eyed stare—and that, too, was familiar enough! The captain chuckled, reached out, took the tip of the big hat between thumb and finger and lifted it gently. Beneath it appeared the delicate nonhuman face, the grass-green eyes, the tousled red mane and pointed ears of the Nartheby Sprite image Goth had assumed in Moander's stronghold.

"Knew it!" he laughed. "Thought you could fool me with that silly hat, eh? What are you two up to now?"

The Sprite face smiled politely. But a deep, gravelly voice inquired from behind the captain's ankles, "Shall I mangle this churl's leg, Hantis?" and a large mouth with sharp teeth in it closed on his calf, though the teeth didn't dig in immediately.

Mouth and teeth! he thought, startled. Tactile impressions were no part of the shape-changing process! Why, then—

"No, Pul," the Sprite said. "Let go his leg! This must be Captain Pausert . . . ." It giggled suddenly. "Goth showed me the imitation she can do of me, Captain. It's a very good one . . . May I have my hat back again?"

So that was how he learned that Nartheby Sprites and grik-dogs really existed, that Goth had hastily copied the images of two old friends to produce fake shapes for the Leewit and herself when they were transported into Moander's citadel, and that Hantis and Pul were the passengers they were to smuggle past the Imperial intelligence agents on the lookout for them to the Empress Hailie . . . .

The *Venture* took off on schedule. The first six hours of the trip were uneventful—

"Somebody to see you, Captain," Goth's voice announced laconically over the intercom. "I'll send 'em forward!"

"All right . . . HUH?"

But the intercom had clicked off. He swung up from the

control chair, came out of the room as Vezzarn and Hulik do Eldel walked into the control section from the passage. They smiled warily. The captain put his hands on his hips.

"What-are-you-two-doing-on-this-ship?" he inquired between his teeth.

"Blood in his eye!" Vezzarn muttered uneasily. He glanced at Hulik. "You do the talking!"

"May I explain, Captain?" Hulik asked.

"Yes!" said the captain.

Both she and Vezzarn, the do Eldel said, had discovered they were in a somewhat precarious situation after the *Venture* landed on Emris. Somebody was keeping them under surveillance.

"Oh!" the captain said. He shook his head. "Sit down, Miss do Eldel. You, too, Vezzarn. Yes, of course you were being watched. For your own protection, among other reasons—"

The disappearance of Yango and his Sheem Robot, while en route through the Chaladoor on the *Venture*, had not required explanation to authorities anywhere. Pirate organizations did not complain to the authorities when one of their members disappeared in attempting an act of piracy. Nevertheless, the authorities of Green Galaine were informed that a man, who represented himself as the Agandar and very probably was that notorious pirate chieftain, had tried to take over the *Venture* and was now dead. It was valuable information. With the menace of Manaret removed, civilized worlds in the area could give primary consideration to removing the lesser but still serious menace of the Agandar's pirates. When his organization learned the *Venture* had landed safely on Emris and that no one answering Yango's description had come off it, they'd wanted to know what had happened.

" . . . so we've all been under surveillance," the captain concluded. "So was the ship until we took off. If pirate operators had started prowling around you or myself, they might have given Emris intelligence a definite lead to the organization."

Hulik shook her head. "We realized that, of course," she said. "But it wasn't only Emris intelligence who had us under surveillance. Those pirate operators *have* been prowling around. So far they've been a bit too clever to provide the intelligence people with leads."

"How do you know?" the captain asked.

She hesitated, said, "An attempt was made to pick me up the night after I disembarked from the ship. It was unsuccessful. But I knew then it would be only a matter of time before they'd be questioning me about Yango. I don't have as much trust as you do in the authorities, Captain Pausert. So I got together with Vezzarn who was in the same spot."

"Nobody's been bothering me," the captain said.

"Of course nobody's bothered you," said Hulik. "That's why we're here."

"What do you mean?"

"Captain, whether you're a Karres witch or not, you were suspected of being one. Now that the Agandar has disappeared while trying to take your superdrive from you, there'll be very little doubt left that you are, in fact, the kind of witch it's best not to challenge. The *Venture* is at present the safest place for Vezzarn and myself to be. While we're with you, the Agandar's outfit won't bother us either."

"I see," the captain said after a moment. He considered again. "Well, under the circumstances I can't blame you for stowing away on the ship. So you'll get a ride to the Empire and we'll let you off somewhere there. You'll be far enough away from the Agandar's pirates then."

"Perhaps," said the do Eldel. "However, we have what we feel is a better idea."

"What's that?"

"We're experienced agents. We've been doing some investigating, And we've concluded that the business which is taking you into the Empire is a kind that might make it very useful for you to have two experienced agents on hand.

Meanwhile we could also be of general service around the ship."

"You want me to hire you on the *Venture*?" said the captain, surprised.

"That," Hulik acknowledged, "was our idea."

The captain told her he'd give it thought, reflectively watched the two retire from the section. "Goth?" he said, when he'd heard the compartment door close.

Goth appeared out of no-shape invisibility on the couch. "They're in a spot," the captain said. "And experience is what we're short on, at that. What do you think?"

"Ought to be all right," Goth said. "They'll go all out for you if you let 'em stay. You kind of got Vezzarn reformed." She rubbed her nose tip pensively. "And besides . . ."

"Besides what?"

"Had a talk with Maleen and a predictor she works with just before we left," Goth told him.

"Yes?"

"They can't figure you too far. But they got it worked out you're getting set to do something—and it could get sort of risky."

"Well," said the captain helplessly, "somehow we do always seem to be doing something that turns out sort of risky."

"Uh-huh. Wouldn't worry too much, though. We come out all right. . . . Before you start to do that, they said, you're going to get together a gang to do it with."

"A gang?"

"Whoever you need. And that was to happen pretty soon!"

The captain reflected, startled. "You mean that in some way I might have got Hulik and Vezzarn to stow away on the ship?"

"Could be," Goth nodded.

He shook his head. "Well, I just can't see—What's *that*?"

But he knew as he asked. . . . A distant, heavy, droning sound, approaching with incredible rapidity. Goth licked her lips quickly. "Egger Route!" she murmured. "Wonder who . . ."

The droning swelled, crashed in on them, ended abruptly.

The Leewit lay curled up on her side on the floor, eyes shut.

The captain scooped her up, was looking around for something to bundle her up in again when Goth said sharply, "She's waking up! Just hang on hard! This one won't be too bad—"

He hung on hard . . . and comparatively speaking, it wasn't too bad. For about ten seconds he had the feeling of clutching a small runaway engine to him, with many pistons banging him simultaneously. There was also a great deal of noise. Then it was over.

The Leewit twisted her head around to see who was holding her.

"*You!*" she snarled. "*What you do?*"

"It wasn't me!" the captain told her breathlessly. He put her down on her feet. "We don't—"

The communicator signaled from the inner room.

"That'll be Toll!" Goth said, and ran to switch it on.

It was Toll.

Half an hour later, the captain sat alone in the control chair again, absently knuckling his chin.

The Leewit was staying. No one had sent her deliberately along the Egger Route to the *Venture* this time; so the witches felt it was something he and the Leewit had done between them. Some affinity bond had been established; some purpose was being worked out. It would be best not to interfere with this until it could be clarified.

He and the Leewit were about equally dumbfounded at the idea of an affinity bond between them, though the captain did his best to conceal his surprise. The smallest witch had accepted the situation, rather grudgingly.

Well, strange things simply kept happening when one started going around with witches, he thought. . . . Then he suddenly stiffened, sat up straight, hair bristling.

Like hearing a whiff of perfume, like seeing the tinkle of a bell—vatches came in all sizes; and this one was no giant. He could make it out now, flicking about him to left and right. A speck of blackness which seemed no bigger than his thumb. It might be as small as a vatch could get—but it was a vatch!

It came to a pause above the control desk before him. A pair of tiny silver eye slits regarded him merrily.

"Don't *you* start making trouble now!" the captain warned it.

"Goodness, no!" giggled the vatch. "I wouldn't *think* of making trouble, big dream thing!" It swirled up and away and about the control room and was gone.

Gone where, he wondered. He couldn't rell it any more. He got out of the chair, paused undecidedly. Then from the passage leading to the passenger section came sudden sounds— a yelp of alarm from Vezzarn, a shriek of pure rage from the Leewit.

The intercom clicked on.

"Captain," Goth's voice told him, "better get down here!" She was choking with laughter.

"What's happening?" the captain asked, relaxing a little.

"Having a little trouble with a baby vatch . . . oh, my! Better come handle it!" The intercom went off.

"Well," the captain muttered, heading hurriedly across the outer room towards the passage, "here we go again!"

The following is an excerpt from:

THE WIZARD OF KARRES

by

Mercedes Lackey, Eric Flint & Dave Freer

hardcover, available in August 2004
from Baen Books

CHAPTER 1

The shrill screaming from inside made Captain Pausert open the cabin door with some caution. Not that screaming was necessarily unusual around his present company—just that it was a good idea to meet screaming with due care.

He ducked reflexively as something went whizzing past his head. Vermilion splattered all over the wall of the *Venture*'s second-best stateroom. It didn't make things look much worse. The eggshell blue paint that Goth had picked out with such care during their refit on Uldune was scarred and splattered with mute testimony to the savageness of the battle which was going on inside.

In the center of what had once been an ankle-deep pale cream carpet was the perpetrator of the ghastly destruction.

The Leewit, the younger of the two witch girls of Karres aboard the ship, stopped drumming her heels on the floor, sat up and glared at him. "What are you doing here, stupid?" she demanded, weighing the next paint-bottle in her hands.

Like the sound of sunlight, like seeing a scent, he was aware of the insubstantial thing somewhere in the room: a thumb-sized vatch, filling Pausert's head with tinkling vatch-giggles. Then he saw it. Around the light, a sheet of paper dragged by that tiny piece of impossible blackness fluttered like a demented moth.

THROW IT AT THE BIG DREAM THING! squeaked the vatch, inside his head, its silvery eyes wide with delight. THROW, THROW!

"Shan't!" said the Leewit, changing her mind.

SPOILSPORT! THROW AT ME AGAIN, THEN! The vatch

swooped down at her, fluttering what had obviously been the Leewit's artistic endeavor inches from the Leewit's nose.

The Leewit snatched at it furiously, nearly dropping the paint bottle. "Mine! Give it!"

The vatch and the picture twitched away from her fingers, and then disappeared, and then reappeared—in four different localities at the same time.

Life with vatches was interesting. So was life with Karres witches. Life with both was . . . *complicated.*

Captain Pausert's life had been very, very complicated for some time now.

The Leewit impotently threatened the dancing vatch quartet with the paint bottle. Then she turned on the captain. "You! You can even handle a giant vatch. Get my picture back from the stinkin' little thing!"

"Seeing as you asked so nicely, child, I will." Captain Pausert was careful to keep a straight face. It amused him to see the Leewit persecuted, for a change, since the Leewit was ever so capable of doing a fair amount of persecuting herself.

Still, vatches were too capable of creating havoc for him to leave one on the loose here. Forming hooks of the invisible stuff that was klatha force, Pausert began to reach with them for the tiny vatch . . . or vatches.

There were four of them and they all looked the same—two inches of blackness and a pair of slitty silver eyes. They all seemed to have the Leewit's picture, too. That was confusing. But vatches did odd things to time and space in human dimensions. He'd just try each one in turn.

He did. To no avail.

"It's doing a light-shift, Captain." That observation came from the Leewit's older sister, Goth, from where she lounged in a formfit chair on the far side of the room. "Splitting its image. Neat trick. Hadn't thought of that," she said, rubbing her sharp chin.

Pausert stared at the four. "So where is it actually?" Light-shifts were one of Goth's klatha skills.

"Got to be somewhere between them, Captain."

Pausert "felt" with the klatha hooks . . . encountered non-material resistance. Suddenly there was only one tiny speck of whirling midnight, and the Leewit's artwork fluttered towards the floor. The little blond witch snatched it out of the air.

Pausert was a vatch-handler. He'd taken on Big Windy, the giant vatch. He could pull them inside out and make them jump through hoops, if he had to. Only . . .

There was one kind of these non-material klatha-creatures that was supposed to be unmanageable—and, unfortunately, you couldn't tell which kind of vatch you had until you had it. Then it could be too late. Klatha was powerful, but also dangerous.

TICKLES, giggled the vatchlet.

Pausert tried to make the little creature move. It was like pushing smoke. With a sinking feeling, he realized that the silvery-eyed mischief must be one of the kind of vatch that none of the witches of Karres could make do anything.

I LIKE THIS PLACE. IT'S FUN! The vatchlet whizzed around his head, then—into his chest.

Pausert's heart stopped for a moment. But nothing else happened, and it restarted again.

Well, at least it hadn't turned on him. And it sounded and acted awfully young. He'd—

Suddenly, the ship-detector alarms sounded through the intercom system. Pausert had set them up to do so when the *Venture* had made her run through the Chaladoor, that region of dangerous space between Emris and Uldune. He'd never gotten around to undoing it.

The baby vatch and Leewit would just have to sort out their own problems. This could be something far worse. The captain left at a run, with Goth hard at his heels. They nearly collided with Vezzarn, the old spacer-cum-spy who was one half of their crew. The other half, Hulik do Eldel, former Imperial agent and citizen of the pirate planet Uldune, was barely moments behind.

The Captain focused the viewscreens on the object—no, objects—the detectors had picked up. They were still almost at maximum range, but were coming in fast.

"Imperial cruisers, Captain," said Goth, looking at the heavily armed spacecraft.

Pausert's heart began doing complicated calisthenics. Pirates would have been preferable. Much preferable.

"There is another one up there coming in the upper quadrant," said Hulik, pointing.

"And another one, dead ahead," added Vezzarn. "I think they've got us boxed, Captain."

They did indeed. Pausert realized that this meant that someone back at the Governor's Palace in Green Galaine on Emris must have passed on details of their plans, including their exact trajectory. This was not good, and he had the feeling it was going to get a great deal worse.

"Do you want me to unseal the nova guns, Captain?" asked Vezzarn nervously.

"Not sure it'll do much good," replied Pausert grimly. The guns were very effective when they worked, but they were also old and erratic—and sometimes downright dangerous to use.

Nevertheless, he nodded his head. "May as well, though. In the meantime, Hulik, try the communicator."

The slim, elegant Miss do Eldel set it to the Empire's general beam length.

A young man in the neatly pressed uniform of an Imperial lieutenant stared out at them from under his regulation cap. " . . . instructed to stop firing your thrust generators and allow us to match velocity and trajectory, and board for inspection."

The man paused, obviously about to repeat. Pausert leaned over and hit the send button. "This is Captain Pausert of the *Venture*. What are you looking for?"

The officer looked faintly startled, as if he hadn't expected them to reply. "Ah. Captain Pausert. Can you give us visuals, please?"

"Our visuals *are* on," said Pausert smoothly. "Sorry. We might be having a malfunction with the screens. Or perhaps you are. But what seems to be the problem, Lieutenant? What are you looking for? We're a civilian spacecraft, on a course from the Empire planet of Emris to the provincial capital of the Regency of Haile. We're not a pirate vessel, I assure you. In fact, we have a letter of safe conduct with the seal of the Empress Haile herself."

The lieutenant was definitely looking more respectful now, but Pausert was not going to drop his guard. A good half of the people aboard the *Venture* were *persona non grata* so far as the Empire was concerned. The last thing he wanted was to have any Imperials aboard.

The Imperial lieutenant hesitated for a moment. Then said: "I'll give you to Commodore Fleser, Sir. If you'll just wait a moment. He'll answer your questions."

Pausert flicked the toggle. "What do you think, Goth? Hulik?"

"Better play along, Captain. Me and the Leewit will get the Sheewash Drive ready." Goth headed for the hatch leading out of the control room. "We can outrun them if we have to, but Threbus said to keep a low profile."

Hulik nodded. "We can outrun them, but they do outgun us. Let's see what they want first."

The Captain decided their advice was good and toggled on the buzzing communicator. The screen now showed a jowl-faced gray-haired man with Commodore's insignia.

" . . . Fleser of the Imperial cruiser, ISN *Malorn*. Reduce thrust or be fired on."

Pausert realized that the Imperials weren't going to pussyfoot. He reached out and began cutting the thrust. "This Captain Pausert of the *Venture*. Why are you interfering with a vessel in the legitimate pursuit of business?"

"We have orders to investigate the possibility that you may be carrying a dangerous criminal, as well as one of the infamous witches of Karres," said the Commodore grimly. "Cut thrust further, Captain. You're within range of our guns now and they're locked onto your ship. Any attempt at escape and you will be fired on. Out." He cut the communicator-link.

Captain Pausert shook his head at the blank screen. "Great Uncle Threbus was dead wrong about one thing. That Commodore knew who we were, and he was still prepared to fire on us. Looks to me like the Empire doesn't plan to leave us alone after all." He stood up. "Looks like they're looking for our passengers. I'm going to have a word with Goth."

"Ought to be all right," said Goth. "I can hide myself in no-shape. You got that safe-conduct signed by the Empress Haile for the passengers. And they won't be looking for the Leewit at all. We'll be ready for them, anyway."

"I don't think letting them find Hantis and Pul is a good idea, safe-conduct or not. You know smuggling them past any Imperial Security Agents is what we're supposed to do."

Goth nodded. "Guess you're right, Captain. I can try a shape-change on them, except . . . I'm still not really good enough at that to use any shape except one I already know well. Not and keep it up for more than maybe a minute. Like I did when I made myself and Leewit look like Hantis and Pul on the Worm World. But any shape like that might also be in Imperial records."

"What about no-shape?" he asked. Goth could bend light around herself so she was invisible.

"Got to do that to yourself." Goth shook her head regretfully. "It's too bad I can't do an age-shift yet, like Toll and Threbus can."

Pausert rubbed his chin, dubiously. A younger—or older—Hantis and Pul would still look like a Nartheby Sprite and a grik-dog. That was too close for comfort. Still . . .

"What about this: could you do a shape-change that *imitates* an age-shift? You'd still be working with shapes you know well, just changing their age. That might be enough to fool the Imperials, if we combined it with disguises."

Goth thought about it for a moment, then smiled. "I think so. That's a good idea, Captain!"

"We'll have to hope so. I don't see anything better, in the time we've got. The Imperials should be in boarding range in a few minutes. You go and talk to Hantis and explain things. What about the Leewit?"

"Can look after myself," scowled the Leewit, gray eyes peering up at him from under lowered brows. "So long as you keep that smelly little vatch away."

The captain couldn't rell the little silver-eyed piece of klatha-blackness anywhere. Even if he couldn't detect it, though, he suspected it was still around somewhere.

"I bet you can, brat." He rumpled the Leewit's hair, which she hated, and ducked around the doorway before she could purse her lips to form one of her supersonic whistles. She could literally bust machinery with them.

Back in the control room he found Vezzarn, returning from the nova guns. "They're all ready, Captain. They might be old but I wouldn't want to have them fire on me at this short range, even if those are cruisers."

"Let's sight them on the nearest of the Imperials. It might remind them of their manners."

The little old spacer gave a crooked smile. "I kind of figured on that, Captain. I've been tracking them in with the rear turret. I reckon we could bring the forward turret to bear too, once they're alongside."

"Do that."

The communicator buzzed insistently. It was the Commodore Fleser of the ISN *Malorn*. "Captain Pausert. You will deflect your guns from my ship!" he demanded angrily.

"Commodore Fleser," replied Pausert in an even tone of voice, "we've had a lot of pirate trouble. We do not, in fact, have any proof you are who you say you are. So our guns will stay locked onto your vessel. Before we open our airlock we'll put the lock-bar in place, and seal up the access codes. Make a false move and you won't have a command any more. At this range—you might destroy us, but we'll take you with us."

The Imperial officer looked like he was going to explode himself. "Over and out," said Pausert, before the man had a chance to reply.

WHAT FUN! squeaked the vatch.

Pausert groaned. That was one complication he could have lived without.

"You agree, our papers are in order," said Captain Pausert stiffly. "You are welcome to inspect our cargo. None of our passengers or crew even resemble these descriptions and holo-plates." He handed back the pictures of Goth, the Nartheby Sprite Hantis, and the grik-dog Pul. "You've been misinformed and sent on a wild-goose chase, Commodore."

Pausert was trying to keep calm. To him, the air in the cabin practically reeked of vatch. He could rell that little quicksilver-eyes in here somewhere.

Bulldog-faced Commodore Fleser in his blue-black gold-braided uniform, of course, would not be able to see the vatch. But he wouldn't be immune to its mischief. At the moment the officer was rather off his stride, knowing his vessel was locked by elec-tromagnetic hull clamps into a death-grip with the *Venture*. That could change in a vatch-inspired instant, though. From what the Commodore had said, the Imperials wanted Karres witches even more than the supposed criminal Hantis.

"We have specific orders from ISS headquarters," said Fleser, equally stiffly, "to stop this ship. They are absolutely certain you have these miscreants aboard."

Pausert hoped the Imperial Commodore took the sudden wid-ening of his eyes for a reaction to the mention of the dreaded ISS . . . and not to the glass of water which the captain could see slowly lofting from his desk. He shrugged. "Go right ahead and search, Commodore. But I'll be making an official complaint to Duke Abelisson, the Empress' comptroller."

The vatch was quite capable of creating trouble just for the fun of it. Likely to, in fact. Vatches regarded human space as little more than an aspect of their dreams, and they regarded people as dreamed-up pieces in their games. It hardly mattered to them what happened to the pieces, when the game got boring.

The Imperial hadn't seen the glass. He turned toward the hatch. "Humph. My men will conduct a thorough search and—"

Pausert practically pushed him through it. "Well, you must see to them, then! A good commander always leads from the front, Sir. Let us take you to it."

Water trickled down Pausert's back. There had to be some way of dealing with the little menace!

CHAPTER 2

Sedmon the Sixth, Daal of Uldune—sometimes called Sedmon of the Six Lives by the witches of Karres—listened silently to the communicator relaying the sub-radio report from his agent on Emris.

Sedmon bit his knuckle.

Sedmon patted him on the back.

Sedmon sighed in sympathy.

The fourth Sedmon flicked the screen-controls to show the star-maps of the route between Emris and the Regency of Haile.

The other two Sedmons continued looking out of the one-way windows of the western tower of the mighty House of Thunders, the ancient castle in the highlands south of Uldune's capital city of Zergandol. They knew what the others were doing and thinking anyway. Ruling the web of power-hierarchies and fierce business-interests that made up the former pirate planet of Uldune was no sinecure. In fact, it would have been too much for most humans. But the hexaperson was the best six people for the job. The clones spoke only because words helped formalize their shared thoughts. Also, it was a good habit. Whichever one was on public duty that day would have to speak to ordinary people.

"A Nartheby Sprite! It would help if we could contact the Wisdoms of Karres."

"Karres has done its disappearing trick again, unfortunately."

"No idea where or why?"

"None. But the rumor of the Worm World having destroyed them is almost certainly a falsehood emanating from the ISS."

"Pausert is in great danger, however. The Agandar's fleet are certainly in hot pursuit."

The Sedmon left unsaid the fact that Captain Pausert being in danger meant that a certain member of his crew was in danger also. They all knew that. They also knew that it had surprised them to discover just how upsetting that was.

"Not to mention the ISS."

"Unfortunate about the sub-radio beeper."

"It has been policy to have it fitted to all ships assuming new personalities here for near on a century. It is the first time it has served us so ill. The fact that the Agandar's pirates had discovered it, and that the late Jonalo had sold the information to Imperials is unfortunate. But that is where things stand. We must make the best of it."

"We're going to have to take action ourselves."

"I suppose we are the only one we can trust."

Two of the hexaperson got up and went to the door. It was unnecessary to discuss the mission and who would go. Or to bid the others farewell. They all knew that the Nanite plague had to be stopped. The other four would have to manage without them.

The Sedmons' ship, *Thunderbird*, did not look like the vessel belonging to a wealthy, powerful planetary ruler. But then, it wasn't supposed to. The ship did have a number of features which were unusual even for a full-size battleship, and simply unthinkable in a scruffy-looking cargo tramp. Right now, what it had that was important was speed. And also a subradio tracker, fixed to the frequency of a certain signature transmission given out by the engines of the *Venture*. Even at this range, the signal and direction indicators were giving readouts. Emris, the world from which the *Venture* had lifted, was three dangerous weeks travel from Uldune, across the zone of space called the Chaladoor. To go around took the better part of a year. However, the *Venture*'s course headed her inward toward the Empire's heart at a tangent which the Sedmons' ship could intersect in little more than two months. The hexaperson could only hope that that would be soon enough.

CHAPTER 3

A full platoon of Imperial Marines were busy with the search. They were being impeded at full volume by the Leewit. The Marines did not know quite how to deal with this miniature empress. In a lacy girl's party-dress, the Leewit looked to be a little blonde girl of somewhere between three and four. With her stuffed fluffy stiff-legged toy puppy under one arm, she stood in the center of the cabin and berated them at the top of her voice. *How dare they make such a mess of her room!*

Her nursemaid was stooped over, as she had been since the Marines entered, trying to put everything in order. She was a skinny old woman with sharp features, wearing a baggy ship's suit. Her head was covered in something like a turban, even her ears and eyebrows. If any of the Marines had noticed something oddly young-looking about the nursemaid's very large, grass-green eyes, the ruckus being caused by the Leewit had distracted their attention.

Commodore Fleser looked at the carnage. He turned to the saluting Sergeant. "What happened here?" he demanded.

The NCO gestured helplessly. "Honest, Captain, I don't know. It was like this when we came in, I swear."

"Was not!" squealed the Leewit. Her accusing finger swept across the squad of Marines. "They did it!"

"My best stateroom!" bellowed Captain Pausert. "There is going to be trouble about this! I gave you permission to search, not destroy the place."

"We have to find the criminal. And the witch. We will take whatever steps we need to!" But even Fleser looked a bit aghast at the paint-splattered walls and the tumbled furniture.

"And I will lodge an official complaint with Duke Abelisson, be sure of it. *Another* one." Pausert scowled ferociously. "Miss Seltzer, take the young lady into the empty stateroom next door. You have finished with that one, Sergeant?"

"Er. Yessir."

"One moment," said the bulldog-faced Fleser. "These people . . . " He pointed to the Leewit, with her stuffed toy, and the nursemaid. Pausert just hoped he didn't put a hand on them. Goth's light-shift illusions didn't stand up to touch. "They are not listed by the officials at Green Galaine. Who are they?"

Captain Pausert looked at the Sergeant and his Marines. "I will explain, Commodore. But confidentially, please. It is an Imperial matter."

The Commodore drew himself up. "I am an officer of the Imperial Space Navy, Sir. You can trust me."

"Good," said Pausert cheerfully. "Then I'll reserve it for your ears only. Sergeant, escort Miss Seltzer and her charge next door, please."

To his horror he began to rell vatch again. "*Vatch*erly there is a good explanation," he added. Goth, cloaked in no-shape, would rell the vatch also. But Hantis might not be able to. Best give her some warning that mischief was around.

All but the Commodore and one rather slimy-looking individual in plain black coveralls left.

Pausert looked questioningly at the man. "And you are?"

"This is Micher," said the Commodore. "Imperial Interservice Security."

"Ah. Now I understand." Pausert's tone was decidedly frosty. "What I have to say is not for his ears, Commodore."

"This is my assignment," said the ISS man, in a rather whiny voice. Pausert knew the type. A bully to those below him and a bootlicker to those above. There was something odd about him, though. Pausert couldn't quite put his finger on it, but the man gave him an uneasy feeling.

"I have orders from the regional chief of Imperial security about this, Commodore," said Pausert firmly. "Goodbye, Micher."

Micher blinked. "But my orders . . . "

The Commodore propelled him firmly out of the door and closed it. "Now, what is this about, Pausert? Whatever it is, the ISS is not going to like it." His expression made clear his own low opinion of the ISS. Fleser was an officer in Imperial service, and thus had to put up with them. Yet, here was Pausert, ostensibly on Imperial service himself, chasing them away. The Commodore was plainly fascinated by such apparently contradictory behavior.

Pausert glanced uneasily at the door. "This is strictly between ourselves, Commodore. A very important Imperial lady's honor hangs on it."

Now the Commodore's curiosity looked about ready to sit up and beg. "Of course. You can trust me."

Pausert did his best to look even more uneasy. It wasn't hard. "Ask yourself just how a nursemaid and a child could get onto a ship in Green Galaine without being on any passenger list, Commodore. Without being observed by security cameras. In total secret. Just who has the influence to do that?"

It was the Commodore's turn to look uneasy. "Something like that could be organized, Captain. But not to keep it secret from the ISS. They have agents everywhere."

Pausert bit his lip and said nothing. Just raised his eyebrows and drew the Charter and Seal of Haile out of his pouch. Tapped it meaningfully.

The Commodore's mouth fell open. "You mean . . . "

"The ISS doesn't handle *quite* everything. The royal family's security is handled by . . . But I never said a word, Commodore Fleser. And if you take my advice, you won't either. The little girl is very *imperious*, though, isn't she?"

He smiled, allowing the Commodore to put his own interpretation on that smile. "The ISS is very jealous about the situation. Speaking personally, I'd be quite happy to hand the whole thing over to them. The girl's a little monster, frankly. I don't doubt for an instant that your Marines were just grossly slandered."

He drew himself up stiffly. "However, that's not my decision—

nor yours—and duty is what it is. But that's what this is all about, Commodore. Not some hogwash about mythical witches of Karres and criminals. The ISS is trying to cause embarrassment within—"

A pregnant pause, here, designed to make the Commodore even more uneasy. "—certain quarters."

Someone knocked, and then entered the stateroom without waiting for a reply. It was the security agent. His moist eyes were alive with suspicion. "A message for you, Commodore. The Chief Engineer from the *Malorn* has come across. He insists on seeing you." The ISS agent looked as if he would have liked to kiss the engineer. "He's waiting. Won't let me pass the message on."

As he spoke, the burly engineer gave up waiting and came in anyway. "Commodore, the *Malorn*'s air-recycler is not working," he said bluntly.

Even Captain Pausert was stunned by this news. Air recyclers never failed. Never. They were the most reliable piece of equipment on any ship. Without them, space-travel would be impossible.

The Commodore looked as if someone had kicked his legs out from under him. All the bulldoggy bluster was gone in an instant. "Can you fix it?" he asked.

The Chief Engineer looked at him gloomily. "It's mostly solid-state engineering, Sir. That's why they don't go wrong. I've got my men busy stripping what can be stripped. But we can't get to a lot of it." He rubbed his jaw. "The auxiliary plant is running, sir. But you know that only gives us thirty-six hours."

At least they had a standby of some sort, thought Captain Pausert. But of course military craft did have, in case of combat-damage. The *Venture* didn't.

"Suit-bottles," said Pausert, thinking back to his own military training with the Nikkeldepain Space Navy. "You've got marines on board. They must have air-cylinders. At least a couple of hours each. And the other cruisers must have the same."

The engineer looked gratefully at him. "I hadn't thought of that. We could transfer all but a skeleton crew to the other ships too."

The Commodore nodded. "We're still six days from base. We'll have to move. Sergeant Harris!" he bellowed.

The Sergeant came at a run, Blythe rifle at the ready. "Sir." He took in the scene and realized that he wasn't being called to arrest anyone, or shoot it out with a dangerous criminal. He lowered the barrel of the rifle.

"Round up your men and get them back onto the *Malorn*. At the double."

"But the search!" protested the ISS man. "The witches must have done this . . . "

"That's enough of that rubbish!" snapped the Commodore. "Move, Micher, before I leave you behind. I'm not abandoning my new command for the ISS's bit of spite. Besides, if these so-called witches can put my air recycler out of order, then I certainly don't want to fight with them."

Unfortunately, the sergeant had left open the door leading to the next cabin. As they passed by in the corridor, Pausert got another scent of sunlight and the sound of violets. He glanced in and saw that the little vatch was here—and was playing lightshift with the nursemaid's headdress. Making it look like an Imperial crown . . .

Even more unfortunately, the Commodore had glanced through the floor also. Fleser stopped in his tracks.

"That enough fooling around, my little lady!" said Pausert sternly. He shouldered the Commodore aside and stalked into the cabin, obscuring Fleser's view. "That thing is supposed to stay out of sight."

Pausert readied his klatha hooks for the little brute. Even if he couldn't catch it, he could maybe squelch it long enough . . .

Behind him, he heard the Commodore mutter something. It sounded like "—glad I don't have to deal with the spoiled—" Fleser's heavy footsteps led away down the corridor.

Pausert sighed with relief. Alas, his klatha hooks once again seemed to be able to do nothing worse than reduce the little vatch to giggles.

A few moments later the outer locks clanged. When Captain Pausert arrived back in the control room, the communicator beebled insistently.

The Commodore's red face was glaring at him. "Damnation, Pausert. Can you deflect your guns?"

"Oh. Yes, certainly. Good luck, Commodore."

After Pausert deflected the guns, he saw that the vatchy patch of darkness was now above the coffee dispenser in the control room.

What was it going to do this time? He began the klatha-reach. It darted away.

I'VE GOT TO GO, BIG DREAM THING. BUT I'LL BE BACK ... BACK ... BAAAAAAAACK ....

That was really *not* what he needed to hear. But at least he could see in the screens that the Imperial flotilla was receding. Quite rapidly, in fact.

"I hope," he said to the indentation on the couch, "that you'll give them back their piece of air-recycler. That was cruel. I think you frightened the Commodore out of ten years of life. Being stuck in deep-space without air is enough to terrify anyone."

"I've teleported it back already. When they try it again it'll be working. And it served them right. You told some awful fibs."

He tried to look innocent. "Just false suggestions, The Commodore fooled himself."

Goth laughed. "Just so long as the Leewit doesn't find out she was supposed to have imperial blood. She's already impossible!"

"Just like that little vatch." He grimaced. That had been a near thing. And the vatch hadn't even been *trying* to create mischief. It had said it would be back; without a doubt it would return at the worst possible moment.

Goth appeared out of no-shape. "They're hunting for us pretty hard, Captain," she said seriously.

"Yes. It's not what Threbus led to me expect."

"I guess this must be more important than they told us," said Goth, biting a strand of hair.

The captain took it gently out of her mouth. "I guess you're right, girl. And I don't like being kept in the dark."

The Leewit and the grik-dog trotted into the control room. Pul was looking even more sour-faced than usual.

"My legs are still stiff," growled the grik-dog. "Posture like that's unnatural."

"You complain?" sneered the Leewit. "Try holding yourself up sometime, pretending you're a third your real size. I'm the one had to do all the work. Fatso."

"That information," said the Nartheby Sprite, making a small moue and wrinkling her foxy brows, "is available strictly on a need-to-know basis. And I don't think you need to know, Captain."

"Well, I beg to disagree!" snapped Pausert. "And as the captain of this ship—"

Pausert felt something close on his leg. Just firmly, but with a hint of immense unused strength. "Shall I gnaw his leg off, Hantis?" asked the grik-dog out of the corner of his mouth.

"Do that and I'll swing you around my head by your tail, Pul," said Goth, crossly. "The Captain has to know what he's dealing with, Hantis. Even if you don't tell him everything, you have to tell him *something*."

The Nartheby Sprite laughed musically, and twitched her long, pointed ears. "Very well. To save my Pul's tail and the captain's leg, I will tell you some of it. Not all of it, mind. I *can't* tell all of it. There is a mind-block so I don't remember parts of it, and won't until I speak to the Empress. It can't even be tortured out me."

"We grik-dogs bite people who swing us by the tail," gruffed Pul. He had, however, released the captain's leg. And the look he gave Goth was a tad uneasy.

"Let's just have the story," said Captain Pausert, peaceably.

"But it goes no further than you and Goth, understand? We don't want to cause alarm and panic. That would serve them better than us."

"I give you my word," said Captain Pausert, curiosity burning at him.

"Very well." She sat down, arranged her graceful legs, and began. "My kind are the last remnant of an old, old civilization. Nartheby is our home-world where almost all of our kind now live, but once we roamed widely, even to your Yarth itself. There are stories about our people visiting—although as you were a young and developing culture we largely left you alone. Then we were afflicted by a plague. It wrecked our culture, our colonies and our star-travel. We only saved ourselves by retreating to Nartheby and destroying any ships that came near our world, for a period of five centuries. Then it appeared that the danger was over. But the only Sprites that survived were on Nartheby." She pinched her fine nostrils. "Now . . . The plague has resurfaced. It is spreading, fast, through the Empire."

Captain Pausert and Goth stared at her. Pausert was the first to find his tongue. "But . . . Surely we shouldn't be keeping it a secret? We should be quarantining the infected areas."

Hantis had always seemed to be smiling. Now, as she shook her head, she just looked sad. "It's not that kind of plague, Captain. That's what we thought it was too, at first. It's an invasion. The invaders are just very small. They attack the way a plague would, but they're intelligent. They invade a host, breed billions of operatives, and then take over their hosts and control them. No quarantine can stop an intelligent disease."

"Does Karres know of this?" asked Goth.

Hantis nodded. "Yes. That's why they've gone into hiding. There are no Karres witches out in the Empire at all right now. Except those on this ship."

"But why?" demanded Captain Pausert. "Why have they just run off and left us to deal with this?"

Hantis shook her head. "They haven't. They certainly haven't! But they have to be very careful. The Nanite-plague feeds on and uses klatha energy. Klatha energies are also the only way to fight them. That makes Karres and her witches the greatest danger in human space to the Nanites. They've been trying to get Karres destroyed. So Karres is preparing a number of defenses—but after the fight with the Worm World they're pretty battered."

Goth nodded. "Threbus and Maleen both kind of hinted at this. So what is it you have to do, Hantis?"

"Yes," agreed Pausert. "Why is getting you to the Empress Haile so important?"

"Because of Pul."

"Pul? Him?" Captain Pausert looked at the blue-furred animal with its mouthful of teeth.

Hantis patted the grik-dog affectionately. "Yes. Grik-dogs were bred to smell out Nanite exudates. Pul here can tell if someone has been infested. No Nartheby Sprite would ever consider leaving home without one."

"And I can tell you that ISS agent from the Imperial Cruiser had been invaded and taken over," growled Pul. "It was all I could do not to bite him."

"Grik-dog fangs can inject a venom which kills Nanites. Unfortunately it kills the host too, and also takes quite a long time." Hantis looked even sadder.

"Which means that anyone who is infected can't be saved." Captain Pausert felt very cold, suddenly.

"The Empress Haile is going on her procession through her territories and dependencies soon. We've learned—suspect, at least—that there is a Nanite plot designed to reach fruition when she returns to the Imperial capital. It is essential that Pul and I get there before that. Unfortunately, the Nanites have obviously taken over some of our own agents. They know who I am and where we are going. They will stop at nothing to prevent us from getting there."

End of excerpt from *The Wizard of Karres*